THE KEEPER OF THE CROWS

KYLE ALEXANDER ROMINES

an imprint of Sunbury Press, Inc.
Mechanicsburg, PA USA

an imprint of Sunbury Press, Inc.
Mecanicsburg, PA USA

For information about special discounts for bulk purchases, please contact Sunbury Press Orders Dept. at (855) 338-8359 or orders@sunburypress.com.

To request one of our authors for speaking engagements or book signings, please contact Sunbury Press Publicity Dept. at publicity@sunburypress.com.

ISBN: 978-1-62006-646-1 (Trade Paperback)
ISBN: 978-1-62006-647-8 (Mobipocket)

Library of Congress Control Number: 2015954539

FIRST HELLBENDER BOOKS EDITION: October 2015

Product of the United States of America
0 1 1 2 3 5 8 13 21 34 55

Set in Bookman Old Style
Designed by Crystal Devine
Cover by Amber Rendon
Edited by Sarah Somple

Continue the Enlightenment!

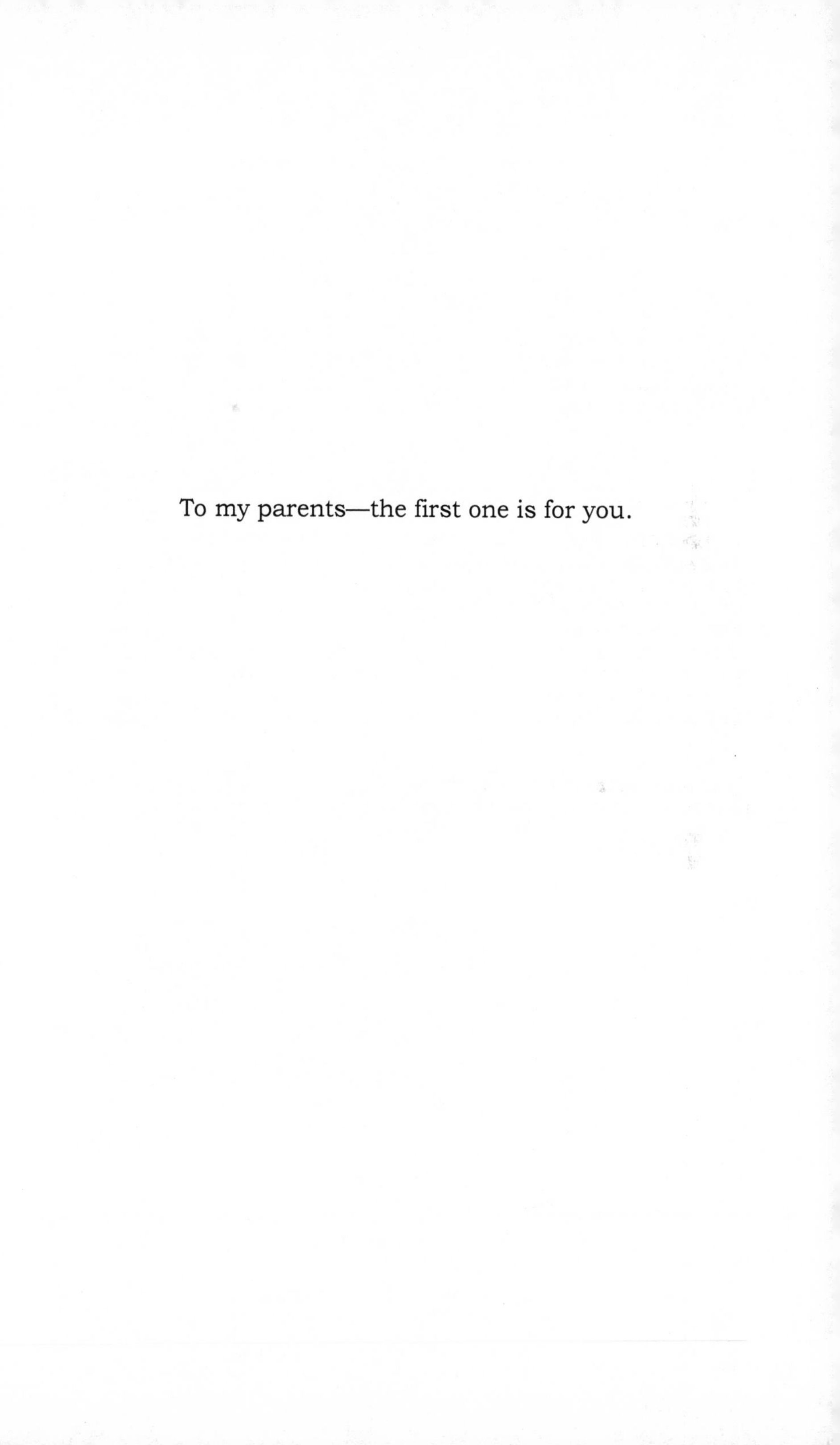

To my parents—the first one is for you.

"And it came to pass at noon that Elijah mocked them and said, 'Cry out loud: for he is a god; either he is lost in thought, or he has wandered away, or he is on a journey, or perhaps he is sleeping and must be awakened.'"

—1 Kings 18:27

PROLOGUE

The days were growing shorter. Dry leaves abandoned the crooked husks of trees in droves, scattered by searing winds. Autumn had crept upon Gray Hollow slowly, draining the life from lush cornfields and pastures.

Jeffrey Daniels eased his truck onto the dirty gravel road without bothering to signal. There was no one around for miles anyway. The truck, an old 1980 Ford F-150, left a thick trail of dust in its wake as it traveled along the road. It took little time for a layer of dirt to cling to the truck's faded brown paint. Jeff didn't care; the vehicle was a relic passed down from his father. If he possessed the money, he would have replaced it long ago. Unfortunately, a series of bad investments, coupled with his failure to advance beyond a high school education, left Jeff without the funds necessary for the upgrade.

Things weren't always going to end up this way. Jeff was a star athlete in high school, and what he lacked in intellect he made up for in work ethic. That was something else he picked up from his father. A widower, Jeff's demanding father taught him the value of hard work. Many of his earliest memories were of working the fields. After his senior year of high school, Jeff left Gray Hollow and never looked back. Until now. He was finally unable to resist the call of the town—and of the Alistair farm.

Jeff hastily brought the aluminum can up to his lips and choked down the frothy liquid.

"Ugh," he grunted. It was warm. The vehicle bounced over the gravel rocks, causing him to spill the remainder of the beer on his jacket. "Stupid truck," he muttered as he glanced at the gas gauge. There was barely enough fuel to get back into town. Jeff hurled the empty can down on the floorboard and brought the vehicle to a halt. A rusty metal gate barred his entry to the farm. Jeff almost laughed when he saw the locks fastened around the wooden post.

Like anyone would want to break in here, he thought.

The sun waned above, casting an orange glow on the farm. An old barn stood nearly twenty feet beyond the fence. Like his truck, the barn's red paint was faded, and planks of rotten wood contributed to a general state of disarray. A cornfield rested just outside the barn, with a small grassy hill overlooking the whole property. Jeff grabbed a cooler from the back of his truck and hoisted it over the gate adjoining the wooden fence. A wave of reluctance washed across him when he rested his hands on the cold metal. After hesitating, Jeff shook his head and yielded to the silent calling that prompted his return to the abandoned farm. It wasn't like anyone was going to find him out here. The farm lay deserted since the last member of the Alistair family passed away almost twenty years ago. The government now owned the property. All the while the Alistair farm lingered in limbo, waiting. Waiting for him.

"Here goes nothing," Jeff said before he began climbing over the fence. A blast of freezing wind sent a chill through him, but it was too late to turn back now. He trudged through thick piles of multi-hued leaves. Dusk was fast approaching over the October horizon. Jeff stared into the thick rows of corn. He remembered all too well what secret lay hidden within. That the corn would still be growing in an ordered pattern after all these years disturbed him for some reason. He caught another chill, this one not from the cool breeze.

The government probably planted them, he thought. Even as the words formed in his head, Jeff found the probability unlikely. He didn't understand why the town would waste money by planting corn in an abandoned field. As he rounded the corner, Jeff spotted a dark figure in the cornfield. He nearly jumped out of his skin before realizing the figure wasn't human. A stitched amalgamation of cloth and straw hung from a pole that towered above the rows.

"It's just a scarecrow," he said to himself, letting out a sigh of relief.

Don't be so uptight, Jeff. The guilt was making him nervous. The sense of relief died when he recognized the design of the scarecrow. Even from this distance, the straw and cloth obscured by the corn in front of him invoked a strong response. He knew all too well who stitched it together.

From what he could see, the scarecrow was marred by time. There were torn patches in its clothes, the colors having faded following years of sun and rain. Somehow the passage of time made the scarecrow seem even more sinister. A snapping sound to his right startled him. Jeff turned and saw a crow perched on one of the cornstalks. The bird fluttered onto the brown grass.

"What are you looking at?" he asked the bird. The crow stared up at him with eyes of swirling blackness. He kicked at the animal, which flew back into the cornfield.

Great, now you're talking to birds, Jeff thought. He frowned and trekked off angrily toward the hillside. The grass under the solitary tree looked at least somewhat inviting. Jeff settled against the tree, greeted by an oppressive silence. *What did you expect, coming back here? You can't change anything.*

Dealing with the tension the only way he knew how, Jeff grabbed a can from the cooler. The liquid fizzed when he popped the top. He threw his head back and let the golden beer flood down his throat.

"Twenty years," Jeff said aloud, as if it made the words more real. The drink wasn't having its desired effect. Rather than fading away, the memories were becoming sharper. He drove all the way from Virginia for resolution. Instead, the tragedy of twenty years ago was just as fresh in his mind as it ever was. Jeff finished the beer and reached for another can.

He looked up at the darkening sky. A deep red hue now dominated the horizon, signifying the impending sunset. Muffled screams echoed in his head, and tears burned his eyes.

"I didn't mean it," he whispered. "Honest."

The crow was standing in front of him again, its head cocked in Jeff's direction. He tried to meet its gaze, but he couldn't. It was just like all the others. Watching him. Judging him.

"You don't know me!" he shouted, hurling the can at the bird. He could see his breath in the cold autumn air. The can sailed over the bird and rolled out of sight in the tall grass. This time the bird didn't move.

A second crow appeared near the base of the hill, followed by a third. Jeff's skin started to crawl as he noticed dozens of the birds forming a circle around the hill. He looked up, following a shadow overhead. The tree's empty branches were covered in even more black crows, staring down at him in unison. The cold air biting his nose let him know this was no delusion induced by his beverage of choice.

With a rustle of wings, the birds began rising into the air. Striking out at him from all directions, the crows enveloped him in a thick cloud, nipping at his skin and clothes.

"Get off me," Jeff tried to yell as he struggled to his feet. The swarm muffled his voice as he fled from the tree.

This is crazy, he thought. It was as if the birds were diseased—or possessed.

Jeff stumbled into the cornfield in an attempt to escape. He tore deeper and deeper into the rows in an effort to find refuge.

Then they were gone. The sound of beating wings vanished, replaced by the eerie silence of the wind against the corn husks.

"Thank God," Jeff muttered while trying to catch his breath. He leaned against a wooden post. That was when Jeff realized something was seriously wrong. He stared up at the empty post.

Hadn't the scarecrow been there before?

In the sky, the sun was beginning to set. Jeff realized he needed to get back to the truck before nightfall. A hiss echoed behind him. He spun around but saw nothing. Footsteps sounded from between the rows. Something was inside the shadowy labyrinth with him. Jeff heard the hissing sound again. This time, out of the corner of his vision he spotted a figure dart past one of the corn rows. Was that laughter he heard?

He was sweating now, his heart pounding with fear. A rustling sound came from his right. This time Jeff thought he saw a hat on top of the figure, which ran with a limp. The shape vanished again. Jeff was too scared to care if he was imagining things. He just knew he needed to get to the truck.

Before he could react, he felt a painful sensation in his left leg. His knees buckled, and Jeff fell forward to the ground. Something had cut him. Jeff looked quickly in every direction in the darkening cornfield and searched for the unseen assailant.

"I'm sorry," he whispered. "I'm sorry!"

Then he heard the voice.

"Jeffrey," something called to him through the cornstalks. The voice was little more than a soft whisper, but he knew it right away. It was the voice he heard in his dreams.

Then rugged cloth scraped past his face, and something jagged slashed against his throat. Jeff gagged and blood began pouring from the cut. He held his right hand tightly against the wound and forced himself to stand. Fear coursed through his veins, and he knew if he didn't get help soon, he would die. Jeff lumbered desperately through the stalks until, miraculously, his truck came into view.

The birds rematerialized in the distance on the horizon. As he emerged from the cornfield, they immediately began flocking toward him. He ran as fast as he could to reach the truck and battled to maintain focus. His body threatened to betray him. Despite his best efforts, blood seeped across his fingers. Jeff flung the door open and stumbled into the front seat. He thrust the keys into the ignition, his rearview mirror reflecting the approaching flock of crows.

The truck refused to start. Jeff cursed and tried again. This time the engine roared to life. Headlights illuminated the impending night as he pressed his foot against the gas pedal, racing against time. Unseen, the creature of straw watched him from the cornfield. It retreated back into the rows until becoming one with the darkness.

The truck bounced over the gravel road, gaining speed with every second. Jeff felt hazy, but the memory of the inhuman voice in the cornfield kept him awake. He wondered if he would ever be able to sleep again. The sense of unease did not lift when he cleared the Alistair farm. More blood was pouring from his wound, and there was not another car in sight. He reached for his cell phone to call for help. In his haste, he knocked the phone below his seat.

Only the pale gleam of the crescent moon lit the black night. Rows of trees lined both sides of the curvy road. Jeff grappled for the phone, taking his eyes off the road to search for it. The moment he succeeded in grabbing the phone, the injured man looked up—just as a flock of crows crashed against the front of his truck, smashing through the windshield. Jeff swerved and felt the Ford tear through a metal guardrail. His vehicle spun out of control and plunged into the forest below. The massive tree was the last thing he saw.

Part One

AWAKENING

Chapter ONE

"Are you sure?" Thomas repeated. Surprise registered on his face.

"Absolutely," replied the voice on the other end of the office phone. "I was riding my bike out in the country when I saw it. There was a truck crashed into a tree in the forest just off Black Gnat Road."

Thomas leaned back in his chair, searching out his notepad from amongst the clutter of his desk. He snatched a pen and cradled the phone against his ear in a delicate balancing act. "Just riding your bike?" he asked, listening to the silence on the other side. "You weren't looking for anything else, were you? I'm not a sheriff's deputy. You can tell me the truth."

"No, I swear. I mean, I stayed the night behind the mill, but that's it. That's just between us, right?"

"Sure," Thomas said, somewhat skeptical of the man's claims. Al Pittman was Gray Hollow's town drunk, a less than illustrious position. "To be clear, you saw a wrecked truck and just wandered down?"

"Maybe I thought there could have been some money or something in the truck, but I didn't know there was a body in it."

Finally, the truth comes out. Thomas smiled. As a reporter, he had always been able to pry information out of reluctant witnesses. In another life, he might've made an excellent lawyer.

"You're positive he was dead?"

"Yeah," the man replied. "His throat was cut. There was blood everywhere."

"When exactly did you find the body?"

"I'm not sure. It took me awhile to ride into town to make the call. Around nine this morning, maybe?"

Thomas scribbled the details down quickly on the notepad. As he stood up, he attempted to nuzzle the phone underneath his chin while he grabbed his things. He swung the brown leather jacket around his shoulder.

"Did you tell anyone else about this?"

"Well, I called the sheriff's department first. I didn't want to get in trouble."

Thomas tried to shake the feeling of disappointment. He had hoped to reach the area first. Now he would have to tiptoe around a crime scene.

"You got my money?" Al questioned.

"Just grabbed it," Thomas said. He stuffed his wallet into his jeans pocket. "And, Al? Thanks."

He couldn't believe his good fortune. If Al was telling the truth, that was. Some might consider it inappropriate to be so animated at the possibility of finding a dead body, but Thomas had been waiting for months for something like this to happen.

This could be my ticket back to New York, he thought.

"I'm going out," he called over his shoulder to Max, the editor of Gray Hollow's only newspaper, *Hollow Happenings*. It still nearly killed Thomas to see his name under the corny masthead.

An unseasonably cold wind hit him as he stepped outside, disheveling his curly black hair. His pale blue eyes appeared darker in the shade provided by the trees outside the newspaper offices. He was surprised that the leaves had clung to their branches as long as they had, as they seemed to be in constant struggle to survive Gray Hollow's seemingly unending drought. In that respect, they reminded him of his own bad luck.

Thomas Brooks was never the most traditional journalist. Others often used that as an insult, but he viewed it as a strength. The actual inner-workings of a newspaper were far different than the false reality depicted in film. Thomas discovered this earlier than most as a member of his high school's newspaper staff. The lackluster experience almost soured him on journalism altogether. Then everything changed.

The student coordinator of the city anti-drug coalition visited Thomas' school periodically to discuss the dangers of substance abuse. Her name was Kandy Wells, a young woman whose personal life told a different story from the staunch anti-substance abuse policies she advocated. Not only did she abuse various narcotics, but she and her boyfriend sold prescription pills to college students at parties. Thomas found the hypocrisy staggering. Although everyone in his small high school knew about the rumors, no one ever did anything about them. After deciding to expose her as a fraud, Thomas convinced his college-aged older brother to get them invited to a party at the local community college—a party he learned Kandy was going to attend.

The following week his story appeared in the city paper, containing incriminating pictures and substantiated quotes. Kandy was fired by the anti-drug coalition amid the allegations, though no charges were ever filed. Thomas' work catapulted him to an internship with the city paper. He earned a journalism degree in college, where a series of journalistic awards brought him to the prestigious *New York Chronicle.*

Then he lost it all.

"I said, where do you think you're going?"

The abrupt question ended his brief foray into the past. Having made his way to his car, Thomas turned around, one hand on the door of his Nissan Altima. Max Harper stood outside the building's entrance, thick arms folded across his chest.

"Sorry, Max. I didn't hear you. What were you saying?"

"You had a deadline on the property tax hike, in case you've forgotten. I expected it on my desk this morning."

"I won't be long," Thomas promised, opening the door to his car.

"Where are you headed?"

"Let's just say I might have found a story that's more interesting than tax hikes. Trust me on this." He slid into the car without waiting for a response, waving as he rolled out of the parking lot. The editor looked on with a scowl.

He'll feel better when I lay a murder story on his desk, Thomas thought. It was probably too quick to jump to the word murder. Even if Al's story was true, the homeless man was hardly an expert on homicide. However, if the man in the truck *was* murdered . . . everything would change.

He slid his sunglasses over his eyes and accelerated. Max was a pushover. Thomas certainly had more demanding editors in the past. Yet the man had done him an enormous favor by hiring him when no one else would. That counted for a lot, as far as Thomas was concerned.

***

Jezebel ducked under the line of yellow tape. Leaves floated gently from the trees above, partially obscuring the truck smashed against the thick oak. She began walking down the steep hill slowly to avoid slipping as she kept her gaze focused on the scene below.

Al Pittman was telling the truth, she thought. When the homeless man phoned the station from the Clayhorn Feed Mill, she was understandably dubious. Now she was glad she listened.

After pulling on a latex glove, she looked over the shattered glass in the truck bed. The leaves crunched under the weight of her boots as she neared the truck.

She radioed one of her deputies.

"Logan, this is Sheriff Woods," she said. "I don't know how to say this, but it looks like Al Pittman was right."

"Is there really somebody dead in there?"

The deputy's skepticism wasn't hard to understand. Al Pittman spent more time in the jail than he did wandering the streets. The man's reputation was less than spotless.

Gray Hollow was a quiet town, largely without violence. This was one reason why her department was so small. With all the cutbacks made by the city council due to the recession, Jezebel was one of only three county officers.

She retrieved a pen from her pocket and jotted down the license plate number of the unfamiliar Ford. As she stared at the passenger side windowpane, Jezebel could barely make out a figure inside. Something stained the window.

My God, she thought. It was all blood.

"Get Pittman down here right away," she said into her handheld radio.

"You got it, Sheriff," the deputy replied.

When Jezebel stared again into the truck, for a moment, she felt as if she were being watched.

Get a grip on yourself, she thought. Jezebel tucked her bangs behind her ears. While on duty, she wore her sandy blond hair tied securely in a bun.

The forest was eerily quiet, as silent as the motionless figure inside the truck. She opened the front door, which creaked slightly when her fingers gripped the handle. It was obvious the truck hadn't been in particularly good condition *before* the collision. She quickly scanned the point of impact, where the front of the truck was bent and disfigured against the trunk of the massive oak tree.

How did this happen? She tried to visualize the truck's path into the forest. The bend in the road could be treacherous in the dark, especially if the man had been speeding or drinking. Even so, she could not remember an accident of such magnitude in this part of the county since she took over as sheriff four years ago.

If the road was more dangerous than she remembered, it might be prudent to do something about it. There were many places in rural Gray Hollow that had fallen into disrepair over the decades, and the county was in desperate need of funding for new infrastructure.

She battled her gag reflex as she pulled the door open. The sheriff stepped back and exhaled into the breeze. The smell of death filled the air.

"That's strange," Jezebel muttered before returning to the truck. The odor was stronger than she expected, especially since it appeared that the wreck took place within at least a day. The corpse was out of the sun and in the cool fall air, which should have slowed down the process of decomposition.

The victim's body was leaning back against the front seat, which also struck her as odd.

Wouldn't the body have been thrown up against the steering wheel?

"Pittman," she whispered. Had the homeless man moved the body? Now that she was certain there was a dead body on her hands, she needed to treat it seriously. Her gaze shifted, traveling down the man's corpse.

There were minor abrasions covering the visible portions of his skin, and his clothes were ripped and torn. His hands and face were covered in dried blood, some of which had clearly gushed down from a wide wound across his neck. Jezebel carefully reached in the pockets of his leather jacket before searching for a wallet or some type of identifying information.

Nothing, she thought. She studied the man. He looked a few years older than she was, perhaps in his late thirties.

"Who were you?" she asked. The sheriff gazed into the body's vacant eyes. There were empty cans on the floorboard of the truck, which strongly suggested he had been drinking. It no longer mattered. She doubted the man inflicted the neck wound on himself, which meant she was now likely in the middle of a murder investigation.

Jezebel braced herself for the task at hand. She hadn't encountered a single murder case in all her time as sheriff. Jezebel was thirty-six years old and had lived in Gray Hollow practically her entire life. After graduating from Hollow High, she obtained a bachelor of science in administration of justice from the University of Louisville and went on to pursue a master's degree in criminology before returning to join the Gray Hollow Sheriff's Department. Later, Jezebel would complete a degree in forensics with online and correspondence courses, but she never regretted the decision to return to her hometown.

Even from a young age, Jezebel instinctually reached out to protect those who were picked on, which deepened into a desire to pursue a career in law enforcement. In high school, she was impacted by a special-needs student who was routinely bullied by some of his older classmates. When he went missing, she blamed herself for all the times she stood by and watched.

Jezebel was so wrapped up in thought that she failed to hear the sound of footsteps behind her. As she looked down, a shadow crept over the ground below.

A hand gripped her shoulder.

She whirled around, pulling her gun.

"Whoa," Thomas Brooks said. The reporter's eyes grew wide when he saw the weapon in her hands.

"What do you think you're doing here?" Jezebel demanded.

"I'm a journalist, remember? Mind putting that away?" he said, looking nervously at the gun. The sheriff holstered the gun.

"Don't sneak up on me next time," she said.

"A little jumpy today, Sheriff?"

"This *is* a crime scene, Mr. Brooks. Didn't you see the yellow tape?"

Thomas made a show of looking around.

"What yellow tape?" he asked. "I don't see any around here."

Jezebel narrowed her gaze. She'd only left one line of tape at the top of the hill, where the truck had gone over the edge.

"I haven't had time to go over the whole area," she said. "Like I told you, this is a crime scene. Someone died here."

"So you're confirming it's a murder?" he replied, as he recorded the quote in his notebook.

"That's not what I said." Jezebel instantly regretted giving out the information. Brooks was a far more competent reporter than she was used to dealing with. "You shouldn't be here," she said. "I'm going to have to ask you to leave, Mr. Brooks. Something very serious took place here, and I don't want you standing over my shoulder while I try to piece everything together."

"Right," he said, narrowing his eyes. "Like I haven't heard that before. Listen, I'm writing this story. You can either include me, and I'll try to be as fair as possible to you, or—"

"You were the one who said you were a journalist," she cut him off. "How do you think it would look if you spent time in jail for interfering with my investigation?"

The two faced each other in the silent forest, with only the wind between them. Thomas watched her carefully. Jezebel Woods was certainly attractive, but that was probably less intimidating to the locals than her sharp intellect. Thomas, on the other hand, was from the city, and he had dealt with strong willed women on a regular basis. He wasn't about to let her cut him out of this story—he needed it too much.

"What will it be?" she asked, waiting for him to reply. "I'm not sure your reputation would be able to handle a short incarceration."

That made him flinch.

"Call me Thomas," he said, offering a smile. "I think we got off on the wrong foot. I'm not here to step on anyone's toes. And whatever you believe about me, I promise you I didn't get into this business to practice sensational journalism." She pursed her lips. Thomas was mostly telling the truth, but he knew she had every reason to be skeptical. "The fact is, I've been around many crime scenes before, and even though you're obviously a very skilled sheriff, I have experience with these types of investigations. I can help."

Jezebel looked into his eyes and searched for the truth. This was the first time she had encountered Thomas Brooks in person. He seemed sincere enough. Besides, with his background, the journalist might have access to resources she didn't. But at the end of the day, rules were rules.

"If you think you have something constructive to add to this investigation, make an appointment. Even if I were willing to collaborate with you on this investigation, it would jeopardize this entire investigation if anyone knew you were here. I don't know what you're used to getting away with in New York, but here in Kentucky, we follow the rules."

She knows, Thomas thought. He raced to formulate a response and found himself at a rare loss for words. Luckily, she spoke again and spared him the trouble.

"By the way, how did you find out about this?" she asked, putting her hands on her hips.

"The same way I suspect you did. Al Pittman told me," he answered quickly. At least he hadn't withheld the source from her, but he could tell her trust wouldn't come easily—especially if she knew about New York.

"I'll deal with Al later," Jezebel muttered. "Now if you'll excuse me, I have an investigation to get back to. I trust you know how to find your way back to the road."

She turned back around and opened the door, and Thomas caught a glimpse of the carnage inside the truck. The body was covered in blood, just like Pittman said. He made a quick note about the cans on the floorboard.

His throat was cut, he thought, *but by what?*

Then Thomas noticed the windshield.

"Did you see this?" he asked her, pointing to the smashed glass.

Jezebel glanced up.

"What are you still doing here?" she asked, narrowing her gaze. "I told you to leave."

"Take at look at this," he said, gesturing at the front of the vehicle.

The windshield was barely intact, very nearly shattered in several places. Jezebel had noted the damage when walking down the hill but ascribed it to the collision. Instead, the cracks were caused by something else entirely. There were several birds partially embedded in the cracked glass. Blood from their dead bodies smeared the windshield. Jezebel kicked herself internally for missing something so obvious, although in her defense she hadn't had ample time to inspect the crime scene.

Thomas knelt down next to the tree and stared at the front of the hood.

"There are more over here," he said, careful to avoid touching the birds and contaminating the crime scene. "Do you think these could have caused him to wreck?"

She didn't answer. Jezebel leaned over the seat and picked up one of the loose black feathers with a gloved hand.

"Crows," she whispered curiously. She could think of no reason that would explain why the dead birds would be encased in the windshield.

It's almost as if they flew directly into the glass, she thought.

"His throat was probably cut before he got in the truck," Thomas added.

"Oh yeah? What makes you think that?"

"See the blood smeared across the outside handle? He was bleeding when he got in, and I don't see any wounds on his hands. Just blood."

"You've got a point," she said. Jezebel checked for blood on the inside handles. "You have done this before, haven't you?" she asked, impressed.

His knowledge surprised her. If she was going to be working with him, it might be a good idea to research the journalist. There was certainly enough information out there, if her guess was correct. She'd heard stories about what happened in New York.

"Yes," he said, nodding. "A few times, in fact."

Before she could reply, Jezebel noticed something on the corpse's pant legs.

"What do you make of this?" she asked, deciding to test him. She lifted one of the pieces of hay with her fingers. After placing the straw in a sealed plastic bag, she held it up for him to see.

"Maybe he was a farmer," he said after a pause. "Half this town is covered in hay bales." Jezebel heard a hint of mockery in his voice.

"Do you have something against small town farmers?" she asked, glaring at him.

"Not at all," Thomas said, realizing too late he might have offended her.

"Good," she replied curtly. "Although I doubt this man was one."

"Why do you say that?"

"If he was a farmer, don't you think there would be more hay in the truck *other* than just on his pants?"

"So you think he may have visited a farm recently. What's with all the smaller wounds?" he asked. "It looks like he was scratched with barbed wire."

"I'm not sure," she said, concluding her search for any trace of identifying information. She'd found nothing to ID the victim.

"Do you think he could have been attacked before the wreck? Maybe he picked up a hitchhiker or something."

"I don't think so. If there were someone with him in the car, they probably would have been injured along with him in the impact. But until we have an ID, it's impossible to determine what might have motivated someone to kill him, assuming we're dealing with murder here."

Twigs snapped on the hill behind them. The pair watched two men walk downhill in their direction.

Jezebel swore. "This is exactly what I was afraid of," she said.

Thomas recognized the profile of Al Pittman as rays of sunlight peeked through the trees. The other man was a muscular officer who had apparently been given the duty of returning Al Pittman to the scene.

"Sorry for not radioing, Sheriff," the officer said. He held his hand over his hat, as if he was worried it would fall off as he neared the base of the hill. "I wasn't aware you had company." He eyed Thomas suspiciously. "What's he doing here?"

Thomas tucked his notepad back inside the duffel bag. The officer sounded polite, but Thomas couldn't help noticing a trace of bitterness betrayed by his tone. He wondered if he was the source of the hostility or if there was already tension between the two.

"This is Thomas Brooks from *Hollow Happenings*," Jezebel said. "Thomas, this is Deputy Logan Randall."

Thomas offered his hand, which Deputy Randall ignored.

"What's a reporter doing at the crime scene?" he demanded.

Jezebel frowned. "Mr. Brooks offered to help," she said. "I explained that if he wanted to collaborate on this investigation, he would have to make an appointment. He was just leaving."

They both looked at Thomas for confirmation, and he nodded quickly.

"Are you sure it's wise to bring an outsider into this investigation?"

"I haven't made any decision yet, but I'll determine what's wise and what's not, *Deputy*." She stared him down. Randall was five years her senior on the force, and clearly resented the fact that he served under her. Unfortunately for her, despite his gruffness, Gray Hollow needed all the officers it could get. She could barely manage everything as it was. With a murder investigation on her plate, she would have to try to keep things peaceful. Jezebel was suddenly glad she made the spontaneous decision to allow Thomas Brooks to stay. He might prove easier to work with than the irritable deputy.

"Thanks," Thomas said to Jezebel. "Sorry for any confusion I might have caused," he added for the deputy's benefit. "I'll be in touch."

He used the opportunity to slip a wad of money into Al Pittman's pocket as thanks for the tip. He had the feeling the sheriff was watching him out of the corner of her vision, but she offered no protest.

"Looks like someone took a nasty spill," the deputy said, looking over at the truck as Thomas started up the hill. "I guess this wasn't a murder after all."

"Wrong," Jezebel replied. "His throat's been cut. Go see for yourself."

While the deputy went over to inspect the truck, Jezebel called to Thomas before he could leave. "One minute, Mr. Brooks." As Thomas made his way back down the hill, she took the opportunity to address Al Pittman.

"Mr. Pittman, if you don't mind, there are some more questions I'd like to ask you."

"I thought I answered over the phone."

"You did, but there are some other things I'm curious about after having a chance to inspect the vehicle."

"OK," Al replied reluctantly. He looked uncomfortable to be back at the crime scene. Thomas wondered why Al was so unsettled and was curious if the sheriff picked up on it as well.

Then Jezebel pulled Thomas aside.

"You aren't planning on running the story yet, are you?" she whispered.

"Why?" he asked hesitantly, resisting the inclination to frown.

"I'm afraid the public might panic if they think there's some crazed killer on the loose. We aren't even completely sure what we're dealing with at this point."

Thomas paused. The police had the power to keep him out of a crime scene, but short of a court order they had no authority to censor the press. In the old days, he wouldn't have hesitated to run the story. Now he was stuck in Gray Hollow, where everything was different. There was a new set of rules to follow. The town was so small, and Jezebel Woods *was* the source at this point. He couldn't afford to alienate her after she went out on a limb for him. Besides that, something about the driven sheriff he couldn't quite put his finger on.

"OK," he finally said. "Here's my number." Thomas passed her a business card. "So are you going to let me in on this?"

"We'll see," Jezebel said. "If you find anything else that's useful, I'll give it some serious thought."

As he turned, leaving her at the foot of the hill, Thomas felt the distinct impression that he had been dismissed.

"All right, Mr. Pittman, where were we?" Jezebel asked.

Before he could answer, she spotted something over his shoulder and stopped cold.

"Is something wrong?" Al asked.

"Nothing," she said, her eyes on the truck. One of the dead crows' black eyes was open, as if staring at her. Ordinarily it wouldn't have troubled her, if not for the fact that she was almost positive its eyes were closed only a few minutes ago.

Chapter TWO

The rusty hinges of the old barn door screeched as if the door itself were reluctant to give way. A strong arm pried the wooden door halfway open. Slowly, light from the outside spilled into the dark room.

Gary tugged at the door and swore when he discovered it would budge no farther. He brushed away a cobweb and stepped onto the dirt floor inside the barn. Particles of lint floated in suspension, dancing in air like they were assembled for a autumn ball.

"What a stupid holiday," he muttered before sneezing from the dust.

Still, if it will shut the kid up, maybe it'll get Mary to shut up too.

He smiled at the thought. Gary had never been a very sentimental man. Farming involved making a living the hard way, and it was a tough life. His son, Ben, had no way of knowing that; Gary provided for him his whole life.

I work myself to the bone, he thought while wiping soiled hands against a formerly white t-shirt. *And for what?*

When he finished his chores on the farm early, Gary expected that Mary would be happy to see him before Ben got home from school. Instead, she sent him out scouring the dark barn for Halloween decorations.

"Halloween's still more than two weeks away," he had protested—for all the good it did him. He sneezed again, his nose crinkling at the intake of stale air.

"Now where did I put that light?" After spending almost two full minutes feeling around for the light bulb, Gary pulled down on the chain. Nothing happened. After years of disuse, the light bulb had finally gone bad. Now it was just something else around the farm needing to be replaced.

Great. Now I have to do this in the dark.

Gary rarely ventured into the room at the back of the barn, which always made him feel claustrophobic. Since the room was just large enough to store Mary's Christmas and other holiday decorations, he had the perfect excuse to leave it abandoned most of the time.

After allowing his eyes to adjust to the shadows, Gary looked under the wooden cabinets and went through stacks of crates. He separated out the Christmas decorations before finally opening the crate containing orange lights and glow-in-the-dark pumpkins.

"It's about time," he muttered, setting the crate aside. He went deeper into the room, combing through the older decorations. The uneven wood of the table felt unsettling to his touch. Gary moved a sheet out of the way as he looked over things stored away so long ago he had forgotten them. He moved his hand under another sheet, one obscuring a man-sized figure.

Something rustled underneath the sheet, brushing up against his fingers. Startled, Gary stumbled back. The sheet fell down off the table, and a black crow fluttered quickly out of the barn.

"Get out of here," Gary yelled after it. If only it was hunting season, he would have had his gun nearby.

Gary looked up, only to find himself staring into a pair of sinister eyes. This time he was not so quick to laugh off the feeling of apprehension. He stared at the straw scarecrow that rested uncovered on the wooden counter against the wall. Gary hadn't seen that particular scarecrow in a long time, but he remembered it all too well.

Gary stared at the wide stitched smile, which seemed to be grinning at him.

It's just a scarecrow, he thought. He grabbed the figure and turned to take it outside with the rest of the decorations. As he started toward the door, he caught a glimpse of its face in a sliver of light; its eyes still appeared to gaze into his. Unnerved, Gary decided to leave the scarecrow in the barn and replaced it on the tabletop.

"Maybe next year," the farmer muttered. Gary shut the door to the back room, crate in hand. He hoped Mary would be appeased.

A few minutes after Gary left, something started scraping against the door. The scratching sound continued for a few moments before slowly ebbing away.

***

"Let me get this straight. The first murder in God knows how long, and you want to sit on the story?"

Thomas cringed at the words but tried to keep his expression emotionless. He had rarely been accused of timidity. Truthfully, he wasn't even sure it was a murder yet, but he needed to sell his boss on the story.

"That's right. Sheriff Woods thinks it might cause a panic."

"Cause a—" The editor threw his hands up in the air. "I would expect this sort of thing from an intern. Of *course* she's going to say that."

Thomas sighed. He knew this was going to be a tough sell. Like him, Max Harper needed a big story. It was a difficult time for all media in general, let alone a rural newspaper with declining readership.

"Trust me, I understand. My gut tells me to wait on this, though. This is more than a simple mugging. You should have seen the man's throat."

Max started to speak, then fell silent. The editor was a husky man, who might have been a linebacker if not for severe asthma. Thomas could see the man's fingers unconsciously reach for the inhaler in his shirt pocket.

"Trust you? That's rich, coming from you." Thomas glared at him but remained silent. Max saw the look on his face and bit his lip. "I'm sorry. That wasn't fair. You've done great work since you arrived. I do trust you."

"Then listen to me now. If we do this right, Sheriff Woods is offering full access to the investigation. She knows I have experience handling this kind of thing." It was an embellishment, of course. Jezebel had offered no such arrangement, at least not yet, but Thomas felt more comfortable lying to his pushover boss than the formidable sheriff.

Max collapsed into his chair and shook his head. "I don't have a choice, do I?" he muttered. "Fine. Have it your way. Just don't expect me to let the rest of your workload slide."

Thomas grinned. "You're the boss," he said cheerfully, heading out the office door.

"And, Brooks," Max called after him. "Keep me in the loop on this. I want a report tomorrow. Remember, that property tax story is still due before you leave."

"Absolutely."

That was easier than I thought. Thomas secretly thought the editor was a little intimidated by his time at the *New York Chronicle*. For all his bluster, Max was very easy to get along with.

Now, he thought, *what to do about Jezebel Woods?* The truth was, he was in a bit of a gray area legally—though that had never bothered him before. There was no statute barring an officer of the law from sharing and receiving information from a reporter, but such collaborations happened more rarely than conveyed in film and television. Thomas' unofficial participation in the investigation was largely within the sheriff's discretion, so he needed to find a reason for her to keep him involved. He could do that by showing her he actually could help her. He might be morally unscrupulous, but he was a darn good reporter, even if other people seemed to have forgotten that fact.

He sat down at his desk and made room amongst the mess for his notepad. After firing up his computer, the reporter stared at the notes he made earlier. He immediately spotted something that bothered him.

"That's just between us, right?" Al Pittman had asked him during their phone conversation. It was a reasonable request given the circumstances. If not for the strange way Al acted in the woods, Thomas might not have thought anything of it. He circled the words with his pen.

Could Al Pittman have killed the man in the truck? Thomas doubted it. For one, Al wasn't covered in blood. More than that, Al called the sheriff's department in the first place, something most killers would be more than reluctant to do.

A killer. Despite his experience, Thomas still had trouble picturing a murderer stalking the quiet streets of Gray Hollow. He wrote the word *motive* on the notepad and underlined it. *Money?* Thomas wondered. That was one possibility, yet the truck didn't appear to belong to the type of person with money to flaunt around.

Maybe it was drug related. He tried doing a search for all the most recent drug arrests in Gray Hollow. Aside from a couple of kids busted for smoking pot, Thomas was unable to find anything. Even when he widened his search, he found little evidence to suggest Gray Hollow had a drug problem.

"Make a note to ask Jezebel about that," he mumbled while reading the rest of the notes. The brutality of the murder stood out. The man in the truck bore several cuts across his body. Thomas recalled his theory that the man's throat was slit before he made it into the vehicle. Then there were the dead crows in the windshield. That stumped even Thomas.

If the murder wasn't about money, was it about revenge? Without knowing the identity of the victim, it was virtually impossible to determine—but that was something he thought he could change.

Thomas took out his cell phone to call up an old number from another life. He wasn't going to sit around and wait for Jezebel to call him. He hesitated, staring at the name in his contact list, and then pressed the call button.

"This is Evelyn."

Thomas swallowed.

"Eve?"

"Thomas? Is that you?"

"Yeah. It's been awhile, I know. How've you been?"

"What is this about? I'm kind of busy right now, and I'm not sure I'm up for a heart-to-heart at the moment."

"It's not that. Listen, Eve, something's going on down here in Gray Hollow, and I could use your help."

"Gray Hollow?"

"It's where I live." The words hung in the air, so he continued. "I'm working for a small paper in Kentucky called *Hollow Happenings.*"

"I didn't know that," she said hesitantly. "Sorry I haven't kept in touch." He couldn't tell if she was being sincere.

"It makes sense," Thomas said. "Things ended badly between us. My fault."

My fault. He closed his eyes, thankful she couldn't see him now. He felt pathetic for having to do this. Time numbed him to the pain of their breakup, but speaking to her brought back memories of the life he once had. Those memories were all too fresh.

"How can I help you?"

"I need a favor. We found a body in the forest today, and—"

"We?"

"I'm working with the sheriff. Can you run a license plate for me?"

"If you're assisting the sheriff, why do you need me to get you a name?"

"You know how this works. Our partnership is shaky at best. It's too early to see how far I can trust her."

Evelyn laughed.

"It almost sounds like you're worried about getting played. This sheriff sounds formidable for the backwoods."

"If she tries to withhold information from me, it would be helpful if I already had a head start on her."

"That sounds more like the Thomas I know. *You're* still trying to play everyone, aren't you? Still not willing to trust anyone. That's why it didn't work out between us."

There were a lot of reasons it didn't work out between them, he knew. It was true he was mostly to blame, but she wasn't entirely faultless either. Still, he couldn't help caring about her, and it felt wrong to him that she didn't feel the same way.

"Will you do this for me?" he asked. He waited while she considered the request.

"Yes," she replied after a pause. "Give me the numbers."

Thomas read the license plate to her.

"I'll see what I can do. I'll call you back when I know something more."

"Thanks. I appreciate this."

He hung up the phone and stared at the blank screen of his computer for a long moment. Deciding it was better to attempt something constructive than to wallow in self-pity, Thomas pulled a meager phonebook out of his desk. He flipped through the book until he found what he was looking for.

Clayhorn Feed Mill, he read, copying down the address. It was relatively late in the afternoon, but Thomas still had time to do a little more investigating of his own before he finished the property tax article for Max. If he timed things right, he could even quell the growling of his stomach while he was at it. He winced, remembering the grotesque imagery of the crows embedded in the truck windshield.

Fifteen minutes and one drive-thru later, Thomas pulled his car onto the gravel road of the Clayhorn Feed Mill. The taste of the sandwich was fresh in his mouth. He placed the sunglasses over his eyes to shield himself from the bright sun.

There is one thing to be said for small towns, he thought. *You can get from one end of town to the other in less than fifteen minutes.*

In actuality, Thomas wasn't all that far from where the body was found. The mill was situated on the outskirts of Gray Hollow. As Al had said, a dense forest surrounded it from behind. After seeing the area himself, Thomas found it easy to believe a habitual drunk would seek refuge there. He needed to be sure Al was telling the truth. Other than Jezebel, the man was his only source of information. Thomas continued looking around. It wasn't surprising that Al's bike was gone. He guessed it was at the sheriff's department.

There were only a few customers at the moment. Two trucks were parked in spaces beside the seed store, and three others were next to the loading area in the back. There were piles of feed and fertilizer stacked around everywhere, left there completely unattended. That would never happen in New York. Thomas shook his head and walked inside the store.

"Can I help you?" a man behind the counter asked in a thick drawl.

"I hope so," Thomas replied. "Do you know who worked the morning shift?"

"You're looking at him. The name's Joel Grayson."

"I'm Thomas Brooks," he said. "Do you mind if I ask you some questions?"

"Sure," Joel said skeptically. He raised an eyebrow.

Thomas was glad he wasn't originally from New York; a northeastern accent would have set him apart from the others.

"Did you see Al Pittman around here this morning?"

"What's this about? Is Al in some kind of trouble?"

"Not at all," Thomas said carefully. "He left his coat at the bar last night, and I thought I'd bring it back to him. I heard he was in the area recently, but for the life of me I can't find him."

It was a lie, but Thomas had the feeling Joel might be less than forthcoming if he thought Al was in hot water with the law.

"That's good to hear," Joel said, coming out from behind the counter. He looked around the store as if scanning for more customers. Seeing none, he turned and faced Thomas. "Al's not as bad as a lot of folks seem to think. Judy doesn't mind me letting him stay here sometimes."

"Judy?"

"Judy Conway. She owns the mill. To answer your question, Al slept outside last night. He comes around this place every now then for some quiet."

"I can see why. It certainly seems peaceful out here."

"That wasn't always the case. Tell you the truth, this place isn't what it used to be. The mill's kind of run down, if you ask me. When I first started here, tons of customers came from all across the county, even though the place is out of the way. Now, not so much."

"Have you worked here long?"

"Eleven years," Joel answered proudly. Then he returned to the reason Thomas was there. "If you're looking for Al, I haven't seen him after this morning."

"So he did come back."

"Yes. Actually, it was odd. Al came peddling in here on his bike, like he was in a hurry to get someplace. He went out there to use the phone," he said, pointing to an old pay phone. "I would have let him in myself, but Judy says phones are for paying customers only." He shrugged as if to say, *rules are rules.*

"What did he say to you?"

"Nothing. He pedaled toward town when he finished."

Thomas stopped. Something in that sentence struck him as strange.

"He didn't ask for money to pay for the call?"

"Come to think of it, he didn't. In the past, he's always been able to get a quarter out of me."

Thomas started piecing together what he had learned. Suddenly, his phone buzzed. He looked down at the text. It was from Evelyn.

The truck is registered to a man named Wilbur Daniels.

"One more thing," Thomas quickly added before he turned to go. "Have you ever heard of Wilbur Daniels?"

"No," Joel replied. "Why do you ask?"

"No reason. Thanks for your help. I really appreciate it."

"Tell Al I said hello when you give him that coat."

"Sure," Thomas said as the door closed behind him.

***

The wind shifted, scattering a carefully raked pile of leaves under a large oak tree in Jezebel's mother's front lawn. Carried by the wind, some of the leaves swept toward the road in front of a discolored white house. The house was of meager size, surrounded by a wooden fence marking the edges of the small property.

As Jezebel walked across the yard, she frowned at the state of disrepair of the fence. A trace of sadness momentarily softened her habitually professional demeanor. She knocked on the door.

"Mom?" she called. "Are you in there?"

It wasn't an entirely foolish question. Emma Woods, Jezebel's mother, possessed no car. Taking the keys away from her mother was a painful decision to make. As

Emma's dementia worsened, however, it was the safest option Jezebel had.

The lights were off inside the house, which wasn't a good sign. Jezebel twisted the knob on the screen door and stepped into the house. It was chilly inside, only a little warmer than being out in the elements. The sheriff raised the temperature on the thermostat while looking for a sign of her mother.

"Mom, you can come out now."

Jezebel never thought twice about returning to Gray Hollow to care for her mother. Like all other teenagers during their adolescence, she once dreamed of getting far away to the big city. The diagnosis of Emma's disease put a definite end to those plans. In the end, Jezebel found her place in the department, and everything worked out for the best.

Jezebel made a mental note to ask her mother's part-time sitter to start locking the door.

"This isn't another game, is it?" she asked lightly while creeping down the dark hallway. Her mother claimed her eyes were sensitive to the light, but Jezebel found the dark house unsettling. She offered to move in with Emma when she first came back to Gray Hollow. Emma, stubborn to a fault, would have none of it. It was an independent streak they shared. Jezebel was born with it. Emma, on the other hand, acquired the characteristic after years of suffering through a disastrous marriage.

Despite her mother's obstinacy, the sheriff made sure to drop by her mother's house regularly. If her mother fell or injured herself somehow, everything would change. Jezebel feared what was to come, though she was powerless to stop it.

She tiptoed through the small living room and looked for signs of her mother. Aside from a whirling fan above her and a stack of unread magazines on a table next to the couch, there was nothing in the room that merited attention. After picking up a blanket from the couch, she left the room.

Jezebel peered inside her mother's bedroom. Again, there was nothing except a pile of messy clothes. She scooped the clothes up and threw them into the laundry bin. When she returned the next day, she would have to tidy up.

Then she spotted the open door in the kitchen. She assumed her mother forgot to close it again. Or perhaps was she unable to? The sheriff headed back into the cold, wandering past the trees in the backyard.

When she leaned against an old oak tree to gather her thoughts, a hand shot out at her from behind the tree's black bark. The hand gripped her tightly around the shoulder. She spun around and found her mother standing there.

"Mom!" Jezebel exclaimed, startled. "What are you doing out here in your pajamas?"

Her mother stared at the leaves blowing around the yard with a vacant expression on her face. Emma's white nightgown was as disheveled, as was the rest of the woman's appearance, giving her an almost savage quality.

Even when Jezebel was a young girl, her mother was always very particular about the way she looked. Emma was a plain woman but tried hard to look her best in hopes of pleasing Jezebel's father. With the onset of dementia, Emma's inability to groom herself showed. Ironically, Jezebel, who was not vain at all, was blessed with such natural good looks she rarely needed to put on makeup.

"Here you go," Jezebel said, wrapping the blanket around her mother. "It's too cold for you to be out here without one of these." She began leading her mother back to the house.

"Jezebel?" Her mother looked into her eyes, a fearful look on her face.

"What is it?"

"It's coming," Emma said. "Can't you feel it?"

"Feel what?"

"Darkness."

"It's only three o' clock. We still have plenty of time until sunset."

"Something's out there. Look at the crows."

The older woman glanced nervously at the windy lawn once more before Jezebel escorted her inside and shut the door. She sighed and sat her mother down in a chair next to the fire. These were the only times she felt like crying; the times she realized she was losing her mother to this new person, the fearful and fragile old woman whose hand shook too badly to comb her own hair.

"I tell you what. Why don't I make you some soup before I head back to the office? How does that sound?"

Emma didn't respond. She merely continued whispering to herself, clutching the blanket. The vacant expression returned. Her mother was deep inside her own world, one part memory and one part mysticism. But this talk of 'darkness' was new. A ringing broke the silence, and Jezebel removed the phone from her pocket.

"This is Sheriff Woods," she said, stepping into the kitchen.

"Print results are in on that suspected homicide," said the voice of Heavy Markham, her other deputy. Aptly named, Heavy was a slightly overweight man in his early sixties. Heavy's calm and steady presence was an asset to the department.

"And?" she asked. If the killer left prints on the victim's belongings or inside the truck, it would make her job that much easier.

"We pulled a partial off the door of the truck. The prints belonged to Alan Pittman, Sheriff."

She frowned. "Al Pittman lied to me. He claimed he didn't touch or move the body."

That disturbed her. Despite being the town drunk, Al was generally considered harmless. From her own interactions with him, she had a hard time believing he was capable of anything truly malicious. Unfortunately, her job wasn't to do what she believed, but to keep the people of Gray Hollow safe.

"Do you think Al killed the victim, Sheriff?"

"I'm not sure. When I arrive in town, I'm going to arrest Pittman for withholding information for a start. We can keep him in the station. That should give us enough time to figure out what to do with him. Do we have an ID?"

"Not yet. This is looking like a real ugly mess."

Jezebel agreed. "Let's pray it doesn't get any uglier. That's why I want to keep this quiet for the time being. I don't want any more dead bodies on my hands."

***

In the corner of the sheriff's office, Deputy Logan Randall listened carefully to the conversation between Heavy Markham and Jezebel Woods. His door was cracked open, just enough so that he could overhear what was being said.

So the sheriff planned to arrest Pittman. It wasn't surprising. Logan had warned her for years that the drunk was a threat to the community. Did Jezebel heed his warnings? No. Logan hated working for the sheriff, hated the very concept of it. He had seniority—even old Markham had seniority. It wasn't just that she was a woman; everything she handled was tempered with flexibility and compassion.

Logan believed the law was not flexible. The law existed for one reason: to punish the guilty, and it was his job to enforce it. The deputy wondered if there was a way he could use this new information to get himself elected sheriff. He had friends in high places.

The sound of the fax machine caught him off guard.

"Finally," he murmured aloud. He had been waiting for the readout to tell to whom the truck in the woods was licensed.

The name sent a shiver down his spine.

Wilbur Daniels.

He suddenly knew the name of the man inside the truck.

"Jeffrey," he said out loud, transfixed. After glancing around to make sure Markham wasn't looking, he tucked the fax into his pocket. He needed to make a call, and it wasn't to the sheriff.

Chapter THREE

Thomas was having a hard time concentrating on his work. It was difficult for him to finish his article, *County votes to increase property taxes*, with images from the gruesome murder scene swimming in his mind. He typed a few more sentences before sighing and stretching his arms in the air.

Outside, the sky was just starting to darken. Thomas gazed out the window after clicking print on his computer. He left the copy for Max and stepped back to his desk. Piles of old articles were stacked next to his computer.

"So much for Wilbur Daniels," he muttered, combing through the papers. The attempt to locate anything in the records of *Hollow Happenings* was proving to be a futile pursuit. Still, if there was one thing Thomas Brooks was once known for, it was his methodical approach to research.

Maybe I should call Eve back, he thought while staring at his phone. Thomas scrolled to the number but stopped before pressing the call button.

"Wait a second," he whispered, returning to the stack of papers at his desk. Thomas pushed the newspapers aside and removed a folder buried underneath.

Before returning from his trip to the feed mill, Thomas had stopped by the courthouse to obtain the public records of farm ownerships around the area where the victim in the Ford was found. He flipped through the records, reading the names of the farms. *Johnson's Dairy,* the *Alistair Farm, 6-R Farms,* and the *Daniels Farm.*

The Daniels Farm, as in Wilbur Daniels. Looks like my hunch was right, he thought. The land was currently deeded to a Paul Morris. More importantly, the farm was purchased from the original owner twenty-two years ago.

"Wilbur Daniels," Thomas said aloud. Was the victim Wilbur Daniels, returned to visit his old farm?

He wrote down the address of the Daniels Farm. If Daniels visited the farm, Paul Morris possibly saw him. From the deed, Thomas could tell the farm was a small one, surrounded by many acres of land owned by others.

This will help narrow the search, the reporter thought excitedly. Returning to the stack of newspapers, he sought out those papers published in the year of 1987.

There should be a record of the transaction, Thomas thought as he flipped through the December 2nd issue.

Dr. Paul Morris has purchased the Daniels Farm, he read in the business announcements page. *The farm, which belonged to Wilbur Daniels, was foreclosed to resolve his debts after his death. Daniels died of a heart attack in November.*

"Looks like I'm back to square one," Thomas said. If Daniels had been dead for twenty-two years, it was impossible for him to be the victim in the truck . . . yet the Ford was registered to Wilbur Daniels all the same.

Unless Daniels passed the truck on, he thought. He searched through the pile for all of the issues in November.

"Obituaries," he said aloud. "I knew it."

Wilbur had a son named Jeffrey, who had probably kept his father's truck. Smiling, Thomas scribbled furiously on his notepad. His theory was back on track.

If he went to the farm, Paul Morris should know.

He looked back at his cell phone, where Eve's name was still highlighted. Thomas wondered if it had been fair of him to call her. She *did* send him the information about the car, suggesting she didn't hate him entirely. At the same time, Thomas admitted to himself she appeared to have little desire to talk to him.

Maybe it was time to move on; Eve certainly seemed to share that sentiment. He sent her a quick text thanking her for the help. As he laid the phone back down on the desk it started to ring.

“Eve?” he asked, answering the phone without glancing at the display.

“This is Sheriff Woods. We found some alcohol in the victim’s bloodstream, but he was probably not inebriated when he died. Also, there have been some other developments you might want to hear about.”

“What developments?”

When she told him, Thomas almost didn’t believe it. He yanked his keys from the desk and grabbed his jacket.

“Hang on, I’ll be right over.”

***

Wind swept the trees as the police cruiser sped down the paved road, kicking fallen leaves in the air behind it. In the sky, pale clouds surrounded the red sun. The car’s lights were turned on in anticipation of the impending night, although the faint daylight managed to linger.

Logan Randall swerved left and continued onto a long driveway leading to a two-story brick house. After putting the cruiser in park, he stepped out of the vehicle. He grimaced at the chilling gusts and stared grimly past the trees lining the forest.

A familiar pain burned in his hands. His skin cracked in the cold weather, bleeding slightly from dryness. Logan realized part of the problem stemmed from washing his hands repeatedly, but he was a man obsessed with cleanliness. So far he was unable to shake the habit.

“Well, well,” said a man walking from the house. “Logan Randall. To what do I owe the surprise?” There was amusement in the man’s voice, yet his face was utterly serious.

“Gary Davis,” Logan said. “It’s been a long time.”

The two made eye contact and held it. Logan’s friend looked every bit the farmer he was, wearing torn jeans and a stained white shirt underneath an open button-up shirt.

“It has,” Gary replied. He wiped his hands on a dirty rag. Logan was temporarily distracted by the glow of orange lights around the lawn surrounding the house.

Several jack o' lanterns covered the porch, along with enormous cobwebs.

"Interesting decorations," he observed in a gruff voice. "The gnome is a nice touch."

"Mary," Gary replied humorlessly. "She's been after me for a week to get out the decorations for Halloween."

"Never figured you for much of a Halloween person."

"I do what the wife tells me. It's the only way to stay sane."

"How's Ben doing? Is he going to be a basketball star like his dad?"

"He's a chip off the old block," Gary said. "What is this about, Logan? I know you didn't come to see me to talk about my son's athletic ability."

Logan frowned. He was never good at small talk anyway. It was better to get straight to the point.

"Jeffrey Daniels is dead."

"What?" Gary blurted out, clearly confused.

"His body is in the morgue."

"I haven't heard from Jeff since his dad's funeral. I thought he moved."

"He did. Apparently, he came home for a visit."

"What does this have to do with you and me? Jeffrey hasn't spoken to me in years. You and I aren't too close anymore either."

Logan straightened his uniform. "It might mean nothing, but it could mean trouble."

"What do you mean?"

"It's not just that he's dead, Gary. It's how he died. His throat was cut, and his body was covered in lacerations. We found his truck crashed into a tree in the forest."

Gary's eyes widened. Logan fought back a sneer. *Now he gets it.*

"So he was murdered?"

"Yes. Jeff came to Gray Hollow without telling anyone and ended up dead. Quite a coincidence, wouldn't you say? Do you know where they found him?"

"Where?" Gary asked, staring intently at him. Logan now held his complete attention.

"Off Black Gnat. And before you ask, I don't think he drove all the way down just to visit his old house."

"Then where—"

"Do you really have to ask? You know what farm borders Black Gnat."

"No."

Logan saw fear in the farmer's eyes. "When we first found the body, I thought Al Pittman killed him. Al discovered the body, and it was easy to see he was looking for money. Sheriff Woods has him in custody right now."

Gary sighed with relief. "Thank God."

"You're not understanding, Gary. I said that's what I thought *at first.* The fact that it's Jeff changes everything."

"It is strange that Jeff of all people would die so close to that particular farm. You think it has something to do with . . ." he trailed off.

"I'm not sure," Logan said, his frown deepening. "But I'll find out."

Gary finally sighed and peered into the distance.

"Why did you come here, Logan?"

"Because if the two are connected, we could be in danger."

"I didn't think anyone else besides the five of us knew what happened that night."

"The four of us, after today. I already called our friend in the courthouse."

"What did he say?"

"He was skeptical. Listen, it could be nothing. Something about it just feels wrong to me. If you see or hear anything out of the ordinary, I want you to call me."

The two men watched the light begin to vanish from the sky as the winds whipped through the trees.

"I've been feeling strange, too," Gary said, scratching his back. "It's like that a lot this time of year."

"You don't have to feel guilty about it. We were teenagers. It's not like we were sober."

"Don't tell me you never think about it."

"Never," the deputy replied. Turning, he opened the car door and said goodbye to his former friend. He had other places to be.

Logan counted himself lucky to be a deputy. He was perfectly positioned to monitor the investigation. Perhaps more importantly, he could keep an eye on Jezebel Woods.

As he drove away, he promised himself the past would stay buried.

At any cost.

***

"Please don't make me ask you again, Al."

Jezebel gazed into the suspect's eyes intently and waited for an answer. Al Pittman shrank back from her, unwilling to meet the sheriff's penetrating stare. No longer bound by handcuffs, his hands trembled visibly on the desk. Seated across from him, she watched those hands shake, as if reaching for a drink to steady them.

"I already told you, Sheriff Woods, I didn't do anything wrong." Pittman followed her line of sight to his hands and tucked them under the table, showing at least some trace of social consciousness. It was too late. She knew he was afraid.

Good, she thought. *Then I'll get the truth that much sooner.* Jezebel never went out of her way to intimidate those on the wrong side of the law. She was, however, a firm believer in standing up to them. It was the only way to earn their respect.

"We're not dealing with disorderly conduct anymore. This is different. Murder is as serious as it gets."

"I told you, I didn't kill anybody!" Al's face turned red. The man seemed genuinely outraged.

Honestly, Jezebel didn't believe Pittman was capable of murder. That wasn't the point. She needed the truth from him, and so far he hadn't given it to her. "You're under arrest for interfering with a criminal investigation, not murder. At least not yet," she added for good measure. "You lied to me. That's why I'm having a hard time trusting you."

She leaned back in her chair when the station's heating system roared to life. Like most of the station's equipment, it was old and almost perpetually faulty. Jezebel knew complaining would do her no good; the struggling town could ill-afford to pay for new equipment. She would make do with the substandard heater until Gray Hollow was back on its feet.

"Now tell me about the wallet, Al."

"Someone dropped it outside the mill. I was going to take it back to them." He averted his gaze.

"Are you sure about that? Because we looked at the license inside the wallet we found on you; it belonged to a man named Jeffrey Daniels. You took his wallet, didn't you?"

When he looked down, there was shame in his eyes.

"OK, maybe I did. I really needed the money. It's hard to live wandering from place to place. You don't know what it's like, living on the street. When I saw that he was dead and found the wallet . . . I didn't think it would do any harm to keep it. Besides, he was dead. What was he going to do with the money?"

There it is, Jezebel thought. She sighed, shaking her head.

"If you lied to me about that, Al, then what else could you have lied about?" She stared at Pittman, waiting for the realization to dawn on him. "We found your prints on the body."

"I told you, I was looking for the wallet."

"Earlier you told me you didn't touch him at all. You propped him up, didn't you? You moved the body."

"Yes."

"That's two lies now, Al. Things aren't looking any better for you."

"I didn't kill him."

"I'm not saying you did, but we're going to keep you here until we figure out what really happened inside that vehicle. If someone saw you get into the truck with Jeffrey Daniels while he was still alive, it won't be hard for someone to put together a case that you killed him for his money. If that happens, you'll need a lawyer. I know you can't afford one, so I'll talk to Judge Underhill about appointing one for you."

"Thanks, Sheriff Woods. And thanks for the towels and mattress, too. You're a real nice lady."

If circumstances weren't so serious, she might have laughed. The absurdity of a potential murder suspect complimenting her during an interrogation was almost too much to bear. As she stood up to leave the room, Heavy opened the door.

"Thomas Brooks is here to see you. I'll take Pittman back to his cell if you want to speak with him."

"Thanks," Jezebel replied as she stepped into the hallway. Immediately, she could tell the journalist was angry about something.

"Thomas," she said. "We received the toxicology report. The victim wasn't over the legal limit, regardless of all the cans on the floorboard. His blood-alcohol was elevated, though."

"What do you think you're doing?" Thomas asked, folding his arms across his chest.

She didn't appreciate his tone. "Excuse me?"

"You know very well Al Pittman didn't kill Jeffrey Daniels. He definitely isn't capable of the cruelty inflicted upon the body. I haven't even lived in Gray Hollow six months, and I know that."

"That's your opinion." She stopped. "Wait a minute. How did you know that the victim's name was Jeffrey Daniels? He wasn't even from Gray Hollow."

"Thanks for keeping me in the loop," he said sarcastically. "Don't worry. I'm more than capable of doing a little research on my own. I've been following up on your leads for you."

"What does that mean?"

"Does the name Jack Grayson ring a bell? The man who runs the feed mill? Did you interview him to confirm Pittman's story?"

"I didn't have to," she said defensively. "We found Daniels' wallet in Pittman's jacket, which proves he lied to me."

The news seemed to catch Thomas off guard. He hesitated for a moment, as if considering whether or not to press the subject further.

"When I spoke with Jack Grayson, he told me Al raced back to the mill on his bike so he could call you. He didn't borrow any money to make the call, which sounded strange. He was using the cash he got out of the wallet."

"Which means he lied about not touching the body," she repeated.

"Jezebel, the man is homeless. Of course he would lie about looking for money. Why do you think I give him tips for information?"

The use of her first name did not go unnoticed by Jezebel. She had done him a favor by keeping him involved, and now he was telling her how to do her job. Thomas was dangerously close to crossing a line from which he couldn't return.

"His prints were all over the body," she said, hoping that an explanation would give him the chance to reconsider his approach.

"Did you find any evidence of blood on Al? If he cut Daniels' throat he should be covered with it."

She paused. "No. We didn't."

"Then you should let him go. Pittman hasn't done anything wrong, and he certainly didn't kill Jeffrey Daniels."

That was the last straw. Jezebel swept a strand of hair out of her face, glaring at Thomas.

"How dare you try to tell me how to do my job? In case you haven't noticed the badge on my chest, I'm the sheriff here, not you."

Thomas laughed derisively. "It's the same story, all the time. You're so worried about 'doing your job,' that you forget about justice."

Jezebel had to battle the urge to strike him. "Before I make you wish you had never showed up here tonight, let's both stop pretending you care about justice, Mr. Brooks. It's certainly not why you're interested in this case."

"You don't know me."

"I know your type. You like to complain about the system, but we're the ones who keep you safe. That's why Al Pittman is staying put. I'm not going to risk this town's safety to prove a point to you."

"Do you really think Al Pittman killed Jeffrey Daniels?" he asked, narrowing his gaze.

"No," she said. "I'm keeping him off the streets until we figure out what's actually going on. I thought you wanted to help with that. If you don't like the way I run this office, though, you're free to leave at any time. By the way, I don't know how they do things where you're from, but I have a title and I would appreciate if you used it. It's Sheriff Woods."

"I don't believe this," Thomas said. He threw his arms up in the air in exasperation. "Just so you know, *Sheriff*—Jeffrey Daniels isn't a stranger to Gray Hollow."

"You have exactly one minute to explain what you meant by that."

He laughed again, the sound of which caused her to see red. "You can read all about it in the paper."

"Fine," she snapped. "And you can spend the night in jail for obstruction of justice."

Thomas wore a look of utter disbelief. "You have got to be kidding me. Those charges will never stick."

Jezebel guessed he wasn't used to being challenged, but that was about to change. "Deputy Randall," she said. "Why don't you show Mr. Brooks the inside of one of our cells?"

***

Dusk ensnared the landscape, cloaking the horizon in a gray pallor. The night was waiting.

Something else was waiting too. An unearthly howl traveled across the sky, carried by the winds. The howl echoed over the fields of Gray Hollow. It was the sound of death.

Dry leaves scattered along the edge of a decaying forest. The forest was incredibly old, home to trees twisted in horrifying positions as if diseased somehow. Their branches stretched out like fingers with talons, waiting to seize unsuspecting prey. Thickets of razor sharp thorns and briars ran the length of the forest, perpetually shielded from the light.

A winged shadow descended from the sky. The crow landed in the center of a patch of rotting pumpkins outside a small cave. Surrounded by brush and fallen leaves, the cave was almost impossible to see. Even in the daylight, the inside appeared completely sable.

As the sky grew black, the darkness within the cave radiated outward. It reached out its consciousness, searching for its vassal. The power was still there, buried in the old cornfield miles away.

The darkness felt the energy of the first sacrifice. Slowly it woke from its slumber. Its return would be much swifter. Decades had passed, and it was hungry. Soon, its servant would feed it once more. That, too, would take time. The darkness did not have the strength to revive the thing buried within the cornfield. Not yet.

When the vassal rose again, chaos would be unleashed on Gray Hollow. More blood would be spilled, offered up to the entity within the cave. It had kept the boy alive for a reason.

Soon, its servant would unleash its dark children on Gray Hollow, and night would be filled with the taste of vengeance.

It was almost time.

Chapter FOUR

The night was pitch black by the time Thomas reached his house. After turning off the car's ignition, he lingered quietly for several minutes. Only by divulging what he'd learned about Jeffrey Daniels had he narrowly avoided spending the night in jail. Thomas realized too late he had taken the wrong approach with Jezebel Woods, who didn't seem swayed in the slightest by his apologies. Even so, there was an unmistakable look of realization on her face when he'd said Jeffrey's name.

A quick glance at his cell phone showed no evidence of a response from Eve. Not that he expected one.

"What a day," he mumbled. He opened the car door and saw a pair of eyes shimmer from behind a bush in front of his house. The reporter fumbled through his passenger seat for the remains of the sandwich he was eating on his way to the mill earlier. He tossed the sandwich to the black cat, which sniffed the bread halfheartedly. Choosing to ignore the sandwich, she brushed against his legs, purring.

"Sorry. That's all I've got this time," Thomas said to the stray. A few days after moving to Gray Hollow, he'd been napping on a lawn chair when the cat came slinking by. Needless to say, Thomas was startled when he woke to find himself staring into the feline's eyes. In the beginning, the two tolerated each other out of necessity. The house he purchased was in a small neighborhood on the edge of town; the stray could have come from anywhere. As time wore on, Thomas warmed to the cat. Maybe it stemmed from loneliness. Whatever the case, theirs was the perfect arrangement. He wasn't home long enough during the day to take care of a house cat.

"I'm home," Thomas said caustically when he entered the dark hallway. The house was a single story, and he had been amazed at the cheap price when he purchased it. Rates in Gray Hollow were extraordinarily low compared with what he was accustomed to in the city.

Aside from a fan spinning in the next room, the house was utterly quiet. Of the two houses next to his, one was currently empty. When Thomas arrived, the owners had a 'for sale' sign out in front. The sign hadn't budged during his stay. The other house belonged to a traveling salesman who was rarely home.

The floorboards squeaked beneath his feet as he made his way over to the light switch. He flipped on the light, illuminating a room devoid of all but the most necessary furniture. At least everything was clean.

Thomas walked into the kitchen and turned on the overhead light. He set his things down on the table before fixing a glass of ice water, then sipped at the drink while wrestling with the questions gripping his mind. The image of the crows in the window kept coming back to him. It was the one detail he had no explanation for. Thomas rubbed his temples in an effort to clear his head. The pill bottle loomed on the counter like a seductive temptress. For as long as he could remember, Thomas struggled with insomnia. Most nights he was able to drift off in a few hours or so. Sometimes it was worse.

As a writer, it was Thomas' memory for detail that plagued him. When he went to bed his mind remained in high gear, continuing to process thoughts from earlier in the day. He just couldn't stop thinking. Considering how busy as he was that afternoon, Thomas knew he wouldn't have an easy time getting to sleep. In the space of one day, he managed to alienate the sheriff, his boss, and Eve. Thomas pushed his notes away. He didn't want to think about the death of Jeffrey Daniels any more.

Jezebel was right to be angry with him. *When am I going to learn to keep my mouth shut?* Thomas wondered. Her comments about his motives were dead on. Why had he marched into the station and demanded the release of Al Pittman? The behavior *was* unlike him. Thomas wanted to believe it was out of a desire for justice, but in his heart he knew otherwise. There wasn't any harm in keeping Pittman in jail for the time being. No, Thomas needed to prove to himself that he was devoted to fairness, to honesty. That was probably because he wasn't actually devoted to either of those things.

"That's the thing about facts," one of his journalism professors said to him once. "Sometimes they're ugly." Which led to the inherent contradiction of twenty-first century journalism, in Thomas' opinion. People wanted a narrative, not a collection of facts, and nine times out of ten they wanted that narrative to be entertaining. That was fine with Thomas; he was very talented at advancing causes. That talent eventually morphed into a thorn in his side. Thomas found it hard to keep himself out of his articles, only able to ignore the urge for a time. Every person, even a journalist, was subjective at the core. Surely he couldn't be expected to avoid *all* biases.

Thomas shook his head. This was the last thing he wanted to think about now. He rose from his chair and grabbed the bottle on the countertop. He swallowed a sleeping pill. The kitchen went dark as he flipped off the switch on his way to the bedroom. Despite the pill, sleep proved elusive. Memories of his past life continued to plague him. Not so long ago, he had everything he always wanted. Then his perfect life collapsed around him.

He only had himself to blame. When a woman came forward claiming that she was involved in an extramarital relationship with a popular attorney general who was speculated to run for Governor of New Jersey, he should have known the story was too good to be true. Thomas wasn't convinced of her story, but she produced suggestive text messages on her phone. He also found a witness who said she could substantiate the claims—an old woman in the alleged mistress' apartment.

Thomas was anxious to write the article. He wanted to get it out before any other reporters caught wind of the story. It was, after all, a twenty-four hour news cycle. At the same time, he knew he was operating with very slim evidence. Thomas went against his reservations and published the story online anyway. Visions of awards and recognition danced in his head. He didn't know his Achilles heel was about to do him in.

"I stand behind what I wrote," he had said firmly to Amy Schiller, the editor-in-chief. Schiller was a stern and demanding woman in her mid-fifties. The story was even more of a success than Thomas anticipated. At first, the attorney general tried to deny the story, but another source confirmed that the texts had indeed come from his phone. His wife left him, and the man was followed everywhere he went by the media. In a tragic twist, the man committed suicide.

There was only one problem with the story. It was completely false. The elderly woman admitted she wasn't sure who exactly entered the "girlfriend's" apartment. Her eyesight wasn't what it once was, she claimed. The text messages indeed came from the attorney general's phone, but were mistakenly sent by one of the aides who managed his many cell phones.

Thomas' career was destroyed. His so-called sources were flimsy at best, and he didn't have a leg to stand on. He was fired almost immediately. Thrust into a limelight he never wanted, Thomas quickly discovered none of the other prominent media outlets would hire him. The resulting bitterness and conflict in his relationship with Eve led quickly to their breakup. A part of him would always resent Eve for not sticking by him when times were rough.

Sure, she said all the right things, made all the right excuses. Things such as, "You know what your problem is, Thomas? You don't trust anyone. You think you're alone, and you're not. You're pushing me away." Deep down, however, he couldn't shake the feeling that she left him because he wasn't successful anymore.

Did I even want her to stay? The medicine was taking effect. *If she didn't really love me, maybe it was for the best.*

He was stuck in a town called Gray Hollow, and it was all for the best? A part of him yearned to return to the city, to his past life. Yet could it ever be the same, after suffering such disillusionment? Thomas worked hard during the day, which left little time to consider such possibilities. It was only at night that he was forced to face himself.

Hollow Happenings was a small paper, but at this point he was willing to take whatever job he could. Thomas worked day and night to prove himself to his new editor. All he needed was one big story. Thomas felt his eyes close. The world was growing dimmer, and it was becoming more difficult to remember the events of the past clearly. Finally, he gave up and yielded to sleep.

***

The scratching started again. In the darkness of the barn, something scraped against the frayed wood of the sealed door. Upon hearing the noise, a curious mouse sniffed at the dirt underneath the door.

Tap. Tap.

The sound grew steadily stronger. Slowly, the door started to pull back. Stale air gushed from the cobweb-covered room as the dark contents of the room were exposed to the night air.

The mouse scurried out of the barn. As it passed the farm equipment and ran toward the cool grass, the mouse found itself staring into the eyes of a large golden retriever outside the barn.

"Get back here, Lizzy!" Gary yelled, calling for the dog. The dog hesitated, stared at the mouse, and then ran back in the direction of the farmhouse.

Save for the dim light provided by the sliver of moon, the sky was perfectly black. A coyote howled somewhere in the distance. Then everything fell silent, like the night was waiting for something.

Gary stood under the flickering porch light, gazing across the farm. Subconsciously, he felt something calling to him, beckoning. The farmer narrowed his eyes, a grim expression on his face.

"What's gotten into you?" he asked Lizzy. He rubbed the dog's thick fur.

Gary stared at the Halloween decorations. In the night, the once benign decorations seemed infinitely more threatening. His skin prickled as his imagination played tricks on him. Logan Randall's visit unnerved him a great deal more than he cared to admit.

A hand wrapped itself around his shoulder. Gary jumped back, startled.

"Are you coming in?"

His wife, Mary, stood in front of the screen door. She shuddered in the cold and folded her arms across her chest.

Get a hold of yourself, Gary thought.

"In a few minutes," he said. Lizzy curled up at his feet, watching the two adults with interest. The dog periodically glanced back at the barn, a gesture neither of them acknowledged.

"Is something bothering you?"

He was tempted to laugh. After all these years, he could never predict what his wife would do in any given situation —but she could read him like a book.

"No," he lied. "I just like watching the farm, that's all. We had a good harvest this year."

Truthfully, something *was* bothering him. He had little inclination to share the subject with his wife. The secret was his burden to carry. Alone.

"Suit yourself," she said. "It's freezing out here. I don't know how you stand it."

He could see her breath when she mouthed the words. A soft sound came from the direction of the barn, and Gary glanced over at the worn building. At his feet, Lizzy finally settled into an uneasy sleep.

When he turned back, the sound of the shutting screen door let him know Mary had returned to the warmth of the house. Gary was glad she chose not to press the issue. Communication was becoming more difficult between them lately. It was something he hoped was not a harbinger of things to come.

It didn't help that he usually grew more demanding during the fall season. For one, the harvest was frequently a stressful time for him. For another, it brought back bad memories from another time in his life.

"Forget you, Logan Randall," he muttered as he lit a cigarette. The farmer inhaled the smoke into his lungs. Gary knew smoking was a filthy habit. He tried to quit several times to satisfy Ben. Kicking the habit was more difficult than he anticipated, especially when things were so stressful.

Jeffrey Daniels is dead. No, not just dead. Murdered. Maybe it means nothing, Gary thought as he sucked down another lungful. As much as he wanted to believe that, he couldn't. *Logan would not have driven all the way out here if it wasn't serious.*

Going into the back room in the barn earlier spooked him enough as it was. He decided not to focus on what happened all those years ago. If Logan was right about anything, it was about not having regrets.

Having a child, though, mellowed Gary. He was no longer immune to doubts. Logan, who never married, was clueless in that department. Gary doubted Logan ever put anyone first other than himself.

Bottling it in is the worst part. Living in fear. Fear that, unlikely as it was, he would be found out. Fear of the unknown. It didn't surprise him that Jeff came home. Jeff was always the one closest to what had happened that night. After all, he was living next to the Alistair Farm at the time. Gary was sure that was why Jeff moved away from Gray Hollow when his father died. He was never close to Jeff, so he couldn't be sure; of all the people there that night, Jeff was the outsider.

"That's it," Gary said. He flicked the cigarette away. He wasn't going to think about this anymore. The door creaked when he opened it, and he left the porch behind.

As he reached for the lock, Gary glanced out the window. He did a double take when he saw what looked like a shadow emerge from the barn. He was certain he was imagining things, but for a moment he thought he saw something like a pitchfork in its grip. Before becoming fully alarmed, Gary blinked hard and rubbed his eyes. He peered out the window again, but all he saw was the dark grass rippling in the autumn wind.

The air was cooler than usual inside the house. Gary turned up the thermostat on his way up the stairs and flipped off the light switch. Outside, he could still see the glow of the Halloween lights. The lights were actually comforting to the part of his brain still disturbed by Logan

Randall's visit. On some childlike level, the lights made him feel safe.

He looked into his son's room. The boy was asleep, curled up next to a brown teddy bear. Gary frowned. In his opinion, Ben was getting a little too old for a stuffed animal. He was almost eight. If he could play sports, he shouldn't be sleeping with a teddy bear.

"Ben's out of it," Gary said when he entered their bedroom. Mary was already in bed reading a book.

"Did you go over his homework?" Mary asked without bothering to look up.

Gary pulled his shirt over his head and grabbed his toothbrush. He was supposed to help Ben with math.

"I was going to, Mary, I promise. He's asleep."

"Why did I have a feeling you were going to say that? You know Ben's struggling. It isn't hard to contribute."

Of course I contribute, he thought, frustrated. *What else do you call rooting around in the barn for decorations?*

"Maybe you should do it," Gary said, taking off his watch. "Aren't you better at that sort of thing anyway? Math has never been my strong suit."

He instantly regretted his words, realizing they would probably start another fight about his involvement in his son's life. With a sigh, he settled into bed next to her and waited.

"That's the truth," Mary muttered dispassionately. Gary waited for the usual crack about his lack of a college education to come up, but it didn't. He wasn't sure if he should take her lack of caring as a good or bad sign.

After a few minutes of total silence, the sound of barking echoed through the night.

Mary looked up at him.

"Are you going to put a stop to that?"

"Honey, Lizzy's probably chasing a rabbit or something."

The barking grew louder and more urgent.

"Gary—"

"Fine," he muttered. Gary slid from under the covers. He looked under the blinds of the window and glanced down at the porch. The golden retriever was growling at something in the field.

Gary's eyes widened when he spotted a shadowy figure walking toward the house under the barn light. It was too dark to see who it was. The figure looked up at him, almost as if whomever it was knew Gary was watching.

Did Logan come back? Perhaps the deputy forgot to mention something earlier. But surely he would have called, were that the case.

"What is it?" Mary asked.

"There's someone outside. Stay here, I'm going to see who it is."

"For God's sake, Gary, call the cops first."

He nodded and grabbed his phone. "That's weird," he muttered. "My phone's not working."

"Neither is mine," Mary said, surprised. "It's dead."

"Try the landline," Gary said. "I'm going to find out what's happening." He snatched his shirt off the floor. Gary was halfway down the stairs when he heard something that sounded like a yelp from Lizzy. He took off running down the steps. When the farmer threw open the screen door, he saw his dog lying on the ground, whimpering.

"Lizzy!" Gary yelled. He knelt down next to her and ran trembling hands through her fur. There was no police car around. This was not the work of Logan Randall.

An expression of horror crossed his face as he drew his hand back. It was wet. In the dim light of the lawn decorations, he could see blood on his hands.

Then all the power went off. The lawn decorations, the barn light, and the house electricity faded. Complete blackness cloaked the farm.

"Gary?" he heard Mary call from the house. "None of the phones are working."

"Stay there," he repeated. Gary ran to the toolbox in the shed close to the barn. He shivered in the cold, his hands shaking. As he turned to go back to the house, Gary heard the screen door slam shut.

He's inside the house, Gary realized, and his skin started to crawl. He cast one furtive glance toward the dying retriever, then threw open the door to his house and stepped inside.

"Mary," he whispered. There was no response. The house was completely dark, with no sign of movement. Everything was quiet.

He crept toward the bottom of the staircase. Gary's eyes slowly adjusted to the darkness, and he carefully inspected the living room and dining room as he passed them. The intruder could be hiding anywhere. He gripped the staircase and made his way up, listening quietly for warning signs.

The door to his son's room was open. Ben wasn't in his bed. Then Gary heard something coming from his bedroom. He tiptoed inside.

"Gary," his wife whispered. She was on the floor next to the bed, holding Ben. Her hands were shaking. "There's someone in the house."

"I know," he replied. "I'm going to sneak back downstairs and get the rifle. You lock the door and don't open it."

The floorboards creaked underneath him when he stepped off the last stair. Every hair on the farmer's body stood on end. He snatched the keys off the counter and ran to his office to get to the safe. His foot caught on something resting in the hallway, and Gary slipped. The key fell out of his hands. He looked to see what he tripped over.

A pitchfork.

"Gary," a strange voice called in the darkness. The farmer scrambled backwards on the floor. A distorted shape stepped out of the shadows. Gary reached out and grabbed the key. The figure started toward him. Gary hobbled toward the safe. His ankle was sprained, maybe worse.

The figure bent down, picked up the pitchfork, and continued walking slowly in his direction. Gary thrust the key into the safe hastily and removed the rifle, fumbling to switch the safety off.

He could feel the intruder closing in on him. Gary swung the gun in the direction of the shadowy figure. His shaking finger pulled the trigger.

The shell exploded out of the gun. It caught the figure squarely in the chest. The figure was picked up by the impact and thrown back into the next room.

How? Gary thought, clutching the rifle tightly. No person would have been sent back that far into the air, even at such close range. He stepped back into the hallway.

Through the window, a beam of moonlight illuminated the hallway. There was no body on the ground. Instead, he could see a lump of what looked like hay strung out over the floorboards.

"Impossible," he said. He ran his hands through the straw. He saw the shadow move on the wall behind him. Gary moved to get out of the way, but he wasn't fast enough. The pitchfork slashed the front of his chest. Gary shouted in pain, firing again.

This time, his shot went wild and shattered the window. A cool breeze swept into the house. Gary slumped to the ground, his head spinning in pain.

Above, Mary screamed from inside the bedroom. The figure turned and headed up the staircase.

"No," Gary cried. He tried to stand, and his weight collapsed due to his ankle. He started to crawl.

The figure staggered to the top of the stairs and pounded away at the door.

***

Inside the bedroom, Mary remained frozen. Ben cried in her arms. Then everything went silent. She started to stand up, unsure of what to do.

"Gary?" she whispered, inching closer to the door.

The spikes of the pitchfork tore through the door. She screamed as the figure on the other side of the door ripped the pitchfork out and slammed it against the wooden door again and again.

"Ben!" she shouted, searching desperately for a way out. Mary ran over to the window and motioned for her son to follow her. She tried opening the window, but it was stuck. Tears streaked down her face. Finally, she succeeded in getting the window open.

"Ben, get out on the roof," she said, urging him forward.

At that moment, the door burst open. Mary screamed as a dark figure slowly walked into the bedroom. As it grew closer, the moonlight from the outside covered it in an unearthly glow. She found herself rooted to the spot, unable to look at anything except its horrifying stitched face.

The pitchfork slammed into her, pinning her to the wall. She felt a sharp pain, and blood gushed from her body. The figure turned to the boy standing next to the window.

A bullet slammed into the intruder. "Come on," Gary shouted. He helped his son out onto the roof. He held Ben's hand tightly, afraid their pursuer would rise again.

Inside the bedroom, the figure picked itself up again.

As Gary turned to move, his eyes locked on the dead body pinned to the wall. He lost his balance and fell off the roof, taking Ben with him. Everything went black.

Disoriented, he opened his eyes. The ground felt hard beneath him. And cold. He could feel his blood leaking through his clothes and into the soil. Every part of his body was in pain. The rifle loomed in the distance.

I fell, Gary remembered when he spotted the roof.

Then he saw his son next to him, face down on the ground.

"Ben?" he asked, trying desperately to wake his son. Gary shook the boy. There was no response.

Gary thought he heard laughter coming from inside the house. He looked up into the window and saw a familiar twisted face looking down at him. When he blinked, the figure disappeared.

For a moment, all was silent once more. Then he heard the creaking sound of the staircase coming from inside the house. The screen door swung open a few seconds later.

Chapter FIVE

It was still dark when Jezebel pulled into the driveway. Located on the western end of the county, the remote farm was almost completely cut off from the rest of Gray Hollow. She quickly decided not to wait for Logan Randall and got out of the car. When he did arrive, Logan was going to be testy. The deputy wasn't happy to take her call so early in the morning. Jezebel put him in his place over the phone. She was the sheriff, and she intended for it to stay that way. Right now, their differences would have to take a back seat to the task at hand. They had work to do.

She cleared her throat.

"Mr. Brinkley?" Walking over to a dirt-covered truck, she found herself looking at a sixtyish man leaning against the vehicle. Jezebel spotted a young boy in the truck staring down at the floorboard.

"That's me," he said in a weak voice, "Mike Brinkley." His gray hair, peppered with remnants of black, was disheveled. He looked genuinely disturbed.

Jezebel paused. The words caught in her throat. This was really happening. Someone else was dead. It was only yesterday they discovered the first body. It was too early to tell if the two killings were connected, but her gut told her they were. Jezebel didn't believe in coincidences.

"Would you mind telling me what happened?" the sheriff asked. "I realize we went over it on the phone, but I need you to go over exactly what you did this morning."

This changed the parameters of the investigation entirely. Jezebel had hoped to catch whoever killed Jeffrey Daniels quickly. Above all, she prayed it was an isolated incident. If other people were being killed, it was more than just some thief looking to score some money. Someone was out there murdering the people of Gray Hollow. Jezebel needed to figure out why, and fast. Before things escalated even further.

"I had just settled down to bed last night," Brinkley said. He stared at the silent house. "We live on the farm over past the creek. That's my grandson, Tim, in the car. If I'd known what was waiting for us here, I never would have brought him."

Jezebel saw the bloodied carcass of a dog close to the barn. The yellow fur was mixed with a sea of red. She felt a stab of pity for the boy in the truck.

"Around eleven or so last night, I thought I heard gunshots. Sounded like it might be someone poaching on Mary's land, but I went over here this morning just to check."

"Mary?" Jezebel asked.

"She brought us banana bread once when we moved here," the old man said quietly. "She introduced herself, along with her boy." The sheriff could hear the regret in his voice. She suspected the man was wondering how things might have been different if he went to the farm immediately after hearing the shots.

"How many gunshots did you hear?" Jezebel asked.

"At least three. Maybe more."

Jeffrey Daniels died from bleeding to death, not from a gunshot. *We need to find the weapon,* she thought. *Maybe we can trace it.*

"So the victims were shot to death?"

"That's the strange thing. I didn't see any bullet holes on the—on the bodies. Though I didn't look too close," he added quickly.

"Two victims," she said. "One in the house, one outside?"

"That's right. The boy is over there under the window. I didn't move the body. Mary is in the upstairs bedroom."

When Brinkley phoned her, Jezebel called in both of her deputies immediately. Heavy was going to the office to start the paperwork, and Logan Randall was en route to the farm.

"My deputy is checking up on the family. It shouldn't take too long to identify the bodies. Did you know the victims well?"

"No, I only met Mary once. We're new here. Moved from Thistlewood last year. They mostly kept to themselves. I can tell you that there were three of them. Two parents and a child."

Which means the man is missing, she thought. *He could be the one who owns the rifle.* On the surface, domestic violence sounded plausible. *But how does that relate to Jeffrey Daniels?* This farm was on almost the opposite end of the county from where Daniels' body was found.

"When did you find the bodies?"

Dust rose in the air on the gravel road in the distance as Logan Randall's cruiser neared the farmhouse. Brinkley paused before answering as Jezebel's deputy pulled next to her cruiser.

"About 6:10," he answered, his eyes on the approaching deputy. "Tim and I wake up early every morning to milk the cows. Checking up on Mary and her family seemed like the neighborly thing to do."

"Why did you wait until morning to call our department?"

"I thought maybe they were shooting at a coyote or some animal," he said. "Nothing around here is in season though."

"Sure you did," said Logan Randall. "Wonder if the kid has the same story."

"Logan, that boy doesn't look like he's in any condition to talk right now," Jezebel shot back. She was not in the mood to tolerate his attitude. Not today. "I need you to go behind the truck and examine the body while I finish up with Mr. Brinkley."

"Of course," Logan replied. He hardly bothered concealing his contempt for her.

"Sorry about that," she said to Brinkley. "We can wait to take a statement from your grandson."

"Thank you. I've never seen him like this before."

Jezebel sighed. She couldn't find fault with Brinkley for failing to call in the gunshots when he heard them. However, if he had, they might have been able to catch the killer in the act.

"If you can, please tell me exactly what you did when you first reached the farm."

***

Logan Randall listened carefully to the conversation as he examined the body of Ben Davis. True, he could always go through the sheriff's report later, but he knew there was always more to be learned from listening to a witness firsthand.

Logan stood in this very location only a few hours ago. That fact unnerved him greatly, which was something he didn't care to admit. Ben was dead. According to what the sheriff told him, so was Mary.

Did Gary do this? Did he kill Jeff too? Logan made a mental note to himself to go through the phone records to see if Jeff called Gary before driving to Gray Hollow. He knew the sheriff would. Given enough time, Jezebel Woods would find the connection between the two men. It might lead all the way back to him. That was why it was critical to slow her down for as long as he could.

Otherwise . . .

Still, why would Gary have killed Jeff? It was in many ways unlikely. When the two spoke in the yard, he seemed sincerely shocked to hear of the murder. Whatever his faults, Gary loved his family.

People snap all the time, Logan thought, grimacing. Things were moving too quickly. There was another possibility he didn't want to consider.

In many ways, it would be easier if Gary had killed everyone. Both of them were in the cornfield that October night. If someone else learned their secret and then committed the killings, *that* would be a real reason for worry.

***

"When I saw the body upstairs, I threw up," Brinkley finished. He gave Jezebel another feeble look. "I'm sorry, but I couldn't help myself."

Is it that bad? Jezebel wondered. This was ugly, which was one thing it had in common with the death of Jeffrey Daniels. Murder was bad enough. The savage nature of these crimes crossed the line in an even bigger way. "Mr. Brinkley, I'm sorry to have to ask you to do this, but I need you to go inside with me to help point out what you did when you went into the house."

"Do I have to?" The color went out of his cheeks. A fat crow landed on the barn light and looked down at the scene below.

"Please. Your help will bring us that much closer to catching whoever did this to these poor people. Otherwise, the killings might spread."

The static on her radio roared to life.

"Sheriff Woods?" It was Heavy.

"Yes," she replied, pressing the call button. "Tell me you've got something for me."

"I have the results for 321 Pale Cross Road. The house at that address is belongs to Gary Davis. It matches the G. and Mary Davis found in the phonebook."

The words struck a distant cord in her memory.

"That name," Jezebel whispered.

"What's that?"

"I know him—Gary Davis." Jezebel turned away from Mike Brinkley, who was looking at her with unabashed curiosity.

When Jezebel was growing up, Gary Davis attended her high school. It was a long time since they last crossed paths, even though she knew he still lived in Gray Hollow.

It means something, she thought, though she could not figure out what. The horror of the scene stopped her from yawning, but her head was spinning. Only the adrenaline was keeping her going. She needed rest, needed to be thinking straight. This case demanded her at her best.

"Do you have anything else for me?" Jezebel asked.

"Not at the moment."

"Oh, wait. There are two cars registered in his name." Heavy gave her the model and license numbers of the van and truck that belonged to the Davis family.

"Excuse me one moment," she said to Brinkley, who looked relieved simply to not enter the house. Jezebel walked over to Logan Randall, who was still standing over the boy's body.

"Did you see any sign of a bullet wound?"

"No," he said, shaking his head. "I think his neck is broken."

Jezebel looked up at the open window.

"That's the room where Mr. Brinkley found the woman's body. It looks like the boy might have fallen from the roof trying to get out. This house belongs to Gary Davis, Logan. Didn't you two know each other at some point?"

"No," he replied a little too quickly. "I think we went to the same school. So did you, if I recall. Most of us in the county did."

"Right," Jezebel said. Logan was three years older than the sheriff. She couldn't help feeling that something about his expression seemed suspicious.

"What are you thinking?" he asked, staring deep into her eyes.

"It's too early to know. I haven't even been inside the house yet."

"Seems pretty straightforward to me. Looks like Davis went crazy and killed his family. They're dead and he's gone."

"Doesn't it strike you as odd that these murders happened so close together with the death of Jeffrey Daniels?"

"It happens." Logan shrugged his shoulders.

"Maybe. I think there's more to the story. Brinkley said he heard gunshots, yet according to him, neither body has a bullet wound."

Jezebel stopped and radioed in.

"Heavy, this is Sheriff Woods again. This means Al Pittman is in the clear, since he was tucked safely away in a jail cell. Thomas Brooks was right."

Thomas Brooks. In all the confusion, she had forgotten about him. He would probably expect her to share something like this with him, but his lukewarm apology for his behavior inside the station had not gone over well with her. As far as she was concerned, Thomas was lucky she hadn't kept him in jail overnight anyway.

Even if he hadn't shown his true colors, Jezebel likely would have kept the news from him. She couldn't take the risk he would spin the town into a panic with a story portraying Gary Davis as some kind of serial killer. The truth was, there weren't enough facts yet to know what exactly happened to Gary and his family. Jezebel was determined to find the truth, and that most certainly did not involve Thomas Brooks.

I can't keep three murders under wraps forever, she thought. The situation was unraveling beyond her ability to control.

"You're letting Pittman go?" Logan asked. "That's a mistake." He grabbed her shoulder. "These could be two separate killings. You don't have any evidence linking the two."

Jezebel pulled free of his grip. "Deputy, the *only* reason I kept Pittman in custody in the first place was to make absolutely sure no one would get hurt. I didn't think he was a killer for one second. Now we've had two more bodies turn up anyway. Al Pittman may be a person of interest, but I'm not holding him any longer. It's not like he has the means to leave the county anyway."

"I disagree—"

"Sorry, that's the way it's going to be."

He shot her a scathing look. Jezebel noticed that Logan seemed to grow increasingly angry as of late when he didn't get his way.

"Now, I need you to go check the barn and the garage for the two vehicles registered to Davis. If he's on the run, we need to be able to find him." As Deputy Randall stalked away in the direction of the barn, Jezebel returned to Mike Brinkley.

"Do you think that man—Gary—did this?" Brinkley asked while leading her into the house.

"Anything is possible," she replied cryptically. The circumstances did look bad for Gary Davis. Still, there were other considerations to take into account, like motive. Jezebel wasn't about to waste time explaining police procedure to the pale man in front of her. The natural light coming into the house wasn't enough, so she used her flashlight to search for signs of a struggle.

"That looks like a bullet hole," she said, pointing to the wall in the hallway. Paint and wood were shattered.

"I missed that when I was in here," he said. Jezebel removed the shell from the wall and placed it in a sealed bag. Then she bent down and inspected a clump of material below the damaged wall.

Straw, Jezebel thought. She picked up the matted hay with her glove. The sheriff wondered if it was part of the Halloween decorations outside. Jezebel tried flipping on the light switch.

"The power's off," she said. If Gary Davis killed his family on the spur of the moment, why would he go through the trouble to shut the power off?

"Up here," Brinkley said. He walked slowly up the stairs. "I checked all the other rooms before this one." He hesitated, then turned to the door on the right.

"My God," Jezebel whispered when she saw the woman in the room. Forcing herself to dust the pitchfork for prints, she watched Mike Brinkley face the door, unable to look. "There's another bullet hole," Jezebel said, pointing to the wall. "You can go back outside, Mr. Brinkley. I can handle it from here."

"Thank you, ma'am," he replied weakly. The old man quickly made his way down the stairs.

"Sheriff Woods," came Deputy Randall's voice over the radio. "I found the vehicles. Both of them."

"Then he's likely on foot. I'll call Heavy and have him put out an APB for Gary Davis. We might be able to get some police officers from Thistlewood to help us with the search." Jezebel put her hands on the windowpane to steady herself. The cool, fresh air relaxed her as it washed over her face. Outside, the sky was beginning to lighten.

The sheriff turned back to the dim bedroom and switched her flashlight off. There was still a lot of work ahead, but then it would be time to start connecting some of the dots. First, she needed Gary Davis in handcuffs.

In the pale light of morning, Jezebel saw something strange. The white sheets of the bed were pulled up over a pointy shape. She walked slowly to the bed and reached out to grab the sheets to reveal what was concealed underneath.

The sheets slid down, exposing a horrific face. Jezebel stifled a scream. The menacing visage of a withered scarecrow stared blankly back at her, a stitched smile frozen across its face.

Inert, the scarecrow fell forward when the sheets slid off, sprawling clumsily across the mattress.

It can't be, Jezebel thought. "Salem," she whispered.

***

His feet crushed the brown grass as he fled through the forest. Gary heard dry twigs snap loudly underneath his feet. He prayed nothing else could hear the sound.

In the distance, he thought he heard sirens briefly. When the bodies were discovered, Gary knew he would be blamed. No one would believe him.

I have to get to Logan, Gary thought. He raced down a steep hill. His injured ankle buckled, and he fell face first into the leaves. He crawled behind a massive tree trunk to catch his breath.

The wound from the pitchfork was deep, and the pain in his chest was intense. Grimacing, he pulled his fingers back from the injury. There was nowhere nearby he could find a bandage. Or stitches.

Where am I? Gary thought, disoriented. Dried sweat covered his shivering body. Nestled firmly in his hands, the rifle felt abnormally heavy.

He had run for hours in the darkness. Something hunted him, stalking him across the forest. Gary peeked out from behind the tree and checked to see if he was alone. He heard nothing aside from the regular sounds of the tranquil forest and the beating of his own heart.

A crow landed on an outstretched branch of a tree not far from him. Gary watched the bird, which seemed to be looking for something. He shook his head vigorously in an attempt to focus. Gary closed his eyes, wondering if he was going insane. It all seemed like a dream, like a vicious nightmare sprung forth to life to devour him.

Crunch.

Gary's eyes snapped open. He listened carefully while trying to remain as quiet as possible.

Crunch. There it was again. Something was walking through the forest. Was it the thing that attacked him in the house?

Why is this happening to me? Gary thought. The answer came to him before he even finished asking the question.

The sound was louder. The thing stalking him was growing closer. Then he saw it. The scarecrow stepped out into a clearing below, surveying the hill Gary just came from.

The farmer realized something was wrong. Something was very wrong. As morning approached, he could see the stalker more clearly.

It wasn't the same as the intruder that invaded his home. The design was similar but different.

Then Gary heard another crunch and looked up. Standing mere feet from him was a second figure. Gary tried not to breathe, unable to avert his gaze from the shadowy form. It stretched out its worn face as if smelling the air.

His heart pounded louder than ever. Surely it would hear him.

The creature stepped farther away and walked down to the creek below. The other figure had already disappeared over the next hill.

Gary shifted just an inch, and another twig snapped under him. The crow in the tree turned its head slowly until its eyes were looking directly into him.

He heard the sound of footsteps in the distance again. They were coming back. The farmer swore. Gary threw himself out from behind the tree and ran as hard as he could in the opposite direction.

The creatures watched Gary emerge from his hiding place. Sunlight began to spread through the forest, and they shrank back toward the dark.

Chapter SIX

It didn't take Thomas long to figure out something was wrong. The day started innocently enough: after allowing himself to sleep in a bit later than usual, he made a quick outline of his notes from the previous night before showering and heading to work. He spotted the latest edition of *Hollow Happenings* propped against the porch on his way outside. His article on property taxes was the front-page story. The innocuous headline gave no hint of things to come. Thomas dialed Max to give him a heads up.

"I'll be at the office in about two hours or so," he said after the editor picked up. "I'm going to spend time in town trying to get a fix on who knew Wilbur and Jeffrey Daniels."

"I'm not sure that's the best use of your time," Max replied. "Didn't you say Wilbur Daniels died over a decade ago? I doubt many people will remember his son."

"If there's one thing I've learned about small towns, it's that people have long memories. If that doesn't pan out, I have another lead. A doctor named Paul Morris purchased the Daniels farm after Wilbur died."

"You think Jeffrey might have visited his old farm the night he died?"

"There has to be a reason he came back. If he showed up at the farm, Morris could have spoken with him. Gotta go." Ending the call, Thomas let his foot off the car's gas pedal as he neared the outskirts of Gray Hollow. The refuel light came on suddenly, and he noticed that he was running low on gas.

"Perfect timing," he muttered aloud. A Minute Mart gas station was only one right turn away. When living in the city, Thomas usually relied on public transportation and rarely went anywhere in his car. His residence in Gray Hollow seemed to require him to drive long distances regularly. Although the town's population was under four thousand people, it spanned a surprising amount of land. Forgetting to pay attention to the level of fuel in his tank was a habit he needed to break.

Thomas turned on his signal before pulling into the gas station. In reality, as long as he was close to town he needn't fear running out of fuel. Gray Hollow was covered in gas stations. The reporter found it almost comical. The town didn't have many nice restaurants or clothing outlets yet possessed a multitude of gas stations.

"Good morning, Mr. Brooks," a matronly woman said from the pump across from him when he began fueling his vehicle.

"Hi," he replied, unable to identify the woman. That was another aspect of small town life that was hard to get used to. So many people he never met somehow knew him by sight.

"I read your article on the tax hikes," the woman continued. "It's a shame. I'm Paulina Gregson, by the way."

"Nice to meet you. Honestly, I'm shocked the topic has gotten so much attention."

"You'd be surprised," the woman replied, removing the cap from her gas tank. "Most of the community's wealth is in land."

Thomas looked out at the town beyond the gas station, which was notably muted in activity. There were a few mechanics and auto repair places on both sides of the road. A small strip mall bordered the community park, which overlooked Town Hall. The other important buildings, such as the county school and local hospital, were out of sight.

"If it makes you feel any better, property taxes are a lot higher where I come from." *That's weird,* he thought, trying to slide his credit card into the pump machine. *It isn't working.*

"I think the machine's out of order," Paulina said. "It breaks down from time to time."

"Thanks," Thomas said before turning to go inside the Minute Mart.

Paulina stopped him. "By the way, what's the story on the truck accident out by the Alistair Farm? My friend, Beatrice, saw the caution tape on her way to bingo."

Word spreads faster than lightning around here, Thomas thought. "Keep reading the paper," he said. "That's all I can say for now." Thomas felt her gaze follow him into the store.

The way Paulina said the words 'Alistair Farm' stuck in his mind while he paid. As he returned to the car, Thomas remembered the name of the property from his research. It adjoined the farm where Jeffrey and Wilbur Daniels once lived.

The woman placed more emphasis on the farm than the accident itself. It almost sounded like she *expected* something wrong to be associated with that area. The crash occurred closer in proximity to the Daniels Farm than the Alistair property, but Thomas couldn't deny the knowing curiosity in Paulina Gregson's eyes.

He considered her expression as he drove farther into town. He eased the car into an empty parking space at the edge of the town square. Cold air gently brushed over him as he made his way across the street to the coffee shop.

"I know what you're thinking," said a man busy reading a newspaper on a bench. "For as small as this place is, the parking spots always seem to be filled."

"You can say that again," Thomas replied. "How are you this morning, Bob?"

Bob Lipton was a regular at Dina's Coffee Diner, the aroma of which drew in most of Gray Hollow's commuters at some point during the day. Even Thomas wasn't immune to its charms.

"Same as always. Give me something to read and something to drink and I get by."

Thomas laughed. He admired the man's easygoing attitude, which was a far cry from his own fast-paced lifestyle. Since *Hollow Happenings* only came out twice a week, Thomas noticed that Lipton often supplemented his reading materials with random periodicals from inside the diner.

"Headed somewhere in particular?" Bob asked, staring out from behind his thick glasses. "Chasing down the latest gossip?"

"You're more right than you know. I was planning on going by the sheriff's office when I finished here. Then it's back to the paper for me."

The residents of Gray Hollow would have plenty to gossip about when the details of the crash were eventually revealed. Thomas hoped Bob and the rest of the town would be able to enjoy the peace for as long as they could. If the murderer killed again, things were going to get ugly. Thomas stepped into the old-fashioned diner and was instantly confronted with the overpowering scent of freshly brewed coffee.

Just what I need, he thought, anxious to get a jumpstart on the day. After finding his place in the small line, the reporter looked at the rows of empty booths. The normally crowded diner was all but abandoned. A broken light flickered near the bathrooms at the end of the hallway. No one seemed in any hurry to fix it, allowing a thin specter of shadow to perforate through the back of the store.

Thomas struck up small talk with several of the other patrons while he waited, hoping to glean some information about the mysterious Jeffrey Daniels. No one seemed to know anything about the murdered man.

It looks like Max was right, he thought when he reached the front of the line. *This is probably a dead end.*

"I'll have the caramel mocha," he said politely. Thomas reached for his wallet. "Pretty quiet in here today."

The man across the counter grunted noncommittally.

"That'll be $3.53," the cashier said, waiting expectantly for payment. Thomas handed over what happened to be exact change and left the diner with his beverage in hand.

The warmth of the diner faded almost as soon as his hand let go of the door handle. Thomas exhaled, his visible breath rising to the level of his eyes. The police station was only a few blocks away, well within walking distance.

"Well, I'm off," he said, waving goodbye to Bob. Then he stopped. "You're pretty informed of what goes on around here," he began. "I'm not sure if you're aware of it or not, but the sheriff picked up Al Pittman yesterday. I heard it might have something to do with some trouble he was in around the Daniels Farm—or the Alistair Farm."

"If you're looking for a news headline, you're looking in the wrong place," Bob replied in an amused tone. "Al Pittman getting into trouble isn't exactly news. That being said, I don't think he would have anything to do with the Alistair Farm."

Thomas narrowed his eyes. "Why not?"

The man folded his newspaper. "Back in the day, there used to be plenty of rumors about that old farm. It's been abandoned for years, and some folks believe it's haunted. Rumors breed superstition."

"Thanks for the tip," Thomas said. He shook his head. Ghost stories weren't exactly the substantial lead he was hoping for.

I think it's time to pay the sheriff a visit myself, he thought. *That ought to straighten things out.* He knew he probably needed to apologize again for his outburst the night before. Touching base with Jezebel might be a helpful start before he delved into the day's work. Other than Paul Morris, Thomas didn't have many leads at the moment. Now that the sheriff's department should've finished their reports, he hoped the results would point him in the right direction.

Thomas took the long route and walked through the county park on his way to the sheriff's office. Small as it was, Gray Hollow had a certain charm to it, he thought as he enjoyed his coffee in the crisp morning air. There was an unpolluted quality to the town, which seemed suspended in time. Thomas wandered down a winding path cut through the grass, surrounded on each side by trees and the occasional bench. The sun peeked out from behind the clouds, giving life to the multicolored leaves of the trees.

Finally he came to the police station, which stood beside Rex's Grocery. Inside, Thomas was greeted with mountains of paperwork and the smell of worn leather seats. In a way, the police station reminded him of the offices at the newspaper. Much like the town itself, the station was virtually devoid of activity.

"Deputy Markham?" Thomas asked the heavyset older man busy with paperwork.

"What's that?" the man replied quickly, as if surprised by the reporter's sudden appearance.

"Sorry if I startled you. I'm Thomas Brooks, in case you don't remember me."

"Not at all, Mr. Brooks. We're in the middle of a big case, and I was a little preoccupied."

Big case? Thomas thought. From the tone of the officer's voice, it sounded like they were investigating something recent. Was the deputy referring to the wreck or something else?

"I don't mean to intrude," he said. "I just wanted to touch base with Sheriff Woods. Is she in?"

"She's out at the moment. Want me to take a message?"

"No thanks," Thomas answered. Something felt strange, but he wasn't sure what. "I'll give her a call later."

He thanked the deputy for his help and made his way outside. Thomas started to call Jezebel before stopping, his fingers still on the cell phone. If the sheriff found out something important about the murder, she would have called him.

Or would she? Their arrangement was fragile at best. Neither completely trusted the other, and their most recent argument didn't help matters. After throwing his coffee cup in a trash can, Thomas walked briskly down the sidewalk in the direction of his car.

Then something behind the grocery store caught his eye. It was an aged mountain bike, stained with rust. He knew that bike. More importantly, he knew its owner. Thomas walked toward the bike, propped up next to a garbage bin. It was quite by accident that he saw the man leaning against the wall.

"Al?" he stammered.

"Hey, Thomas," Al Pittman replied, waving lazily at him. Thomas stared at Pittman, surprised.

"What are you doing out here? I thought you were in jail!"

"The deputy let me out early this morning. Gave me my bike back."

There is no way Jezebel did this to appease me, Thomas knew. *Not when she was so adamant about keeping him in custody. She said she wanted to be sure Al wasn't related to the killing.*

If she was willing to release Al, the sheriff must have known something he didn't. Something new. Perhaps even another murder.

"That's what she's investigating," he muttered, stunned. What if Jezebel was playing him, looking further into the murder without keeping him informed?

"What did you say?" Al asked, keeping one eye open. The man looked like he was on the verge of drifting off to sleep. That surprised Thomas, who would have guessed that the level of comfort in the jail cell was better than sleeping on the street.

"Nothing," Thomas said. "They didn't happen to mention why they let you go, did they?"

Al shook his head. Thomas excused himself and tried to put the pieces together. Whatever development had occurred was fairly recent, since Pittman wasn't released until that morning, which suggested the big case Deputy Markham referenced was indeed related to the murder of Jeffrey Daniels.

The simplest solution would be to call Jezebel Woods and demand answers. Thomas knew that strategy wasn't going to work on the sheriff.

Besides, he thought, *she kept me in the dark. Now it's my turn. Two can play at that game.* An idea crept into his mind, and he veered off in the direction of the courthouse while scrolling for his editor's number. Max picked up almost immediately.

"Thomas? What is it?"

"You're not going to believe who I just ran into outside Rex's Grocery. Al Pittman."

"The sheriff let him go?"

"Yeah." Thomas briefly recounted the details of his agreement with Jezebel once more, this time adding in his argument with her the previous night.

"Max, something bad is going on. The sheriff is dead serious about protecting Gray Hollow—I'm thinking she believes it's bad enough to cause a panic."

"Another killing?"

"That was my guess, too. It would explain why she's trying to keep me in the dark. She wants to suppress the story as long as she can."

"If she's locking us out, we have to go to press. Special edition. The public will force her to come clean. I don't care if she blames you."

"Not just me. Us. I'm going to need your help on this."

"What for?"

"If we're going to print this, I want the *whole* story. Including what she's investigating now."

"If she isn't sharing with you, there's not much we can do to force her hand."

"Let me finish. If someone else is dead, Jezebel may have a suspect this time. That might explain why she wants to keep it so hush-hush. And if she is looking for that suspect then she probably obtained a warrant."

"A warrant," Max repeated. "Brilliant. Where are you?"

"Outside the courthouse. You've dealt with these people far longer than I have. An expert touch is in order, and not one from a stranger."

"Let me grab my jacket," the editor muttered hastily. Thomas could hear rustling in the background. "I'll meet you in ten minutes."

The day was warming up faster than Thomas anticipated. He enjoyed the change in weather and waited outside the courthouse at the center of the town square.

Town Hall was usually a calm place. Most of the elected officials worked other jobs during the week, and many meetings were held in the evening. Everything revolved around a slow but steady pace. All in all, it made for a boring experience when Thomas found himself assigned to cover those meetings.

Even so, despite the laidback attitudes of many of the participants, politics was a serious business in the tiny community. Connections were incredibly important, something that depended on the fact that everyone seemed to know everyone.

Except me, Thomas realized. Being an outsider wasn't always a good thing, which was one reason he needed Max.

The editor would know exactly how to find the information they needed to obtain.

"Speak of the devil," he said while watching the stout editor jog toward him, coffee in hand. "I see you took time to load up on the caffeine."

"Didn't take two minutes. The diner was quiet today." His expression grew suddenly serious. "Are you ready to get down to business?"

"Absolutely. Where do you propose we check?" Thomas asked. He held the door open for his boss as the two passed under the giant clock affixed to the top of the courthouse.

"I say we start at the source." The two newsmen walked over to a desk in the front hallway. "We're here to see Judge Underhill," Max said to the receptionist inside. "I called ahead."

"You managed to set up an appointment in ten minutes?" Thomas asked incredulously. Max deserved more credit than he gave him.

"It doesn't hurt that Judge Underhill gets sinfully cheap rates for ads when he runs for reelection."

The two went up a flight of stairs. After stopping outside a massive wooden door, Max knocked gently.

"Come in," bellowed a voice from behind the other side of the thick door.

The editor opened the door and stepped into the darkened room. A robed man sitting at a desk looked up and set his pen down in front of him.

"Hello, Judge Underhill," Max said. "Thank you for seeing me on such short notice."

"Not a problem," the judge said as he stood. "Please, come in. And I told you to call me Charles."

Thomas was surprised at how young the judge appeared. Somewhere probably in his early forties, he guessed.

"Thomas Brooks, meet Judge Charles Underhill," Max said.

Thomas shook the judge's outstretched hand. His attention was drawn to a line of portraits on the walls overlooking the room. All were of former judges. The one closest to the judge's desk was of a Jeremiah Underhill. Thomas guessed that he was Charles Underhill's father.

"This one might be a keeper," Underhill said with a warm smile. "I read your article on the tax hikes. I suspect it will stir up certain members of our little community, but that's the price we pay for keeping the politicians honest, eh?"

Thomas wasn't sure how to reply.

"I seem to be getting a lot of reaction from that article," he said. Underhill cocked his head and returned his attention to the editor.

"Now, what can I do for you two?"

The judge listened as the two men began with the tale of the discovery of the wrecked Ford truck and of the body of Jeffrey Daniels.

"Poor Al Pittman," he said. "Most people treat him nicely, but he doesn't have it very easy. Always getting into trouble. I got into trouble myself every now then in my youth. My father used to sit me down and say, 'Son, if you're ever going to follow in my shoes, you're going to have to start opening your eyes to the needs of people other than yourself.' And you know what? It worked."

Thomas fought the urge to roll his eyes. Max finished the story by recounting the events of the morning. While attentive, Judge Underhill didn't seem to be the most sincere person Thomas ever met. Unlike the story he told, he seemed to be focused on his own interest, though he hid it very well.

"This story is important not just for the paper, but for the safety of the community. If there is someone out there killing people in Gray Hollow, the people in this town have a right to know so they can protect themselves."

"We can't publish anything based on theory," Thomas interjected. "We need facts."

"So you want to know if Sheriff Woods has asked me for a warrant?" The judge pieced things together quickly.

"Yes."

"Sheriff Woods is fairly popular around these parts. The people trust her to keep them safe. Having said that, I'm not a politician. I trust you, Max, and I'm happy to do you this favor.

"There's no warrant, but I can tell you there's an APB out on a man named Gary Davis. He's a person of interest in a case the sheriff is looking into, and that's all I can tell you."

"Thank you," Max said. He shook the judge's hand again. "I owe you for this, Charles."

"I know," the judge replied with a smile. "Nice meeting you, Mr. Brooks," he called as the two men left the room.

"Wow," Thomas said. "I take it you and the judge are friends?"

"Judge Underhill is everyone's friend, Thomas. That's why he's such a good politician."

"I thought he wasn't a politician," Thomas replied.

"Don't believe a word of it. He's the best one there is. He likes to pretend that as a judge he's somehow above the fray. His position is an elected one, and he's more involved in local affairs than you might suspect."

"I'll keep that in mind." Thomas made a mental note to stay on Judge Underhill's good side. "Whatever the case, we have a name. I'll find out where Gary Davis lives. If we're lucky, we could have our crime scene."

"I'll go with you," Max said. "With any luck, the sheriff will be gone by the time we arrive. Let's stop back at the office so I can pick up another camera."

I can't wait to see Jezebel's face when she reads Thursday's paper, Thomas thought. A grin spread across his face. "We have work to do."

***

A storm was brewing.

Hours after Thomas' discovery, night crept over the barren forest. The dim light of the waxing moon was not enough to penetrate the darkness swimming inside the cave like a vortex.

A ripple ran through the grasses of the lifeless forest, and the animals in close proximity of the cave quickly scurried away. The deformed branches of the trees remained frozen in place.

The blood of the newly dead fed the darkness, giving it form. Form enough to fulfill its task.

It was time.

Hundreds of crows poured out from the confines of the cave. The birds tore through the forest in a whirlwind and formed a cloud in the night. It was the darkness that kept them and now guided them toward the place where it all began.

The moon shone more brightly over the abandoned pastures of the farm, glowing over the silent cornfield.

Shrieking, the throng of crows descended into the cornfield and swarmed the dead earth below. Thunder coursed through the sky, followed swiftly by a torrent of rain.

Then came a faint echo from below. The echo grew stronger as a force unseen pounded against the wet soil. Finally, a white hand erupted from the ground. Rain dripped down the sharp black nails on the hand's twisted fingers.

A second hand wrenched itself free of the soil. In the dead of night, a body emerged from his shallow grave. He dragged himself across the mud. Lightning flashed, illuminating mud, flesh, and straw. The corpse opened his eyes. He sought out a puddle of water clear enough to see his reflection in.

The corpse struck out at the puddle with a scream. He battered the reflection with his heel until the mud churned. Then he walked toward the barn, through the rows of pumpkins. The pumpkins glimmered in the moonlight, raindrops sliding down their slick skins. Tearing a pumpkin from the patch, he smashed the bottom against the ground and ripped out the insides. The figure hacked at the shell of the pumpkin with its nails. Within minutes he had holes to see through, and a mouth to breathe.

As the lightning lit up the darkened field, the figure placed the pumpkin over his decayed face.

The walking corpse looked up at the moon with glowing eyes. Then he faded into the darkness.

The Keeper of the Crows was free.

Chapter SEVEN

Jezebel lunged forward in bed, breathless. Her hands were tightly clenched around sheets drenched in sweat.

"Just a dream," she whispered to herself. Save for the continual whirling of the fan, the house was totally quiet. "It was just a dream," she repeated.

The nightmares had started again. Jezebel climbed out from under the sheets. There was no way she was getting back to sleep, no matter how tired she was. She trudged to the kitchen and rubbed her eyes. It was still pitch black outside.

Jezebel was frustrated by her inability to recall the dream that disturbed her so intensely. It bothered her that she couldn't remember any details. Nightmares were nothing new to the sheriff. The end of her freshman year in high school had been marked by a series of frightening dreams serious enough to prompt her mother into seeking treatment for her. Luckily, the nightmares faded with time.

What time is it? She checked the clock on the microwave when she entered the kitchen.

"4:30 in the morning," Jezebel said aloud. She hadn't had a decent night's sleep since they found the body of Jeffrey Daniels. The stress of the case was starting to get to her. "Get a grip on yourself," she muttered. Jezebel traced the outline of the coffee pot next to the stove. This would mark the second day in a row she was off to such an early start.

A soft noise outside startled her. Jezebel walked to the window, her nerves on edge. Other than piles of fallen leaves below the trees, there was nothing on her back lawn.

There it was again. She spotted a large crow a few feet from the window. Jezebel watched the bird for a few moments before shivering and closing the blinds. After what she had seen of the wreckage of Jeffrey Daniels' truck, the sight of the crow was unsettling.

Suddenly she felt very alone, although such a feeling was not unusual for her. Even though Jezebel was both well-liked and well-known in the community, she didn't have many close relationships. It wasn't that she was incapable of making friends; Jezebel was very popular in high school. Unfortunately, her current position left her with little free time. What time she had left was often devoted to looking after her mother. Whenever she tried to reach out, her other obligations always seemed to get in the way. She could count on one hand the number of serious relationships she'd had since college.

Jezebel stretched and grudgingly started the coffee pot despite the unforgiving hour.

"Good morning, new best friend," she muttered.

Today is going to be a long day. There was certainly more than enough on her plate. So far the search for Gary Davis was proving futile. The police in Thistlewood promised to keep an eye out for him, although Jezebel doubted he could make it that far on foot. Logan Randall assured her he would handle the search, and she reluctantly agreed. That would permit her to focus on the investigation and collecting evidence.

It was too early to jog, the one regular indulgence she allowed herself. Jezebel took pride in being athletic. Muscle came in handy to a woman in law enforcement. Her athleticism had helped her several times over the past few years, like when dealing with out of control patrons at Dale's Bar.

Moving to the living room, she turned on a lamp next to her favorite recliner. Jezebel bent down and rooted through picture albums and records from the past in a cabinet below the television. Finally she found it. Her hands closed around the old yearbook, worn with time.

After flipping through its contents, Jezebel located Davis' picture with ease. It was only a few pages away from her photo. He looked just like she remembered. When she said, "I know him," it might have been an overstatement. More like she *knew* him, once.

Her memories of Gary Davis were foggy; they hadn't been friends. From what she remembered, he was a bully. Since the two had been in the same grade, they shared a few classes together, and Jezebel could recall arguing with Gary when he picked on some of the more unpopular students.

Even if Gary remained just as cruel as he was in the past, Jezebel had a hard time believing anyone could do what he did to his family. Anger rose up within her at the image of the boy lying on the ground.

Why would Gary have wanted to kill Jeffrey Daniels? That was the real question. Regardless of the lack of physical evidence linking the two, Jezebel knew deep down the murders were connected.

Maybe he killed Daniels and his wife found out about it, she thought. *That still doesn't explain why he killed his son, too. Not to mention the fact that he didn't even try to hide it.*

She hoped Logan Randall would find Gary soon so she could start getting some answers. Jezebel retained deep reservations about letting Randall head the search. While he may have denied it earlier, she knew Logan Randall and Gary Davis were once friends, which was fitting, since the two were both miscreants during their adolescent years.

The potential conflict of interest troubled her. Regrettably, there was little she could do about it, since she lacked the manpower to keep him off the case. Her out-of-shape deputy Heavy Markham certainly wasn't up to such an arduous physical task, and she needed to conduct the rest of the investigation herself.

It'll be fine, she told herself. Gray Hollow was such a small town that almost everyone knew everyone anyway. Jezebel was certainly familiar with most of the people she put away. Just because Logan knew Gary didn't mean he would break the law for an old high school buddy. *I'll just have to keep a close watch on him.*

She closed her eyes for a moment to clear her head in an attempt to make sense of it all. The startling image of the withered scarecrow flashed in her mind. Seeing it in the bloody farmhouse bedroom had shaken her to the core. Jezebel was almost sure she had seen the scarecrow, or one just like it, years before. The connection was left out of the report because she wanted to be sure. As disturbing as the scarecrow was, Jezebel wasn't sure how it related to the case.

Outside, the sky was beginning to grow lighter. Sunrise was on its way.

Find connection between Daniels and Davis, she wrote before heading to the shower. The words Thomas Brooks said to her still rang in her ear.

"Just so you know, sheriff, Jeffrey Daniels isn't a stranger to Gray Hollow."

She decided to give Thomas a call later and ask him what he meant. He could provide her with the link between the two men. Jezebel realized she needed to be careful with how she worded the request; the last thing she wanted was to tip off the attentive reporter to what was going on with Gary Davis before she had someone in handcuffs.

Hopefully, she thought while turning on the hot water, *we'll have this case wrapped up before anyone even has cause for alarm.*

***

"I have a bad feeling this isn't legal," Max complained. The editor straightened his tie.

"Of course it's not legal," Thomas replied. "Do you think the sheriff would just let us waltz into the morgue?"

"I'm not sure I'm comfortable with this," Max said as the two headed for the hospital doors.

The Gray Hollow Memorial Hospital was one of the larger buildings in town, which was ironic for something that started out as an animal clinic. Even into the early twentieth century, the hospital served as a veterinary clinic. Most patients traveled to the nearby hospital in

Thistlewood to receive care, unless they wanted to wait for a weekly visit from one of the doctors at St. Francis' Hospital.

Eventually, two doctors began sharing offices with the veterinarian when the small community began expanding. Two became four, and it wasn't long until the successful practice led to renovations of the new hospital. After twenty years, a corporate hospital chain from the north, which provided new and desperately needed equipment, bought out the close-knit community hospital.

"Last chance," Max said before the pair passed through the mechanically operated doors. "Sure you don't want to give the sheriff a call? Haven't we bent the rules enough already?"

"Not a chance. If she hadn't moved the bodies already, we wouldn't even be having this conversation."

When the two arrived at the home of Gary Davis the previous day, it was evident Thomas' timing was perfect. Jezebel and the other officers were nowhere to be found. Thomas had no problem crossing the caution tape. Max required a bit more prompting. They took pictures of the two outlines at the crime scene, then split up to ask the neighbors if they heard anything about what happened the night before.

The search didn't last long. There were only three neighbors who lived anywhere close to Gary Davis' large farm. After talking to a middle-aged woman named Cindy Williams, Thomas learned a great deal about Gary and his family. He'd had a wife named Mary. They'd had a son together, Ben. It was Max, however, who found the most valuable witness. Mike Brinkley told Max everything that he saw when he went into the house, including his conversation with the sheriff. Thomas couldn't believe their luck.

"Remind me again why we need to be doing this? We *have* Brinkley's statement."

"Brinkley also told us we couldn't quote him. It's easier this way. Relax. It's not like we're breaking into the morgue to see the bodies for ourselves. Although it would make for an explosive front page . . ."

"Don't even joke about that," Max said, turning white. "You may be new here, but I have a reputation to uphold."

"Trust, but verify."

"More like if I trust you, I'll get *crucified* if we get caught."

"What's the worst that could happen?" Thomas asked. "We've already got the hard part out of the way. The most they could do is to refuse to give us the information. Besides, don't forget about the First Amendment. I've been involved in a few lawsuits myself, and the press usually prevails."

"What do you mean, 'usually'?"

It was too late; Thomas strolled inside the air-conditioned entry hall. Max shook his head and quickly followed.

"Hello," Thomas said to a man behind the directory counter. "I'm Thomas Brooks with the Shelbyville Funeral Home. We're here to pick up your cadaver release forms."

"Why didn't you request the forms in the mail?" He looked confused.

"I'm a close friend of the family," said Max. "They requested I attend to all the details personally to make sure everything went smoothly."

"You're going to need clearance to fill out the forms," the man said. From the look on his face, he remained unconvinced.

"I spoke to Janice last night about it over the phone," Thomas said. The sentence was partially true; the reporter *did* call the hospital directory to find out who was working the counter the night before. "Didn't she leave a note?"

"I'm sorry, sir, but I don't see it anywhere," the man said after searching vigorously for the note.

Max sighed.

Thomas ignored the sign of disapproval from his editor. "This is very disappointing. We drove all the way from Shelbyville to take care of this ourselves."

"Well, I guess I can make an exception, if you talked to Janice. Can you give me the names?"

"Absolutely. Mary and Ben Davis."

"I have them listed right here. Here are the forms," the man said. He handed a thick stack of papers to Thomas.

"Thank you," Max replied. "I appreciate this. We will complete and verify the forms at the office."

"Glad I was able to help."

"See," Thomas whispered as the two men headed outside, "that wasn't so hard."

"Sure. We had to impersonate funeral home directors to find something out we already know, which I'm pretty sure is illegal. I can't believe I let you talk me into this. Is this how you did things in New York?"

Thomas shrugged. "Things are faster my way, and it's always worked out for me before."

"If that was true, you wouldn't be here."

Thomas ignored the pointed barb. "Now we know for sure that Brinkley was telling the truth. Mary and Ben Davis are dead."

Max nodded. "Add that to the APB for Gary Davis, and it starts to fit together. She thinks Davis murdered his family. There's only one problem I can think of with that scenario."

"What's that?" Thomas asked, nearing his car.

"How does this relate to the death of Jeffrey Daniels?"

"That's what we have to find out. For now, we have enough to run an article exposing what we know. There will be more to come as we confirm it."

"Confirm?"

"When Jezebel sees what we've printed, she's going to have to start coming clean with answers. In the meantime, I still have some other leads to pursue."

He waited for Max to slide into the passenger seat before starting the ignition. After putting the car in reverse, he glanced over his shoulder and left the hospital parking lot.

"Start the presses, Max. Things are about to get heated."

***

"You're sure?" Jezebel asked. The information over the phone disturbed her. It was only noon, and already it was already shaping up to be a long day. At the moment she was in her car, chasing down a lead.

She waited for the officer from Thistlewood to respond.

"The pitchfork had no fingerprints belonging to Gary Davis matching the prints your department sent us."

Unlike Gray Hollow, the city of Thistlewood devoted a great deal of money to the police budget, which boasted a relatively well-equipped forensics department.

"He could have been wearing gloves," Jezebel said. She paused to let the woman on the other end of the line finish.

"The shells recovered all matched the same rifle, the same type as the one registered to Gary Davis. The autopsy showed no trace of bullet wounds in either corpse. In fact, Sheriff, there was no sign on either of the bodies indicating prolonged struggle."

"When I was at your department earlier, I was told the blood on the first floor didn't belong to either of the deceased."

"That's correct."

"Then the blood probably belonged to Gary."

If no struggle took place, why was Gary bleeding? There was no weapon recovered, such as a knife with Gary's blood on it. Only the pitchfork, which held traces of both Gary's blood and that of his wife.

Something else bothered her. Why did Gary fire his rifle? If he really wanted to cover up the crime, why risk alerting the neighbors? Especially since neither of the victims was killed with the rifle anyway.

"Was there any indication that someone else was involved, other than the three members of the Davis family?"

"Not from the samples you sent us."

"OK. That's all for now. Thanks for your help. Tell Chief Barnes I appreciate his assistance."

"Will do. Good afternoon."

For every question answered, another question reared its ugly head. Jezebel felt a new sense of urgency, and she stepped on the accelerator. She continued driving until she reached Old Main Street. The street was in the oldest part of town, home to many buildings in disrepair. Most stores in the area were out of business altogether, boarded up and sealed off from the world.

From her parking space, Jezebel initiated a quick phone call to Heavy Markham to let the deputy know she would soon be on her way to the office. Heavy told her that after following her research into Jeffrey Daniels, he confirmed that the victim's father, Wilbur, once owned land in Gray Hollow.

Confident that she missed no other significant updates in her absence, Jezebel ended the call and made her way toward the antiquated store a few feet away.

Novelty Store, read the simple sign in faded black letters. She peered through the grimy windows as if waiting for something to happen. When nothing did, Jezebel entered the store, which caused a small bell to ring on the other side of the door.

"Hello?" Jezebel looked around for the proprietor. "Is anyone there?"

She wiped her nose and stifled a sneeze. The store was covered in dust, which lined each row of books with a thin veil of gray. Dim lights burned constantly above her, barely illuminating all of the items in the shop. The novelty store was overstocked with items of all shapes and sizes for sale, stacked from wall to wall.

Despite its worn appearance, the store had changed very little from when she was younger. It was always filled with peculiar products, which earned a well-deserved eerie reputation with children. She could still recall some of the creepier rumors her friends used to tell her about the shop. According to one story, from time to time the proprietor locked children in a cellar under the store, and they were never seen again.

Jezebel passed down an aisle of bookshelves, temporarily distracted by the various pieces in the store. Strange antiques were everywhere, from old wooden masks to Persian rugs. A bronze oil lamp resting next to a lounge chair loomed in front of her. Jezebel advanced in the direction of the light and the empty chair. A strange-looking doll rested on the shelf next to the lamp. The doll was carved from dark wood, with strands of what appeared to be human hair framing an intimidating face. Transfixed, Jezebel reached toward the doll.

"May I help you?" a baritone voice replied from behind her. Unable to help herself, Jezebel jerked. She turned around and found herself staring into a pair of narrow, dark green eyes.

"I apologize for startling you, young lady," the man continued, the hint of a smile on his dry lips. "My name is Percy Durer. How may I be of service?"

"I know who you are, Mr. Durer," Jezebel said. She stared at the storekeeper. If the novelty store was infamous among the children of Gray Hollow, so was its owner—a white-haired man with a lean, wiry frame.

Durer was part of the reason for the stories; one of the more popular myths was that he abducted children who came into his store after sunset. When Jezebel was older she realized the story was of course false (the novelty store wasn't even open after sunset), but that didn't make Durer any less ominous.

"I am Sheriff Jezebel Woods. If you don't mind—"

"Jezebel Woods?" The storeowner's eyes lit up. "Yes, I remember you now. A small little fidgety thing, that's right. You used to take turns peering into my windows with your friends, didn't you?"

Jezebel was stunned.

"I'm not sure, Mr. Durer. That's not why I'm here. If you don't mind, there is something you might be able to help me with. I'm looking into a crime."

"That's right. You said *Sheriff* Jezebel Woods. Whatever happened to that Ramsey fellow?"

"Sheriff Ramsey died over four years ago."

"Forgive me; I'm not as up to date on current affairs as I once was. The store has been so quiet since all the shops moved to New Main Street. I receive few customers now. Some days I don't even bother to come out of my room." The old man pointed at a door at the top of the stairs.

Jezebel could hardly bring herself to believe anyone would sleep in that place.

"But I'm distracting you with my prattle, I can see. What brings you here?"

"An item was found at a crime scene I was investigating. Something very old. It was something I hadn't seen in a long time. I knew if anyone could help me determine where it came from, it was you."

"You are too kind," Durer said as he watched her. Jezebel could tell he was intrigued. "What item was it?"

"It was a scarecrow," she finally said after a slight pause. She stopped. "I expected you to laugh."

"Why would I?" asked Durer. He seemed completely unfazed.

Jezebel wasn't sure how to respond.

"Can you describe the scarecrow for me?" he continued. "There must be a reason why you sought me out in particular."

She took a picture out of her wallet and placed it on the counter. "I thought I had seen it before—or something like it. But I have to be sure."

A strange look came over the proprietor's face as he looked at the picture. For a moment, Jezebel thought he was about to grin. "You mentioned you saw it before. What *exactly* did the scarecrow remind you of?"

Jezebel shied away from telling this man what she really thought. She kept her words impersonal and casual. "When I was younger, there was a boy who made scarecrows. It was his hobby. Many farmers bought them from him. The scarecrows sprung up all over the town. I thought maybe you might have one, by some chance."

"And what was the name of the boy?" Durer asked in a hushed voice. He studied her closer than ever.

"Salem," she said. "Salem Alistair."

"Salem," he repeated in a whisper. "Come with me, Miss Woods. I have something I would like to show you."

Jezebel followed the old storekeeper down an aisle of books leading to a winding staircase near the back of a store. The two walked down the staircase.

"What is this place?" Jezebel asked as Durer opened a door. "I never knew this was down here."

He replied with a thin smile, "This is my special place. I keep only my rarest and most fascinating possessions in the cellar."

He flipped on a light, revealing a cluttered, colorless room filled with even more peculiar objects. Many of the books on the shelves were about New Age and the occult, and there were several unfamiliar charms and symbols hanging from a shelf.

"Don't mind those," Durer said. "I've long been interested in spirituality. It is part of the culture, after all."

Jezebel let the comment pass, as she did not fully understand what he meant. An image flashed through her mind of Durer trying to lock her inside the cellar, and chill bumps covered her arms. At times like this, she was glad she was allowed to carry a gun.

"Over there," Durer said. The old man pointed to a shelf near the back of the room.

Jezebel gasped. She hoped the storekeeper might have come into possession of one of the scarecrows, but she never would have guessed this. Sitting on the shelf were five hideous scarecrows.

"This is what you're looking for. You'll notice that all of them are different. You will also no doubt recognize the design as similar to the picture you showed me."

"They're horrifying."

Durer smirked. "Some might call them that. I regard them as works of art, expressions of the darker part of a young man's soul."

"Salem gave these to you?"

The storekeeper cackled. "Not exactly. In the beginning I was very interested in the young Mr. Alistair. We spoke often. Like me, he shared an interest in the supernatural. I believe I frightened him in the end, and he stopped coming by my store. I acquired these scarecrows from others, mostly farmers who purchased them from the lad. When they saw the price I offered for them, they sold the scarecrows gladly. Salem never charged much for them, I believe."

"Salem designed the scarecrow we found," Jezebel said aloud, as much to herself as to the man watching her. Durer led her back up the stairs.

"Before you are on your way, there is one thing I would very much like to know."

"Yes?" Jezebel asked.

"What sort of crime scene did you find one of these scarecrows at?"

"I can't comment on that," she said. "And now I really need to be going."

Durer remained nearly motionless. "It must be fairly serious then, judging by your demeanor. Can you imagine why one of these scarecrows would be at such a place? Just a thought."

"Good day, Mr. Durer. Thank you for your time."

"No, thank you, Sheriff Jezebel Woods," Percy Durer said. "Perhaps we will meet again soon."

The bell sounded again as she left the store.

"Wow," Jezebel said once she was within the confines of her police cruiser. "That was even creepier than I remembered."

Just as with the Thistlewood forensic information, she was now filled with more questions. Durer's question reverberated in her head. What did a scarecrow made by Salem Alistair have to do with the murders of Jeffrey Daniels and Mary and Ben Davis?

This day is filled with old memories, she thought. *I need to check the case files on Salem Alistair when I get back to the station.* Ironically, since she had become sheriff, she had never looked into that particular case, despite her personal investment—or perhaps because of it. After all, it was over twenty years old. The disappearance of Salem Alistair was a mystery that was never solved.

Now it was dangerously close to being reopened.

***

Logan Randall removed his gloves and carefully applied sanitizer to each hand. The wind picked up, which chilled the air of the hill he was climbing. He ignored the wind easily; the deputy's focus was elsewhere.

A day of searching yielded no visible results. Even though he wasn't sure what he would do if he actually *found* Gary, Logan was disappointed his friend hadn't tried to contact him. If Gary was on foot, it was possible he didn't have a phone. He thought of the blood on the floor of the house, and the deputy wondered if Gary was injured. Perhaps he was dead already.

That might even make things easier for me. Just as Logan opened the door to his cruiser, his cell phone rang. "Hello?" he said after recognizing the number.

"Any sign of him yet?"

"Not a trace. It's like he's gone invisible."

"That's impossible," said the voice on the other end of the line. "There have to be some footprints somewhere, or something."

"If there are, I'll find them."

"You have to. If this gets out, it could destroy us both and everything we've worked hard to create."

"I understand."

"Do you? Logan, you have to be prepared to deal with Gary when you find him."

"What do you mean, 'deal with' him?"

"You know exactly what I mean. I don't know if Gary killed Jeffrey Daniels or not, but either way, what he knows puts us all at risk."

"So you want me to kill him?" Logan said, as if asking for permission.

"If it comes to that. You can ask Rick for help if you need it. We're all in this together, Logan. Now find him."

The line went dead.

Chapter EIGHT

He was lost. Gary dropped to his knees in exhaustion. Sounds and sights blurred together as he drifted in and out of consciousness. What day was it? After traveling for so long, he couldn't be sure. He crawled to the creek and gulped down as much water as his weary body could handle. His instincts told him to press forward, but Gary could not muster the energy to move.

They stalked him at night. Somehow, they always found him. So far he had managed to elude them. That might not be the case much longer. Gary's injuries were getting worse with time.

He needed medical care and food. Gary's stomach rumbled with hunger. Even though they would be looking for him, it was worth the risk. Survival was the only thing on his mind now. He felt trapped in a strange nightmare, unable to wake up. At night he scrambled through the woods, rifle in hand. During the day he could feel the eyes of the crows following him.

Most of all, he couldn't shake the feeling that the death of his family was his fault. Perhaps the best course of action would be to admit everything to the police. What else did he have to lose?

A horn sounded in the distance. Was he close to the road? Gary slowly picked himself up.

As always, the crows followed.

***

"I'm sorry," Max said into his office phone, grinning. "The story is an exclusive. You'll have to read about it in *Hollow Happenings.*"

Thomas shook his head once again at the name of the newspaper. Corny though it was, if the paper propelled him back into the big leagues, he would never laugh at it again.

"You're a genius," Max said as he placed the phone in its cradle. "Without a doubt, this will be the biggest story in the history of this newspaper. The best part is, there's still more to come."

A few months ago, Thomas had persuaded Max to start a website for *Hollow Happenings*. The traffic was slow, which was expected, but the web address now afforded them a unique opportunity. When Thomas finished his story, they were able to send it online to every news agency in the region. In addition to being seen in Gray Hollow, the chilling tale of the murders would be read by people across the state.

"Thank you," Thomas said seriously. "I mean it. If you hadn't hired me . . ."

"Don't mention it," Max replied. "The way I see it, I owe you one. This story hasn't been in print over two hours, and already our phones are ringing off the hook."

I bet the phones are ringing off the hook in the sheriff's office as well, Thomas thought with a smile.

"Let's not get carried away, boss. There's still a lot of tough work ahead of us. As far as we know, Gary Davis isn't in custody yet, and we don't have the slightest idea what his motives are."

"Leave the motives to the police. I just got off the phone with the publisher of *The Capital.* This could be bigger than we thought, Thomas."

Thomas could feel the excitement radiating from his boss. All of the nervousness Max experienced in the hospital had vanished. Unlike Thomas, Max wasn't hoping to be snatched away by a prominent media outlet. He was passionate about one thing: bolstering the circulation of the small town newspaper he already ran.

After working with Max one-on-one for several months, Thomas was starting to learn what made the man tick. Since there were only two full-time staff members of

Hollow Happenings, they were in frequent proximity. It was hard to spend so much time with someone and not get to know him.

Like Thomas, Max was not originally from Gray Hollow. Once he graduated from a community college in the Midwest, the editor became a reporter for a large newspaper in Springfield. He worked at the paper for nine years, until one day he came home to a note from his wife and an empty house. Opting for a slower pace, Max left his career and his former life behind when he moved to Gray Hollow. Max grew to love working in the tiny community and threw himself into his work. When he took over as owner and editor, he worked tirelessly to revive the failing paper. That was probably the only reason he hired a scandal-ridden reporter like Thomas.

"I'm going to be honest," Max had said when he hired him. "I'm not just hiring you for your skill, I'm banking on your notoriety to pick up a few readers."

Thomas came to admire Max's courteousness and relaxed demeanor. Both were characteristics highly unusual for a newspaper editor anywhere. Max genuinely loved Gray Hollow and its people. He never married again; Thomas suspected that he was still in love with his ex-wife. But that was in the past. *Hollow Happenings* was Max's life now. A revival of the newspaper's local popularity would literally embody the realization of all of his dreams.

The phone rang again.

"I've got to take this," Max said, practically skipping back to his office. Thomas decided to keep his cynicism to himself for once and let Max enjoy the moment. After returning to his own desk, he decided to continue his break a moment longer before jumping back into the investigation.

That's more like it, he thought as he stared at his computer screen. There were twenty-five messages in his inbox already. The story was already big; the fact that his name was attached to it helped even more. Despite his fall from grace, Thomas' infamy would help the story spread.

"Wait a second," he muttered. He frowned when he began reading the tenth email. The email was from a television news reporter in Springfield named Chuck Howard.

It's a little too early for the TV crews, Thomas thought. The idea was unsettling, and for good reason. At this stage in the investigation, it would be all too easy to get scooped by an ambitious television reporter with resources Thomas no longer possessed. The email was polite, but Thomas had no doubt that if this Chuck Howard became involved things would get messy. It would turn into a competition—and print rarely fared well against television media.

Even though the email was tentative, Thomas knew the fact that Howard had jumped on it so early was not a good sign. He sighed and quickly sent a delicately worded response designed to diminish the reporter's curiosity.

The phone rang again.

"Max," Thomas called out, amused. "Your adoring public demands more answers!"

He peered through the open blinds to the editor's office. Max was still on the phone. Buzzing on Thomas' desk was his own cell.

"Hello?" he asked, picking up the phone.

"Thomas, it's me. Is it true?"

"Eve?" Of all the people he expected to have heard of the story, he would never have guessed this. "How did you hear about it?" Thomas managed, fumbling for words.

"You're not as cut off from your old friends as you think," she said. "When the words 'Thomas Brooks' and 'murder' appear in the same article, some people are bound to notice."

She must have checked into me after I used her as a source for the license plate, he realized.

"What do you want?" His voice sounded colder than he intended.

"To talk. I've been thinking about us since you called me."

"I don't know what to say," Thomas replied.

"Don't you miss it?"

"Miss what?"

"Everything. New York. Working for a *real* paper."

"Maybe," he said after a pause. "Gray Hollow is starting to grow on me though."

"Is that what this story is about?"

"What do you mean?"

"I read your article, and I have to ask. Is everything in your story factual?"

"What? Of course it is!"

"With your history, you know there are bound to be questions."

"We've been over this. My sources lied to me. It was one time. Once. I've suffered for it long enough. How many times do you have to bring this up?"

"There's no need to get so defensive. Believe me, I feel sorry for you. It's doubtful I would last ten days in a place like that."

"So what is this about? I've got work to do. I suspect you do, too."

"Like I said, I wanted to talk. You may find this hard to understand, but you're not the only one with regrets."

What does that mean? Thomas wondered. Was she sincere, or was she after something else? After all they had been through, he had a hard time trusting her.

A prolonged silence occurred as he waited for her to finish.

"If you need any more help on this, Thomas, please let me know. Call me."

"I will," Thomas replied mechanically. He wasn't sure he meant it.

***

The air was unusually warm for the fall season. Sunlight beamed down from the cloudless blue sky. Weather so perfect seemed made for relaxation. Unfortunately, Jezebel didn't have that luxury.

Things were not exactly going her way. Hours of working late finally caught up with her, and the sheriff stumbled out of bed over an hour late that morning. To make matters worse, she was forced to deal with a case of domestic abuse before even making it to the station.

"Jeez, lady, are you trying to kill me? I'm dying back here!"

Jezebel kept her jaw clenched tightly shut and mobilized every ounce of energy to repress her anger. She was almost to the breaking point. It didn't help that Eric

Sizemore, the man she arrested for spousal abuse, wouldn't stop badgering her.

"For God's sake, at least put the window down!"

"The air conditioning is working fine. If you have an aversion to being handcuffed and incarcerated in the back of a police vehicle, then I suggest you avoid giving your wife black eyes."

"This isn't Constitutional. Torture's illegal."

Jezebel turned around, her eyes flashing with anger. "Mr. Sizemore, you've been told you have the right to remain silent. I *highly* recommend you exercise it." She sighed deeply and returned her attention to the road. She slowed the car down when she neared the town square. Ordinarily she didn't mind waiting for the pedestrians to cross the street; it gave her a chance to wave at the people she recognized. But today she couldn't wait to get out of this car and into the office.

On the bright side, at least this day can't get any worse.

Then the station came into view.

"What on earth?" she muttered. Several people were waiting outside the police station, and the parking lot was full. She could see Logan Randall arguing with one man next to the front door. Reluctant to be caught in the crowd until she knew what was going on, Jezebel pulled into the back of the station. She prayed there hadn't been another murder.

Eric Sizemore allowed himself to be led into the station easily, perhaps intimidated by the crowd out front. Most wife-beaters weren't too keen on publicity. When she walked into the front of the station, the room was filled with the sound of ringing phones. Deputy Markham was seated at the desk, where he was attempting to manage all of the lines.

"What's going on out there?" she asked, concern in her voice.

"Sheriff Woods, thank God you're here. I've been trying to get a hold of you for the last half hour."

"Sorry about that. I got into a scuffle with Eric Sizemore. Remind me to call Judge Underhill and set up a hearing for that sleazebag later."

"We have bigger problems than that," Heavy said, handing her a newspaper. Her mouth nearly dropped open in shock when she saw the headline. Jezebel had to read over the words twice before they managed to sink in. This was exactly what she hoped would not happen.

"Brooks," she muttered darkly. *How did he find out?* Jezebel couldn't believe she underestimated him this much. "They have everything! Almost every detail we've already gathered from this investigation! Do you know what this means?"

"I have a good idea," Heavy replied. He gestured to the phones, which had not stopped ringing since Jezebel entered the room. "Everyone is worried that Gary Davis or someone else is going to turn up at their doorstep with a pitchfork. Deputy Randall and I have been trying to sort it out since this mess started."

Jezebel heard the front door slam shut. Thomas Brooks could not have picked a worse time to release his information. Not when she was starting to suspect there was even more to the murders than she originally thought. Her conversation with Percy Durer had given her a lot to dwell upon.

Now, thanks to Thomas, she had no time to think. She could only react. That was a problem. Her number one duty was to keep the people of Gray Hollow safe. That task just grew a great deal harder.

"I hate to ask this, Heavy, but would you continue to work the phones?"

"Of course," he said without hesitation.

"Thanks. I'm going to find Thomas Brooks and kick his—"

"Well, well," Logan Randall said, walking inside. "What do we have here?" He crossed his arms.

"Not today, Logan," Jezebel said.

Logan shrugged and shook his head at Heavy. Not even a minute after the deputies heard the front door close, it opened again.

"Correction. We are going to deal with all the people outside, then I am going to take care of Thomas Brooks."

***

The Daniels farm was much smaller than Thomas anticipated. Like most of the farms in the rural areas of

Gray Hollow, a thin dusty trail covered in gravel led from the road to the two-story house looming in the distance.

Of all the drawbacks to the community, the gravel roads bothered him the most. Thomas was accustomed to having his car clean, since he rarely used it in the city. Now the vehicle was almost always dirty. Dust surrounded the car in a cloud as he traveled down the winding roads.

Tall trees loomed on each side of the road, which served as a reminder that the cleared land was once part of the massive tapestry of forests covering the town. It was no small wonder the police were unable to find Gary Davis. Anyone familiar with the woods would be able to vanish into its vastness, or so it seemed to Thomas.

He finally reached the end of the road at a place where the trees gave way to pastures. The Daniels farm was located in the middle of nowhere. Thomas was alarmed at just how isolated the property was. If Al Pittman hadn't stumbled across the body of Jeffrey Daniels, it might have been weeks before someone noticed the crash.

Gathering his notes into a folder, Thomas surveyed the land with a watchful gaze. An old barn, much smaller than the one belonging to Gary Davis, was about sixty yards from the farmhouse. From the looks of things, the barn had fallen into disrepair. He got out of his car and began the journey on foot.

For a moment, Thomas imagined he saw someone staring at him from a glass window on the first floor of the house. When he blinked, the figure was gone.

He started walking toward the house. A large cornfield rested about ten feet from the brown house. The cornfield stretched on as far as he could see, ending at the edge of the forest. Thomas looked at the tranquil cornfield to his right as he neared the door. The dry stalks of corn were motionless in the calm of the warm day, yet something about the land made him uneasy.

Thomas frowned. The lights were on outside the house. Although Paul Morris might have simply forgotten to turn them off, the sight of the light aroused his suspicion. Tearing his eyes away from the lights, he rapped loudly on the screen door.

Almost as soon as he knocked the door opened, revealing a stocky older man with peppery hair. The speed with which the door opened made Thomas wonder if the man was watching for him at the window.

"Dr. Morris?"

"Yes," the man answered. Paul Morris looked him over carefully. "Are you the reporter?"

"Thomas Brooks," he answered, sticking out his hand. The old man shook it and motioned for him to come inside. Morris peered intently outside before shutting the door once more.

"Thank you very much for allowing me to speak with you, Dr. Morris. I appreciate it."

"It's not a problem. Truth be told, I'm glad for the company. It can get pretty lonely out here sometimes, especially lately. Can I offer you something to drink?"

"No, thank you," Thomas said. "Do you mind if I ask you a few questions?"

"That's why you're here, isn't it?" the man asked. Thomas thought he detected a note of worry in the doctor's voice.

"According to my notes, you purchased this farm in 1987. Is that correct?"

"Yes. That was the year I closed my practice."

"Did you ever know Wilbur Daniels?"

"That's the name of the man who owned the farm before I bought it, isn't it?"

Thomas nodded the affirmative.

"No, I never met him. I heard about his heart attack when we purchased the house. My wife and I never had children, Mr. Brooks. Over twenty-five years in Detroit left us both wanting a respite. Somehow we found Gray Hollow. I saved up a lot of money while I was practicing, and the Daniels Farm had been foreclosed upon. It was one of the best bargains I've ever found."

"Does your wife live here with you?" Thomas asked. He searched the room for a sign of the woman. Other than in old photographs, he couldn't see any trace of Mrs. Morris.

"She died of breast cancer six years after we moved here."

"I'm sorry."

"Don't be. The last years we had were the best years of my life. If we hadn't moved out here when we did, we might have never shared that time together."

"Did you ever meet Jeffrey Daniels, Wilbur Daniels' son?"

"Yes. He stopped by a couple weeks after his father's funeral to pick up some of his dad's old things, although he left some things behind. I always told him to come back for them, but he never did. It was easy to tell his father's death was hard on him. Even as old as I am, I still remember the look on his face. He was . . . haunted. That's the best word for it."

"It probably wasn't easy to lose his father and have his dad's property foreclosed on."

"Apparently the man was up to his eyes in debt, though I don't remember the son asking for very much. In fact, it seemed like the boy just wanted to get away."

It was time for the big question.

"Have you seen him recently?"

"Who, Jeffrey Daniels? No. Why do you ask?"

Thomas was crestfallen.

"You didn't read about it in the newspaper? Jeffrey Daniels' body was found not far from here. He was murdered."

The old man stiffened, genuinely shocked.

"That's terrible. I didn't know. I don't subscribe to the local newspaper though, and I rarely go out. Since my wife died, this house has become a refuge of memories."

"Did Jeffrey Daniels ever try to contact you? To call you?"

"I'm sorry," the old man said as he shook his head, "but I haven't seen or heard from him since he left. Why?"

"Daniels didn't live in Gray Hollow anymore. When I found out he used to live at this address, I assumed that he came back to see the house he lived in as a boy. Now I'm starting to think there was another reason he came back, although I don't have the slightest idea what that is. Have you encountered anything suspicious at all around here?" Thomas asked as he reached for his folder. Sadly, it looked like his conversation with Morris was leading nowhere.

The doctor paused before glancing out the window. This time, Thomas picked up on it.

"I notice that you keep staring out the window. Is there a reason for it?"

"Well, I wasn't going to say anything before, but yes, I have seen something strange. When you mentioned murders it really got me thinking. This house is almost completely isolated. The adjoining farm is the Alistair Farm, which was also foreclosed on. No one lives there anymore, so I'm totally alone, which is fine with me. Trouble is, recently, this feeling has been growing in my mind that there is someone else here. Like something is watching me. A few nights ago, there was a sound outside of my window that was almost like an inhuman scream. In the morning I found a trashcan next to the porch knocked down. There were birds everywhere."

Thomas recalled the crows embedded in Daniels' windshield. "Do you have problems with predators? I imagine that in a remote place like this you would have plenty of animals around your cornfield."

"You're right. In the past there have been issues with coyotes, and I thought that might be the case again. So the next evening I waited outside on the porch, but I fell asleep. A strange noise startled me from my nap. Night came while I was sleeping, so I switched the porch lights on. Something was walking in the cornfield—on two legs."

"You saw someone?"

"Not that night, no; I only saw the dim outlines of whatever was out there. I kept the porch lights on the next two nights. Nothing. Then, last night, I saw something in the shadows just outside the porch lights. Someone was out there waiting for me. I prayed I was seeing things, but I left the lights on in the hopes it would scare whoever it was away."

"This could be dangerous, Dr. Morris. You have to report what you've seen." Finally, they were getting somewhere. If Davis thought he committed the murders in front of Morris, the killer might want to cut the loose end. Even so, how did Davis find out Jeffrey Daniels was coming to the house? There was still a connection missing.

Someone in the town has to have known Jeffrey Daniels, he thought. *I won't stop until I find them. If Daniels didn't go to his farm, he had to go* somewhere.

***

Outside the brown house, the day was growing late. A sliver of darkness crept into the horizon, waiting for the remainder of the overpowering sunlight to fade.

Through the crow perched on the fencepost on the road, the Keeper watched the two men talking inside the house. Soon, the man who owned the house would be dead. The presence of the reporter, however, troubled the Keeper. The crows saw him near the body of Jeffrey Daniels days ago, and again at the Davis farm.

The reporter was getting closer to the truth. If Thomas Brooks became a threat, he too would be dealt with. For the time being, the Keeper would keep an eye on him. He had plenty to spare.

The crow flapped its wings and flew into the forest. In the darkness of the barn, the Keeper waited for nightfall. It was only a matter of hours until the day faded away.

There was blood to be spilled.

Chapter NINE

The tea on the stove wasn't ready. Paul Morris returned to the window, staring off into the darkening sky. As if waiting for sunset, the fields were perfectly still—almost unnaturally so.

There's nothing out there, you silly old fool, he told himself as he peered into the impending night. The doctor made his way back to the kitchen. Surely the only things waiting outside were apparitions construed by the overactive imagination of a lonely old man. The visit with Thomas Brooks frightened him, though he would never admit it out loud. Unlike many of the other local farmers, Paul was not trained in the use of firearms.

It was just him, all alone in an empty house. Paul was being honest when he told the journalist he rarely ventured out of the house other than to buy groceries or get gas. Even at his age, the doctor could still run the tractor, and that was all he needed to do anyway.

"Just a little hot," he said aloud before pouring the tea into a pitcher next to the stove. Although his wife was long dead, the doctor had developed a habit of speaking as if she were there.

Paul was setting the table for himself when he passed by the kitchen window and saw them. He stepped closer, still clutching the hot pitcher of tea. A flock of birds near the Alistair farm approached from a distance, as if they were flying straight for him. Suddenly, one bird flew against the window. Startled, Paul dropped the pitcher.

Glass shattered as hot tea spilled over the floor. Sounds echoed outside the farmhouse.

What in the world? The old man opened the front door and walked outside. His nerves were raw. *What is going on?*

Dozens of crows covered the thin fence separating the yard from the cornfield in front of the forest. Paul saw the birds watching him with black eyes. He shuddered.

A low hiss, almost snakelike, emanated from the cornfield. In unison, the crows lining the fence cocked their heads in the direction of the stalks.

Something was moving in the cornfield. Or perhaps *someone.* Paul tried to shout a warning, to move, to do something. Instead, he found himself rooted to the spot in fear.

From its own perch in the sky, the fiery sun began its descent. The faint outline of the moon appeared above, and the hissing grew louder. Paul heard a cackle from within the stalks, carried by the silence of the evening.

A pumpkin head emerged from the stalks, its frozen smile full of mockery. Paul's heart beat faster than he thought possible. A tall scarecrow stepped out of the cornfield, wearing something that looked like a twisted jack o' lantern for a head. The scarecrow stood like a man, but there was something inhuman about the way it moved.

For a moment the scarecrow stood motionless at the edge of the cornfield. It stared at him. Paul remained transfixed. His gaze settled on the black holes carved into the pumpkin where eyes should have been. The scarecrow's patched clothes were stained with blood. Instead of the hands of a man, the scarecrow's arms ended in branchlike claws of hay.

"Flesh," croaked a hideous voice from inside the pumpkin, and Paul knew he had landed in a nightmare. The crows looked on as the scarecrow renewed its march forward.

After regaining his sense of self, Paul stumbled backwards, his gaze locked on the creature staggering forward up his lawn. Moving as fast as he could, the doctor ran back into the house. He dashed into the living room, where he tried to stop gasping long enough to call the police.

There was no dial tone. The line was dead.

***

The Keeper of the Crows could hear the old man scrambling around frantically inside the house. He lumbered up the steps to the door, the sunset at his back. The lights the farmer had used in a pathetic attempt to ward the Keeper away fizzled and went out.

The Keeper hit the door with force. The blow knocked the door off its hinges. The scarecrow stepped inside the dark house. He could smell the old man's fear and savored the taste. The night was ripe for sacrifice.

Paul fell again. This time he landed hard on the wooden floor. He crawled back and tried to fend off the creature with his hands. The Keeper stopped when he saw his face.

"You're not Daniels," the scarecrow roared. The Keeper had mistakenly believed the vision from the crows was of Wilbur Daniels, but this old man wasn't even from the town, he sensed.

A new farmer lived in the old Daniels house. Wilbur Daniels, like his son Jeffrey, was gone. The scarecrow shook with rage. This was not why he had come.

He watched the farmer run into the kitchen. The need was overwhelming, even if the scarecrow did not know the old man. Feeding his children had left the Keeper drained, and the darkness demanded sacrifice.

The old man continued running away. The Keeper followed after him.

***

Minutes after leaving the Daniels Farm, Thomas was no closer to finding the truth. Dr. Morris was as helpful as possible. He had answered all of Thomas' questions. Unfortunately, the answers Thomas was seeking simply weren't there.

There were a thousand different pieces, and so far they seemed to be from different parts of the puzzle. Unable to see how things were connected, Thomas knew the story would remain unfinished. His article was a good start, but it was far from enough. People wanted an entire tale. A collection of facts was no good without a more substantial narrative.

He took one hand off the wheel and reached down to check his cell for messages. Almost immediately, the phone began ringing in his hand.

"Brooks? I knew I'd find you eventually."

"Sheriff," Thomas said with a grin. "How nice to hear from you!"

"'Nice' my left foot. Do you have any idea what you've done?"

"Let's see. I've provided an invaluable service to the citizens of this community in accordance with the rights and responsibilities of the press under the first amendment?"

"Laugh all you want, but you'll pay for this."

"Threats, too? Nice. I think I'm going to have to revise my earlier opinion of you, Sheriff Woods. What exactly are you going to do? Arrest me?"

"It was a mistake not locking you up for obstruction of justice in the first place—a mistake I'll soon rectify."

"You can come and get me if you'd like. I'm headed back from the Daniels Farm, where I just interviewed Paul Morris. That's something you might want to check on, if you get the time. I have to warn you though, if you're planning on bringing me in, you might want to kiss your job goodbye. Regardless of all the legal ramifications such an action would surely bring, how do you think it would look to the fine citizens of Gray Hollow if you arrested the one person who actually told them the truth?"

"You didn't tell them the truth. You spun Gary Davis as some kind of serial killer and sent this town in a panic, which is exactly why I didn't want to work with you in the first place. I had you pegged from the first moment I set eyes on you, Brooks. You're so wrapped up in trying to get the story you didn't take the time to care that you might be getting the facts wrong. And for the record, we already interviewed Morris. I handled it myself right after we found Daniels' body."

Interesting, Thomas thought. Morris hadn't mentioned that to him. Even if Jezebel hadn't figured out the connection between Jeffrey Daniels and his father's old house, Morris still lived in close proximity to the murder scene.

He decided to change his tone and adopt a less combative stance.

"Listen, I understand that you want to protect your town. I'm not trying to fight with you. But honestly, don't you think it might help to have told them that Gary Davis might show up in their back yards with a gun?"

"That wasn't your call to make. I had this investigation under control until you got involved."

"With all due respect, I don't think you did. Do you even know *why* Davis killed those people? Every single person I found that knew Gary Davis told me point blank that he would *never* have harmed his family. None of this makes sense. Why would he kill Jeffrey Daniels? Why leave his vehicles behind?"

"You're the one who painted Gary as a murderer in your story. I'm still treating him as a missing person. Don't think for a second you're not going end up with egg on your face when this is over, if you don't end up in jail. You know what else? Suddenly I feel like having this conversation face-to-face."

Thomas grimaced. Jezebel clearly wasn't backing down, and her repeated references to jail time were starting to unsettle him.

He heard her siren from the other end of the phone before she hung up. Thomas swore and tossed the phone into the passenger seat. He suddenly regretted telling her where he was. She'd called his bluff, and now she was going track him down. He had seen her on the verge of anger before, and he wasn't eager for it to be directed at him.

Thomas kept his eyes peeled for any sign of car lights and eased his foot off the accelerator. The last thing he needed was for her to catch him speeding too. As usual, his conversation with the sheriff left him angry. Making things worse, her points struck a little too close to the truth. In the past few days, he had impersonated and lied to others in hopes of getting information. The old Thomas

Brooks was still alive and well, despite what he promised himself when he came to Gray Hollow.

So much for turning over a new leaf.

She was wrong about one thing, though: The murders weren't just parts of a story for him. This was personal. Even if he didn't know the victims, Thomas felt more connected to this case than any he ever worked before. It didn't matter that he wasn't from Gray Hollow; as much as he wanted to deny it, the town was becoming a part of him.

I should probably call Max, he thought. It was hard to imagine the laidback editor faring well in any heated conversation with the formidable Jezebel Woods. Thomas was grateful he hadn't told Max where he was heading when he left the office. Otherwise he might already be in handcuffs.

Then Thomas stopped. Something about what he said to the sheriff came back to him. What was it he said about 'connections?' Flipping on the light above him, he hastily pulled out his interview notes from his visit with the doctor. In all his time speaking with Morris, he never once asked about Gary Davis!

"I can't believe it," he said out loud. He was approaching it from the wrong angle. Paul Morris may not have seen *Jeffrey Daniels* before the murder, but that didn't mean he couldn't have seen *Gary Davis*. It was a long shot, to be sure, but it was one that was worth taking. If Jezebel interviewed Morris right after the first killing, she wouldn't have had a reason to ask him about Davis either.

His hand flew to the phone he had thrown into the passenger seat. Although the sun was setting in the sky, it was probably early enough that the doctor would not mind taking his call. Hurriedly, he dialed the number and punched the call button.

Rather than the ringing noise Thomas expected, he was greeted by an operator's voice.

"We're sorry, but this call cannot be completed as dialed. Please hang up and try again."

The words the old man said less than an hour before returned to him.

"Something was walking in the cornfield."

"The killer," Thomas exclaimed. Morris was in danger.

There's no one else around for miles, he thought, *except me.* Thomas knew he had to go back for the old man. After wheeling the car around, he put his foot down hard on the gas pedal.

A few minutes later he heard the roar of a police siren. *Impossible,* he thought, trying to get a better look at the driver in his rearview mirror. *There's no way she could get here that quickly.*

"Jezebel," he whispered. He blinked at the flashing lights. She was trying to pull him over. The sheriff could not have picked a worse moment to find him. Thomas was going seventy-five miles an hour. He didn't have time to stop; not when someone's life depended on it. So he did the only thing he could think of to do. He kept going.

Hopefully, he would lead Jezebel back to the doctor's house. Gaining speed, he glanced over his shoulder. She was getting closer. Thomas could see the sheriff's perplexed expression in the mirror and forced himself to look at the road in front of him. The forest appeared to stretch out toward him, with each new twist or turn in the road bringing him closer to careening down the same hills that led to the demise of Jeffrey Daniels.

His phone was ringing again. This time, he knew exactly who it was without speaking. Trying not to look away from the road, he answered the phone and managed to switch it to speaker.

"What in God's name are you doing?" she shouted through the phone. "Pull over!"

"I can't do that!" he shouted. "Paul Morris is in danger! He told me he thought he was being watched, and now there's no dial tone at his house."

Thomas turned quickly onto the road leading to the Daniels Farm. Jezebel, who was not prepared for the turn, passed the road by. In his rearview mirror, he saw that she threw down the phone, came to a screeching halt, and threw her vehicle in reverse.

This time, the dust from the gravel road was the least of Thomas' worries. As he jumped out of the car, he prayed he wasn't too late.

***

Inside the house, the scarecrow wrapped fingers of straw around the old man's throat. Pinned against the living room wall, the doctor's struggles were becoming weaker and weaker. The Keeper paused, staring into the old man's eyes. The need for the offering was overwhelming.

"Help," Paul tried to say as his eyes started to close. "Please, God."

"Save your prayers," the scarecrow said, squeezing harder on the man's throat. "There's no one who can hear you now."

The old man slumped to the floor.

Grabbing Paul's foot, the Keeper began dragging the man behind him. The scarecrow walked through the glass door at the edge of the living room, sending shards of glass spilling to the ground as they passed into the cool night air. In the sky, the sun had almost completely vanished.

The Keeper walked toward the cornfield, still dragging the body. There was more work to be done. His children were waking, and the crows were his eyes.

"Stop!" a voice shouted. The Keeper turned until his black eyes were staring at the reporter standing on the shattered glass.

"Get away from him," Thomas yelled, his voice betraying fear.

"As you wish," the scarecrow hissed. He released his grip and allowed the doctor's body to rest on the grass. The man's blood ran into the ground, which was enough.

Then the Keeper turned his full attention to Thomas. The man had stuck his nose where it didn't belong too often, and now he would pay the price.

***

Thomas didn't know why the killer was dressed up like a scarecrow, and at that moment, he didn't care. Paul Morris lay on the ground, bleeding. The doctor wasn't moving.

Thomas grabbed a large stick from the ground and swung at the intruder as hard as he could. Moving faster than Thomas could believe, the scarecrow caught the stick and ripped it from his hand. Then the killer caught him in the stomach with a punch that sent him reeling backwards.

Thomas tried to crawl away from the house to catch his breath, but the killer followed him. The scarecrow lifted him into the air as easily as someone might pick up a piece of paper. As he stared into the swirling darkness inside the pumpkin, Thomas struggled vainly to free himself. The killer's breath was rancid, like the smell of death.

The sound of a gunshot pierced the silence of the night. Thomas felt the bullet whiz through air, passing by him.

"Put him down!" Jezebel Woods shouted, standing outside the doorway. She held her pistol in both hands, her hair blowing in the wind.

"Put him down," she repeated. "Or this time I won't miss."

The Keeper stared at the sheriff. Part of the scarecrow's brain was filled with memories of another time—*his* memories. It knew the sheriff. *He* knew the sheriff.

"You," the Keeper hissed. He watched the woman inside the house. Before Jezebel could fire again, the scarecrow threw the reporter toward the house.

"Thomas!" Jezebel shouted, her voice filled with concern. She ran toward him, her gun raised. The killer disappeared into the cornfield. "Are you all right?"

"Yeah, I think so," he said as she helped him sit up. "I don't think Morris is, though. You need to call an ambulance!"

"No," she whispered after feeling for the doctor's pulse. "He's dead."

"I—I can't believe it," Thomas said. "We just spoke an hour ago. He was right across from me."

"What was that thing?"

"Whoever he is, he's strong. If you hadn't come along, he would have killed me too. You saved my life."

"Stay here," Jezebel said. "I'm going after him." Before he could say another word, she vanished into the cornfield, holding her gun at the ready. He waited for what felt like hours until finally she returned.

“He’s gone,” she said, staring into the cornfield, as if expecting the killer to return from his hiding place within the stalks of corn. Thomas followed her gaze. Together on the grass outside the brown house, the two stared at the cornfield until the darkness of night finally claimed possession of the sky.

Chapter TEN

"Something's going on in Gray Hollow," Chuck Howard said. The surface of the conference room table felt cold under his hands, as if the frost from outside had managed to find its way inside the news station. Most of his important colleagues sat gathered around the conference table. Susan Washington and Fred Keller, the two lead anchors, were watching him skeptically.

Let them stare, Chuck thought. He fought the impulse to smirk. The anchors both knew the ambitious young reporter was angling for a spot at their news desk. In fact, Chuck planned to advance far beyond the limitations of RB-KAR. If not for the media's current financial crisis, he told himself, he would already be on the ascent. At least he was in television.

Chuck felt that waiting for Jim Doyle, the associate producer, to finish discussing increasing the time devoted to national issues amounted to little less than torture. Now that it was Chuck's turn to speak, he intended to woo the crowd. Or at least the people he needed to persuade. The RB-KAR channel television news station wasn't particularly large. Despite this, the news program was carried by most of the south-central portion of Illinois.

Chuck pointed to the screen from the website of *Hollow Happenings*. He had checked into the small town newspaper. *Hollow Happenings* was a joke, employing only two full-time staffers. It would be child's play to scoop the newspaper.

"In the last week there have been three murders in Gray Hollow."

"There's violence all across the state, Chuck," Jim Doyle said. "These are hard times. I don't see why that warrants sending a news crew to Gray Hollow for an extended amount of time."

Of course you wouldn't agree, Jim, Chuck thought, irked. The associate producer had never liked him. Chuck kept his eyes trained on Eric Howard, the executive producer, who also happened to be his uncle.

"'Extended' is hardly the word I would use. The article makes it sound like this could all be over shortly."

"Sounds like a waste of time to me," Susan Washington said.

"My gut tells me that this could be huge. This man, Gary Davis, is suspected of murdering a stranger, as well as his wife and son. He's been hiding in the forest for days, potentially armed. More than that, the story left a lot out. The reporter didn't seem to know why any of this was happening. There is a story here. I can feel it. Besides, what do we have to lose? Other than the town newspaper, no other news organizations have jumped on this yet."

"What do you want to do?" Eric asked. The producer lowered his glasses. Chuck grinned, realizing he had won the argument.

"Go to Gray Hollow for three days to see how this plays out. I'll only need one cameraman and one assistant. Jennifer Dunlap can handle my assignments when I'm gone."

Jennifer would depart from the station in three months for maternity leave, which meant she wouldn't threaten to eclipse him in his absence. Chuck had planned for everything.

"Fine," the producer said.

Sitting through the rest of the meeting was excruciatingly painful. Chuck practically ran from the conference room when the meeting was over, stopping only to thank Eric for his support. It was good to have an uncle in the business.

***

Thomas slumped back on Jezebel's couch. He had only just arrived at her home and sat in the living room, waiting for her to return from the kitchen.

Unnerved as he was after his assault by the killer, it was all he could do to retain his composure. When Jezebel allowed him to leave the crime scene the night before, Thomas headed for bed as soon as possible, but sleep proved impossible. He found himself rising out of bed at the slightest of sounds.

That was one of the reasons Thomas was relieved when she scheduled their meeting for noon. After the sleeping pills he'd taken, even the continual beeping of his alarm clock hadn't been able to rouse him until eleven.

Like his own residence in Gray Hollow, Jezebel Woods' house did not have a very homey feel to it. Other than a few sparse framed photographs on the wall, he could see very little evidence of a life beyond her job.

When Jezebel welcomed him inside only a few minutes ago, she had offered him a cup of coffee, and he gladly accepted. As he reached for the cup on the table across from him, Thomas noticed that his hands had finally stopped shaking. In the aftermath of Paul Morris' death, the two agreed to meet to air out everything they knew about the case. Initially, Thomas was surprised when she invited him to her house, but he realized why she picked that particular venue when he saw the crowd outside the police station on his way through town. He couldn't imagine being able to accomplish anything inside the swarmed station. Thomas also realized that was probably the fault of his article, although Jezebel kindly chose not to comment on it.

He took another sip of the black coffee. The caffeine stirred him from his near-catatonic state, which left him free to reflect on the events of the previous night. In the background, he could hear Jezebel running the sink water.

Suddenly, an old woman stood several feet from him. Thomas watched the woman, who returned his gaze with a vacant expression.

"The darkness is watching you now," she whispered. She pointed at him with an arthritic finger. "It knows who you are."

"Excuse me?" Thomas asked, shocked at what the strange woman said.

"Mom?" Jezebel said, concern in her voice. She quickly walked into the living room from the kitchen, drying her hands with a rag. Jezebel gently took the old woman by the hand and led her from the room.

Thomas watched the two until they were out of his line of sight. After a few minutes, Jezebel returned to the living room.

"I'm sorry for that," she said. "My mother has dementia. She probably just sensed something was bothering you, that's all."

"No worries," Thomas said. "Does she live here with you?"

Jezebel shook her head. "Not yet. She has a part-time sitter at the moment, but I'm not sure that's enough anymore. I picked her up earlier for a checkup later today."

Thomas felt a new tinge of pity for the sheriff. He briefly wondered how hard it would be to manage all of her responsibilities and deal with a sick mother.

"Thanks for the coffee," Thomas said, taking another sip from the cup.

"No problem. You looked like you could use it. I know I did, after last night."

Thomas caught a glimpse of his eyes in the mirror. They were bloodshot.

"Before we start, I need to get something off my chest. I owe you an apology for the way I've acted toward you. You were right when you said I was acting in my own self-interest. I guess I managed to convince myself that wasn't true."

Jezebel laughed. "I guess that's a start," she said. "Why don't you tell me everything you've found, and we'll see how it goes from there?"

Thomas held his notepad carefully in his hands. He stared at some of the most pertinent questions. "Let's start from the beginning."

"This all started when Al Pittman found Jeffrey Daniels."

"Somehow I think this hinges on Daniels," Thomas commented. "His death started everything else. Someone wanted him out of the way badly enough to risk all of this. Otherwise, there is also the possibility of a serial killer operating here."

"I don't even want to contemplate that," Jezebel said. "What have you found on Daniels?" she asked. "Thanks to you, we know Jeffrey Daniels once lived in Gray Hollow with his father."

"Wilbur Daniels. He died of a heart attack in 1987, I believe. No one I spoke to had any contact with Jeffrey after that. Morris implied he left town and never looked back."

Jezebel started pacing. "I did some digging myself," she said. "There is no mention of a Jeffrey Daniels in the local school records. So even after they moved here, Wilbur kept Jeffrey in whatever school he was in at the time. As it turns out, a Jeff Daniels attended high school in Thistlewood, just outside the county lines."

Thomas looked up from his notes. "That's close to the Daniels Farm. I think you're onto something. What else did you find?"

She finished pacing and sat on the chair across from him. "Surprisingly, there was a lot of information in his record. Most of it wasn't useful. Daniels was apparently very popular in Thistlewood; he was a star athlete in multiple sports. I think that was why I remembered his name. His father practiced law in Thistlewood but later moved his practice to Gray Hollow."

"He probably kept Jeffrey in school at Thistlewood for sports. That's pretty much everything about Daniels, isn't it?" Thomas asked.

"I think so. Soon after we found him, Ben and Mary Davis were murdered."

"What kind of weapon did Gary Davis use at the house?"

"A rifle. Why is that important?" she asked, raising an eyebrow.

"Because the man we saw last night was unarmed. He killed Paul Morris with his bare hands. If Gary was the killer, why wouldn't he just use his gun?"

"Maybe he stashed the rifle away in the woods, where no one would ever find it. In these types of investigations, it's common practice for a suspect to try and hide the murder weapon."

"Then why wear a mask?"

The jack o' lantern wasn't exactly a mask, but Thomas didn't know how else to describe it.

Jezebel watched Thomas. "What?" she asked, but then it appeared to dawn on her. Thomas spoke her thoughts aloud. "Davis has to know we're looking for him. He can't survive in the forest indefinitely. Where did he have time to get a scarecrow costume?"

"Davis has to know we're looking for him. He can't survive in the forest indefinitely. Where did he have time to get a scarecrow costume?"

"Or why bother to conceal his identity?"

"Exactly. How much do you know about Davis?"

"We went to school together, actually. He was a creep, as far as I can remember. I see what you're getting at, Thomas, but the evidence that Gary was involved is very suggestive."

"Or circumstantial. Did he kill his wife and son with the rifle?" Thomas already had an inkling of what the answer might be due to Brinkley's testimony, but he wanted to hear it from her directly. Thomas kept those details out of the story that appeared in the newspaper.

"No. There were shots fired in the house, but we think Ben Davis was killed in a fall from the roof. The wife, Mary, was nailed to the wall with a pitchfork."

Thomas flinched. If Gary Davis indeed killed his wife in this manner, the man was without question a psychopath.

"We found no sign of fingerprints on the pitchfork, in case you're interested. Wiping prints is consistent with someone who would go through the trouble of hiding a murder weapon," she said before he could interrupt. "It doesn't prove his innocence or guilt."

"The man lives on the other side of the county. How could he have reached the Daniels Farm without a vehicle?"

She paused. "How did you know he was on foot?"

"It wasn't hard to check how many cars were registered in his name. You still haven't answered my question."

"The truth is, I'm not sure. You may have a point. As much as I hate to admit it, my instincts have been telling me all along there's more to this than it appears." She stood up and started pacing the room again. "Why would he leave the house on foot in the first place? He had two cars. The man could've been out of the country by now!"

"I don't understand," Thomas said.

"I've been approaching this from an angle of finding Gary Davis," she said. "What if that's the wrong way of looking at it? Why didn't he leave? The murder wasn't even reported until early the next morning. That's more than enough time to get away. Unless . . . Gary didn't have that time. Maybe he had to leave right away. What if someone was after him?"

"Like the man who killed Jeffrey Daniels and Paul Morris?" Thomas asked.

"Exactly," Jezebel said. "If your theory is correct, and at this stage that's still a big *if*, then someone *else* is out there with reason to want Gary Davis and his family dead."

"So you're thinking that the killer came to the farm and murdered the wife and son, but Gary escaped?"

"It's too early to know for sure. Either way, we still need to find Davis as soon as possible. Logan Randall is in charge of the manhunt. That leaves one substantial missing piece," she said. "We still haven't found the connection between Daniels and Davis. Something to prove that this isn't all disconnected."

They sat in silence a moment. Both contemplated the weight of her words. If there was a serial killer at work in Gray Hollow, the deaths might be just beginning.

"There is a link," Thomas said finally. "Between the first and third attacks. Paul Morris owned the house Jeffrey Daniels use to live in. That's too much of a coincidence for me."

"You're right," she said. "We still have to find out how Gary Davis ties into all this."

"You have me there," Thomas replied. He sighed. "Nothing I've found comes close to suggesting a relationship between them."

"Morris didn't know anything? No saved papers or photographs from either of the Danielses?"

"He didn't live long enough for me to ask him."

"Surely there has to be something. The house is a crime scene. I'll go back and search it when I drop off my mom."

Thomas didn't like the idea of her going back to that house so soon after what transpired there the night before.

"Be careful," he said.

"Don't worry. I'll be carrying a loaded weapon. What are your plans?"

Thomas was so occupied with their discussion that he hadn't thought about it. There was a lot to do, and time was fleeting. Sleeping in was a luxury he probably shouldn't have allowed himself.

"I called Max last night to give him an update, but it's probably best for me to show up at the office for a quick word. Then I think I'll head to the Thistlewood Public Library to do some research on Gray Hollow."

"What are you looking for?"

"Wilbur Daniels had his heart attack in 1987. That's when Jeffrey moved away, and all the evidence indicates he hasn't been back since. Until now. Whatever caused this, I think it has something to do with the history of this town. I've been living here for months now, but I still don't know much about the history of Gray Hollow." Suddenly, Thomas recalled another detail from the murder scene he neglected to share with her. "Remember," he said. "You might be in danger. Last night, when you appeared, the killer spoke. I think he knew you."

"What exactly did he say?"

"Just one word: 'You.'"

Jezebel's eyes narrowed. He could tell she was troubled by something, although he wasn't sure what it was. As if sensing his gaze, she shifted her attention to her watch.

"It's almost time for Mom's appointment. I'm sorry I have to cut out on you when we obviously have so much left to discuss. Do you have any more questions for me before we head out? You have my number."

"There is one thing, but I doubt you'll know the answer to it," Thomas said. "Why on earth would the killer dress up like a scarecrow? It doesn't make sense to me. Surely there's a reason for it."

Jezebel nodded. "Actually, I might know more than you think. When you said you were curious about Gray Hollow's history, I think you were on to something. Since this case started, I've been exposed to small reminders from this town's past. At first, I thought it was just coincidence. Now I'm starting to realize this has more to do with history than I thought."

Thomas stared at her. "What aren't you telling me?"

"When we went into the Davis house, we found something at the scene of the murder. Something I didn't expect."

"What was it?"

"A scarecrow. It wasn't the same as the one we saw last night—for one thing, it didn't have a pumpkin covering its head. All the same, it was put there for a reason. I'm starting to think I may know what that reason is."

He scratched his head. "Care to tell me what it is?"

"Not yet," she said. "I have to be absolutely sure before I bring this back up. Small towns have long memories. Some scars heal quicker than others. And some wounds never close entirely."

"What does that mean?" he asked, trying hard to keep the sarcasm out of his voice.

When she looked into his eyes, Thomas thought he could see sadness on her face. "While you're at the library, try researching the name Salem Alistair."

Thomas tried to extract more information from Jezebel but found her defenses impregnable. Finally they parted ways, and new questions filled his mind.

Who are you, Salem Alistair?

***

Light spilled across the dense forest and trickled down to the small creek at the mouth of the stream. Logan Randall climbed down the hill in his attempt to locate the suspect's trail. Footsteps sounded behind him, and Logan became aware of a nearby presence.

"It's about time you caught up with me," he said tersely. He shot a glance back at the tall man walking across the stream.

"Sorry," Rick Pepper said. "I thought I heard something back in the bushes. It was just a deer." He took a drink from the water bottle in his gloved hand. His other hand held a small caliber pistol.

"I told you to be careful with that thing," Logan snapped. "Keep it out of sight until we find Gary. The last thing we need is for you to be seen with a gun. Our friend went through a lot of trouble to get us two untraceable guns."

The deputy was on edge. It was hard enough dealing with all the whiners at the station, but to have wasted so much time searching for Gary on top of that? His hands were sweating profusely under the gloves, but Logan didn't dare take them off. At least they kept his hands clean, aside from the sweat.

"Relax," Rick said. "I'll just tell them I was hunting."

"Yeah, I'm sure Jezebel Woods is going to fall for *that,*" he said sarcastically. Logan waited for his companion to finish his drink before continuing. He stared at Rick, who had always been tall, even during high school.

Ironically, Logan would much rather have been stalking Rick through the forest than Gary. Of all the friends in their group, Rick was his least favorite. There was a thickness to the man, a brash attitude that Logan simply could not stand. The tall man had been given the nickname "Peppers" in high school because of his last name, although his fiery temper also had something to do with it.

"Still working for the chick?" Rick laughed. "How does it feel to be a lapdog for a woman that's younger than you are, Logan?"

Logan clenched his fists silently and gave no sign of acknowledgement. He would shed no tears if anything happened to Rick during the manhunt. He closed his eyes and listened to the wind shift.

"Quiet," he whispered. He held a finger to his lips. "Did you hear that?"

A few hours ago, Logan received a report of a break-in at a farm about fifteen miles from Gary Davis' house. One of the owners, a woman, returned to the house after having lunch with a friend. That was when she found a broken window and some missing food. As she stared outside the farmhouse, she saw a man running into the field with what she thought was a rifle or shotgun.

The description matched Gary Davis. In case his old friend really was in the woods behind the farmhouse, Logan wisely kept the report to himself. No sense in alerting the sheriff just yet. He would wait until Gary was dead or in handcuffs. Without question, Logan was prepared to kill his friend, though he hoped it wouldn't come to that. If Gary came clean and told him what was going on, perhaps he could help him.

They went deeper into the forest, far deeper than Logan had ever been. This was an untamed region of town, completely undeveloped and unsettled. They were on their own in the thick woods. No witnesses.

It was hard to pinpoint the source of the sound he heard over the roar of the river in the background. In the distance, Logan could see a dark patch of forest covered in briars. He followed the sound, turned, and went the other way.

"Split up," he whispered to Rick. "I think I heard him up by the waterfall. I'll walk up on this trail, and you go down around the other side. Look out for him and watch for my signal. Do not shoot unless I give the go-ahead."

Rick nodded, suddenly serious. Grateful for the tall man's silence, Logan advanced onto the trail leading along the river. With the onset of autumn, most of the plant life was withered, which made it difficult for him to avoid being seen. Gary, who had been in the forest for a week, was probably an ace at blending in.

When he heard the sound again, the deputy knelt behind a tree trunk and made sure his gun was loaded. Then he saw Gary. He was standing next to a tree beside the waterfall, running his hands through the water.

Gary looked bad. The man's clothes were ripped to shreds. His shirt was stained with blood, and it looked like there was something wrong with his leg. Still, he had the rifle resting only a few inches away. That made him dangerous.

Easing closer, Logan contemplated going ahead and taking the shot. He didn't know where Rick was, but it was probably for the best. If anyone could reach Gary, it would be him—not Rick. As his fingers inched closer to his gun, he struggled with indecision.

"Logan?" Gary asked, sitting straight up. "What are you doing here?"

***

Rick cursed loudly, then wished he hadn't. If Gary Davis happened to be nearby, he would've easily heard his voice.

Logan would be furious, Rick thought. Then again, Logan was not lost. Rick was. It was almost funny. Rick liked to brag to his friend about his outdoor skills. While it was true he was a talented hunter, Rick was not so skilled at finding his way around strange surroundings.

The waterfall wasn't anywhere in sight by this point. In fact, the forest seemed to be growing darker. He stepped on a pile of leaves and gritted his teeth at the crunching sound. Brushing his way through a briar patch, Rick stumbled down the shadowy trail. He was almost tempted to call out to his friend.

The longer he traveled, the more it dawned on him that he was getting even farther away from where he was supposed to be. A sticky string-like substance attached itself to his face, and Rick tried in vain to tear a spider web from his skin. Failing to do so, he swore again, this time quietly.

"Logan?" he finally whispered. "You there?"

Nothing. Not even the birds. He couldn't see anything moving in this part of the forest. It was almost barren. Pumpkins grew wildly across the thin soil, which created a mass of vines he was forced to tiptoe through. The pumpkins struck Rick as out of place. He wouldn't have guessed they could grow in the woods, without sunlight.

Rick tripped on a vine and went sprawling perilously close to a ledge. While staring down into the pit of earth, Rick thought he could see the dim outline of a human figure. He stood and dusted himself off.

About time, Rick thought as he waited for his eyes to adjust to the shadows. Even though he was lost, he had still managed to find Gary! He would get the credit for taking care of the problem. *Wait until Logan finds out I was the one that tagged Davis.*

He remained as quiet as possible. Rick turned the safety off his pistol. He peered down into the pit, trying to discern the face of the figure below. It was too dark. Rick bent down closer. He cautiously watched the stationary figure. Was Davis wearing some kind of pointy hat?

A large black crow fluttered up out of the branches at the top of the pit, flying right past his face. Thrown off balance, Rick slipped and fell forward into the pit. The last thing he remembered before falling unconscious was staring into a motionless face of cloth.

***

"Logan? What are you doing here?" Gary repeated.

The deputy tucked the gun away and hesitantly stepped outside the line of trees. He tried to betray no sign of how upset he was at being spotted. To his relief, Gary didn't go for his rifle. In fact, he seemed glad to see him.

"I could ask you the same question. I've been looking all over for you. I saw your house. Did you think the department wouldn't find out?"

"Find out? Do you think I killed them? Logan, you have to believe me, I had nothing to do with it!"

"Calm down, buddy. I'm here alone. Just tell me what happened."

"The scarecrow."

Logan saw the scarecrow at the crime scene, but he wasn't sure of its significance. "What about it?"

"Don't you get it? Don't you know what it means? They're everywhere! They're following me through the woods. The scarecrows are trying to kill me!"

For the first time, Logan was convinced his friend was utterly insane. Despite himself, the deputy felt a pang of pity for his friend. Gary had obviously snapped and killed his family, although that didn't explain what happened to Jeffrey Daniels.

"What do you mean, Gary? Did the scarecrows kill Jeffrey Daniels?"

"Maybe," Gary said, his face ashen.

Logan glanced around for Rick. What was keeping him?

"You know what the scarecrow means. I'm not crazy," Gary said. "Look, I know all this sounds incriminating. But I didn't do anything."

"Then who did?"

"*He* did."

"Who?" Logan asked, confused.

"You really have to ask that question? Who would want to kill both Jeffrey and me? What did we have in common?"

"What are you talking about?" Logan muttered.

"That night back in high school. You remember. There was always something wrong with him, Logan, you know that. We all did. He brought Jeffrey Daniels back, then he went after my family."

Now Logan was worried. "You think someone found out? Is there anyone who knows what we did? Talk to me, Gary. I can help you. Your friends can help you."

"I don't think I deserve help," Gary said. "I've been alone in the woods for days without anything to eat until I broke into that farmhouse. All I can hear are my wife's screams. Sometimes, I just want to confess it all. That might be the only way to get him to go away."

"Don't talk like that, Gary. You know what that would mean. Do you want to spend the rest of your life in prison?"

"Do you think I care about that anymore? My family is gone."

"What about us then?" Logan asked. "Your decision will affect all of your friends. Surely you don't want us to get locked up. Think about it."

This conversation was quickly taking a turn for the worse. He and Gary paced around each other in circles, surrounded by the forest. Logan kept one eye trained on the rifle resting atop the moist soil. He wondered if the gun was loaded.

"Do you want me to go to prison because of your actions, Gary?"

Gary bowed his head. "I'm sorry, Logan. I've got to do what is best for my conscience. It's what Mary would have wanted."

"Then I'm sorry, too," Logan replied, seizing his opening. He punched Gary as hard as he could in the jaw, and Gary stumbled back.

"What are you doing?" he shouted while trying to regain his footing as Logan kicked the rifle down the other side of the hill.

"You're a threat to everything," Logan said. "I didn't want to do this, Gary, but you've left me with no choice. I'm not going to prison."

Just as Logan reached for his pistol, Gary threw himself at the deputy's legs. Logan stumbled back, which gave Gary enough of an opening to grab at the pistol. The two struggled over the gun as each attempted to gain an advantage over the other. Finally Logan's grip failed, and the gun toppled over the waterfall.

Before Logan could recover, Gary's arms were around his neck. He pushed Logan back toward the edge of the deafening waterfall. Logan grabbed his friend's injured leg, squeezing as hard as he could. Gary screamed in pain and released him.

"I'm sorry it had to come to this," Logan said. He jumped on top of Gary and hit the man again and again. "Too bad you had to open your mouth."

Gary snarled before butting heads with him. Logan winced and released the man. Then Gary tackled him, and the two men rolled down the muddy hillside in the direction of the darker portion of the forest.

Logan found himself lying facedown in the mud at the foot of the hill. Gary, only a few feet away, crawled toward an object resting in the mud. When he realized what the item was, Logan jumped to his feet. He was too slow.

"That's what you get, you piece of filth," Gary said, his outstretched hand grabbing the fallen rifle. He swung the rifle in the air, pointed it right at Logan's chest, and pulled the trigger.

Nothing happened. The rifle didn't fire. Gary's eyes grew wide.

Logan removed his service revolver from behind his back, nestled safely away while he had used the replacement weapon now lost in the waters. The sound of the gun echoed throughout the forest. Logan stared at the corpse of his friend for a few moments, watching the blood sink into the soil. He could feel the mud clinging to his skin. The feeling of contamination made him queasy. He needed to wash off, and quickly. Logan wasn't about to wait for Rick. He had brought his own vehicle.

Logan turned around and left.

***

Having joined his family in death, Gary Davis sunk slowly into the scarlet-tinted mud.

The darkness welcomed him.

Chapter ELEVEN

When Thomas passed over the lake, gray clouds covered the sky, ushering in a dull pallor over the town reflected in his rearview mirror. His tires kicked up mist from the morning's small rain shower, which sprayed the sides of the concrete bridge. The reporter glanced out the window at the sky. Over the past few days, he noticed that the weather was growing murkier as the month stretched on.

The dark recesses of Cavern Lake loomed below the large bridge, trickling into the rivers and tributaries that ran throughout the town. Cold water rushed harshly against the shoreline beneath the massive concrete structure, stirred by the fierce winds. Cavern Lake separated Gray Hollow from the nearby city of Thistlewood. Only by traveling across the bridge could a car reach the city on the other side. In this respect, the community was virtually isolated from the outside world. Gray Hollow was for the most part an inaccessible location.

After flipping off the radio, currently playing unintelligible static, Thomas' thoughts kept returning to the twin pools of darkness inside the horrific jack o' lantern. Outside the car, thunder roared across the heavens.

Maybe I can get inside before it starts raining, he thought as he pulled onto the street on the other side of the bridge. In contrast to Gray Hollow, the city of Thistlewood was brimming with scores of bustling homes and businesses. Despite the influx of traffic, Thomas located the city library with little difficulty.

"Max, it's me," Thomas said into his cell phone on his way out of the car. "I'm heading into the library in Thistlewood." He ducked inside the building and out of the worsening weather. "Would you mind looking up a name for me?" he asked.

"What do you need?" his editor replied.

"Go back through the newspaper archives and find everything you can about someone named Salem Alistair. I don't know how long I'm going to be at the library."

"All right," Max said.

Thomas hung up the phone and walked into the sparsely populated library. Having to travel twenty minutes to Thistlewood was still a minor inconvenience compared with his commute in New York.

Gray Hollow had yet to catch up to the Age of the Internet. Lacking a library of its own, the town's historical documents were located in the Gray Hollow Primary Sources section of the Thistlewood Public Library. Since Thomas possessed a keen eye for seeking out information anyway, the task at hand didn't pose too much of a problem for him.

The public records area of the library was empty, which didn't surprise Thomas. Although Thistlewood was larger than Gray Hollow, it was by no means a big city. Settling into the small room, Thomas swung his jacket over a chair and began selecting books from the shelves.

He started with some of the most recent books he could find. Many texts contained tedious information pertaining to financial transactions unimportant to him. The general books covering town history were more gossip oriented than Thomas expected. One section over a series of church fires in the sixties surprised him. Each of the seven churches were set on fire and completely razed to the ground. From what Thomas gathered, the fires appeared to be the result of arson, although the culprits were never caught.

"Weird," Thomas muttered. His own parents had taken him to church often as a child. Thomas fell out of the habit in recent years, likely attributable to the hectic nature of his career. Upon surviving his near-death experience, he was seriously rethinking that position.

After retrieving an older book from the shelf, Thomas delved deeper into the town's past. This particular volume contained a wealth of information about the early development of Gray Hollow. Located on fertile ground and bordering Cavern Lake, the town prospered for a long time from agricultural output and commerce. The lake and nearby rivers allowed for extensive fishing. Finally, he came to a passage that was particularly of note.

In the early nineteenth century, the economic success of Gray Hollow was largely inhibited by its geographic isolation. Regardless, the town was self-sufficient enough to support its growing population. A period of drought heralded famine at the end of the decade, prompting a rise in unemployment and crime. This may have contributed to records of renewed practice of pagan rituals among some citizens. It is well documented that these practices resulted in conflict throughout the territory. All of the factors outlined above are generally held to be responsible for a mass migration of individuals to what became the city of Thistlewood. Positioned in an area more accessible to trade, the population of Thistlewood eclipsed Gray Hollow within two decades.

Thomas read the paragraph twice before skimming through other sections of the book. What did it mean by "renewed interest" in pagan rituals? Were there pagan rituals before? It sounded out of place for nineteenth century America. Then again, the dated book's definition of paganism was probably antiquated at best. He flipped back across the pages of the book but could find no other sources to back up the claim.

"Maybe the scarecrow has some significance to the town's pagan history," he said to himself, scribbling the thought down on a notepad. He returned to the bookshelf and removed a new stack before placing the well-weathered volumes on the table. It took him brief forays into all the books to find what he was looking for.

Two primary groups settled the town that would come to be called Gray Hollow: traders pressing westward from the colonies, and colonists from a fort in the vicinity. Due to a lack of preparedness and an extensive drought, the small settlement's population was reduced to sixty-three people sometime around the late eighteenth century.

According to popular myth, around that time a man named Bartholomew appeared in the settlement. Claiming to have escaped an Indian encampment, Bartholomew showed the settlers agricultural practices he learned during his entrapment to help them survive the drought. Bartholomew also introduced the settlers to what he claimed were Indian rituals he had witnessed designed to make the land fertile. The documented rituals, however, show little resemblance to known Native American practices.

There was little church influence at the time. As a result, there was no resistance to Bartholomew from the desperate settlers. It is unknown what happened to Bartholomew, but at some point in the winter he disappeared.

The next spring the harvest was plentiful, and the townspeople survived. The influence of Christianity returned as more settlers arrived into the town, and the rituals heralded by Bartholomew were largely abandoned. Many in the town believed, however, that there were those who continued to practice pagan rituals. Indeed, there are at least three documented outbreaks of witchcraft practiced in Gray Hollow since that time.

Some of those accused of witchcraft claimed they were worshiping the demon Baal of the biblical Old Testament. These practitioners were driven underground with fierce resistance, and for good reason. The Baal worshipers believed that successful rituals required blood sacrifice to the demon in order to fertilize the land. A few of the cultists declared to have been "touched" by the demon, asserting they were given special knowledge and abilities—to date these claims have not been properly documented.

"Wow," Thomas said as he set the book down. This wasn't what he was expecting. While the bit about Baal didn't make sense to him, the town legend potentially explained the scarecrow costume. Maybe the killer was trying to use the legend about the pagan rituals to frighten his victims. Thomas doubted that was actually the case. It sounded too far out there. The people of Gray Hollow had their own superstitions, but from what Thomas had seen, they wouldn't panic over someone dressed in an admittedly realistic Halloween costume. As the reporter waited for Max's call, he continued reading.

He didn't have to wait long. In the middle of scanning some pages of interest using the library's copier, his phone started vibrating. Thomas answered the phone and turned around just in time to find himself starting into the eyes of a stern-looking librarian.

"Sorry," he offered apologetically. Thomas attempted to speed up the process of copying. He glanced out over the rows of computers. Several people were looking at him with irritated expressions. "I hope you have something good for me," he muttered quietly over the line. "Half of Thistlewood is staring at me right now."

"'Good' might not be the word I would pick, but I definitely have something for you," Max replied. "You've really got me scratching my head on this one. There are literally dozens of articles on Salem Alistair, but I'm not sure what it has to do with *this* case."

"Jezebel said it was important, so it probably is. What have you found?"

"This happened several years before I came to Gray Hollow. It's no small wonder I haven't heard of this before now. Despite my love for this town, there are a lot of closely guarded secrets around here."

"You're telling me. I just spent the last hour learning about early colonial demon worship in Gray Hollow."

"You're kidding."

"I wish. So what's so big about this old story?"

On the other end of the line, Thomas could hear Max take a big breath before continuing.

"Salem Alistair was a teenager who disappeared in 1987. He lived in Gray Hollow all his life, at the Alistair Farm. Now that I think about it, the Alistair Farm is right next to the Daniels Farm."

Then it's also close to where Jeffrey Daniels' body was discovered, Thomas thought.

"There are no coincidences in this town, Max. Is this the same Alistair Farm everyone seems to think is haunted?"

"The very same," the editor replied. "From my understanding, it's a silly local superstition."

"Of course it is. It looks like this story was the reason for it. When did Salem disappear?"

"Around Halloween, according to the articles. Most of them don't say much about him, other than to update the readers on the search. It quotes several police officers commenting on the case every so often. In the last few, the police indicate that they believed he was dead."

OK Jezebel, you've got me on this one, Thomas thought. Other than the proximity of the two farms, he had no clue what bearing Salem Alistair had to the current murders. "Anything else? You were right, I'm not seeing what's so important about this case either."

"Salem lived alone in the house with his elderly aunt, who died two years later. Both his parents were already dead. When he died, the estate was left without an heir, and no one has been able to sell it since. No wonder. The farm is worth a fortune, and there aren't that many people in Gray Hollow with that much money."

Maybe Jezebel believes that Salem was murdered, and whoever did it is the same killer active today. The idea seemed far-fetched, but so had his theory about the scarecrow costume.

"Thanks," Thomas said as he left the library and moved outside into the wind. "I'm on my way back to the newspaper. We can catch up when I get there. I have another meeting with Jezebel after that." He crossed through the parking lot and returned to his car.

"Whatever it takes," Max said as Thomas started the engine. "As long as the stories are coming in, I'm happy. You are running behind on a few deadlines, but we don't go to press until Monday, so I'm not worried."

"Trust me, this story is bigger than all the rest. Remember the response we got yesterday? It's only going to snowball from here. Anyway, I'll be there in half an hour."

Thomas hung up hastily before punching another number into the phone and starting on the road back to Gray Hollow. As much as he hated to admit it, he had liked hearing Eve's voice on the phone, regardless of the mixed emotions it created. The saga of Salem Alistair provided him the perfect opportunity to call her back; if anyone could unearth something beneath the surface of the case, it was Eve.

"Hi, it's me," he said after succeeding only in getting her voicemail. "I thought about what you said, and it made a lot of sense. I'm going to take you up on your offer to help with the case. There is an old local mystery I'm looking into about a teenage boy named Salem Alistair, who disappeared in Gray Hollow. The sheriff suspects the disappearance relates to the current string of deaths.

"I was hoping you could find any regional or state stories dealing with Salem Alistair or any of his relatives. Are they still out there? Has he resurfaced? I don't really know that much about him at this point. If you could do this for me, I would really appreciate it. Thanks."

The car raced toward the impending storm building over Gray Hollow. In the distance loomed the bridge, overlooking the dark lake. The killer was out there somewhere, and Thomas intended to find him.

***

Jezebel was starting to get seriously worried. With strong misgivings, she had shared the name of Salem Alistair with Thomas Brooks. The sheriff prayed Salem's disappearance wasn't related to the killings, but seeing the murderer at the Daniels Farm had convinced her otherwise. For years, the mystery of what happened to Salem had gone unsolved. Now the cold trail was hot once more. While Jezebel wanted to solve the mystery more than anyone, she also needed to stop the killings. If she caught the man who had murdered Paul Morris, maybe she could do both.

Since his disappearance, Jezebel had avoided thinking about what might have happened to Salem. The past was back in full force, and there was no escape from it. As she stepped out of the police cruiser, she folded her arms across her chest to keep warm. The clouds in the sky were ominous, and she could tell a storm was coming.

With any luck, I'll be out of here and back with Thomas Brooks before the storm hits, she hoped.

Her thoughts settled on the reporter. His information and analysis of the situation were proving helpful. Jezebel was glad he hadn't pressed her about Salem when she gave him the name. The sheriff was not lying when she told Thomas she needed to take her mother to her appointment, but she was also thankful for the excuse. She had never opened up to anyone about the events of the past before. Doing so to anyone, let alone a complete stranger, would be painful for her.

Then again, Thomas Brooks was no longer a stranger. The concern he showed for Al Pittman, and the way he had bravely confronted the individual who attacked Dr. Morris was impressive—and Jezebel wasn't easily impressed. In many ways, the reporter was frustrating for her to characterize. At times he seemed capable of thoughtfulness and intelligence. Other times, he struck her as selfish and overly ambitious.

Jezebel had researched Thomas' fall from grace. She wondered how losing such a prestigious career would affect someone's sense of identity. Thomas was still probably coming to terms with what happened to him. That didn't excuse his unprofessional behavior, but at least she knew where he was coming from.

There was a draft inside Dr. Morris' house. She looked at the broken glass and demolished door and was reminded once again of the killer's ferocity. The crime scene wasn't as grim as the Davis household, yet it seemed to leave a greater impression on her. For one thing, she had come face-to-face with the killer just outside the house. It was also isolated, cut off from most of the closest neighbors.

After her encounter with the masked figure, Jezebel swept the scene for prints. Again she was thwarted, just as she was at the Davis house. There was nothing to be gleaned from the forensic evidence at the moment, though she kept her fingers crossed that circumstances would change.

If I were Paul Morris, Jezebel thought, *where would I keep Jeffrey Daniels' old things?*

There was one thing working in her favor: according to Thomas, the house was foreclosed on and purchased very quickly after the funeral of Wilbur Daniels. Like Thomas said, the speed implied that Jeffrey left Gray Hollow as soon as he could. Jezebel hoped it also meant that some of the Daniels' possessions were left behind.

It all comes down to whether Morris threw them away. Twenty years is a long time to hold onto someone else's possessions.

If Morris kept some of the Daniels' belongings, chances were they would be in the tool shed outside the house. Thankfully, Jezebel found the door to the shed unlocked. The small building was crammed full of old files and books from Morris' medical practice. After searching for several minutes, she found signs of Wilbur and Jeffrey Daniels in a group of boxes against the back wall. Aside from several first place sports trophies with 'Jeff' inscribed on them, the boxes were filled to the brim with various documents, books, and other papers. Most of them bore the signature of Wilbur Daniels, although there were a few photo albums. Wilbur was a lawyer in addition to managing the farm.

Jezebel fingered through an album quickly, studying the image of a younger Jeffrey. In none of the photos did she see his mother, which led her to think she either left the family or died young. She made a mental note to check for a certificate of death or divorce when she returned to her office. Then Jezebel spotted a picture that captured her attention.

"Bingo," she said. Jezebel tucked the album under her arm, having found what she was looking for. It was a photograph taken in 1986, featuring Gary Davis, Jeffrey Daniels, and a third adolescent at a basketball game between Gray Hollow and Thistlewood. There were a number of pictures with Gary Davis, who was sometimes pictured with a younger Logan Randall.

That's the connection, she thought. *They were friends.*

"Now to get out of here," she said to herself. Being alone in the tool shed was starting to creep her out.

As she returned to her car, Jezebel looked down at the first photograph, studying the third individual in the picture. She knew him too.

"Rick Pepper," she muttered. Jezebel thought of the tall student from her high school. Of the three friends in the picture, she knew him the best. They clashed regularly when they were students. Jezebel could clearly remember Rick bullying Salem Alistair.

"Are you involved in this, Pepper?" she whispered while starting her engine. The man was certainly large enough to have worn the scarecrow costume and was probably strong enough as well. It was time to do some more investigative work before she reconnected with Thomas Brooks.

There was a flash of lightning as the car pulled out of the driveway. A drop of rain fell from the sky, and the storm began.

***

It was pitch black when Rick came to at the bottom of the pit. Only the light of the moon provided any illumination in the dark forest. After opening his eyes, he shook his head groggily. Something wet trickled down from his hair to his face. He forced the other eye open. His face was swollen.

Rain poured down hard around him, forming large puddles in the thick mud. *Where am I?* Rick thought. He tried to remember what happened. A memory of the crow flashed through his head, which prompted a wave of pain.

"Logan," he called out. Rick prayed his voice carried beyond the sound of the rain. Distant thunder rumbled, permeating into the woods. Where did the deputy go?

Rick attempted to stand, but the pain in his left leg was overpowering. He was sure he had broken it in the fall. After fumbling around, Rick fished around in his pocket for his cell phone. If he could only get his girlfriend to pick up, she would drive him to the hospital without questions. If she could find him in the forest, that was. The phone was not in either of his pockets. He quickly realized it must have gotten lost when he fell. Unable to find the cell phone, Rick looked around in desperation.

That's when he remembered what else was missing. Rick sat up, startled. He recalled the twisted face of cloth belonging to the motionless figure. It was nowhere to be seen.

The roar of the thunder echoed again, joining with the rainfall and the darkness in a terrifying symphony. Rick heard a crack outside the pit. Upon hesitantly peering outside, he saw nothing other than piles of leaves being flung around in the violent winds.

Then he heard the sound again. Panicking, Rick clawed his way out of the pit. He fell outside the wall of mud and hit the wet earth with a thud. He spent enough time in the woods to know that something was very wrong. In his free time, he enjoyed hunting, both in and out of season. He knew now that he was not alone in the forest—there was something out there.

The leafless trees were crooked, blackened mockeries of their former selves. As his eyesight adjusted, he could see hundreds of crows lining the withered branches. Underneath the trees loomed not one but four darkened, man-sized figures. None of them were moving, yet Rick could feel their invisible eyes watching him.

A soft hiss echoed from deeper within the woods. Lightning flashed again, illuminating the forest long enough for him to see the darkened figures for what they truly were: scarecrows, each as frighteningly grotesque as the next. Rick closed his eyes in terror. He prayed when he opened them that he would emerge from this waking nightmare.

Instead, a new source of dread appeared in the distance. A fifth figure, taller than the others, stood underneath a tree. Three crows perched on the figure's shoulders. When the lightning flashed a third time, revealing the menacing head of a carved pumpkin, Rick let out a scream.

The figure twisted its head in his direction. Impossible as it was, the creature was staring directly at him.

"Hello, Rick," creaked a raspy voice.

Using a tree trunk to lift himself up, Rick hobbled away on his right leg as quickly as he could. He didn't get far. A tree root erupted from the mud and wrapped itself around his left foot. Rick was thrown to the ground. Moaning, he turned in the direction of the scarecrow still watching him.

"I don't think so," the monster said. The crows on the scarecrow's arm seemed to follow him with their eyes. "You're not getting away from me that easily. Not when I went through so much trouble for this reunion."

"What—what are you?" Rick gasped. He frantically searched for some way out. He saw none. If only he still had his gun . . .

The creature seemed to laugh, a shrill, horrifying sound echoing outside the jack o' lantern.

"You of all people should know. After all, it was you and your friends who created me."

What? Rick thought, too terrified to make sense of the monster's words.

Suddenly standing above him, the scarecrow bent down until his carved mouth was directly next to Rick's ear.

"I am the fear that has haunted your dreams for twenty years," the scarecrow whispered. "You know my name."

"I don't—"

"Say it!" demanded the scarecrow.

"Salem Alistair," Rick said. Tears welled up in his eyes. *I don't want to die,* he thought.

"The boy that was Salem Alistair is gone now. I am something wholly new, a mixture of his former self and the Lord of this forest. I am the Keeper of the Crows."

"What do you want?" Rick trembled. He feared the answer. The Keeper scraped a blackened fingernail against the tall man's cheek. The scarecrow held the drop of blood for Rick to see and whispered into his ear again.

"This," the Keeper said. "All of it. For the twenty years the darkness kept me alive, I've thought of nothing else."

"You came back for all of us? All five?"

"No," the monster replied. "I want the whole town, and every soul in it. With each death, my power grows. In time, I will bring Gray Hollow to its knees."

"Please, Salem," Rick stammered. "I'm sorry. Please, don't do this."

With a roar, the Keeper of the Crows threw Rick against one of the withered trees. The white hands disappeared, replaced by claws of straw. As the storm raged, the scarecrow advanced slowly toward the helpless man. Suddenly, the straw seemed to flow and ebb, as if it were alive somehow.

"That's not my name," the Keeper hissed. The straw claws tore their way into Rick's chest. Rick screamed, his cries joining the sounds of the storm.

Chapter TWELVE

Steam rose out of the shower and fogged the glass on the bathroom mirrors. Logan Randall enjoyed the cleansing feeling of the hot water washing away the grime, but more than that, he *needed* it. Deciding that fifteen minutes would provide adequate cleanliness, he turned off the faucet and snatched a fresh towel hanging over the shower. Logan touched his bruised cheek, wincing at the tenderness. His fingers traced the outline of his bloodied lip. The left side of his face was swollen as a result of one of Gary's kicks.

Other than the death of his friend, nothing had gone according to plan. Logan lost his spare weapon, and while he doubted it could be traced back to him, he despised loose ends. In addition, he had been separated from Rick Pepper, a man he considered a loose end in and of himself. It was after eight and completely black outside, but Rick still hadn't called him back. Logan hoped Rick was not foolish enough to get himself caught. The more he thought about it, the more Logan believed Rick was another potential problem that needed tending to. He had already killed Gary. It would be even easier to eliminate Rick.

Logan heard a knock from outside the house. His heart raced. Logan was not expecting company, and Rick or anyone else surely would have called first. Gary's paranoia was affecting him. With a frown, Logan walked into his bedroom and picked up the gun resting on the dresser.

"Coming," he said gruffly before answering the door. The familiar face that greeted him at the door was no threat. "What are you doing here?" he asked. Logan placed the gun down and motioned for his friend to come inside. The man sat on the couch while Logan listened from the kitchen.

"We needed to talk, and I didn't want to do it over the phone again so soon after the last time. We've both worked too hard to have this come back and bite us in the rear now."

Logan returned to the living room and handed his friend a drink. He took a seat on the couch opposite from the man and sipped his own drink quietly.

"So tell me, how did everything go today?"

"Wait," Logan said, arching his brow. "Didn't Rick tell you?"

"I haven't heard from Rick all day," his friend replied curtly. A dark shadow passed over his face.

"Neither have I. We were separated in the forest."

"Separated?"

"Don't worry. I handled Gary myself. You were right about him. He was planning to confess everything."

The other man looked incredulous. "Don't worry? I've tried calling Rick several times. He hasn't answered. I thought he was with you."

"Like I said, we got separated in the woods," Logan repeated, reluctant to admit that he elected to return alone rather than searching for Rick. He didn't plan on revealing that he left so he could get the mud off his body as soon as possible. He also decided it might be best to omit the part about the lost gun for the time being.

"I don't like this. Rick is getting dangerously close to entering the same category as Gary Davis."

Logan noted the casual nature with which his friend addressed a subject as intense as death. Both men shared cold and distant personalities. Both were survivors willing to make any necessary sacrifice.

"What about the sheriff? How much does she know?"

"I'm not sure," Logan answered honestly. "I've been watching her carefully, but I've also spent too much time tracking Gary down. Luckily, she seems to be butting heads with that reporter, Thomas Brooks."

"Brooks?"

"You know him?"

"We've met," his friend said. "Is he a threat?"

"To tell you the truth, I think he's more dangerous than the sheriff. According to Jezebel, he used to be a big-time reporter in New York. She kept him in the cold and he still managed to break the story."

"If you think he's getting too close, you know what to do. Now, why don't you tell me what else you've learned?"

***

Thomas finished the draft, printed it out, and threw it away. Returning to his desk, he shook his head and started typing again. Aside from his lamp, all the lights in the office were turned off. Max had left hours ago, before Thomas even showed up. Thomas admired the editor's work ethic. The two of them were the only reporters for the small paper. Anna Feather, the graphic designer who pieced the paper together, lived three counties away and did her work over the Internet.

It had been a long day. There were many things he'd learned that he wanted to tell Jezebel Woods. Some of the information wasn't necessarily pertinent to the case, like the stories of the pagan rituals, but all of it was starting to finally resemble a narrative. He hoped the sheriff's day was just as productive.

The light at his desk flickered and went out. Thomas stopped, gazing out the darkened windowpane in the back of the office. Suddenly, he remembered the image of the scarecrow and wondered if Paul Morris' murderer was something more insidious than a killer of flesh and blood. The reporter dismissed the notion, stood up, and walked across the room. He rummaged through the hall closet until he found a new light bulb.

It was just an old bulb, Thomas thought as he screwed in the light.

He was planning on meeting Jezebel at 8:30, which was close to fifteen minutes away. While he anticipated the meeting, Thomas was having a difficult time catching up on his deadlines. He even made an effort to return early from the library to tackle some of his assignments ahead of time. That way he would have more time to devote to tracking down a murderer who had already killed four people.

That story was already in the computer, just waiting to be updated if they discovered new information over the weekend. He would print the story covering the death of Paul Morris in the Monday edition of *Hollow Happenings*. Jezebel agreed with his decision to publish the piece. They both seemed to be of the opinion that since the cat was already out of the bag, there was no harm in continuing to inform the public.

His cell phone rang, which startled him. Amused at being unable to finish another sentence, Thomas leaned back in his chair, closed his eyes, and picked up the phone.

"Sheriff Woods?" he asked as he waited to hear what Jezebel had to say.

"That's the second time you've answered the phone that way when I've called," she said.

Thomas' eyes snapped open as he sat up straight at the sound of Eve's voice.

"Do you and this sheriff have something going on I should know about?" Although Eve's tone was playful, Thomas sensed an undercut of irritation in her voice.

"Sheriff Woods and I are hardly even friends," Thomas replied. "We're just working on this case together." He wasn't sure why he was being so defensive. Did he really believe he and Eve still shared a future together?

"That's good to hear," Eve said. "Like I said before, I can't see you settling down in Gray Haven and raising a couple of kids."

"Gray Hollow," he corrected. "Thank you for returning my phone call."

"Of course," she answered. "I wish I was more help. There are virtually no records of newspaper stories at any level mentioning Salem Alistair."

"That was my fear. Even Thistlewood's paper archives in the library didn't have anything on his disappearance, and the city is only a few miles from Gray Hollow."

"The information you sent me wasn't really enough to go on. Other than the state record of his birth certificate and the names of his parents, Joshua and Bethany, there was practically no information about him. No driver's license, no speeding tickets, nothing. It's actually really weird."

"You're telling me. My editor was equally surprised. He thinks it's some kind of town secret or something. A few people I've spoken to in town believe the Alistair Farm is haunted—maybe this relates to that."

"Maybe. I'm surprised you have an editor in Gray Hollow. I thought maybe you country folk operated on a communal system."

"Ha, ha," Thomas replied flatly. "That joke doesn't even make sense."

"How do you think Salem Alistair relates to the three murder victims?"

"Four," he said. Thomas instantly regretted sharing the information.

"Four?" she asked. "Your article only mentioned three."

"A doctor named Paul Morris was killed since then," he added reluctantly.

"What happened?" she asked, cutting to the point. He normally admired that skill, except when it was pointed at him. "What are you leaving out?"

"I visited Morris earlier in the day for an interview. He was a potential witness. When I tried to call him back, his phones were down."

"What?" Eve sounded skeptical.

"It's true. When I went back to his house, I found the man's body—and the murderer."

"You've got to be kidding. What happened?"

"The killer was dressed up like a scarecrow. He almost killed me," Thomas admitted. "Luckily, Jezebel fired at him and scared him away."

"What?" Eve shouted into the phone. "You could have died! Thomas, what on earth were you doing?"

"I thought confronting the killer would give Morris a chance to get away," Thomas said. "As it turns out, he was already dead."

There was a small pause on the line.

"How could you do something so foolish? Now this psycho knows who you are!"

Thomas could see a pair of headlights approaching the newspaper office. He held the phone against his ear and mouthed a disheartened protest while peering out of the window blinds. "This isn't the first time I've put myself in danger for a story. You know that."

The car belonged to the sheriff. Thomas gathered his things, heading out to meet Jezebel as he continued to talk to Eve.

"Sorry," he mouthed to Jezebel when he got outside.

"No problem," she said, allowing him to walk alongside her on the sidewalk.

"Listen, I have to go. The sheriff needs me. Thanks for your help."

"Thomas Brooks," Eve retorted angrily. "Don't you dare cut me off—"

He hung up and slid the phone into his pocket. Leaving their cars behind, the pair walked in the direction of Dina's Coffee Diner.

"Sorry again," he said. "That was a friend."

"Didn't sound friendly to me," Jezebel replied. She looked amused. "It's nice to see that I'm not the only person you don't get along with."

"Actually, that was my ex-girlfriend. Compared to you, she's an angel."

Jezebel punched him in the shoulder. Thomas couldn't tell if the action was meant to be playful; it actually hurt his shoulder.

"Thanks for the compliment. How long has it been since you two split up? It sounded like you were talking about the case."

"Eve works for my old paper," Thomas confessed. "That's how we met. She's helped me out lately with some searches involving the murders."

"That's how you keep one step ahead. It must be good to be friendly with an ex."

"To be honest, we haven't been on friendly terms for a long time now. We've hardly talked since we broke up. Things ended badly between us."

"Sorry," she said. "I didn't mean to pry."

"It's no problem. I'm sure you've had similar experiences."

"Not really," she muttered.

Thomas opened the door to the diner, and the two walked inside, greeted by the pleasant aroma of coffee.

"While we're being truthful, I haven't really dated all that much, even before I became sheriff. And now, with all of my duties, I really don't have time for it."

Thomas took a seat across from Jezebel. He noticed her lay a book down on the table.

"What's that?" he asked curiously. He pointed to the book, which appeared to be a black photo album.

"These are pictures I found at the Daniels Farm," she said, opening the album. "In case you can't identify the person with Jeffrey Daniels in the photos here, the man is Gary Davis. When he was younger, that is. They were friends, which explains the connection between them, if not their connection to the killer. Notice this third individual in these four photographs? His name is Rick Pepper."

"Should I recognize him?"

"Probably not. Like Gary Davis, he went to school here in Gray Hollow. He was known for being a very violent bully, so much so he almost got kicked out of high school once."

"What does that have to do with the murders? Being in the same old photo doesn't make Rick Pepper a killer."

"Maybe not," she said. "That's not the end of the story. One of the people Rick used to bully more than anyone was Salem Alistair."

"Again with Salem Alistair," Thomas said. "I looked up the story, just like you said. What is with the fascination around his disappearance?"

"Remember the scarecrow we found at the house of Gary Davis? I showed you a picture of it? Salem Alistair designed it."

Thomas was taken aback. He had been prepared to tell her he believed the scarecrow was related to Gray Hollow's pagan history. Now he was even more confused than ever.

"How can you be sure?"

"Salem was my age. He was . . . different and got picked on a lot. His parents' farm was the largest in the town, and they had a big problem with crows. Salem built scarecrows to scare the birds away. At first no one thought anything of it, but the scarecrows were so enormously successful that other farmers began offering to pay him to make them scarecrows as well. We're not talking generic scarecrows either. Salem's creations were monstrous. Their grotesque appearance was matched only by their collective success in frightening away the crows."

"So you think this bully, Rick Pepper, might be responsible for Salem's disappearance? Now he is killing his old friends, dressed in a scarecrow costume? That's hard to believe, Jezebel. I mean, for goodness sake, this kid's body was never found. He could still be alive for all we know. Maybe Salem even came back to Gray Hollow for a little revenge. Were Gary Davis and Jeffrey Daniels bullies, too?"

"Gary was. I'm not sure about Jeffrey Daniels. And you're wrong about Salem. Even if he did survive, the Salem Alistair I knew couldn't hurt a fly. He was very kind and gentle. He loved animals. Salem said he could hear their feelings."

Thomas raised an eyebrow. "You seem to know an awful lot about him. It doesn't sound like you learned all this from the town gossip."

"When we were little kids, I lived close to the Alistair farm. After my parents separated, my dad continued living in his old place until he died in a tractor accident a few years ago. Salem and I used to be friends. When I got older, it was harder. None of my other friends liked Salem because he wasn't like everyone else. In retrospect, I wish I had tried to be closer to him. He didn't have any other friends. I did try to stick up for him whenever I saw anyone harassing him."

"Sounds like you feel you didn't do enough," Thomas said. Suddenly, he thought he knew the reason why Jezebel Woods went into police work.

"You're right." Jezebel looked away. "That year in high school, anyone could see Salem was having a really tough time. Instead of reaching out to him, I pulled back. Then he was gone. The police said they never found out what happened, but in my dreams I could see him all the time. He didn't run away, Thomas. Someone killed him. And I could have done something."

"Jezebel, there is nothing you could have done," Thomas said. He leaned over the table, putting a hand on her shoulder. "You were just a teenager."

"If I'd said something—anything—he might still be alive today. Now someone is leaving scarecrows behind at murder scenes. They're taunting us."

Jezebel thinks this could be her chance to seek justice for Salem Alistair, Thomas thought. *She's probably right. If Jeffrey Daniels or his friend, Gary Davis, knew who murdered Salem Alistair, the killer would have good reason to want them dead.*

Thomas wasn't convinced the killer was Rick Pepper, but Jezebel's lead was as good as any.

"So what do you want to do next?" Thomas asked. "I'm completely on board with you on this. You're not going to have to go through this alone." Despite the assistance of her two deputies, Thomas had already figured out that she was severely understaffed, similar to his situation at the newspaper.

"Thank you," she said, smiling again. "Maybe you're a better man than I gave you credit for. When we finish here, I think we both need a good night's sleep. Then I suggest we meet in the morning, track down Rick Pepper, and see where that leads."

"Good," Thomas replied. "In the meantime, I would like to hear everything else you know about Salem Alistair and his disappearance."

"Fine," she said. "But you're in for a long story."

Part Two

SALEM ALISTAIR

Chapter THIRTEEN

1987

It was a typical fall day in Gray Hollow. Cool October winds swept over the orange-colored leaves remaining on the trees, and farmers all across town bailed hay in preparation for the winter season. Halloween was approaching, which as always prompted a wave of excitement throughout the town.

Jezebel Woods was excited, too. As the teenage girl hurriedly threw open the door to her house, she didn't bother to remove her shoes before crossing over the white carpet. If not for the music in her ears from the cassette player she got last Christmas, Jezebel would still be able to hear the loud sounds of her peers on the school bus as it passed the two-story home. She paused and inhaled the rich aroma of freshly baked cakes in the kitchen.

Mom must have just left for work, she thought. Jezebel toyed with the idea of sneaking down to sample some of Emma Woods' work. Since her parents' marriage deteriorated, Jezebel had watched her mom struggle to keep them afloat financially. The paltry sum Emma received from her former husband in alimony and child-support was hardly enough to make payments on the new house. In fact, Jezebel once heard her mom speak to someone on the phone about possibly having to sell the house if business didn't pick up.

Jezebel knew her mom kept quiet about her difficulties so that she wouldn't alarm her daughter, but she wished her mother would open up to her. She didn't want her mom to worry so much. Outwardly, Emma Woods was a constant optimist, always saying that her pastry business would pick up soon. Unfortunately, it had been 'soon' for almost a year now. Jezebel loved living in the new house, especially given its proximity to town. She vowed that if her mother ever forced her to leave, she would buy a house just like it when she left Gray Hollow.

As she danced down the hall, Jezebel quickly forgot about her mother's financial woes while dwelling on the anticipation of Halloween. Although she hadn't enjoyed Halloween since she was a child, she knew this year would be different.

My first high school party, Jezebel thought, almost singing the words in her mind. Along with most of her friends, she had been invited to a Halloween bonfire out by Cavern Lake. She never thought she would get the invitation. For one thing, the party was Friday night, just one day away. The prospect was exhilarating. Finally she had something to do other than bemoaning the lack of things to do in Gray Hollow.

Jezebel removed the cassette tape from the player and searched for another artist. She saw the bright blue truck pull into the driveway from her upstairs window, and she groaned inwardly. Jezebel remembered that she'd promised to help her father pick up hay bales for the horses. Her plans to call her friends and talk about the party were instantly dashed. The horn honked loudly. Through the blinds, Jezebel could see her father staring up at the closed window.

"I'm coming!" she shouted down, delving into her dresser drawers for an old pair of jeans. Jezebel kicked off her sneakers and grabbed a pair of gray boots on her way out the door. She thought about leaving a note for her mother but decided against it, hoping she would be finished before her mother returned home.

"It's about time you got your butt down here," Buck Woods said when she climbed into his truck. "I didn't want to come in after you in these clothes, not with your mother's obsession with cleanliness." He stuffed a wad of chewing tobacco in his mouth.

Jezebel sighed, disgusted by the gross habit. She didn't respond. She knew the real reason he didn't want to go inside was that her parents still didn't get along very well. It didn't help that Buck was largely absent from Jezebel's life, which led Judge Jeremiah Underhill to rule against giving him custody of the girl when the couple first split up. Although she loved her father, Jezebel was all too aware of his flaws. A rough man with a tendency toward outbursts of temper, Buck Woods was not easy to live with. The only thing the two really shared in common was their mutual love of riding horses, which seemed to bring out a gentler side of her father.

Jezebel gazed outside as the truck left the suburb. Gray Hollow was alive with activity. Buck slowed to allow a few pedestrians to cross the road. Eventually, the truck left the buildings behind for the soothing sights and sounds of nature in the countryside.

"Aren't you going to say anything?" her father asked as they continued down the winding road. "I rarely get to see you enough as it is."

"What do you want me to say?" Jezebel asked, turning to face him.

Buck paused, as if deep in thought. "You know, I hadn't really thought about that," he said with a chuckle. He grabbed a spit cup for his tobacco. "How're you doing in school?"

"All As and Bs, same as when you asked me three weeks ago," she answered flatly.

"Wow. I don't know where you got those brains from, but you sure didn't get them from me."

You said that last time, too. Wisely, Jezebel chose not to say it out loud. She knew her father meant well, and she didn't want to start a fight.

"I already pulled the wagon in next to the barn before I picked you up, so we don't have to stop by the house," Buck said. He pulled the truck onto the familiar gravel road leading to the Alistair Farm. Like many small farmers in the area, Jezebel's father purchased a lot of his hay from the large Alistair Farm. When Joshua Alistair ran the farm years ago, it was the most profitable farm in the entire community. Joshua and his wife, Bethany, died in a car accident a few years ago, leaving control of the farm to Joshua's aunt, Cornelia, and their fortune to their young son, Salem.

When the blue truck reached the barn, the pair could see a tall, elderly woman standing in front of the hayloft with her arms crossed. She wore a plain dress, which waved about by the wind, and a severe expression on her face. Cornelia Alistair approached Buck as they got out of the truck.

"Buck Woods, I thought I told you that you can't have the rest of the hay until you pay for it."

"Cornelia, when I have the rest of the money I'll give it to you," Jezebel's father protested. "Right now, I need the hay for my horses."

"That's not my concern," Cornelia said. Her arms remained crossed.

"Jezebel," her father said. "Why don't you wait in the truck while Ms. Alistair and I discuss this?"

Instead of obeying her dad, Jezebel walked off into the large field. She closed her eyes and stretched her arms out toward the warm sun. With her father and Cornelia far behind, she smiled as she passed a hill overlooking the cornfield. The tall grasses of the field were still a vibrant green, and everything on the farm seemed filled with life.

Ahead, she saw a teenage boy in the pasture. He was walking alongside a white fence. His eyes lit up when he saw her.

"Jezzie?" A wide smile formed on his face. He ran over to her.

"Hi, Salem," she said, scratching the back of her neck. Salem, who was unusually tall for his age, looked down at her like he was surprised with an early Christmas.

"Hello," he replied. In addition to being extremely tall, Salem was also very thin. He was so thin that the kids at school had given him the nickname 'scarecrow.' It didn't help that it was well known that Salem built scarecrows for fun. No one dared call him that around Jezebel, however.

"What are you doing here?" he asked her.

She joined him on his walk. Salem's thick black hair was disheveled, like he hadn't combed it in days.

"You know, the usual. Dad is buying some hay from your aunt, and he asked me to come along."

"I'm glad you're here," Salem said. "I saw you the other day at school," he added quickly. "I tried to wave at you, but I guess you didn't see me."

"Sorry. I guess I was too busy to notice." Jezebel looked away quickly, blushing. She had indeed seen and heard Salem. She suddenly felt guilty for lying to him. "What's that?" Jezebel asked. She pointed to his right arm, where Salem kept his fist in a ball.

"It's a secret. Would you like to see?"

"Sure," she said, a bit curious.

"Then you'll have to catch me!" he said, running into the field while cradling whatever was in his hand. Jezebel watched him with a look of bewilderment.

"Salem, I'm not going to chase you!" she called after him. He gave no sign of having heard her. "Fine," she muttered with a shake of her head. She chased him through the field and easily gained on the tall boy. The grasses and weeds brushed alongside her legs as she followed him to the edge of the cornfield.

"Caught you," she said when Salem stopped, out of breath. Even when they were children, Salem had suffered from severe asthma. Panting, he held out his hand. Two pinkish worms crawled across a grainy clump of dirt.

"Worms? Why on earth do you have worms?"

They both laughed. Salem knelt down silently in the cool grass outside the cornfield. With his left hand, he formed a small hole in the soil. Then he steadily lowered the two worms into the hole, smoothed dirt over the top, and wet the mud with spit.

"It's for the birds," he said, walking over to the hill. She joined him underneath the calming shade of a big oak tree.

"Salem, I don't think—"

"Watch," he said, holding a finger up to his mouth. Only a few seconds later, a blue-colored bird swooped down from the sky and pecked at the soil.

"Salem, that was amazing," Jezebel said. "How did you know to do that?"

"The bird likes it," he shrugged. "Didn't you hear it chirping when we were in the field?"

"No," Jezebel replied. She wasn't sure if he was teasing her.

"It was saying it was hungry."

"You can't know what birds are saying, silly," she said, gently punching him in the shoulder.

"You can if you listen hard enough," he replied softly. He looked at her with deep green eyes. "I'm not very good at it, but I'm getting better."

Before Jezebel could respond, a large black crow flew out of the nearby forest. It plummeted down from the sky and spread its wings menacingly in front of the blue bird, which took off into the sky. The crow watched the two humans and picked the worms out of the soil.

"No, no, no!" Salem shouted. His expression grew angry. He ran over to the crow, kicking at it. The bird vanished into the cornfield.

"What's the matter?" Jezebel asked, following him. She put her hand on his shoulder, and Salem turned to her, looking as if he had snapped out of a trance.

"I'm sorry. I'm just so stupid! I took down the scarecrow earlier today to sew it back up and didn't put it back!"

"Relax," she said, patting him on the back. "It was just a crow." Together they walked back toward the white fence.

"These crows are bad," Salem replied. He stared into the forest. "Really bad. They're not like normal crows." Jezebel watched his troubled expression, confused. "That's why I made all those scarecrows," he said. "To keep them away. To keep them in the forest, where they belong." Salem's scarecrows were well-known sentinels around Gray Hollow ever since he started making them right before his parents died.

"You don't want to go into the forest?"

Salem stopped, looking at her as if she was out of her mind. Jezebel could tell he was shocked. "No way! Even when we were kids I was scared of the forest. The forest is evil!"

"What?" she said, laughing. "How can you say that?"

"I can sense it," he said. "It makes my head hurt. There's something in there that talks to me the same way I can talk to the birds. It wants me to come into the woods. It always has, for as long as I can remember. But I'm never going to go. That's why I built the scarecrows. Now I wish I hadn't, though."

"Why not?" she asked.

"The other kids tease me sometimes because of them, and because of the way I look."

She smiled in an attempt to lift his mood. "Everyone loves your scarecrows! Just the other day I heard Ray Adams talking about the difference one of them was making in his field. I even heard Mr. Durer has one on display in his store."

"I don't like Mr. Durer," Salem said. "He makes me feel uncomfortable."

"I'm sorry for mentioning him," she said. "I didn't know."

Salem looked aghast, like she just suggested something horribly wrong.

"Don't be sorry. You've always been really nice to me. Just like my parents were." He looked down. "When they used to tell me I was special, they didn't mean it in a bad way. I miss them."

"At least your aunt still lives here," Jezebel said.

"Aunt Cornelia? She doesn't like me because I'm not smart."

"Well, I think you're great. I'm sure your parents would say the same thing if they were here right now."

The two continued walking in silence on the dusty road. Jezebel noticed that Salem kept looking back at the forest over his shoulder. She wondered if he really believed the things he told her. At that moment, Jezebel wished there was something she could do to make him feel better.

On the other side of the fence, Jezebel saw another boy riding a tractor. He looked a little older than she was, but she had never seen him before.

"Who is that, Salem?" she asked, pointing at the stranger. "I've never seen him at school before."

"He goes to Thistlewood. He and his dad moved here awhile ago. I think he plays basketball or something."

A butterfly floated in their path. Jezebel reached out to catch it, but it slipped away.

"Don't worry," Salem said. "I can get it for you." He stood perfectly still and intently watched the butterfly floating in the air. Jezebel was about to ask him what he was doing when Salem started whispering, but then the butterfly turned around in midair and began flying in their direction. Just before it reached them, the butterfly flew back into the sky. "Almost," he said. "It's hard to get things to move on their own. Things that aren't alive are easier than animals."

He noticed her bewildered expression. "I shouldn't have said that. You think I'm weird, don't you?"

"Maybe a little," she replied. "But I like you anyway." Salem beamed. A few seconds later, a loud voice bellowed from the other side of the field. "Well, that's my dad," Jezebel muttered. "Looks like I've got to go."

He looked at her with a pained expression. "I enjoyed seeing you again."

"Me, too. Who knows, maybe we'll run into each other at school."

"Maybe," Salem said, his voice betraying doubt. Jezebel waved as she walked back across the field.

***

Salem stood still, watching sadly until Jezebel Woods finally disappeared from sight. He wondered what she would have said if he told her he could make the scarecrows come to life. She would never believe him.

When he blinked again, it was as if Jezebel had never been there at all. One second she was there, the next she was gone. Just like a dream. Sometimes Salem had a difficult time separating dreams from reality. What he saw in his dreams were visions of such intensity it took him awhile to differentiate between the two. Lately, many of his dreams were coming true, starting with the death of his parents.

He tried not to think about that as he stood in the warm field. The sun was out, and nothing could hurt him in the light. The darkness was where the thing in the forest belonged, trapped inside the cave. Salem wanted to focus instead on the happy memory he just made with Jezebel Woods. Many of his happiest childhood memories were of the fun they used to have.

Salem heard swearing over the fence. He turned around and watched the boy in the pasture next to his farm attempting to squeeze water out of an empty bottle. The boy was covered in sweat and looked very thirsty.

***

"Hello, Jeffrey," Salem said as he walked over to the fence. The boy looked up and noticed him for the first time.

"My name is Jeff," the boy said. "What do *you* want?"

"You look thirsty," Salem said.

"What gave you that idea?" Jeffrey asked. He threw the empty water bottle on top of the tractor. Since his dad bought the farm in Gray Hollow, Jeffrey heard stories from his friends about the strangeness of the Alistair boy. Jeffrey now had some stories of his own. The tall teenager behaved like a child, often remaining completely motionless for hours at a time in the field. At other times, Jeffrey actually saw Salem talking to animals!

"I was just wondering if you wanted a drink," Salem said. "We have plenty of cold water in a faucet next to the barn." The boy smiled.

"Thanks," Jeffrey said. For a moment, he wasn't sure about crossing over to the Alistair Farm, but Salem seemed genuinely happy to help him out. He swung himself over the fence and followed Salem to the barn.

"Who's the chick?" he asked as Salem poured him a drink, noticing a cute girl and her father gathering hay nearby. "Your girlfriend or something?"

"She's my friend." Salem blushed and handed Jeffrey the glass of water. The boy drank it all in seconds.

"Thanks a lot, Salem."

"No problem," Salem replied.

Jeffrey turned and headed back to the tractor. Then he paused, looking back at the boy in the barn. Salem Alistair wasn't what he expected. He was nice, even if he was a little strange.

"Hey, Salem!" he called to the boy, who was already walking back to a large house in the distance.

"Yes?" Salem asked.

"If anyone rings your doorbell tomorrow night, don't answer it."

"What do you mean?" Salem asked.

Jeffrey didn't answer.

Chapter FOURTEEN

Salem opened his eyes and stared at the vast darkness on the other side of the window. Outside, the wind whistled against the exterior of the large house, as if offering a cryptic warning. Peeking out from under the covers, Salem could see nothing except for the infinite blackness. As his eyes adjusted to the night, he heard a quiet scraping somewhere below his room.

Was something else inside the house? Salem slipped out of bed. He attempted to flip on the light switch, only to discover the power was out. Careful to avoid being heard by a potential intruder, he eased the door open and crept into the hall.

"Aunt Cornelia," he whispered. He knocked on his aunt's bedroom door. There was no answer, and Salem remembered that his aunt had departed from Gray Hollow that evening to visit with an old friend in Ohio. She would be gone for the weekend, leaving him alone to fend for himself.

Lightning cracked outside the old house, covering the interior in a dim light. Startled, Salem turned and started down the stairs. He felt drawn by the sound that roused him from bed. In the back of his mind the boy could feel a familiar throbbing pain. Salem chose to ignore it and advanced down the winding staircase.

A wet trail ran across the carpet underneath his feet. Unlike water, the puddle felt sticky. In the darkness, Salem could barely discern the red hue of blood on the white carpet. His skin began to crawl. The pain inside his head grew.

The boy froze halfway down the staircase. Two shadowy figures huddled just inside the frame of the front door. An involuntary scream escaped his lips. Then the lighting flashed again, revealing the faces belonging to the shadows.

His parents were standing at the bottom of the staircase.

"Mom? Dad?" Salem said. He almost shouted the words as he started running down the stairs.

"Salem," his mother whispered. "Come."

Salem stopped. The sound didn't match his mother's voice.

"Yes, son," his father added. "Come to us."

Salem knew something was wrong. He remained motionless, unable to move in any direction. Again lightning exploded downward from the sky.

Salem stared at his parents in horror. His mother's face was cut down the middle, her bloodied arms twisted and broken. Salem tore his gaze away and looked at his father. Large shards of glass protruded from Joshua Alistair's body, which was covered in gaping wounds pouring blood.

"We've missed you, Salem. Won't you come to us?"

They watched him intently. Neither was blinking. Both Alistairs had pale, translucent skin that was flaking off in front of him. The figures were rotting corpses.

Salem knew he was in one of his dreams, but he was powerless to wake from it. In fact, the realization made the boy more afraid than ever.

Joshua Alistair inhaled sharply, as if he could smell Salem's fear. "Why won't you come to us, son? You're breaking your mother's heart."

"What are you?" Salem whispered. Everything went deathly quiet.

"That's not important," Joshua said. "Everything can be just like it was."

"Better," his mother added. "We always knew how special you were. With our help, you can do things you've never even dreamed of. We can teach you, help you."

The two moved slowly, their decaying bodies inching forward. Salem started backing up the stairs, aware there was no line of retreat.

"We can show you, if you would like," they said in unison. "Come into the forest. You know the way."

"Never!" Salem shouted. "I'll never go into the woods! You can't have me!"

His parents' faces contorted in anger. For a moment, Salem was afraid they were going to race after him, but then the front door exploded open. The two wraiths were pulled into the black recesses of the night.

"Why won't you just leave me alone," Salem pleaded, practically immobile on the staircase. The surroundings seemed to vanish around him, leaving him alone again.

"What do you want from me?"

"You," the voice answered, and his mind was gripped with agony.

***

When he woke, it was already morning. He put his hand to his heart, expecting to hear it racing furiously. Instead, there was nothing unusual about the ordinary rhythmic beating. Salem got out of bed. He realized he would have to get ready quickly if he was going to make it to the school bus from the gravel road.

Salem knew the nightmare was not an ordinary dream. It was one of the visions sent from the thing in the forest. The darkness used his parents against him, as if it knew that he told Jezzie how much he missed them.

The boy also knew the darkness was always watching him, and that it was getting desperate. He could feel it whenever his head started hurting. It called him special. Salem wished he was smarter, so he could better control what he was capable of. He just wasn't bright enough to understand it. Salem felt like someone who had a great singing voice but could never remember the words to a song.

Most of the time, Salem never wanted to be like the other kids. Despite the thing in the forest, he was happy. The animals were always nice to him, and he loved living on the big farm. Other times, he wished he could just be normal. He felt that way at school. Salem hated school. He didn't have any friends except Jezzie. Most of the teachers didn't understand him, so they were mean to him too.

Just because his grades weren't good it didn't mean he was not intelligent. Salem was simply smart in other ways. How many of his teachers could nurse an injured kitten back to health? Salem wanted to yell. He wanted to shout out and say that he wasn't an idiot, but no one ever listened to him. When he was at school, Salem missed his parents a lot. He found it strange that his mom and dad could be related to Aunt Cornelia, with whom they shared so little in common.

When he left the bedroom and ran down the stairs, Salem hesitated slightly at the staircase when he remembered his dream. Then he smiled at the sunbeams pouring into the house and allowed himself a sigh of relief. Walking into the kitchen, he grabbed a box of cereal from the pantry and silverware from the drawer. Although his aunt was a severe woman, Salem found himself missing her while he ate his cereal alone. Having grown used to her presence, he found the lack of it surprisingly unappealing.

"Hey there," he said to the scarecrow perched on the couch. After his experience with Jezzie in the cornfield, he had quickly returned to the old house and finished patching up the scarecrow. Sewing was hard for him to learn, but Salem's mother had showed him how. While his parents laughed the first time he told them he wanted to build a scarecrow, they both later said they were proud of how talented he was.

He winked at the scarecrow, delighting in its gruesome features. This was definitely the scariest one yet. It even gave him the shivers, and he crafted it! Aunt Cornelia, of course, detested having the straw figure in the house.

"Salem, you had best move that thing before you go to bed," his aunt had ordered before she departed the night before. Unfortunately, he waited too long and it had grown dark before he could move it outside.

"I'll take you back to the field today," he said, waving a hand at the scarecrow. The figure's arm, which had been propped against the couch, swung down next to its side as if moved by an unseen force. Salem giggled and accidently spilled his cereal all over the table. He cleaned up the mess and snatched up the scarecrow.

Salem raced outside and located the long wooden pole where he left it next to the barn. After wading past the stalks of corn, he planted the scarecrow in the heart of the cornfield. There were no crows anywhere around. Maybe the thing in the woods had given up, but Salem knew that was probably wishful thinking. He returned to the gravel road and waited patiently for the school bus.

Today was Halloween, he remembered as he walked down the road. Since he didn't like going out after dark, Salem didn't celebrate the holiday—although he did like seeing many of his creations prominently displayed in yards on his way to school. In his opinion, most scarecrows were silly-looking, oddly-shaped things with funny smiles on their faces. How was that supposed to scare away crows?

Ahead, the school bus pulled up to the edge of the road. Although Gray Hollow boasted a small population, the town covered a relatively large amount of land, which made timing an issue for the six public school busses. Shivering from the cold, Salem stepped onto the bus when the mechanical doors opened.

"Hello, Salem," said the bus driver.

"Hi, Mr. Hartman!" Salem replied. He took a seat near the front of the bus. Mr. Hartman was once a friend of Salem's parents and always looked after him on the bus. This was often a daunting task on the crowded vehicle.

"Hey, Salem," an older boy said, pointing at his feet. "Your shoe's untied!"

Instinctively, Salem looked down. He was wearing his brown Redwing boots from the farm. They didn't have any strings, which was probably why the other boy immediately started laughing. Mr. Hartman gave the boy a reproachful stare, and the agitator fell silent.

"Look at that," Mr. Hartman said a few minutes later. "I've never seen so many scarecrows outside at once! I think you've become a celebrity, Salem."

Salem laughed. Mr. Hartman was actually right, in a way. A lot of people Salem didn't know seemed well-acquainted with him. He understood that his parents' wealth and subsequent deaths were big news in the small town. Some people liked to tell stories that his house was haunted. Although there were lots of rumors about him, Salem tried not to care what other people said.

When the bus doors opened again, he waited for all the others to leave before making his way to the exit. He said goodbye to Mr. Hartman, bent down to exit the bus, and stepped onto the sidewalk in front of the school. Salem's height made him instantly recognizable among the cluster of students walking into school. He was halfway into the school building when he dropped his books. As he stooped down to pick them up, he stumbled into the person in front of him.

"Watch where you're going, Scarecrow," a boy named Keith snapped.

"You tell him, Keith," came a voice from behind him. Rick Pepper, walking in from the student parking lot, stood at the door.

"I'm sorry," Salem stuttered. He tried to move out of the way. Gary Davis blocked his path.

"Why so frightened, ugly?" Keith sneered. He flashed a set of white teeth. "Today's your day of the year, isn't it?"

"Yeah," Rick said, stepping closer. "I saw your scarecrows propped up all over town. You must be pretty messed up in the head to have dreamed those things up."

"Tell me about it," Keith said. "My dad actually bought one of those things."

A flock of students passing from the next bus into the school failed to deter the two bullies. Rather than coming to Salem's defense, many of the other students started to watch.

"Let me go," Salem said. He made an effort to run to his left. Keith stuck his foot out, causing Salem to trip. Rick offered his hand to Salem but withdrew it as soon as the boy attempted to grab it.

"My friends and I have some fun plans for you, Scarecrow," Rick whispered, glancing at Logan Randall, who was eagerly watching them from within the throng of students.

"That's enough!" shouted an angry voice. Jezebel Woods made her way through the crowd, helping Salem pick up his books.

"Come on," Rick said. "We're just having a bit of fun. Tell her, Scarecrow."

Jezebel's eyes flashed with rage. Before Rick could react, she jumped up and slapped him hard across the face.

"How dare you," she snapped. "Don't you ever call him that again."

"Jeez, what's your problem?" Keith said. "Why do you always have to be such a spoilsport?"

"When you stop trying to beat kids up, I won't have to be," she said. The two stared at each other for a moment, their faces both lined with rage. Keith finally backed down, turning and walking away. Rather than joining him, Rick Pepper sought out Logan Randall and Gary Davis, who were standing nearby.

"You should get to class before the bell rings," Jezebel said once Salem was back on his feet. "Are you OK?"

"Yeah," Salem replied. He rubbed the back of his head. "Jezzie?" he asked as she started to leave.

"Yes?"

"Would you like to come to my house tonight? My Aunt Cornelia left me by myself, and I don't want to be alone for Halloween. I'm a little scared," he whispered, checking to make sure no one else could hear him.

The image of the tall teenager cowering at the idea of Halloween would have sounded absurd to her if Salem had not said it himself, but Jezebel thought she could see fear in his eyes. She looked down. If she had stood up for him more strongly before now, maybe this wouldn't have happened. Unfortunately, she couldn't be everywhere at once. The fact was that what Keith Sanders and Rick Pepper had done was considerably less serious than some of the other bullies. Zack Davidson, for example, locked Salem in the gym locker room after class three months ago. Salem screamed for two periods before someone let him out. There was no shortage of people lining up to pick on Salem.

Just as Jezebel looked at Salem's expectant gaze, she saw her friends approaching. They were looking at the two of them with strange expressions.

"I'm sorry," Jezebel said, trying not to notice the look of betrayal on his face. "I have other plans tonight."

She wasn't lying, she thought to herself as she left to join her friends. After all, Jezebel did indeed have plans. She barely slept last night because she couldn't stop thinking about the bonfire.

"Hi," Jezebel said to her friends when she reached her locker.

"'Jezzie?'" asked Katy Johnson, a slender African-American sophomore. Katy was slightly older than Jezebel, but both had been good friends for a long time. They shared a passion for soccer and track, although their school lacked a girls' soccer team.

"Yeah," Victoria Kelsey added. The tall redhead crossed her arms. "What was up with that?"

"Salem and I were friends when we were kids," Jezebel said. "He still calls me by my old nickname, that's all."

"Is that why you stood up for him?" Victoria asked skeptically. Jezebel could see Salem slinking away in the distance.

"You know how I feel about bullying," she said.

"Jezebel, it's *Salem Alistair.* He's practically the definition of the word 'creepy.'"

"He's not that bad," Jezebel protested. She felt guilty. She remembered how sad Salem sounded when they were walking through the field.

Katy looked bored with the subject of conversation. "Are you still going to help me study for the American History test during lunch break?" she asked.

Jezebel laughed at the quick change in topic. She loved her friends, who could so easily sense when she was uncomfortable.

"I don't see how you can even think about studying," Victoria said. "Not when we have tonight to look forward to. Tell me you're not excited."

A freshman cheerleader, Victoria was the one who had managed to get the trio invited to the bonfire. Although Jezebel hadn't known Victoria for long, she already seemed firmly a part of their group.

"It's going to be awesome," Jezebel said. "I can't wait."

"Who knows?" Katy teased. "Maybe you'll run into Aaron Benton."

Jezebel tried not to blush. Aaron was an attractive older student who held the locker above her. Once more thinking about the party, Jezebel quickly forgot about Salem Alistair.

Tonight is going to be a great night, she thought, grinning.

***

The demon inside the cave was starving. For hundreds of years, the darkness waited, trapped in the cave. The shred of the demon's consciousness had faded over time, until the settlers came. Their sacrifices stirred the darkness from its sleep. The darkness blessed the harvest and in turn fed off the settlers' growing depravity. With each drop of blood they spilled, the being within the cave grew stronger. Its powers over the forest returned.

Then, almost without warning, the sacrifices ceased. Even the demon's most loyal worshipers were killed or driven away. The pagan practices and rituals faded into lore. The demon became hungry again.

The darkness waited for so long. Sustaining itself on the lives of animals lured too far into the forest, the demon used its crows to strip them of their flesh, but even that was hardly enough. Most creatures feared the cave, preferring not to go near it. For a time, the demon almost gave up hope.

Then Salem Alistair was born. His arrival awakened the spirit in the cave once more. Over the millions of years the darkness had roamed the earth, it had encountered many humans blessed with special gifts, including some far stronger than Salem. The boy could serve its purpose nonetheless.

The demon's own spirit was fragmented, unable to leave the cave or take physical form. It could not possess Salem or even touch him as long as he was able to resist its influence. And resist he did. Despite Salem's mental impairments, the boy could sense that the darkness desired his abilities.

Even now, Salem's resolve showed no signs of deteriorating. The entity was hungry, and it was impatient. It would wait no longer. It would have Salem's strength, one way or another. The demon would harness Salem and in doing so unleash a second great darkness over the town. A darkness that would finally give the Keeper of the Crows the power it needed to leave the cave.

The demon was ready. All it needed was the right opportunity. The entity possessed eyes everywhere and knew all the pawns were in play. It was time. When the night fell to the dark, so would Salem Alistair.

Chapter FIFTEEN

The scarlet moon peeked out from behind a wall of black clouds, creating an ominous backdrop for Halloween night. A cold chill descended over Gray Hollow. Tendrils of fog slithered over dry patches of grass trodden by exuberant trick-or-treaters.

Outside the town, the last vestiges of sunlight faded as the darkness grew. A flashy red car zipped out of the fog on a country road, gathering speed. The blaring music surging from the speeding car shattered the tranquility of the surrounding forest. The five occupants of the car shouted loudly, telling jokes while consuming beer after beer.

Suddenly, a torrent of flashing lights appeared from the hill behind the car. The siren of the police car drowned out the screeching tunes as it approached them. The five boys in the car all seemed to notice the cop at the same time, which prompted an equally shocked reaction in each of them.

Gary Davis swore loudly. "Hide the cans!"

Scrambling to gather the aluminum cans covering the floorboards, the boys packed in the backseat worked at a furious pace while Logan Randall pulled over to the side of the road. The smell of the crisp air drifted into the car from the farms with freshly cut hay.

"Everyone shut up," Logan ordered as the police officer approached his car. He turned on the compartment light and quickly retrieved his license and insurance card.

"Is there a reason you were going so fast?" the officer asked. The man seemed perturbed.

"Just late to a party, that's all. How fast was I going?" Logan asked, belatedly adding the word "sir."

"Fifteen miles over the speed limit," the officer replied. Logan handed his license to the policeman, who shined a flashlight into his eyes. Logan blinked and held his hands out in front of his face.

"You boys haven't been drinking, have you?"

"No sir," Logan said. "We're underage." He could see Rick Pepper rolling his eyes in the rearview mirror and wanted to strangle him.

"All right. Here's your ticket," the man said after a few minutes. "You can pay it in the court clerk's office. You all be safe tonight. We've already had reports of underage drinking. We'll be on the streets all night. Don't let me catch you speeding again."

"Of course," Logan said politely. He waited until the policeman returned to his vehicle. The red car roared back to life when he put the vehicle in gear and stepped on the gas pedal.

"That was close," Jeffrey Daniels said from the back seat. He grabbed a full aluminum can from underneath the blanket at his feet.

"I'll say," Gary Davis added. "It's a good thing he didn't shine that light back here. Rick's already had way too much to drink."

"I still haven't had enough to think your mother is good looking, Davis," Rick slurred. That prompted a barrage of laughter.

Gary ignored the comment. "Look at the big man in the front," he said. "Way to handle the situation. I don't think I've ever heard you say the word 'sir' to anyone before."

"Yeah, yeah, laugh it up," Logan replied. He was glad the cop hadn't noticed the odor on his breath. "At least you didn't get a speeding ticket. Look at how fast *he* sped away. It must be great to be able to go as fast as you want."

"Relax, my friend," said the older boy sitting in the passenger seat. "My dad can take care of that ticket for you." Logan's friend, who was twenty-two, had purchased the drinks for the boys in the car.

The car plowed through the thickening fog, heading farther out into the country. All the while, the moonlit sky grew darker still. Eventually, Logan turned the car onto a long gravel road in the middle of nowhere.

"Are you all ready for this?" the boy in the passenger seat asked as the others put on their costumes. "As soon as we get to the house, we're going in just like we planned."

"He might not even be home," Jeffrey Daniels interrupted, clearing his throat. The others couldn't see it in the shadows, but his eyes were full of concern. "Are we sure we want to do this?"

"What are you talking about?" Gary asked. "This was partly your idea, Jeff. Besides, that freak needs to be taught a lesson." He shook his head and pulled the skeleton mask down over his face.

"Too bad we can't do the same thing to Jezebel Woods," Rick muttered. "Why anyone would stand up for that scrawny creep is beyond me."

Logan checked to make sure all of his friends were in costume before shutting off the lights and easing the vehicle into the driveway. Jeffrey considered protesting again, but the sight of the massive house took his breath away. In the moonlight, the old house really was scary. He could see why all the locals thought it was haunted. Vines crept up the house's weathered exterior, which had been left largely untended after the deaths of Salem Alistair's parents.

Jeffrey thought back to his conversation with Salem from the previous day. The boy wasn't at all what he expected. Jeffrey was starting to realize that the new 'friends' he made when he moved from Thistlewood might not be his type of people after all. Unfortunately, the timing of that realization couldn't be worse.

Logan parked the car next to a metal gate near the barn. As the five boys left the car behind, Jeffrey could see a scarecrow in the field. The sight caused the hair on the back of his neck to stand on end.

Those things are a lot scarier at night, he thought to himself. None of the others said it aloud, but their hurried glances at the cornfield spoke volumes in a way their voices never could. Although the wind had died down, the stalks seemed to sway to and fro with life. Jeffrey half-expected to see a pair of eyes appear at any moment.

Logan and Rick removed a sixth costume from the trunk. Both were having a hard time fighting back laughter. Plenty of planning went into the prank, and the fear added to the thrill pulsing through their veins. This was going to be a night to remember.

"I'll go in first," Logan whispered, advancing toward the house. "Wait here for my signal. If the door is locked, I'll just knock and wait for him to answer."

Unseen by the boys, a black crow landed on the tree next to the barn. The bird watched them with dark, unblinking eyes.

Jeffrey prayed Salem remembered his words of warning. Steadily, Logan Randall advanced on the dark house. Only a few lights were on inside, and Salem's aunt's car was nowhere in sight. Salem was alone.

The door was locked. Logan knocked on the door, the other boys waiting tensely for Salem Alistair to appear. Footsteps pounded down the stairs on the other side of the door. After a few moments, a light near the door went on.

"Hello?" Salem called, hesitating to open the door.

Logan knocked again.

"Who is it?" He clearly wasn't expecting any visitors.

Logan swore silently and shook the door handle. It was no use. Salem wasn't going to let them inside. From the window, Jeffrey could see Salem head toward the stairs. Then he heard a soft sound behind him, like the rustling of wings. The lock clicked. As the door swung open, the lights in the house went off.

***

Salem stood in horror, unsure if the creature standing in the doorway was another vision or something real. Before he could run, he found himself surrounded on all sides by masked figures all dressed as gruesome monsters.

"Stop it," he cried, trying to get away. "Leave me alone!"

"Get him," one of the costumed figures hollered. The pain exploded in Salem's head, leaving him too weak to struggle. These creatures weren't from the evil in the forest. They were real. They could hurt him.

They dragged him kicking and screaming from the house. Aside from the light of the moon, it was completely dark.

"Who are you?" Salem asked as they started binding his arms with ropes. "Why are you doing this?" The words stuck in his throat. He was too terrified to speak.

"What's the matter?" asked someone wearing a pumpkin mask. "Are you scared, Scarecrow? Well guess what? The fun is just getting started!"

The others howled with laughter. Salem could see them drinking out of shimmering cans, shouting and growing more violent with each second.

***

Jeffrey felt increasingly uneasy. The others started kicking Salem while some threw cans at him. He wanted to say something but was afraid of what his friends would think. So he watched as Logan Randall and Rick Pepper forced the costume over Salem Alistair's clothes. They had driven three counties away to find the perfect costume, and it looked strangely appropriate on Salem's rail-thin frame.

***

Salem was stuttering now, unable to form coherent sentences. All he could feel was fear. The thing in the woods was there somewhere, watching him. Waiting. He felt himself being dragged backward again, this time over rough ground. Suddenly he realized they were taking him to the cornfield.

Salem looked around, his eyes wide with fear. Above him loomed the scarecrow he placed on the pole that very morning. In the light of night, it looked truly terrifying. Salem tried to call on his gift to make the scarecrow move. Behind the boys, the scarecrow's arm started to rotate, then stopped.

Someone behind him pulled a sheet of cloth over his face. Salem peered through two eyeholes. A rope tied his arms, and he was inside some kind of costume of ragged clothes.

"Do you know what you're dressed as?" one of his tormentors asked, smiling through a black hood. "A *scarecrow*." Grabbing new drinks, the other boys laughed again. Salem was filled with terror. He could hardly breathe in the mask. The more terrified he became, the shallower his breathing became. His asthma was beginning to act up, and there was no way to get to his inhaler.

"Stop," he tried to say as a rag was stuffed into his mouth.

***

"I think he's crying!" Rick Pepper said with a laugh. Jeffrey started to shake, unsure of how much longer he could handle this. He could tell that Gary Davis was no longer amused either. The other three, filled with anger and drink, seemed fine continuing. From above, the crow stared down with cruel eyes.

***

Salem felt himself sliding in and out of consciousness. The shadow seemed to be growing around him, waiting to strike. He wanted to burst free of the ropes, to rage against the costumed figures who were hurting him. He found himself too weak. Despite their masks, Salem recognized their voices. They were the same voices of the people who bullied him every day at school. For the first time in his life, the boy felt hate.

The cool air calmed him enough to slow his breathing down, and his eyes started to open again. Then he saw the shovel. The pointed metal dug down into the brown soil, unearthing layers of dirt. They were digging a hole. A hole for *him*. As the hole started deepening, Salem lost all control. He started panicking, thrashing around as hard as he could.

The rag in Salem's mouth muffled his screams, but his shaking still earned him a kick in the side from Logan

Randall. Gary Davis helped roll his body into the hole, and the figure in the pumpkin mask started piling dirt on top of him.

"That's right," Logan said. "We're going to bury you *alive.*" He grinned underneath his mask, delighting in the utter fear they had evoked in the boy. Of all the pranks they had ever pulled on Salem Alistair, this was by far the best. The boy eventually stopped squirming as the soil was heaped over him. They kept at it until only his head remained above the earth, and even it was almost covered by the dirt.

"Enough," Jeffrey Daniels finally said, wresting the shovel away from the figure in the pumpkin mask. "It's over." He took off his mask.

"Sure," Logan Randall said before popping open another can. "We got him good." He ripped off his own costume mask. "I bet he wet his pants, didn't you Salem?" He turned around to look at Jeffrey, hoping for a laugh from his tense friend.

Jeffrey wasn't laughing. His face was wrapped in an expression of horror. He toppled to the ground, the shovel falling with him.

"What's the matter?" Gary asked.

"He's not moving," Jeffrey whispered. Jeffrey worked swiftly to try to free Salem from the earth. When he cleaned off the last level of dirt, he held his ear to Salem's chest. There was no heartbeat. He pulled off the boy's mask.

Jeffrey's eyes widened. What had they done?

"Jeff? You're joking, right?" Gary asked. He knelt over the body. When he checked for Salem Alistair's pulse for himself, he turned deathly white.

Salem Alistair was dead. Suffocated.

"What are we going to do?" Jeffrey shouted. "We *killed* someone."

"We're going to prison," Rick mumbled, holding his head in disbelief.

This wasn't happening. Surely they'd just had too much to drink, and this was a dream. Only it wasn't a dream. He could feel the cold air, could hear the silence of the night.

"They're going to find us," Gary said. "We were pulled over!"

"So?" asked Logan, frowning. He and his friend seemed calmer than the others.

"So, that policeman will remember us. He has your name, Logan. The police might figure out we were headed here!"

"No, they won't," the figure in the pumpkin mask said, finally removing his mask. "My dad will take care of that. You all just have to keep your mouths shut, and we'll all be OK."

Jeffrey's mouth fell open in shock. He was trembling. "How can you even say that? This *is* our fault. We did this. We have to take responsibility for it."

"Are you sure that's what you want, Jeff?" the boy asked bluntly. "To spend the rest of your life in prison? You know what they do to people convicted of murder? You're pretty close to eighteen, aren't you? Do you honestly think you can just go back to playing basketball after something like this?"

"He's right," Logan said. "Salem's aunt is out of town. Most of Gray Hollow thinks his family is cursed, anyway. You know the stories. If we hide the body, no one would ever know it was us."

"There are tons of other kids who picked on him," Rick Pepper muttered, almost to himself.

"I'm not sure," Gary said, shooting a quick look at Jeffrey. "How are we just going to 'hide' the body so it won't be found?"

Logan Randall smiled. He pointed down at the hole in the ground. "We already have an answer to that," he said. "That hole is already almost three feet deep. We have plenty of time to bury the body even deeper. It will be awhile before anyone finds out he's missing. Then they will probably search for him outside the farm, thinking he's gotten lost or something."

"Remember," Logan's older friend added. "Just because he's missing, that doesn't mean everyone is going to assume he's dead. Given how unpopular he was, I could easily see people thinking he ran away. All the while, the cornfield will help decompose his body and hide the evidence."

Gary stared at the ground. "Fine," he said finally. "I don't want to spend the rest of my life in jail."

"Jeff?" Logan asked. "We're all in agreement. What do you say?" The other boys turned and looked at him.

"I'm sorry I ever met any of you," he whispered, near tears. "Salem Alistair didn't deserve this."

"Think about what you're doing. What would your father say?" Logan asked.

Jeffrey lowered his gaze.

"I won't say anything. I promise. But I never want to see any of you again."

Forming a circle, the boys took turns enlarging the hole, sealing the bond between them. Salem Alistair's body was lowered unceremoniously into the hole, still dressed as a scarecrow. Jeffrey clutched the mask in his hands. Salem's eyes, not yet closed, seemed to bore into him as if the boy was still alive.

***

It didn't take long to fill the hole. Soon Salem's body was buried deep under the earth, where they hoped it would never be found. The search for Salem Alistair would instead lead nowhere, becoming yet another unsolved missing persons case. After checking to make sure there was no sign they were ever at the Alistair Farm, the boys piled back into the car and began the protracted drive back to town. It was all over.

Except it wasn't.

Deep in the cave, the demon roared in triumph. Its moment had come. Darkness poured from the cave, taking a good deal of the demon's remaining power with it. The darkness slowly slid into the grave, reaching out for the boy who had denied it. He could deny it no longer.

The corpse was still for a moment. Then its heart thumped loudly, echoing through the earth. The entity would keep the boy's body alive. Though the demon could not take the soul itself, it could fill the vessel with evil, creating a new servant for itself. It would be a servant with more than enough power to deliver Gray Hollow back to the dark.

Drained from the depletion of its energy, the demon rested. It would take time to gather its strength back. In time, the demon would harness the boy's powers from the grave. When the moment arrived, the new Keeper would be reborn into the world.

Salem Alistair was dead, but the darkest part of him survived. Hidden under the ground, the monster waited to be awakened. The corpse fed off its own memories. With each day, its desire for revenge grew stronger. In time, Gray Hollow would burn, and the demon would be set free.

Part Three

THE KEEPER OF THE CROWS

Chapter SIXTEEN

Crows poured from the sky as the gray RB-KAR van sped across Gray Hollow. Chuck Howard stared at them through the window while adjusting the heater. The small town's chilly air seemed to seep into the news van, which agitated the reporter.

"What's with all the birds?" he asked, putting his hands up to the vents.

"They must be moving south for the winter," a squeaky voice said from behind him. Chuck turned back and looked at Elaine Ferris.

"I'm sorry," he said contemptuously. "Did you film a documentary on birds?" Already he was regretting his choice of camerawoman. At the time, Chuck picked her for her looks, like he usually did. That was before he realized how vocal she was.

"No," she said. "I just thought it was common knowledge. Birds migrate south for the winter. That's where they're headed."

Chuck rolled his eyes at Clark Dickenson, who was too busy driving to notice. They were only in the van for a couple of hours, and already the camerawoman was proving to be incessant. He didn't consider himself to be the type of reporter who cared about getting to know his colleagues. Chuck didn't even bother with those who weren't movers and shakers at the news station, and he liked even fewer. He wasn't inclined to hear Elaine's life story, and he certainly didn't want to hear her *opinions*.

"Welcome to Gray Hollow," Clark said as the van passed over the bridge. "Also known as the state's outhouse. Remind me to thank you again for dragging me all the way out here."

"Trust me, you'll thank me later," the reporter replied. "This is going to be huge. When the next victim is found, we will be the first television news station to cover the emergence of the state's latest serial killer."

"Where to?" Clark asked after driving around the town to familiarize the news crew with Gray Hollow.

"Let's stop at the town square," Chuck answered while watching Elaine prepare the camera equipment. He found her infinitely more appealing when she wasn't babbling. Chuck knew he would have to be careful around her. He didn't want any more harassment accusations against him, not when his uncle was still angry over the last time.

"This diner looks like a nice place to start," Chuck said. It looked like one of the few places in the community that wasn't a hole in the wall. Clark pulled the van off into a narrow parking spot while Chuck noticed a man sitting at a sidewalk bench as he exited the van. He walked over to the man, who seemed amused when he noticed Chuck's suit. The reporter resisted the impulse to scowl at the man and grabbed a microphone from the truck.

"Get me over here, Elaine," he said. "Excuse me, sir," he said. "This is Chuck Howard, reporting in the town of Gray Hollow for RB-KAR news. Are you concerned about the rash of recent murders in Gray Hollow?"

"What do you think?" the man replied sarcastically.

Chuck sighed at the tedious response. "Is the camera bothering you?" he asked. "We won't put you on television if you don't want, Mister . . ."

"Lipton," the man said. "Bob Lipton."

"Right," Chuck said. "As I was saying, Mr. Lipton, we've come a long way to assist the people of your town, and I was just hoping you would be able to help us out."

"I only know what I read in the papers."

"He's not going to be any help," Chuck whispered into Clark's ear. The reporter was not looking forward to dealing with the rest of the locals. Sadly, it was necessary. "Let's head into the diner. Maybe we'll have more luck in there."

Unfortunately, Chuck could tell things were not going to turn in his favor from the second he stepped foot in the diner. When the doorbells jingled, every head seemed to move in his direction. All gazed skeptically upon the man in the suit. Once inside, he introduced himself one by one to successive locals. Other than a few good video clips showing how frightened some of the people were, Chuck failed to learn anything new. Finally, he noticed a well-dressed man in a black jacket standing just outside the coffee line. The man was studying him carefully.

"Hello there," Chuck said in an effort to introduce himself to the man, who looked like someone who might know what he was talking about. "I'm Chuck Howard," he added, extending his hand.

The man shook his hand.

"So I've heard. You're here to investigate the murders?"

"That's right."

"What about Thomas Brooks?" the man asked. "I thought he was looking into the killings."

Chuck flashed a wide grin. The reporter walked over to the man, microphone in hand, winked, and looked him in the eye.

"Let me let you in on a little secret," Chuck said. "Thomas Brooks is a has-been. You know why he's in Gray Hollow? He got caught faking sources in a big New York newspaper. You can't count on him for fair, accurate reporting. *I'm* here to get to the truth of the matter."

The man laughed, and Chuck could see some of the people standing next to them laughing too. He frowned, looking at his camerawoman in an effort to see what was so funny. Elaine shrugged.

"That's news to me," the man told the reporter. "I'm Thomas Brooks."

Thomas watched Chuck Howard's expression turn to shock. Then, just as quickly, the television reporter composed himself once more. Smiling again, Chuck slapped Thomas on the back.

"Well then, it's good to meet you. No hard feelings about that little speech, I hope? Just trying to get a leg up on the competition. Not that I need to."

"What does that mean?" Thomas frowned.

"Look at this place. You reach what, six hundred people an issue, tops? Even with the internet, there's no way you can manage to go toe-to-toe with a television broadcast station."

"Try me," Thomas said. "I've been around a lot longer than you."

Chuck Howard leaned forward and whispered in his ear.

"And where are you now? This must be one of the smallest towns in the state. You're a fallen star, Brooks, and mine is on the rise."

Thomas laughed again and shot Chuck an equally forced grin. Just before leaving the shop, he cast a look over his shoulder.

"That might be true, but for all of your cameras and airtime, only one of us is working with the local sheriff inside the investigation. Only one of us just published a new story that has had over a thousand online hits in an hour. So if I were you, I'd stop making accusations and start doing some reporting. If you were a real journalist, you would know that there are people out there dying. So instead of trying to score points at my expense, you might try showing some compassion around these people."

Chuck wanted to pick up a coffee cup from the table nearby and hurl it at Thomas as he walked away. Instead, he clenched his fist and watched Brooks head down the street. After a few minutes, he followed out the door, motioning for his crew to join him. There was no way anyone in the diner was going to talk to him after *that.*

"Can I see that paper you're reading?" he asked Bob Lipton politely.

"Sure," Lipton said. "If you buy it from me."

"What?" Chuck said, his eyes widening. "I'm not going to pay to—"

"Then you don't get to read it," Lipton said flatly.

"Fine," Chuck said, hastily thrusting a five-dollar bill into the man's hand. "I don't have change. Now let me see that." He grabbed the newspaper.

Fourth victim found dead, read the title of the lead article. *Journalist and sheriff witness attack.*

The reporter crumpled the paper up in his fists. After realizing he needed the information, he tucked the section inside his jacket pocket.

"Wow," Elaine said. "Brooks is actually heading for the police station. He's already got the best scoop."

"Shut up," Chuck shot back. "This isn't over yet. Not by a long shot. Get the van, Clark. If Brooks knows the town so well, maybe we'll just tag along for the ride."

***

Thomas couldn't suppress a sense of pride as he approached the sheriff's desk. The line outside the station had only thinned slightly, which made it difficult for him to gain entrance. Luckily, Deputy Markham was kind enough to unlock a side door for him.

"Sheriff Woods is on the phone," he said, gesturing to her office. "You're welcome to wait here."

"Thanks." Thomas studied the layout of the station. The faint aroma of breakfast lingered in a small lounge across from a reinforced door that led to the holding cells.

"Look who we have here," a bitter voice said behind him. Thomas turned just in time to see Logan Randall emerge from the room, a bagel in hand. Logan stared at the journalist. He walked up to face Thomas until they were almost standing chest-to-chest.

"You're lucky you have Sheriff Woods watching your back. If *I* were in charge, you'd be rotting in a holding cell right now. First Amendment or not," he snarled, as if baiting Thomas to strike.

From close up, Thomas could see a host of abrasions covering the deputy's face. Half of his face seemed swollen, and his mouth was bruised. The reporter wasn't sure, but it looked like Logan had a few scratches on his arm as well.

"You do anything to make my life harder again, and I promise you, you will regret it," Logan finished. "Any questions?"

Thomas didn't back down. "Just one," he replied. "Are you wearing makeup? It looks like you're covered in cuts. Get into any fights lately, Deputy?"

Logan instinctively touched his hand to his face but quickly moved it back down to his side.

"Mind your own business," he snapped before turning away. "I've got work to do."

Thomas stood there for a moment and watched Logan Randall head for his office. It suddenly occurred to him that not only did he dislike the deputy, he also didn't trust him. He wondered if Jezebel felt the same.

"What was that all about?" Jezebel said, opening her office door.

"Just your deputy being his regular charming self. Actually, while we're on the subject, has Logan Randall been involved in any arrests lately?"

"No," Jezebel said, confused. "He's heading the search for Gary Davis. You already knew that."

"Are you sure you haven't received *any* reports from him lately?"

"None," Jezebel replied. "For once, he seems focused on the task. In fact, Logan has hardly spent any time at the station since the Davis murders. Today is the first full day he's spent at the office in a while. Why so curious?"

Thomas finally looked away from the blinds covering the Logan's office windows. He couldn't quite put his finger on what was bothering him, but his instincts told him something was out of place.

"His arms are covered in scratches, and there are bruises on his face. Unless he tripped and fell down the stairs, the deputy got into a fight with someone who hit back."

"That's odd," Jezebel said. "He's such a neat freak, it's hard to believe he would even risk a fight."

"Neat freak?"

"That's putting it mildly. The man is obsessed with cleanliness. He always carries hand sanitizer around with him."

Thomas laughed. "That man has issues."

"I could tell you some stories. Back in high school—" She froze.

Now it was Thomas' turn to be confused. "Jezebel? What is it?"

"Maybe nothing. In high school, Logan Randall was a senior when I was a freshman. One of the students he was friendly with was Gary Davis."

"What?" Thomas said. "And you let him run the search for Gary? How do you know Logan isn't *protecting* him?"

"I asked him about it when we were investigating the murders at the Davis Farm. Logan insisted the two were never that close. At the time I gave him the benefit of the doubt, even though I thought his answer sounded a little evasive. Now I'm not so sure."

"That's the understatement of the year," Thomas muttered, quick to look away when he saw the sheriff scowling at him.

"Don't worry," Jezebel replied. "There is something we can do." She scribbled something on a sheet of paper and passed it to Heavy Markham, checking to make sure Logan Randall wasn't watching from his office. Markham looked at her quizzically but nodded to indicate he understood.

"Come on," Jezebel said to the curious reporter. "Let's go to the courthouse."

Thomas was thankful for the warmth provided by his black leather jacket; the weather was colder than ever. He kept his hands tucked in his pockets, wishing he had possessed the foresight to bring gloves. In contrast, Jezebel was already wearing a pair.

"Mind telling me what that was all about?"

"I told Heavy to check Logan Randall's cell phone records," she said. "If he called Gary Davis before or after the murders, I want to know. I should have done it from the beginning."

"So, why are we headed to the courthouse?" Thomas asked while he tried to keep up with the athletic sheriff. He remembered Jezebel saying she used to run track. Thomas wondered how anyone could show so much energy when it was so cold.

"Because Rick Pepper works there, of course."

"Right," Thomas said. "I knew that."

"I'm sure you did," Jezebel retorted sarcastically. "For your information, he's a paralegal, and not a very good one at that. Judge Underhill was crazy for hiring him, in my opinion."

"Judge Underhill? We've met."

"Frankly, it would be more surprising if you told me you hadn't," she said as they walked briskly down the sidewalk. Thomas struggled to keep up. "The judge makes it his business to get to know as many people as possible. Always a plus for reelection."

"That sounded awfully contemptuous," Thomas said. "Don't *you* have to run for sheriff?"

"Point taken. Actually, we have a good working relationship, even though I find him to be a little pompous. He always seems to say exactly what he thinks you want to hear. Most people like that. I guess I'm just too much of a straight shooter for it."

"Funny," Thomas said. He suppressed a grin. "I thought the same thing when I met him. Except for the straight shooter part," he added swiftly.

"Anyway, I tried calling the judge last night, but he had his cell phone turned off."

The two walked inside the courthouse.

"Hello, Sheriff Woods!" the young woman at the desk exclaimed brightly.

"Hi, Sarah," she said. "How's your dad?"

"He's recovering, thanks to you. The doctors said he probably wouldn't have made it if you hadn't gotten him to the hospital as quickly as you did."

"Tell him I asked after him," Jezebel said. "Can you let Judge Underhill know I'm here?"

"Of course," Sarah replied. Thomas shot Jezebel an inquiring glance as they headed up the stairs.

"Her father flipped his tractor in a sinkhole," she said. "He managed to dial 911 before he passed out."

"Wow," Thomas muttered. "That sounds terrible."

Jezebel nodded. "My father died in a similar accident," she said.

"I didn't know that," Thomas said. "I'm sorry."

"It was a long time ago. Finding Sarah's dad like that brought it back."

"I keep forgetting what a local hero you are," Thomas replied.

Jezebel's expression darkened.

"I'm no hero," she whispered.

Thomas wondered what she meant, and if it was connected to what she'd told him about Salem Alistair. Thomas didn't have to wonder what it would be like to search for redemption for past mistakes. That was the reason he was working in Gray Hollow. He wanted to say something to reassure her, but Jezebel knocked on the judge's door before he had the chance.

Charles Underhill opened the door. Thomas could see the beginnings of a beard on the man's face and wondered if the judge was having problems sleeping lately. "Jezebel. What a nice surprise."

"Charles," she said politely.

"Along with Gray Hollow's newest reporter," Judge Underhill said. "We meet again." His eyes narrowed. "I was a little disappointed in the public outcry your story inspired. Surely it must have crossed your mind that it might be more prudent to sit on the story for awhile?"

"We've discussed it," Jezebel said. "It's too late to go back, but I think we're on the same page now."

"That's right," Thomas piped in.

Thomas was surprised she would speak so warmly of him. Maybe her attitude toward him really was changing.

"If it is indeed water under the bridge, then I am dreadfully sorry to bring it back up," Underhill replied. "Consider the subject dropped. Hopefully we can all work together to end this sorry affair. Have you come any closer to catching the killer?" He asked the question delicately, but Thomas could tell the judge was very curious.

"Let's hope so," Jezebel said. "That's why we're here. Can you help us get in contact with Rick Pepper?"

"Is something wrong?" Underhill asked. Concern crossed his face. "Rick does good work for me. I hope he isn't in any trouble."

"We just need to talk with him for now," Jezebel said. "There are a few questions I need to ask him regarding his activities over the past few days."

"I'll have Sarah give you his cell phone number on the way out," Underhill said. "I'm afraid I don't have it with me. She'll have his address as well, in case you don't have it already."

"Wait," Thomas interrupted. "Doesn't Rick work here? Is he off today?"

"Actually, no one here has heard from Rick all day, as far as I know. He didn't show up for work today."

"Is that unusual?" Jezebel asked.

"Not entirely. Rick loves to hunt, although he normally calls when he wants to take a day off."

"And he didn't call today?" she asked.

"No."

"Any idea where he might be?" Thomas asked.

"If he isn't hunting, he might be at his girlfriend's house. If I recall correctly, her name is Michelle. I'm not sure what her last name is."

Jezebel's face fell. Thomas could tell she was hoping for a new lead. His mind raced furiously. While he was admittedly skeptical of Jezebel's theory at first, the timing of Rick Pepper's disappearance was unusual, if not outright suspicious.

"One last question," Jezebel said. "Has Rick said anything about Salem Alistair or his disappearance lately?"

For a moment, Thomas spotted a flash of recognition in the judge's eyes. The name clearly startled him.

"I don't understand," Judge Underhill said. "Weren't we discussing the recent murders? What does that have to do with Salem Alistair?"

"Maybe nothing," Jezebel muttered. "It's just a feeling I have."

Underhill waited for her to elaborate, but Jezebel thanked him and left, Thomas following after her. After stopping by the front desk in the lobby, she pulled out her cell and dialed Rick Pepper's number.

"He's not answering," she said. Jezebel glanced at the address on the paper and walked swiftly out the courthouse doors. "Come on," she said. "We only have a few hours left before it gets dark."

Thomas followed after her.

Chapter SEVENTEEN

Gathering clouds swarmed over the horizon. Whispers of the darkness to come echoed through the fields. Slowly, the mass of thorns, vines, and pumpkins began expanding outward, animated by an unseen force. An evil power moved through the soil, deforming the trees while sapping their lives.

Jezebel and Thomas failed to notice the flock of crows spilling out of the forest behind them; they were far too engaged in the discussion at hand. Nor did they spot the gray van parked idly across the street from the two-story brick house.

***

"This is where we should find Rick Pepper," Jezebel said. "Hopefully, anyway."

"What if he doesn't want to answer your questions?" Thomas asked.

"Trust me, I can be very persuasive when I want to be," she replied. The pair walked down the sidewalk toward the house.

"I'll vouch for that," Thomas said.

"If I know Rick Pepper, it shouldn't be too hard to tell if he's lying. You can help me verify everything he tells us. We can have Heavy put him under surveillance if necessary."

"If he is the murderer, it would be nice to get a chance to put him behind bars," Thomas said.

"And find out what he knows about Salem Alistair," Jezebel added.

Thomas remained quiet, as if unsure how to respond. She knew he was hesitant to bring up that sore point with her. She was sensitive about the disappearance of her childhood friend. Despite seeing a possible link between Rick Pepper and his school friends, aside from the scarecrow angle, there wasn't that much substantial evidence linking either Rick Pepper or Gary Davis to the boy's disappearance.

"You're absolutely sure this might not be one of Salem's friends looking for justice?" Thomas finally asked, evidently unable to stop himself.

"You should have listened to me the first time. Salem didn't have any friends," Jezebel snapped. "Except me."

And I let him down, Jezebel thought. She appreciated Thomas' efforts to comfort her when she told him about what happened in the past, but nothing he could say would erase her remorse. In her mind, it would always be her fault that something happened to Salem. If she had been there with him, instead of at that stupid party, everything might have turned out differently.

Salem's disappearance had changed her life. Jezebel started having recurring nightmares. She grew depressed, losing interest in her friends. Things didn't get any easier when her father died. In her heart, Jezebel knew she never quite resolved her issues with her dad. After graduating, she focused like a laser on becoming a police officer. She told herself that if she helped enough people, somehow it would make up for failing Salem Alistair when he needed her. So far, it never had.

"Fair enough," Thomas said, retreating from the line of questioning. The pair reached the house. There was no sign of life evident from the outside. All the lights appeared to be turned off. The sheriff knocked on the front door several times.

"Mr. Pepper, are you in there? This is Sheriff Jezebel Woods. I would like a word with you." She rang the doorbell. There was no answer, so she tried it again. Still there was no answer. Then she heard a sound inside the house that sounded like breaking glass. The sheriff looked at Thomas and quickly removed her gun from its holster.

"Stay here. I'm going in to make sure it's safe," she said.

Thomas looked at her like she was crazy. "No way. I'm not letting you go in there alone."

"You're unarmed," she whispered harshly. "You'll just hold me back. Now stay—"

She heard the shuffling of feet inside. Not willing to wait, Jezebel kicked the door open. The sheriff advanced slowly into the house, her gun held steadily in front of her. Thomas followed her inside before she could say no.

A comely brunette with pale brown eyes stood in the middle of the hallway, staring wide-eyed at the sheriff. A broken vase lay on the floor below her. The woman tried to speak, but the sight of the gun made her stutter. Sensing her unease, Jezebel lowered the gun. Whoever she was, the woman didn't look like a threat.

"Who are you?" Jezebel said as she lowered her weapon. "What are you doing here?"

"My name is Michelle Riley," the woman said, a torrent of words gushing out of her. "I'm Rick's girlfriend. He gave me a key to the house," she said, holding up a keychain. "Is he in trouble? He hasn't been answering his phone."

"We don't know," Jezebel replied. "I've tried his cell phone too. He never showed up for work today."

The woman fell back on a chair at the news, and her eyes began to water.

"I knew this would happen," she said.

"What do you mean?" Thomas asked, clearly studying her.

"Since the murders started, I've been afraid for him. I've heard rumors that something in the woods is alive, and there's something evil wandering through the cornfields after dark. Something that's not human."

Thomas returned Jezebel's doubtful look. She had no doubt Rick's girlfriend believed what she was saying, but it didn't help the two of them to hear stories about local superstitions.

"Michelle," Jezebel said. "If anyone has been killing people, it's a human being, not some kind of monster." She almost added 'we've seen him,' but decided it would be best not to tell the woman her boyfriend may have dressed up like a scarecrow and butchered four innocent people.

"I believe what I've heard," the woman said defiantly. "Something is out there."

"If you want to help us find your boyfriend, you have to talk to us," Jezebel said. "When did you last see Rick?"

"Yesterday," Michelle replied. "We were here together, until he had to leave."

"Where did he go?" Jezebel asked.

"Did he say why he had to leave?"

Michelle hesitated. Jezebel could tell she was holding back, and from the look on his face, Thomas could too.

"No," the woman said.

Jezebel folded her arms across her chest. "Michelle, it doesn't look good to lie to the police. Wherever Rick is, you can't protect him by keeping information from us. What if he's hurt?"

The woman looked doubtful. She bit her lip, looking fleetingly around the room. "He told me not to say anything."

"Michelle," Thomas said, looking her in the eye. "We aren't here to hurt you, but someone is out there killing people, and anyone could be next. Are you ready to accept responsibility for the next death, if you could have helped us prevent it? Besides," he added slyly. "It wouldn't look that good in the paper to everyone else if they found out you hindered the investigation."

"You would print that?"

"I would have to," he said in a serious voice. "It's my responsibility."

That obviously worried her, Jezebel noticed.

"If you help us, I promise I won't breathe a word of any of this," Thomas added.

"Fine," the woman said. "Yesterday when we were having lunch, someone called Rick on his phone. Rick sounded frustrated and left the room. When he came back, he had a gun."

"Was he going hunting?"

"No. The gun was a pistol, not a rifle. That's why I was upset. We actually go hunting together sometimes, and I know Rick only has two rifles. He doesn't even own a pistol. He tried to tell me he had always had it, but he was lying. It was new."

"Why would he lie to you about having a new pistol?" Jezebel asked. Things weren't looking good for Rick Pepper.

"I don't know," Michelle said, looking downcast. "Sometimes we fight a lot. He doesn't always tell me everything. There might be other women."

"I'm sorry," Jezebel said. She felt a pang of sympathy for the woman in front of her. "Was that the last time you saw him?"

"Yes."

"And did he say where he was going?"

"I heard him mention it over the phone. 316 Four Winds Acres."

"Thank you," Jezebel said. She turned to leave.

"Sheriff," Michelle shouted out when the pair was back on the sidewalk. "If you find Rick, will you tell him to come home?"

"I'll do what I can," she said softly, gazing down at the street. There were days she hated her responsibilities. No matter what happened, more than likely Michelle Riley would end up a heartbroken woman. As they walked to the parked car, Jezebel removed the paper Sarah had given her from Judge Underhill and looked over it carefully. Rick owned a green SUV, which was how she would know to look for him.

"Why did you do that?" she asked Thomas when they were back inside the cruiser.

"Do what?" he asked, looking confused.

"You threatened to leak her story in the paper."

Thomas shrugged. "It was just easier, I guess. It helped get us what we needed to know."

Jezebel turned on the ignition. "Sometimes I really don't understand you. Making the effort to do things the right way is better in the long run than cutting corners."

Thomas sighed. "Why don't we stay focused on what we learned in there? What Michelle said doesn't prove anything. Remember, no one has actually been killed with a gun. If having a gun meant so much, Gary Davis would still be our prime suspect."

"As someone involved in law enforcement since I graduated from college, trust me," she said. "Having a gun means a lot."

"Just don't get so caught up in this that you make Rick Pepper out to be the killer."

Jezebel stomped on the brake, and the car tires squealed. She looked at Thomas, her eyes full of resentment, and brought the car to a complete halt. "What did you say to me?" she demanded.

"You heard me," Thomas said. "I think you're making a mistake to convict Rick Pepper before we've even found him. I'm worried that you're too caught up in solving this Salem Alistair case, and it's starting to impact your judgment."

"You don't know me very well then," Jezebel said, taking a deep breath before she continued. "There is nothing more important to me than the safety of the people in this town. As much as I want to solve Salem's case, that is not my first priority. But if there's a possibility the crimes are connected, I'm going to do my best to get to the truth." There was a moment's silence in the vehicle, and Jezebel stared down at the floorboard with her eyes closed. She put the car in drive and headed in the direction of the address Michelle had given them.

"I'm sorry," Thomas said finally. "My concerns were real, but they weren't just for you. They were for me, too. I loved being a reporter in New York. It was the experience of a lifetime. You probably know this already, but my firing came after publishing an article exposing a gubernatorial candidate's affair.

"The trouble was, there was no affair. My sources lied to me. Even though there were obvious holes in their stories, I believed them. I *wanted* to believe them. Now look at me. Even if this story somehow becomes a national sensation, I'll always be known as the man who faked his sources. Don't make my mistake, Jezebel."

"I already made my mistake," she said. "A long time ago."

The two spent the rest of the ride in silence. When they finally reached 316 Four Winds Acres, Thomas immediately pointed out the SUV. The green vehicle was parked just a few hundred feet from the road leading to a large farmhouse in the distance. Jezebel pulled the police cruiser up to the grassy area, and the pair exited the car.

"There was another vehicle here," Thomas said, pointing to the dry grass a few feet ahead of Rick's car. "See the tire marks?"

"Someone might still be in the woods," Jezebel said. "Or in the house. I see footprints over here in the mud. Let's see where they lead." The two followed the muddy prints until they vanished. They slid under a barbed wire fence that led onto the farmland. After walking through an overgrown field, they waded through the tall grasses toward the forest.

"Michelle said Rick received a phone call," Jezebel said. "Then he came out here with a gun. Do you think he came to kill the person on the other end of the line? We can get the phone records."

"I'm not sure," Thomas replied. "The two cars were parked close together. Whoever was here with Rick is gone, which suggests he might still be alive. They could have been working together."

"To what end?" Jezebel asked as they neared the edge of the forest.

"I haven't put that together yet," he answered, grabbing her hand when she helped him descend the steep hillside.

"When we get back to the house, we need to interview the owners. They might know something." She would have interviewed them right then and there, but she didn't want to give Rick the opportunity to escape before nightfall. "Watch your step. It will get dark quickly." She tossed him a flashlight.

***

Thomas caught the flashlight and tucked it away inside his jacket. He was glad Jezebel wasn't angrier over their argument in the car. He was actually starting to like her, against his better judgment. In contrast to some law enforcement officials he worked with in the past, she was honest, smart, and dedicated. He stared at her for a moment before venturing into the forest.

***

Clark pulled off to the side of the road. "What now?" he asked Chuck. Following the sheriff's car was a difficult proposition, especially due to the isolation of Gray Hollow's back roads. It was a good thing the van's driver was well experienced in pursuits. Chuck Howard wasn't about to give the man any praise though. He *expected* all of his colleagues to live up to his own standards.

"I guess we go back to the hotel," Elaine replied, offering up a yawn. "I don't know what time it gets dark around here, but the sky already looks stormy, and it isn't like we're going to follow them into the forest."

"Wrong again," Chuck said contemptuously. He was truly beginning to despise the camerawoman. The day spent in the vehicle with her following Thomas Brooks and Jezebel Woods was agony. Chuck did not intend for all that time to be wasted. He slid off his jacket and pinned the portable microphone to his dress shirt.

"We're going in after them," he said. "Or at least, you and I are," he added, looking at Elaine. He would rather take Clark with him, but that wasn't in the cards. "Stay here, Clark. Be ready to start the van. I'll be in touch via cell phone." As he picked it up, he noticed the phone screen go fuzzy for a moment. Then it cleared, like nothing had ever been wrong with it in the first place.

That's odd, Chuck thought as he placed the phone in his pocket.

"Do we have to do this?" Elaine asked.

"Trust me," he muttered. "I wish it were otherwise. Now grab your camera."

Elaine was right about one thing, he thought, looking at the sky. *It is getting darker.*

***

Thomas couldn't shake the feeling something was wrong. The farther they walked into the forest, the stronger the feeling grew. He couldn't tell if it was due to the paranoid words of Michelle Riley or the ominous weather, but his hair was standing on end. A quick glance in Jezebel's direction told him she was experiencing something similar. At least she was used to the country. Thomas wasn't accustomed to treks through the woods, and all the unfamiliar sights and sounds made him uncomfortable.

After a few minutes, the forest started to change around them. The trees appeared warped, their thin branches curved outward like claws. There were briars everywhere, something he didn't remember from the forest where they discovered Jeffrey Daniels' truck. They were numerous miles from that location now.

Jezebel stooped down, studying something on the ground. She squinted in the dim light and motioned for him to join her. Thomas jogged over to the spot, anxious to see what she had discovered.

"Blood," she said, pointing at crusted droplets hardened over dried leaves. "There's a trail in the direction of that waterfall."

"Good eye," he said. Thomas doubted he would have spotted the trail.

The pair advanced cautiously, scanning in every direction. The wind blew softly around them. Leaves fell from the clustered trees, which created a thick maze that limited their visibility. Thomas was glad Jezebel wore a gun.

Thomas saw the body first. It was resting in a puddle of mud at the bottom of the hill. Four crows were picking at the body with their beaks. The birds scattered when the two humans approached.

"Is that normal?" Thomas asked. His voice wavered. "For crows to eat human flesh? They aren't vultures."

"It must be. Try to keep focused. We have to watch out for the *real* enemy here. Whoever killed this man might still be around." She stopped and looked down over the body.

"What is it?" Thomas asked.

"This man *was* killed with a gunshot," she said. "It's Gary Davis."

The name of the dead man shouldn't have surprised Thomas, yet it shocked him all the same. This was the man once suspected of murdering his family—the man half the town searched for over the course of a week. Now he was dead.

"Come on," she said, pulling her gun. "Let's go. I have to call this in."

"Wait," Thomas said as they climbed back over the hill. "Over there. I see another set of footprints." He pointed to the tracks and led Jezebel down by the stream below the waterfall. The two walked around the stream. Thomas could hear the rustling of wings behind him. He turned around quickly, but there was no sign of life other than the twisted trees.

When he looked back at Jezebel, he saw that she had holstered her gun and was wearing a plastic glove on one hand. She knelt down next to the bed of the stream and picked up a metal object that glimmered in the remaining sunlight.

"Look," she said after sliding the object into a bag. She held the bag open for him to see. It was a pistol.

"Do you think it's the murder weapon?"

"There's only one way to find out," she said. "We'll have it looked at when you and I get back into town." Even through the canopy, Thomas could see the sun starting to fade. He suddenly experienced the same sensation he felt when he saw Paul Morris' killer. Despite being unnerved, Thomas was drawn to the trail in front of him. Anticipation tingled in his veins.

"We need more light," Jezebel said. She switched on her flashlight after a few minutes. "Are you sure you don't want to head back?"

"Not yet," Thomas replied. "Not until we reach the end of this trail." He brushed a group of vines out of his way while stepping over a mound of dirt, and Jezebel moved to his side. Suddenly, she stumbled and almost lost her balance, and Thomas reached out quickly to pull her back. She fell on the soft earth in front of the ledge.

"Thanks," she said. "That would have been a nasty fall." Jezebel peered over the side, shining her flashlight. She moved her light to the bottom of the pit.

Another body, covered in leaves, lay at the bottom. The twin light of their flashlights revealed a reddish hue clinging to the body. The man was obviously dead evident by the fact that he was contorted in a horrifying fashion.

"Is that Rick Pepper?" Thomas asked Jezebel, recognizing the face from her photographs.

"What happened to him?" Jezebel muttered. "What could do something like this?"

"Help me make sense of this," Thomas whispered, unsure why he was speaking in a hushed voice. "At first we thought Gary Davis killed Jeffrey Daniels then killed his family. Then we thought maybe Rick Pepper killed them all, along with Dr. Paul Morris. They're all dead, Jezebel. We're out of suspects."

"As much as I hate to admit it, you're right," she said. "Who wanted all these people dead?"

Thomas glimpsed movement to his right. He spun around, holding the flashlight out in front of him. The beam shone only on trees and leaves.

"What is it?" Jezebel asked, her eyes widening.

"There's something out there," the reporter answered. Thomas heard the leaves crunching nearby.

Jezebel held her flashlight in one hand and took out her sidearm. "Come into the light!" she shouted. "I am Sheriff Jezebel Woods, and I am armed!" They heard a soft hissing sound, almost like laughter. "Thomas, we need to get out of here."

He nodded and backed away alongside her. The two kept their flashlights out in front of them while searching for the silent attacker. Thomas thought he saw a face in the path illuminated by Jezebel's flashlight. Slowly, he shined his own light in her direction, his skin crawling.

"Thomas, what is it?"

The light stopped. Mere inches behind Jezebel loomed the horrifying face of one of Salem Alistair's scarecrows.

"Get down!" he shouted. Jezebel swung around, but the scarecrow disappeared. Then Thomas felt something strike him from behind, cutting into his arm. He tripped and fell to the ground. Moving faster than he would have thought possible, Jezebel ran at the scarecrow, firing her gun three times into the assailant's chest. The scarecrow was knocked back into the shadows of the forest.

"Thanks," Thomas said, breathing heavily. He stood up and shook the leaves off him. "You saved me again."

The sheriff was pale and visibly shaken. Thomas could see her trembling.

"I've never killed anyone before," she said.

Just as Thomas walked over to comfort her, the scarecrow regained its footing. The frozen grin was still wrapped around its face. Jezebel shot it again and again, but the creature kept moving toward them. It was gaining speed.

"It's not working," Thomas shouted. "Run!"

The two fled through the forest in the direction they'd come. Casting his light back behind him, Thomas saw two more scarecrows join the first one. One of them was holding something resembling a scythe. Jezebel followed his gaze, and her face contorted with fear. The scarecrow she shot was not bleeding. Instead, there were only empty bullet holes in the straw. There was nothing inside the suit.

Salem Alistair's scarecrows had come to life.

Thomas tried following the path of the stream. He didn't even want to consider what would happen if he got lost now. Jezebel was at his heels, no longer firing her gun. He guessed she was trying to conserve bullets.

The scarecrows were gaining on them. Dozens of crows spilled into the sky above the forest, and Thomas was reminded of the crows embedded in Jeffrey Daniel's windshield. He dodged an outstretched hand, plowing through the briar patch ahead of him. The thorns tore into his skin, but he didn't care about the pain. Not when his life was on the line.

As he stumbled up the hill, he grabbed Jezebel and swung her up to his level. Gary Davis' corpse remained exactly where they'd left it, indicating they were close to the forest's edge. His light flashed on a small metal object near Gary's pants pocket. Turning the item over in his hand, he examined the lighter quickly.

"What are you doing?" Jezebel shouted. "Come on!"

Thomas looked up just in time. He fell back as one of scarecrows clawing its way up the hill reached for him. Thomas pushed himself up and took off in Jezebel's direction. The two other scarecrows scaled the mound of earth and lumbered after them. Thomas grabbed a tree before finally stumbling back out into the field beyond the forest.

It was pitch black, with only the light of moon to guide them. The scarecrows were almost impossible to see in the thick field, disappearing within the tall grasses. Thomas tripped on a fallen branch and landed on his face. He picked up the branch and crawled forward in the grass, out of sight.

***

Jezebel was suddenly aware that Thomas was gone when she turned around and noticed he was no longer behind her. Unfortunately, she could still see the scarecrows. They were getting closer, each with an almost hungry expression on their distorted faces.

"Thomas?" Jezebel yelled into the night. "Thomas!" She fired the gun, weaving through the grass. The scarecrows disappeared. The sheriff's heart beat faster. She was alone. Suddenly, everything was quiet.

With a hiss, a scarecrow appeared behind her. The creature knocked the gun from her hand with the scythe. Jezebel lashed out and kicked the scarecrow in the face. The creature's head snapped back, and its pointed hat tumbled off. Then it turned around, staring at her with dead eyes. The creature knocked her off her feet and raised the scythe. She watched helplessly from the ground.

Before the scythe fell, the scarecrow burst into flames. The creature writhed in pain and tore at its straw body. Thomas grabbed Jezebel and pulled her to her feet, holding a makeshift torch in his free hand. Jezebel pushed away from him and grabbed her gun. She blasted away at the burning creature. When she pulled the trigger, nothing happened. The gun was empty.

"Run!" Thomas shouted. "There are two more out there!" The field around him began to catch fire from the embers of the withering scarecrow. As they raced away, Thomas and Jezebel saw the two remaining scarecrows watching them just outside the forest.

"What are those things?" Thomas asked Jezebel when they reached the police cruiser. "Whatever they were, they seemed afraid of the fire." He clutched the lighter tightly in his hand.

"I don't know," she said. "But I know someone who might."

***

Percy Durer sat at the desk in his bedroom over the store, where he continued scribbling furiously in a book. For years he expected a wave of death to envelop Gray Hollow. Now that time had come. The results would be interesting to observe, at the very least.

The storekeeper had grown up in Great Britain. In his younger years Durer found himself drawn to the occult. When he became a professor of theology, the influence of the occult found its way into his spirituality lectures, which resulted in his expulsion from the Christian seminary where he taught. At the time the removal angered Durer. In retrospect, it was the beginning of his true calling.

Durer traveled the world to seek out stories of folklore and myth at their sources. He had seen things most people would never imagine in their wildest fantasies. Then something exceptional happened. He was in Ireland, pursuing a particularly harrowing tale of the Morrígan, a local banshee. He could feel that the town was somehow different from the others. There was a presence he couldn't explain.

He learned from a barman the story of a group of witches who supposedly lived in the area centuries ago. Durer spent months trying to locate a set of rare books he believed belonged to the witches. Finally, in a hidden location far from town, he found one of the books he sought.

Then something found him. A stranger crossed his path in the dark of night. Under the light of the moon, the man's dark clothes seemed to bleed into the blackness. His jacket appeared to swim around him like a pair of wings. A silver badge of some kind shimmered on his shirt.

“I know what you seek,” the man said, his eyes invisible in the dark. “We share a common purpose.”

“Who are you?” Durer blurted out, overcome with fear. He could sense something wrong with the solitary figure.

“You may call me Bartholomew,” the man replied. The stars appeared to vanish from the sky.

“What do you want?” Durer demanded, shaking.

Even in the dark, it was obvious Bartholomew sensed his fear.

“You have lived your life in shadows,” the man said. “You seek a knowledge that is beyond you, and for that you have been rejected by others.”

“How do you know about me?”

There was silence for a few moments. Bartholomew seemed to be contemplating his next move. For some reason, this frightened Durer even more. “What would it be worth to you to have your eyes truly opened to the spiritual realm?”

Durer did not ask how it was that Bartholomew could offer this gift. He could feel power in the stranger’s words.

“Anything,” he found himself saying.

“Finish your travels and seek out a town in America by the name of Gray Hollow. You will know it when you find it. Offer sacrifices to the Keeper of the Crows. Only then will the scales fall from your eyes.”

“How will I know what to do?”

“Keep the book you have found,” Bartholomew said softly. “It will tell you everything you require. I do not yet have need of it.”

He never saw Bartholomew again. Durer did as he was told, opening his novelty store in the small town. He could sense the power of the being in the forest and feel its strength in the crows. Although Durer himself held no power other than sensing the emotions and feelings of others, he now found himself able to sense the spiritual world around him.

When Salem Alistair was born, Durer could feel the boy’s power as well. He knew it was the will of the Keeper of the Crows that the boy should join him, so Durer did everything he could to persuade the boy to enter the forest. At first, Salem was delighted that someone understood him. Later, the boy seemed to realize Durer's intent and stayed away from the store.

Durer could sense death the night Salem Alistair disappeared. He continued offering sacrifices to the Keeper of the Crows. Jezebel Woods was right: something was walking through the forests, but it was no man of flesh and blood.

He heard a loud clang from below him. The storekeeper frowned and set aside his books. He hoped no one was foolish enough to try to rob him. The old man snatched a letter opener from the desk, opened the door to his room, and walked down the stairs into the dark store.

"Who is there?" he demanded, his voice no longer possessing its characteristic softness. "Show yourself!" There was silence. For a moment, he considered going back upstairs, but then he heard it again. A scratching noise coming from below. Had someone broken into his special room?

Still wielding the letter opener, Durer walked down the second set of stairs. He unlocked the door and turned on the light. The bulb fizzled on and off, as if there were a problem with the electricity. The old man looked around the room. Something was missing. Something was out of place.

The scarecrows, he thought. Someone had moved the scarecrows. They were gone!

Then a sinister face appeared in the darkness, hovering above him. Durer dropped the letter opener in shock. A second scarecrow slammed the door shut behind him. Another picked up the letter opener. Staring at him with grins long ago stitched shut, the scarecrows advanced.

"What are you doing?" Durer pleaded. He shrank back against a bookshelf. "I've always done what you've asked! I offered your sacrifices! I worshipped you—"

The tallest scarecrow stabbed him in the heart with the letter opener. Durer fell to the floor, blood gushing from his chest. He wanted to crawl away, but his body refused to move. The storekeeper heard laughter, then nothing at all.

The demon had taken its power back. It didn't need the old man anymore.

Chapter EIGHTEEN

Bony fingers shakily unlatched the screen door leading outside the kitchen. The worn flannel nightgown swept around the old woman who crept out onto the lawn. Vacant eyes searched the gray sky for an invisible sun. It was morning in Gray Hollow, but the sun was nowhere in sight. Emma Woods sensed what was coming.

"It's here," she whispered in a tone completely devoid of emotion. The sentiment was not quite valid; the dreary morning horizon still boasted at least some light. Emma knew it would not last for long. Not while the darkness continued to spread.

The crows were everywhere. They would not go away. Unnatural gloom was closing in fast on Gray Hollow, early as it was. To Emma it seemed neither fall nor winter. The town had entered a twilight that was in between. When the darkness fell on Gray Hollow, it would not lift again until all life in the town was extinguished.

Night was coming. Somewhere in the recesses of her mind, Emma began to feel fear. Even while her body began to chill in the freezing weather, the woman remained motionless on the barren lawn. She was waiting.

***

Thomas tugged at the leather jacket, which had suddenly become sticky and uncomfortable. Even so, he was reluctant to remove it. It was freezing inside the cramped lounge in the sheriff's offices; the heaters were having difficulties. The expensive jacket was also another reminder to him of his former life. Not that it was worth much anymore. It was matted with leaves and dirt from his terrifying foray into the forest the night before.

"I've never seen Gray Hollow this dark so early in the day before," Jezebel was saying. Neither of them had been able to muster an expression even distantly resembling a smile since their brush with death.

"Another storm?" Thomas wondered what else could happen to make the new day even worse.

"No." Jezebel shook her head. The light bulb above flickered for a second. "It's something else," she whispered. "The black clouds are there. I've never seen so many. The wind is blowing hard, but I can't see the first trace of rain."

Thomas moved from the lounge chair where he'd slept the night before. He was unable to recall precisely when he finally dozed off. Thomas wondered if he looked as tired as he felt. He glanced over at Jezebel as she stared at the window. Unlike him, she showed no sign of having spent the night in the police station. She seemed shaken, yet he sensed an undercurrent of energy boiling under the surface.

Heavy Markham brewed coffee in the corner of the room. Thomas had probably consumed enough caffeine over the course of this case to last him a lifetime, but he had to admit that he needed it again. On a shelf next to the coffeemaker lay the evidence bag with the gun found in the forest. It had not moved from the spot Jezebel placed it when the pair stumbled into the station the night before.

Thomas' gaze returned to the window. Gone were the onlookers who lined up behind the station after the murders became public knowledge, driven away, no doubt, by the atrocious weather. Thomas would have liked to hide, too. When the deputy left the room, Jezebel finally spoke again.

"We have to warn the town about what we saw last night. Everyone is in danger."

"They might be, but I highly doubt anyone is going to believe us when we tell them we were attacked by scarecrows." Thomas was still having a hard enough time accepting it himself.

"We have to try," Jezebel said, unwilling to concede the point. "There is something evil in Gray Hollow."

"A week ago I never would have accepted any of this. Even the most superstitious people in the town will have a hard time believing us. We aren't even sure what we saw."

Jezebel's eyes narrowed. She turned away from the windowsill and faced him. "I know what I saw."

"That's not what I mean. Have you stopped to think about what we're dealing with? It was one thing when we were investigating a simple murder. Killers have motives. They leave evidence. What do these things want?"

Jezebel shook her head. "I've never bought into any of Gray Hollow's local superstitions," she said. "Until now. I should have seen it sooner. It started with the crows. It never made sense why they were in the windshield of Jeffrey Daniels' truck. Something guided them there."

"What could control the crows?" he wondered aloud. "What could bring scarecrows to life?" Although Thomas believed in God and the existence of evil, he never would have imagined that such a supernatural force could appear in Gray Hollow.

Deputy Markham stepped back into the room again, and the two fell quiet. Each silently contemplated the question. All possible answers were equally horrifying. As if he sensed that the two were in the middle of an important conversation, Heavy retrieved the pistol and retreated out of sight.

"When I was in the library," Thomas said. "I read a passage about early cults in Gray Hollow in the 1800s. The cults offered blood sacrifices to the demon Baal. Do you think it's possible those sacrifices played a role in all this?"

"Those settlers have been dead for hundreds of years. Most of us don't even know those stories. Until you brought it up, I had never heard of it."

"Then maybe I'm approaching it the wrong way. Who have the monsters killed so far? Jeffrey Daniels, Rick Pepper, Gary Davis and his family, and Paul Morris. What farm is everyone around here scared of? The Alistair Farm. Who built these scarecrows in the first place?"

"What are you saying?"

"Would Salem Alistair have any reason to want any of these people dead?"

"We've been over this. Gary Davis and Rick Pepper bullied Salem all the time."

Salem Alistair created the scarecrows. Salem was also bullied frequently before mysteriously disappearing. Thomas was willing to bet Jeffrey Daniels also picked on his neighbor. Jezebel had already provided him with photographic evidence linking Davis, Daniels, and Pepper.

Jezebel knows it, too, he thought. "The scarecrow with the pumpkin head is obviously different than all the others. Why? There is a body in there, Jezebel. I think it belongs to Salem Alistair."

"I don't believe that," Jezebel said. Her lower lip quivered. "I can't."

"Fine," Thomas replied, switching gears. He knew he was finally closing in on the truth. "Then why target those particular people? We know Salem Alistair links them. Who else links them together?"

"There's one little problem with your theory," Jezebel said. "The scarecrow that attacked you killed Dr. Morris. Morris didn't move to Gray Hollow until *after* Salem went missing."

"Maybe he isn't just killing for revenge. He might be after something more. These deaths are only the start." The proposition was horrifying.

"We have to stop them," Jezebel said. "Do you know how many scarecrows Salem made? Dozens. We need answers." She stood up and grabbed her gun. "We're going to see Percy Durer."

Thomas frowned. He had never heard the name Percy Durer before, but something about it was unsettling. He glanced out the window at the mounting darkness again. *If this keeps up, it'll be as dark as night in a few hours,* he thought. *It isn't even noon yet.*

Jezebel put her hand on his. "And, Thomas? Thank you for saving my life." Thomas could see gratitude in her eyes. He realized he liked seeing it there. There was something else, too. Coffee or no coffee, Thomas suddenly felt completely awake. The moment ended quickly, but he was sure there had been a spark.

"Don't mention it. We're even. Do you mind if we swing by my house first so I can change clothes and get a new camera battery? We're going to need proof of this if we're going to convince people to believe us."

Jezebel nodded. Having stored a change of clothes in her locker, she had already showered and changed before the reporter woke up. Thomas stepped out of the lounge and removed the cell phone from his pocket as Jezebel conversed with Heavy Markham. He couldn't hear what they were saying for certain, though it sounded like Logan Randall hadn't shown up for work yet.

"Max," Thomas said into the phone. "I need you to pick up." There was a considerable amount of static on the line. For some reason, the sound reminded him of the forest stalked by the living scarecrows. His phone hadn't worked there either.

"Thomas!" Max said loudly. "I haven't heard from you since yesterday."

"I've been pretty busy," Thomas replied.

"The article about Paul Morris is bigger than you know," Max said. "Sales have skyrocketed, and it's all thanks to you! We've also heard from a television station that says they sent a crew down."

"I know all about Chuck Howard, after having shared the unfortunate pleasure of his company. That's not really important right now."

"If we get scooped—"

It was Thomas' turn to cut off the editor. "Max, we're down at the sheriff's department, and we need all the help we can get. I'm going to need you on this."

"Why? What's happening?"

"You wouldn't believe me if I told you."

"What's that supposed to mean?"

"Pray you never have to find out. I need you to drop whatever you're doing and come down to the police station. We need you to track down the owners of the farmhouse on 316 Four Winds Acres. Jezebel and I looked their names up last night when we got back. Dirk and Nina Edwards. We tried calling them, but they weren't at home."

"Did you check the house? Maybe they weren't picking up."

"We did a quick check last night before we got here. The house was empty."

"OK," Max said. "I'll see what I can do and meet you two at the station. Where are we going from there?"

"I wish I knew," Thomas said. He followed Jezebel outside into the cold darkness.

***

Chuck Howard was already tired of searching the forest. It was hard to admit it, but it had definitely been a mistake to stop following Thomas Brooks and Jezebel Woods the previous night. The decision seemed wise at the time. It was nearly pitch black by the time Chuck and Elaine could hear their voices ahead. If he couldn't film it, Chuck didn't want to pursue it.

What a stupid error, he thought bitterly. A gunshot erupted the very second the reporter set foot in the news van. At first Chuck thought he might be mistaken. Then a series of gunshots echoed in the night. Chuck ordered Clark to drive onto a nearby road where he could spy on the police car through the trees.

They waited for what seemed like half an hour. Eventually a fire broke out in the field next to them. Within minutes, Thomas and Jezebel came running toward the police cruiser. The pair drove away into the night.

"Let's wait right here," Chuck had said. "If someone was shooting at them, they'll be back with reinforcements. This time I'll be the one who scoops Brooks out of his own story."

It was only after sitting in silence in the van for over three hours that Chuck realized the truth. They weren't coming back. Whoever was in the forest was dead, wounded, or had escaped. That made the area below a crime scene. Why wouldn't the sheriff have sent more officers to a crime scene?

The truth was so simple Chuck couldn't believe he hadn't thought of it sooner. It came to him as the others were sleeping in the hotel, while he was trying to come up with an excuse to placate his uncle for time wasted. There was a reason why the two had not returned with others to the farm. They didn't *want* anyone to know about what happened. It was a cover-up. The sheriff and Brooks were in it together!

"It's their secret," he had muttered aloud. *Well,* he thought at the time, *it won't be a secret for long.*

Now Chuck found himself in the forest for a second time. He would find what the two left behind one way or another. While the forest was unfortunately still quite dark, the prospect of what he might discover in the woods compensated for the effect on image quality on his equipment.

"It's so murky in here," Elaine half-whispered. "Watch your step."

"Your concern is touching," he said sarcastically. He had already made up his mind he never wanted to work with the camerawoman again if he could avoid it. For some reason Clark didn't agree with him; he even went so far as to hint that it was Chuck who needed to lighten up.

Chuck did agree with Elaine on one thing: it was getting darker. In fact, the farther they traveled into the forest, the darker it seemed to become. Despite the relatively early hour, the sky looked like evening was approaching. Chuck didn't have time to dwell on the thought. Not when he stumbled across the swollen corpse resting in the dry leaves.

Chuck ran to the body and knelt down to study it. He barked an order to Elaine to take pictures. When the day grew bright again, she would be able to get some great footage in the forest. Even in the dim light, he could see that there was blood everywhere. Chuck saw a gunshot wound on the body. If the bullet came from Jezebel Woods or Thomas Brooks, why had they not returned for the body?

It was evident his earlier suspicions were correct. *They were trying to cover it up. Brooks is a has-been. What if he and his girlfriend the sheriff tried to spice things up to put Gray Hollow on the map?*

"This story just got a lot bigger," he whispered excitedly.

"Chuck," Elaine said slowly, trying to get his attention.

"Not now! I don't have time for this!"

"Chuck," she whimpered. He turned around to snap at her, but the camerawoman paid no attention to him.

Instead, she was staring at something in front of them. Two shadowy figures were perched under a tree. Without warning, they started to move.

***

The darkness came alive. The Keeper of the Crows roared, no longer bound by the rising of the sun, which had forced him to slumber in the shadows during the day. Enough sacrifices had been made to give him the power to usher in permanent night. Although the shadows had not yet entirely surrounded the town of Gray Hollow, they were closing in fast. The forest and the crows were at his full command.

***

Chuck saw the two figures on the ground twitch and rise. He screamed when he saw their terrible faces. The creatures looked at him for a moment then started moving toward him. Chuck grabbed Elaine, pushing her in front of him to shield himself. As he backed away, she fell to the ground. Chuck turned and ran. The drumbeat of his roaring pulse failed to drown out Elaine's cries in the background. He gained enough courage to cast one look back. The scarecrows descended on Elaine. Her screams soon faded away.

Panicked, Chuck focused on running faster. Above him, crows spilled out of the forest in every direction. His heart pounded. He could hear the things moving again behind him.

Clark was waiting for him at the forest's edge. "What's going on? Where's Elaine?"

Before Chuck could answer, the scarecrows spilled outside the woods as the clouds above blotted out the remaining light. Chuck kept running toward the van, but when Clark moved to follow him, he tripped and lost his balance. Chuck cast a nervous glance over his shoulder and threw open the door to the driver's seat. Luckily, the keys were sitting in the ignition. He jumped inside the van and turned on the engine.

"Wait for me," Clark called, climbing to his feet, but Chuck was already speeding away.

In the rearview mirror, he could see crows swarming around Clark as the scarecrows advanced on him. Even from the increasing distance, he still heard his screams. Chuck forced himself to look away and pounded on the gas.

***

By the time Jezebel finished telling Thomas about Percy Durer, he could see what she thought was so strange about the man. According to the sheriff, Durer was the only person in Gray Hollow notably interested in the occult. More convicting was the interest he apparently showed in Salem Alistair. When Jezebel told Thomas the storekeeper kept four scarecrows locked away in a secret room, he knew she was onto something. They planned to return to Thomas' house so he could gather his things before confronting Durer.

"Pull over here," he said, and Jezebel moved the cruiser into his driveway. The two got out of the car and walked up to the door. After removing the keys from his frayed jacket pocket, Thomas slid them into the lock and opened the door.

He froze as he peered into the shadows inside his house.

Something inside was waiting for him.

Chapter NINETEEN

The figure sitting in the shadowy chair rose and stepped in front of the window.

Jezebel held her gun in front of her while Thomas flipped on the light switch.

"You really should learn to lock your door," said the woman at the opposite end of the room.

"Eve?" Thomas blurted out. Evelyn Saddler was the last person he expected to turn up in his house. Her appearance caught him off guard. "What are you doing here?"

"Who is this?" Jezebel demanded. She looked reluctant to lower her weapon.

"I can guess who you are," Eve said. "The infamous Jezebel Woods, right?" She returned her attention to Thomas. "You'd think a sheriff would do a better job of telling you to lock your front door. You never had that problem in the city. You were always very good at locking doors, as I recall. Your power's not working, by the way."

Jezebel turned to him. "It's like meeting you all over again. Please tell me you want to press charges. Just say the word and I'll arrest her for trespassing," the sheriff pleaded.

Thomas was struck by the absurdity of the situation. He didn't know why the two women had taken an instant dislike to each other, but he didn't care.

"You still haven't answered my question, Eve. What are you doing here?"

While waiting for her to reply, he picked up a fresh battery from the table next to the cabinet with his camera equipment. When Eve glanced back at him, her expression softened. Thomas detected another emotion. Was it regret? He wasn't sure.

"What did you expect? You called me and told me you were almost killed. Then you hung up, and you haven't returned any of my calls."

"You've been calling me?" Thomas asked. "That's odd." He hadn't received any of her calls.

"We might not be together anymore, Thomas, but I still care about you. I got here an hour ago, and my rental car is parked on the curb."

"*That's* your girlfriend?" Jezebel asked.

"Ex-girlfriend," Thomas corrected her. He wished he had never mentioned Eve to Jezebel at all. A strange combination of emotions washed over him. Before he met Jezebel Woods, Thomas would have given anything to reconcile with Eve. Over the last week, things had changed.

Now his former girlfriend was standing right in front of him. It was the first time they had seen each other since the breakup. The fact that Eve traveled so far just to see him was not lost on him.

"Whatever she is," Jezebel said. "You can talk, but please hurry. We don't have much time."

"She's right," he said apologetically. He shot fleeting glances at each woman. They were starting to stare more at each other than at him. "This case is dangerous. If we don't do something soon, more people will die."

"You really have changed," Eve said, as if noting the sincerity in his voice. "Or maybe you were like that all along, and I just didn't see it."

Thomas let out an exasperated sigh. Of all the times for Eve to delve into deeply held feelings, this was possibly the worst.

"We need to leave," Jezebel said. "You should get your things."

Thomas nodded and stepped into the laundry room for a quick change of clothes.

"I'm going with you," Eve said to the sheriff. The two women stared each other down.

"No offense, but I've already got one civilian to look after. I don't need a second."

"Listen, I'm going to follow you either way. I do this for a living. It's the easy way or the hard way. Your choice."

"I don't respond well to threats—just ask Thomas."

"I just want to make sure Thomas is safe," Eve said. "And to help him with this story."

"So you want the credit for yourself? That's altruistic of you."

Thomas walked out of the laundry room wearing a new set of clothes, save for the dirty leather jacket. "Enough with the bickering," he said. He turned to Jezebel. "We could use her. Eve is a good reporter. Max is going to have a hard enough time managing *Hollow Happenings* and helping us as well." He noticed Eve smirk again at the name of the town newspaper. *Some things never change*, he thought.

"This isn't about me," Eve said before Jezebel could reply. "If Thomas' story is successful enough, there's a chance he can go back to his old job. That's what would make you happy, right?"

"We don't have time to debate this," Jezebel said. "We need to leave now."

The awkward trio marched back into the elements outside the reporter's meager home. Thomas pulled his jacket up as the fierce winds whistled around them. It was colder than ever.

Thomas was suddenly gripped with remorse for having not discouraged Eve from going with them. Whatever evil they were dealing with was extremely dangerous. Jezebel was armed and capable of handling herself. Eve, on the other hand, probably wouldn't even believe Thomas if he told her about the scarecrows.

Even if he said something, it likely wouldn't have changed anything. He saw the fire in her eyes when Eve announced she was going to stay. If Eve was one thing, it was stubborn. It was a quality she shared with Jezebel.

She'll see for herself soon enough, Thomas thought. He hoped he was wrong. He didn't want to put Eve in danger.

Thomas was still trying to process the internal conflict presented by his ex's sudden appearance when his phone rang mere moments after the sheriff started her car. He grabbed the phone and looked outside the car window at the vast gray horizon. This time the static in his phone was more pronounced. He could barely hear the voice on the other end of the line.

"I said this is Max," the editor said loudly. "Thomas, is that you?"

"Yeah, I'm here. What'd you find?" He put the phone on speaker.

"Where are you two? I just got to the station a few minutes ago, and Deputy Markham is the only one here."

"Sorry about that. We're running a bit behind schedule. I went home to change my clothes. Anyway, we're en route to the novelty store," Thomas said. "We'll drive back to the station after finishing up there."

"Fine," Max said. "It's too bleak outside for me to do anything useful anyway. Plus, you two can fill me in on all the new developments when you get here."

"What did you find, Max?"

"It took me awhile to track down Dirk Edwards. He and his wife are staying at Morgan's Motel. Dirk said his wife was coming back from lunch last week when she saw a man with a gun running through the field."

"Gary Davis," Jezebel muttered.

"That's who they thought it was, after reading Thomas' article. They decided to stay in the motel until Gary was caught. I guess they were afraid he'd come back."

"Why didn't they report the break-in?" Jezebel asked. "Surely they can't expect my department to catch the killer if they don't call us."

There was static on the other end of the line. Thomas shook the phone, and by some miracle Max's voice roared back to life.

"Can you repeat that?" Thomas asked.

"Dirk said his wife *did* call. Logan Randall answered the call. He even waited for them to leave the house before searching for the suspect. You knew that, right? Don't you have Deputy Randall searching for Davis, Sheriff Woods?"

"Gary Davis is dead," Jezebel muttered. Her eyes grew wide as the realization hit her. "The gun," she whispered. Before she could say anything else, static took over the phone again.

“Call him again!” Jezebel said. She wheeled the car around.

“I’m trying,” Thomas exclaimed. “I’m getting nothing but static!”

“Give me the number,” Eve said. “I’ll use my cell.” After punching in the number, she frowned. “That’s weird. I’ve got static too.”

Jezebel tried her own phone. It failed as well, as did her attempts to radio in to Heavy Markham.

“We have to get to the station,” Jezebel said. “Something is very wrong.”

“What is it?” Eve asked curiously. “Gary Davis is dead? I thought he was your suspect.”

This time, Jezebel answered her. “When they were in high school, Gary was a friend of Logan Randall, one of my deputies. Against my better judgment, I let Logan lead the search for Gary. Yesterday, Logan showed up with lacerations on his face and arms.”

Thomas finished for her. “Gary Davis died of a bullet wound, unlike the other victims. If Logan received those wounds after going into the forest after Gary . . .”

“With Rick Pepper, who was also Logan’s friend. Logan must have given him a gun. It all fits together.”

“Why would they want to kill Gary Davis?” Thomas asked. “If Gary is his friend?”

“There is only one thing I can think of that would explain that,” Jezebel said. “Gary must have known something that put Logan in danger. Something that had to do with Jeffrey Daniels, and whatever happened to make Jeffrey leave town.”

“Don’t you see?” Thomas asked. “All of them bullied Salem Alistair. Jeffrey Daniels moved out of Gray Hollow only a few *months* after Salem’s disappearance.”

“Salem Alistair?” Eve asked. “The boy who went missing?”

“The very same,” Thomas replied.

“They know what happened to Salem Alistair,” Jezebel said. “They might have done it themselves.”

“And now Logan Randall is the only one left,” Thomas said. “The scarecrows started the murders, and Logan thought the others might talk, so he finished their work.”

“Wait a second,” Eve finally said. “I’ve tried to keep silent here so far about things I don’t yet understand, but what’s this about *scarecrows*?”

“The question is,” Jezebel asked, ignoring Eve. “What will these things do after Logan is gone?”

“I have a feeling that’s what we are about to find out,” Thomas said.

“Would one of you mind filling me in on what’s going on?” Eve asked. “This wasn’t exactly in your last article, Thomas.”

Thomas hesitated a moment and looked at her sheepishly. There was no way Eve was going to believe him.

“It’s kind of a long story,” he said.

***

Logan knew the sheriff was onto him. If she weren’t, she would be soon. It was all Thomas Brooks’ fault, of course. The second the reporter grew suspicious of the bruises on his face, Logan realized it was only a matter of time before he put it all together. Logan should have put a bullet in Thomas’ head long ago. Luckily, it wasn’t too late to rectify that mistake.

He also knew he needed to act quickly. Logan was not stupid enough to overlook all of his own flaws. He realized his obsession with cleanliness, as well as his paranoia, were often shortcomings. There were times, however, when the paranoia ensured that he checked and double-checked everything so that his actions always met with success. This allowed him to tie up several loose ends regarding Salem Alistair. It was fitting, since his unnatural aversion to muck and grime began the day they buried Salem Alistair under the earth.

Unfortunately, Logan had committed one big mistake, and it was going to cost him dearly. There was still a way out, to be sure. He had friends in high places, which was partially why he made a call to the final member of the group that killed Salem Alistair before coming to work. His friend would make sure he’d escape this mess.

The one thing that still troubled Logan was why the killings had started in the first place. After finishing Gary, he now believed him to have been incapable of killing his family or Jeffrey Daniels. So who started the killings? His money was on Rick Pepper. Rick was now dead as well, so they would never know. Logan heard the news of Rick's death when he slipped into the station after Jezebel left with Thomas.

That was when he realized the critical error he had committed. Logan thought the gun he used to kill Gary Davis was his own service revolver. In the heat of the murder, and his subsequent panic to remove the mud covering him, Logan had not removed his weapon from its holster until *after* the killing two days ago. That's when he discovered that the weapon in the holster was not his service revolver at all, but the duplicate weapon given to him by his friend. Logan had mixed the weapons up. He knew what he had to do now; retrieving his own gun from the river was a must. Logan took a flashlight down to the stream below the waterfall before daybreak. There was no trace of it. He'd been forced to leave early when he heard voices in the woods.

Logan walked casually in through the back of the station, keeping out of sight. He needed time to think things through. He was glad Jezebel Woods was gone.

"Good morning, Heavy," he said when he passed him in the hallway. "Any news?" He noticed another man sitting across from Heavy; Logan recognized the man as Max Harper, Thomas Brooks' editor. *Why is he here?* Logan thought suspiciously.

"Not much," Heavy replied.

Logan frowned and backed away. He walked toward the printer in the corner. He turned around as if to speak then walked into the lounge.

"Thanks for letting me in earlier," Max Harper said to Heavy. "You don't mind answering a question for me, do you?"

"What is it, Mr. Harper?"

"Before I got cut off, Sheriff Woods asked me why the Edwards family didn't report the crime at their farmhouse. You know the one I'm talking about?"

Heavy nodded.

"Dirk Edwards told me Logan Randall answered the call. Didn't he give a report on it?"

"I'm not sure," Heavy replied. "I can check when the sheriff returns if you'd like."

From the lounge, Logan heard every word said between the two men in the isolated station. Other than the sounds of the impending storm, the town was perfectly quiet. It was deathly quiet, in fact.

"That's odd," Heavy said. "I can't even get the sheriff on the radio. There's nothing but static." Heavy sighed. "Logan, is your cell phone working?" Heavy called out.

Logan walked slowly into the office space. "No," he said, toying with the bottle of sanitizer in his hand. He could see Max Harper watching him carefully. As soon as he looked the editor's way, Harper avoided his gaze. Logan knew something was up. "Sorry I came in late," he said. "This weather is perfect for fishing. I went out early this morning and lost track of time."

"Funny," the old man lazily replied. "I didn't know you liked to fish."

Logan realized his lie was indeed a poor one and returned the sanitizer to his pocket. That was when he noticed the evidence bag on Markham's desk. His gun was inside it. Jezebel Woods hadn't noticed its significance when she picked up the weapon.

Heavy belatedly realized Logan was staring at the revolver, and he followed the man's eyes down to the gun. He looked at the weapon for a few moments, a strange expression lingering on his face. "Where is your service weapon, Logan?" the old man asked. His face was almost white with seriousness.

"Right here at my belt," Logan replied calmly. "Why do you ask?"

"May I see it, please?"

"Of course," Logan replied. The two men stared at each other for what felt like a minute without blinking. Logan saw Heavy inconspicuously sneaking a glance back at his holster draped across the desk.

Logan Randall moved swiftly. He pulled his gun out and fired into Heavy Markham's chest. The old man choked blood and tumbled from his chair, gasping for air. Logan shot him again. The second shot silenced the older deputy's cries.

Max Harper broke for the door as fast as he could. Logan Randall was faster. A single well-placed bullet in the editor's back dropped Max to the ground. Logan fired another shot into the man's skull. He wiped the weapon clean before switching it with his service revolver. The echo of the gunshots melded with echo of the growing thunder rippling across the sky. Logan heard the same sound when he killed Gary Davis.

This time there was no Rick Pepper to pin his crime on. Even though Logan was sure he had taken care of the problem with the gun, it was still possible for Jezebel Woods to link him to the crime, especially if she suspected him already. He would have to kill her as well, and the reporter with her.

Everything was snowballing out of control. It wasn't supposed to be this way. After making his way to the bathroom, Logan cursed loudly. His uniform was splattered with the blood of his victims. He splashed water over his face. The desperate craving for a shower consumed him. He felt filthy.

Logan forced himself to press on, although the irritation of dirtiness dug in his mind like a burr. *It will all be fine,* he told himself. He just needed time to plan everything out.

Outside, the screeching of tires sounded above the storm. Logan moved to the window. As impossibly bad as the timing was, the sheriff had just arrived. He saw her run from the cruiser, holding her own weapon out in the air. She looked fierce in the sweeping winds. Thomas Brooks followed closely behind her, followed by a third woman Logan had never seen before. Fleeing, Logan made his way outside through the back. He needed to get away while he still could.

***

When Jezebel stepped into the shadow-covered station, the pale light above fizzled and then went out.

"Heavy!" she called. "Are you there?"

There was no answer. They were alone in the station.

"Oh God," Thomas cried out. "Max!" He ran over to a body on the floor.

"We're too late," Jezebel said. She looked at the corpse of Heavy Markham. Anger boiled within her. She knew who did this, and he was going to pay.

She glanced over at Thomas, who looked numb, likely a reaction to all they'd witnessed recently. In contrast, Eve seemed palpably shocked. She paced back and forth, muttering to herself. Jezebel fought back her own rage toward Logan and started to say a word of comfort on Eve's behalf, but Thomas interrupted her.

"You might want to look at this," he said. He stood at Heavy's bloodied desk. "These are the phone records for your Deputy Randall. It looks like someone put in a phone call to Gary Davis on the night his family was killed. If that's not suspicious, I don't know what is."

"I'm sure he wiped the weapon," Jezebel commented. "Whatever else he may be, he's not stupid." She stood up and walked over to the desk. "Get back," she added before kicking the door open to Logan Randall's office.

The room was empty.

"He isn't here," Thomas said.

"These bodies haven't been here long," Eve said. "We spoke with your editor less than fifteen minutes ago, which means he couldn't have gotten far."

"Good work," Thomas said to Eve, trying to ascertain her current state of mind. She seemed skeptical of everything he told her about Salem Alistair, even though he omitted the most fantastical elements of the story.

The look on Jezebel's face pulled his attention away from Eve. He didn't know how close Jezebel was to Heavy Markham, but she looked devastated by his death. Thomas could relate. The man who gave him a second chance was dead. Max died while helping Thomas with the same case that led to his untimely demise.

Something else worried Thomas too, and it stopped him from going over to console the sheriff. The book he read in the Thistlewood library said the pagan settlers claimed that blood sacrifices strengthened the entity worshiped by the early settlers of Gray Hollow. Two more people were now dead. Inside the station, all the electricity was out. Their cell phones weren't working. Outside, it was almost pitch black.

"You two," he heard Eve say. "We may have other problems to worry about."

Jezebel and Thomas saw her point out the window. Crows filled the blackening sky, flocking from every direction. In the streets, dozens of scarecrows emerged from the shadows.

***

Chuck Howard was almost home free. For the better part of an hour, he had been certain he was going to die. Lost on the backcountry roads, he could see the mounting storm in his rearview mirror.

Now, as he sped through the town, the nightmarish landscape was nearly behind him. He could see the massive bridge leading out of Gray Hollow in the distance. The crows were too far behind to pursue the vehicle over the bridge.

In the rearview mirror, he could see several scarecrows walking into the town. Chuck no longer cared how he was going to explain this to his uncle. He only wanted to live. The van left the barren road behind and passed onto the old bridge.

Then a wall of blackness plummeted from the sky and surrounded the bridge, forming a wall of pure shadow in the bridge's center. Chuck cried out, unable to see the city on the other side through the fog. He felt the bridge splinter and give way under the weight of the black presence. Chuck felt around for his seatbelt, but it was too late. The van tumbled into the icy depths of the lake below. His screams died when he hit the water.

***

Inside the forest, the Keeper of the Crows stepped free; now that all was darkness, there were no shadows. There was nothing to keep him from sacrificing all the people in the town.

But first, there was still the matter of revenge to attend to.

Chapter TWENTY

The wind pounded against the exterior of the Clayhorn Feed Mill. Joel Grayson went outside to secure loose bags of grain in case of rain. The threatening sky raged above as layers of black clouds blotted out the sun. Joel felt a chill coming on. He pulled on a pair of gloves and grabbed one of the heavy bags.

He could've used help, but Luke Jesse didn't show up for his shift. In fact, he hadn't even called. Joel frowned as he hoisted another bag over his shoulder. It wasn't like Luke to be this irresponsible. He intended to talk to Judy about it. Despite the storm, Joel's eyes brightened when he thought of Judy Conway. The two had grown much closer in the years since the mill owner first hired him.

The wind picked up again, howling with each new attempt to penetrate the mill's walls. The storm almost seemed alive. Even though it was only a few hours into the afternoon, Joel knew it was time to close up shop. There were no customers, and there weren't likely to be any more in this weather.

I should go check on Judy, he thought. Joel glanced back at his truck. The radio sat lifelessly on the counter inside the store, full of nothing but dead air. Joel wondered if a tornado was on the way.

"Al," he shouted, in an effort to rouse Al Pittman. The homeless man had slept behind the building again last night. Joel wasn't sure how Al could stand the biting cold, but he didn't have the heart to wake the man. With the storm approaching, he decided it was better to make sure Al was safe.

"We need to get inside!" he yelled. When Joel rounded the corner, Al was gone.

What on earth? Other than sheltered bags of grain, mulch, and seeds, he saw no trace of the homeless man. Then he saw something standing in the shadows at the edge of the forest behind the mill. As Joel walked in its direction, the figure slipped behind a tree.

"Al," he said, starting to get angry. "We don't have time for this." Joel could see his own breath. "Come out of there."

He squinted to see farther into the darkness and he saw Al's body lying on the ground in a heap, a frozen expression of horror on his face.

A scarecrow stepped out from behind the nearby tree, its hands covered in blood.

***

Jezebel's eyes mirrored the swarming darkness outside the window. Her face tightened with resolve.

"Come on," she said to her companions. Thomas and Eve went after her, stepping over the dead bodies on the floor. After sliding a large key into a door near the back of the station, Jezebel used her flashlight to illuminate the room.

"This is the armory," Jezebel said. "I hope you both know how to use a weapon."

"I do," Thomas said. "I can show Eve," he added. He looked at his ex-girlfriend. Eve appeared shaken by the sight of the monsters lurking outside and the dead bodies in their midst.

"This doesn't make any sense," she whispered. Her shaky voice grew stronger. "Things like this just don't happen."

"The scarecrows are alive," Jezebel said plainly. "There is no other explanation." Eve started to protest, gave up, and fell silent. Wasting no time, Jezebel began loading rifles, shotguns, and ammunition into a duffel bag on the floor.

"You know the rifles might not be enough to keep the scarecrows back," Thomas said. He recalled their last encounter with the monsters all too well.

"Maybe not," Jezebel replied. "But the guns might slow them down long enough for us to get to the novelty store."

Thomas looked around the room. As he picked up a revolver, a thought occurred to him.

"Get the flare guns," he said. "We know they're vulnerable to fire."

"Good idea, but be sure to conserve them. We don't have many."

From the shadowed room, the three could hear the swelling storm gathering around the town.

"What are you planning to do?" Eve demanded. "What are these things?"

Jezebel was busy adding lighter fluid canisters to the duffel bag, so Thomas decided to answer Eve's question. "They were built by Salem Alistair. Now they've come to life. One of the scarecrows seems to be human underneath. I think he's behind this, although I'm not sure we want to run into him again." Thomas stuffed the pistol in his belt and picked up a shotgun. He looked at Jezebel. "Do you still think Percy Durer knows what's going on?"

"If anyone can help us, it's him," Jezebel said as she zipped up the duffel bag. She tossed both reporters flashlights. "He knows more than he told me. I could see it in his eyes when we spoke. I'll understand if you don't want to go with me." She stopped and gazed down at the floor. "Logan Randall is still out there somewhere. There's no telling what he plans for us. You're not from Gray Hollow, either of you. What happened to Salem . . . it's my responsibility to protect these people, and mine alone."

Thomas stopped her. "I'm not going anywhere. I told you when we first met that you weren't going to be able to get rid of me, and I meant it. You are one of the most stubborn people I've ever encountered, but you're not doing this alone."

Her eyes moistened. At that moment, Thomas finally realized how alone the sheriff truly felt. Jezebel had blamed herself for the probable death of Salem Alistair for years. She devoted her entire life to protecting others to compensate for that guilt, in effect punishing herself by not living her own life. Thomas understood that guilt better than most.

He wrapped his arms around her and hugged her close to him. They stood locked in a tight embrace for all too brief a time before Jezebel pulled away. Thomas was sure Eve was staring at them with righteous indignation.

"Thank you," Jezebel said. "Now let's get out of here while there's still some light in the sky." The three ran out into the sweeping winds toward Jezebel's car. Thomas took a few moments to show Eve how to use the gun. There was no anger in her expression, only another look of regret.

"I'm sorry," he thought he heard her whisper. He couldn't hear her above the sound of the thunder. Although Eve flew from New York for a reason, Thomas was now afraid to know what it was. She seemed on the precipice of saying something but stiffened each time he looked at her. He decided to give her time. If she had something important to say, she would tell him eventually.

"Stay in the light," Thomas yelled. "For as long as you can, anyway."

"Why the light?" Eve asked as she looked up at the sky. Night surrounded Gray Hollow in a circle that was growing closer to the town square by the second. There was only a sliver of gray light remaining in the center of town, looming like the eye of a storm.

"Every time we've encountered these scarecrows, it was night," Jezebel said. "Each of the murders occurred when the sun was down."

They continued racing toward the police car parked nearby. Just as Eve started to climb into the passenger door, an immense flock of crows rose from the roof of the station behind them. Thomas saw the crows flow into the air like a living cloud. He was too far away to reach her in time.

"Get down!" he shouted. Eve spun around and found herself face to face with the impending attack. She pulled the trigger of the gun Thomas gave her. The gun was silent, and she realized she had forgotten to turn the safety off.

Jezebel tackled Eve to the ground before the swarm could reach her. The flock tore into the cruiser instead and crashed through the windows. Unlike the scarecrows, the birds did not appear to be inhibited by the light. Thomas fired the shotgun repeatedly into the air to provide cover for the two women by the car.

"Go!" he shouted as some of the dead crows dropped from the sky. Jezebel swung the duffel bag back across her shoulders and ran with Eve across the parking lot. The swarm of crows spread off into the sky, vanishing into the blackness that continued growing closer.

"Thank you," Eve said weakly to Jezebel.

"We need to get out of here before they come back," Jezebel said with a nod.

"I'm not sure they're coming back," Thomas said. "At least not yet. The scarecrows seem to be able to think for themselves, but I don't think the crows are that smart." He wasn't completely convinced of his theory, but at the moment it was all he had to go on.

"Durer's shop is on Old Main Street. That's several blocks from here. We have to hurry." Jezebel looked at the battered cruiser. "It looks like we'll have to go on foot, for now. Until we can get another vehicle."

The three ran down the deserted street. Thomas searched for any trace of life. He saw one frightened man through the glass windowpane of the grocery store. There were also screams in the distance where the scarecrows roamed freely.

As they hurried away from the station, Thomas noticed the dark cloud envelop the building. The three ran toward the park outside the station. They were careful to remain in the ever-shrinking light outside the stores at the end of the town square.

The crows returned. Shrieking, the birds dived toward them. Thomas and Jezebel discharged their weapons into the air, which scared the crows away.

"Look out!" Eve shouted. One of the scarecrows had noticed the gunshot and was now lumbering toward them. Thomas fired his shotgun. As the blast knocked the creature back, a blunt instrument struck Thomas across the face. He dropped his weapon and fell to the ground. A second scarecrow stood nearby. The creature swung a wooden club at him, which barely missed him. Eve shot at the monster with her pistol, but the bullet merely passed through straw.

"Thomas!" Jezebel yelled. As she lifted her shotgun to blast the creature away, yet another scarecrow burst out of the window of the department store on her left. Jezebel spun around and fired. The shot took one of its legs off. Jezebel dropped the duffel bag and started to run toward Thomas. From the ground, the damaged scarecrow wrapped its gloved fingers around her ankle. Jezebel tripped and fell against the hood of a car. She tried desperately to pry herself free of the creature's grip.

"Get back!" Eve shouted, firing one of the flare guns from the duffel bag at the monster's back. The scarecrow erupted into flames. Now free, Jezebel dived for her shotgun. She shot the next scarecrow with the weapon, ripping it to shreds.

Separated from the others, Thomas crawled under the belly of an abandoned van at a nearby gas station. He could see his pursuer pacing around the van, dragging its club on the ground. He prayed the scarecrow couldn't see him. Gasoline trickled from several nozzles, left unattended by customers who had fled when they first saw the scarecrows approaching. The gasoline formed a stream flowing from the gas station.

Not all the customers had escaped; from underneath the car, Thomas saw at least two dead bodies. More screams rang out in the background, and he could see a small group of people scurrying for their lives. More scarecrows spilled onto the street by the second, drawn by the unseen force responsible for the chaos. There were more of them than Thomas thought possible.

Thomas blinked and looked again for the scarecrow. He stuck his head out from under the vehicle. Was the creature gone? Suddenly, he found himself staring into its terrifying, stitched eyes. The monster reached under the van and pulled him out. He kicked the scarecrow in the chest, and the monster stumbled back. Although the creature was strong, it was nowhere close to the thing that had almost choked him to death at the Daniels Farm.

Spurred on by a burst of strength, Thomas seized the club and in one fluid motion struck the monster's body with enough force to remove its head. He dropped the club, pulled out his gun, and ran over to his friends. Jezebel and Eve were firing into a wall of twelve advancing scarecrows. Even with his help, they were hopelessly outnumbered.

"I'm out!" Eve shouted, looking down at her weapon. There was no time to reload.

"Use one of the flares," Jezebel said.

The scarecrows surrounded them in a semicircle. Their horrific faces remained frozen in twisted grins, all staring at the three people stranded in the heart of the town. A figure approached in the distance.

"You," Thomas muttered. The scarecrows parted in the middle, allowing a tall figure to pass through. The jack o' lantern head seemed to glow supernaturally, as did the eyes of the crows perched on the living scarecrow's shoulders.

"The time has come," the Keeper hissed. "For Gray Hollow to be cleansed. The crows will feast on the flesh of all its inhabitants, and the darkness will be sated." In his right hand was a razor-sharp scythe.

"Who are you?" Jezebel whispered. She stared at the monster with an intensity Thomas had never seen.

"Don't you recognize me?" the monster replied. "It's me, Jezzie."

"No," she stammered. Her eyes went wide with shock. "You can't be . . ."

"Alive? Your friends took care of that. They buried me alive while you had fun at Cavern Lake. You said you would protect me. You shouldn't make promises you can't keep."

"I'm sorry, Salem," she whispered, rooted to the spot.

Thomas watched her carefully. Whatever this creature was, Salem Alistair or not, his words were evil. He was paralyzing the sheriff with her own guilt. When the Keeper was finished toying with them, Thomas was sure Salem would kill them all. He inched away and moved back toward the van parked under the gas station. He had a plan.

"You failed me when I needed you most," the Keeper said to Jezebel. Then you forgot about me, never even bothering to search."

"I thought you were dead."

"My corpse lay in the cornfield, trapped. The spirit of the forest kept my heart beating, combining my body with its power. Now I am the Keeper of the Crows. My vengeance is at hand. The harvest will be reaped."

"This isn't you," Jezebel whispered. There were tears in her eyes. "Don't do this. You aren't evil."

"I will plunge Gray Hollow into eternal darkness. Already the bridge to the lake has been destroyed. Any attempt to escape through the roads on the other side of town will be in vain. The very forests themselves answer to me, with the branches, vines, and thorns. Just like you failed to protect me, you will fail to protect this town." The Keeper raised the scythe in the night sky. Jezebel remained frozen, unable to move.

Thomas spotted the stream of gasoline leading out from the gas station. He reached into his jacket, careful to avoid being seen by the terrifying sentries. He still had Gary Davis' lighter in his pocket. He pulled it out and started the flame.

"Get back!" Thomas shouted to Jezebel and Eve.

He dropped the lighter. The Keeper's glowing eyes shifted to the ground, and he roared with rage.

Instantly, a wall of flame shot up between Jezebel and the Keeper of the Crows. Thomas grabbed Jezebel and pulled her back just as the gas station exploded. Flames erupted across the street in a brilliant display.

"Grab the duffel bag," he said to Eve while picking up Jezebel's fallen shotgun and pointing it at the scarecrows. The twelve monsters that had surrounded them writhed in pain as their straw bodies turned to ash. The Keeper of the Crows, however, watched them, unharmed, through the flames.

"This isn't over," the Keeper hissed. "There are dozens more of my children roaming Gray Hollow. I will have blood." The red fire was reflected in the Keeper's black eyes. "There is no way out."

Thomas didn't stick around to argue with the thing that was once Salem Alistair. There wasn't time. The wall of flame wouldn't protect them forever, and he was sure of one thing: more scarecrows were coming.

We're not finished yet, Thomas thought. There was still the chance that Percy Durer might be able to help them, although there wasn't time to pursue that lead at the moment.

At least they were alive, albeit temporarily. Eve looked worried, but she was unharmed and reasonably self-possessed. Jezebel, on the other hand, was stunned. The fierceness about her he had long admired was shattered.

"Make sure she keeps going," Thomas said to Eve. Eve nodded and wrapped an arm around Jezebel's shoulders. She continued glancing back as they retreated farther into the heart of the town. They ran through the park, which was fortunately devoid of scarecrows. The unnatural darkness spread across almost the whole city and was on the verge of covering Gray Hollow completely.

"The courthouse!" Thomas shouted. He ran as fast as his legs could carry him. In the very center of the town, it would be the perfect place to regroup and make a temporary shelter.

"Thomas!" Eve yelled when they had almost reached the courthouse.

A new cloud of crows swarmed toward them, easily passing over the wall of flame.

Chapter TWENTY-ONE

Abandoning any pretext of shooting at the storm of crows quickly approaching, Thomas raced over to the park trail leading to the courthouse. He could hear his heartbeat echo over the sound of the storm. By the time the three neared the doors of the courthouse, the birds were almost upon them.

He wrenched the doors open and made sure Eve and Jezebel got through safely before pulling them shut. A screeching sound reverberated outside when the wave of crows broke against the building. The thick glass doors mercifully remained intact.

"I think the doors are bulletproof," Eve said. She tapped against the thick glass with her fist. "Thank God. I didn't think this small town would have that kind of security." Eve's arm was wrapped around Jezebel, who remained in a trance.

"The birds are leaving," Thomas muttered. He backed away and kept his eyes on the front door. They passed through a second set of doors and walked carefully into the quiet building. The lights were shut off. Thomas suspected the power was out across Gray Hollow.

They were safe for now. He didn't know how much longer that would last. The gleam of light above the courthouse was fading fast. Despite making it to safety, Thomas couldn't help feeling a sense of defeat.

The trio stood quietly for a moment, unsure of what to do next. Thomas stared outside.

"Come on," he said. "We need to reload."

"This can't be happening," Eve whispered. "Thomas, what happened to the all people running through the streets?" Distant screams had given way to an eerie lull.

"Maybe some of them found refuge," Thomas said doubtfully. "The scarecrows can't be everywhere."

"We're practically still out in the open," Eve replied. "Those things are all over the place. What are we going to do?"

"I don't know. Jezebel, do you still want to make a run for Durer's shop?"

Jezebel didn't respond. Instead she slumped against the wall and sank to the floor.

Eve pulled him aside. "Let her be. She needs time."

"We may not *have* time," Thomas said. "Every second we wait the darkness grows closer to this building." Thomas inspected the area, searching for any trace of life. His footsteps echoed loudly in the silent hallway. He clutched the gun in his hand, ready to use it.

Eve followed behind him. "If we're running out of time, there's something I want to tell you," she said.

Thomas was unable to see her face clearly in the shadowy recesses of the room. "Are you sure this is the best time?" he asked. Jezebel was already in a state of shock; he wasn't sure he could handle a new revelation from Eve.

"There might not be another chance," she said. "I just wanted to tell you that you were right."

"About what?"

"About everything that happened between us," she replied.

"What?"

"When your sources were exposed, the fallout was too much for me to handle. I didn't want to deal with it. Leaving you gave me an out."

Thomas wanted to tell her that such details didn't matter when their lives were in jeopardy, but he couldn't say the words. If she had stayed by his side, he might have never come to Gray Hollow.

I needed you, he wanted to say. *And you gave up on me.* Thomas shook his head. "I can't do this right now." He turned back toward the center of the room.

"You have to know," Eve replied. She caught up with him. "I tried to tell myself that it was your fault. It was easy to think you couldn't get over the past. I made myself believe that you became too bitter after you were fired. In the end, I just didn't want to be with someone who was in disgrace. I wanted to make sure that *my* career stayed on track. So I tried to cut you out and get on with my life."

"Eve—"

"It didn't work, Thomas. No one else could help me forget you, not even for a second. Suddenly, my career didn't seem as important either. When you called me, I wanted to block you out, but I couldn't. That's why I followed you here."

Thomas hadn't expected this. "Eve, I—"

He heard footsteps approaching, bent down, and looked around the corner. There wasn't a hint of movement in the corridor. Thomas glanced up at Eve.

"Wasn't that door shut a few seconds ago?" he whispered.

Eve nodded. "Someone followed us here." The words hung in the air.

"Get Jezebel up the stairs," he whispered to Eve. "I'll be right behind you." He reloaded the revolver, looked for a trace of anyone in the hallway, and then scurried up the staircase after the two women. As he made it to the top, he saw Logan Randall emerge from the shadows. Logan's uniform was covered in blood. The two men made eye contact, and a cruel grin spread over the deputy's face.

***

"I told you that you would regret getting in my way," Logan said. He knew he was becoming unhinged. The filth covering him gnawed at his mind like a rabid animal.

Logan had followed Jezebel and the others from the station, watching from the safety of the back alleys while they fought for survival against the scarecrows.

When Thomas turned and ran, Logan continued moving at a constant pace. There was nowhere for him to go.

Scarecrows, he thought, unable to believe what he saw. They were the creatures that killed Jeffrey Daniels, Rick

Pepper, and Paul Morris. Gary was telling the truth all along, and Logan had killed him for it. The world had gone mad. Salem's scarecrows always disgusted him, but he never imagined in his wildest fears that they would rise to life. Logan had also heard the words of the thing claiming to be Salem Alistair.

Why couldn't the freak stay dead? Logan thought as he advanced up the stairs. The deputy would just have to put him back in the ground after he took care of Jezebel and the others. With all the chaos, there would be no way anyone would be able to tie the murders back to him.

***

Thomas tried opening a door at the top of the stairs. It was locked. Spotting the open door to Judge Underhill's office, he led the other two inside. Logan's footsteps echoed against the stairs.

"It's Logan Randall," he whispered to the others. "He's coming." At the mention of the deputy's name, Jezebel seemed to snap to life.

"Logan?" she asked. "Here?" Her anger overrode the impact of Salem's haunting words, and she grabbed the revolver at her side.

"Yes," Thomas whispered. "Are you OK?"

"No," the sheriff replied. "I keep hearing Salem's voice inside my head. It's all I can think about."

"You saw that thing for yourself. Whoever the Keeper of the Crows is, he's *not* your friend."

"Salem is in there somewhere. This thing has twisted him into something evil."

"Forget about your friend," Eve said. "There are too many of those monsters for us to fight. We don't even know if Durer can help us. Maybe we should just try to leave. The sun has to come out eventually. If we can get out of Gray Hollow, the scarecrows may not be able to follow us."

"You heard that thing," Thomas replied, his eyes searching for a sign of movement. The sound of footsteps stopped. "There's no way out."

"Don't move," a dry voice ordered. Logan Randall crept out of the darkness and pointed his gun at Eve. "Drop your weapons," he said to Jezebel and Thomas.

"Don't do it, Thomas," Jezebel said. She kept her gun trained on the deputy. "He'll kill her anyway, and us too."

Thomas couldn't take that chance. He saw the fear in Eve's eyes, and the madness in Logan's. He released his grip on the gun. The weapon clattered to the floor. Now Randall pointed his gun at Thomas.

"I'll kill him," he said to Jezebel. "You know I will."

Jezebel weighed her options carefully. "How could you do it, Logan? Salem was just a defenseless boy. He never harmed anyone in his life."

"We didn't mean to kill the little freak," Logan spat. "It was a prank. By the time we figured out he was dead, it was too late. That's why I had to kill Gary. He was going to tell everyone what had happened. You think I *wanted* to kill him? Gary was my friend."

"Some friend," Thomas muttered.

Logan snarled. "I wasn't about to spend the rest of my life in prison because Gary suddenly grew a conscience. I'm a survivor. That's what separates me from people like you and Salem Alistair. You wouldn't understand that, city boy."

"Stop," Eve pleaded. "You don't have to do this."

"Oh, but I do. In fact, I'm looking forward to it. If it weren't for this stupid reporter sticking his nose where it didn't belong, I wouldn't even be in this position right now. You deserve what's coming. Now put down the gun, Jezebel."

Suddenly, an explosion rocked the room. Logan Randall stumbled forward, a red hole in his shoulder. Behind him, Judge Underhill stood at his desk, a gun in his hand.

"You?" Logan questioned with wide eyes. He tried to raise the gun again at Thomas, and Jezebel ran at him and pushed him through the window. Shattered glass flew everywhere. Logan Randall landed on the ground two stories below with a thud.

The judge walked to the window, where the deputy was moaning weakly below.

"He's alive," Eve said.

"Not for long," Thomas responded. He knew what was coming, and he suspected Logan did, too. "Not once the Keeper gets here."

"Who?" Judge Underhill asked.

"The creature responsible for this chaos," Jezebel said. "Salem Alistair."

"Salem Alistair?" The judge's eyes grew wide. "That's impossible—he's dead."

"Have you seen what's going on out there?" Thomas asked. "Those scarecrows are his handiwork."

"I heard some reports on the radio before the power went out, but it sounded unbelievable. You can't seriously expect me to believe that inanimate objects have suddenly come to life."

"Up until a little while ago, I wouldn't have believed it either," Eve said.

"Not to change the subject," Thomas interrupted. He looked at the judge suspiciously. "But what are you doing here? The rest of the building is deserted."

"I was hiding when you came in. While you were talking, I saw Logan Randall approaching with a gun. As it so happens, I'm a strong believer in the Second Amendment."

"We need to get out of here before Salem returns," Jezebel said. She glanced out the broken window. "We can't cover the distance on foot."

"We don't have to," Judge Underhill replied. He brandished a set of keys.

"Let's go," Jezebel said, and the group hurried down the stairs. Outside, the final shred of light succumbed to the darkness. Two scarecrows lumbered through the parking lot, searching for prey.

Thomas threw open the courthouse doors.

"Now!" he shouted. They raced through the parking lot. The scarecrows quickly followed, moving with inhuman speed. As Judge Underhill tossed the keys to Jezebel, Thomas and Eve fired at the monsters repeatedly. Each shot missed, and the creatures grew closer to the group.

"Get in!" Jezebel yelled. The engine roared to life.

***

From the ground, Logan Randall watched the car speed away, its lights tearing through the night. The scarecrows chased after it but proved unable to catch the vehicle. As he crawled across the ground, the deputy fought to stay conscious. His gun lay just out of reach, not that it would do him any good now.

Blood poured from his bullet wound, mixing with blood splattered over his uniform from killing the two men at the station. The wound didn't seem to be fatal. Maybe there was still a chance he could make it out of this yet, if he could find a way to stop the blood loss. He pulled himself along, grunting from the pain of his injuries. Logan couldn't bring himself to look at them. Near the back of the courthouse, he spotted the parking lot. Logan told himself that if he could just get to a vehicle, maybe he could wait out the crisis until the next morning.

A hiss sounded nearby. Suddenly, Logan felt a presence behind him. He cocked his head and searched for the source. When he reached out for the gun, he found himself staring into the demented face of the Keeper of the Crows.

"Stay back!" he screamed. Logan pointed the gun at the Keeper. The black eyes carved into the pumpkin lit up with fire. The monster took a step toward him. Logan fired directly into the Keeper's chest. A black substance like blood oozed from the Keeper's rotten flesh onto the stained patchwork of cloth and straw.

"Logan," the monster hissed, continuing to walk in his direction. "I've waited so long for this moment."

The deputy noticed a long scythe in the monster's hands.

"Get away from me!" Logan shouted. He fired again and again into the Keeper's chest. More black blood leaked outward, failing to deter the thing that was once Salem Alistair.

"You reap what you sow, Logan."

Moments before the jagged metal severed his head from his body, Logan thought he could see the pumpkin's carved smile widen.

"Bury him in the ground," the Keeper hissed, sending the crows to pick the flesh from Logan's body. "As he once buried me." It was a fitting end for Logan. His body would spend eternity in dirt.

There were two lives left to take. Then the Keeper would raze the town to the ground with fire and death.

Chapter TWENTY-TWO

"Stay quiet," Jezebel whispered. She focused the beam from her flashlight across the deserted walkway. "Old Main Street was always tranquil," she muttered. "But now it's practically a ghost town." She knocked as loudly as she dared on the door of the novelty store. There was no response from inside. Like all the other buildings across Gray Hollow, it was pitch black inside.

Thomas wondered how many people were hiding within those dark buildings, praying the scarecrows wouldn't come for them.

When Jezebel was confident Percy Durer would not answer the door, she smashed through the display window with her shotgun.

Thomas cringed at the sound. He half expected to hear the rustling of wings behind them.

"Follow me," Jezebel said before stepping deftly into the store. "Make sure to reload your guns. Be careful with your ammo. It won't be long before we start to run out."

Thomas watched Judge Underhill, who was staring intently at Jezebel.

Under the circumstances it shouldn't have been surprising, but Thomas found something about the judge's demeanor unsettling. Why hadn't Underhill shown himself earlier in the courthouse? More disturbing was the way Logan Randall looked when Underhill shot him. Thomas knew a look of betrayal when he saw it. Still, he kept his suspicions to himself. Now was not the time for accusation

—not when there were scarecrows on every block looking for them.

"Wow," Eve muttered. "This place is almost as eerie as the scarecrows." She brushed a cobweb from the wall. "Who is this Durer guy anyway?"

"He's been around for longer than I can remember," Jezebel said. "He was pretty old even then. To tell you the truth, Durer always frightened me a little. When I asked him about the scarecrows earlier, he almost seemed glad to hear of them. Like he'd been expecting the news." She flashed her light over dusty bookshelves in an effort to find the storekeeper.

"He obviously has issues with décor," Eve replied. She held up a skull-shaped candleholder. "I'm guessing he didn't sell children's books."

Thomas nodded. "You're definitely right about that. Look at some of the books on these shelves. This is some pretty dark stuff."

"We don't have time for this," Judge Underhill said. "You told me Durer was the one who could stop this. You all should be focused on finding him."

"That's what we're doing," Jezebel replied with a frown. "And I said the old man *might* be able to help. No guarantees. Luckily for us, Salem seems to be out for revenge first and foremost, so that ought to buy us some time."

The judge didn't respond. The wary expression remained on his face. The four people split apart and began searching the expansive store individually. They inspected deserted aisles, bookshelves, and rows of antiques.

"What's up here?" Eve asked, pointing to a flight of stairs.

"That's where Durer sleeps," Jezebel answered.

***

Eve looked shocked. "He actually *lives* in this place? Creepy." She walked up the staircase while Thomas followed Jezebel into the back of the store. Eve wasn't sure if it was primarily out of jealousy or fear, but she wished Thomas had followed her. She eased the creaky door handle open to the storekeeper's room.

"Mr. Durer?" Eve asked. She shined the flashlight into Durer's bedroom. "Are you here?" There was no one inside empty room. Percy Durer's room was even more disturbing than the floor below, if that was even possible. There were hundreds of drawings covering the wooden planks on the walls. Eve walked closer the papers on the wall. She focused the beam on the uneven drawings.

Why did I have to choose this of all days to come here? she wondered.

Her skin crawled as she looked at drawing after drawing. They were all of a cave somewhere in the forest. Durer penciled in blackness pouring out of the cave, stretching outward like an enormous clawed hand. Crows surrounded the cave in most of the pictures. There were also plenty with dead animals outside the cave, where their blood seeped into the earth. Surprisingly, none of the drawings featured scarecrows at all.

"Gross," she said. She snatched a few of the pictures off the wall. The others would want to see this. Some kind of bird skeleton was nailed to the wall above Durer's bed. Eve was willing to bet that it belonged to a crow. There were several chalices next to a group of candles on a wooden cabinet. She didn't even want to know what was in the cups. Shining her light on the opposite end of the room, Eve spotted a wooden desk.

What's this? she thought. The desk was covered in old papers, manuscripts, and books. One stack of papers seemed to be the storekeeper's financial records, which were full of useless information. Some of the texts were in a strange dialect that she was unable to decipher. When she cleared the papers away from the center of the desk, Eve discovered something new.

It was a book, or at least it looked like one. Like many of the antiques in the novelty store, the brown leather binding of the book was faded. She trained the beam of light on the words on the cover. *The Keeper of the Crows,* read the title.

"Bingo," Eve whispered, flipping through the pages. They all appeared to be handwritten, mostly in cursive. Durer's handwriting was at times neat, other times erratic. Several pages depicted drawings of ritual circles and strange symbols. Eve also saw an odd-looking map spread over two pages near the center of the book. She tucked the book into a bag and left the eerie bedroom.

***

Thomas could hear Eve's footsteps above as he followed the sheriff down the stairs. He was no longer thinking about the disquieting behavior of Judge Underhill. Instead, he was preoccupied with the concerned expression on Jezebel's face. It was easy to guess why she was worried. If Percy Durer was inside the store and had not responded to them, there was a chance he was gone. Even if he was, there was also a chance he was dangerous, given all Jezebel had said about the man. In searching for a way out of their current predicament, it was possible they placed themselves in even greater danger.

"Be careful down here," Jezebel whispered. She gazed into his eyes in the dim light. The door was already open. "The last time I was down here, Durer showed me his collection of Salem's scarecrows. They could still be here."

"Now you tell me," he said weakly. Thomas held out his flashlight to light the way for her.

"Mr. Durer?" Jezebel asked. "Are you here?"

The small room had been overturned. Unlike the largely undisturbed and deserted levels above, Durer's secret room was covered in ripped paper and broken antiques. Jezebel's light came to rest on top of two overturned shelves splintered on the floor.

"Over here," she whispered to Thomas. Together, the two propped the shelves up, exposing the body of Percy Durer. The dead man's expression was frozen in a look of pure horror. Dried blood streaked out from multiple wounds over his chest.

"These are stab wounds," the sheriff said. She moved over to the front of a series of shelves for a better view.

"My guess is someone or something didn't want Durer talking," Thomas said. "That means you were right. He must have known something important."

"Now we'll never know," Jezebel said. She sighed.

Time was running out, and they were no closer to destroying the evil cloaking the town.

While she spoke, a dark figure sitting in the shelf behind her stretched out a withered hand in her direction. Thomas saw the scarecrow's face looming behind her before Jezebel noticed. As he swung the flare gun up to shoot the creature, a knife stabbed his left arm. The flashlight hit the ground and went out. Reeling in pain, Thomas fired the flare gun blindly. The light from the gun temporarily illuminated the room. Two more scarecrows rose from the dark corners of the secret room. Another stood behind him with a knife. Jezebel pushed the shelf over, which collapsed on the scarecrow holding the blade.

"We have to get out of here!" Thomas shouted. The two ran swiftly up the stairs, the sounds of the creatures following behind them. Then Jezebel tripped on an old step, dropping both her gun and flashlight. Thomas saw Judge Underhill in the shadows. The man was staring dispassionately at Jezebel, holding a flare gun. The scarecrows passed through the doorframe and began walking up the stairs.

"What are you waiting for?" Thomas shouted incredulously. "Shoot them!" The judge didn't move. Running as fast as he could, Thomas doubled back and grabbed Jezebel's hand as one of the withered scarecrow hands wrapped itself around her ankle. Pulling furiously, Thomas barely managed to free Jezebel from the creature's grip.

"What's going on?" Eve asked. She raced up to them from the other side of the store.

"Run!" Thomas and Jezebel shouted in unison. The four took off for the car outside. Thomas was glad Jezebel took the chance of leaving the engine running. He could see the scarecrows through the window as the sheriff shifted the vehicle into gear. Sitting in the back seat, Thomas looked up at Underhill with eyes full of rage.

"Why didn't you shoot?" Thomas shouted. "She could have been killed!"

"It wasn't my fault," the judge said tensely. "I froze."

"It's OK," Jezebel said. "We're all alive, aren't we?"

"Where are we going?" Underhill asked.

"I don't know," Jezebel answered. "Getting to Durer was as far as my plan went."

"Did you find anything downstairs?" Eve asked. "Other than the scarecrows, I mean."

"Durer was dead," Thomas said. "He was murdered by the scarecrows in the basement, which means his secrets died with him."

"That's not entirely true," Eve replied. She held up a faded book for him to see. "I have his journal right here. It's called *The Keeper of the Crows,* so I think it might have what we need."

"I never thought I'd say this," Jezebel said. "But thank God your girlfriend decided to tag along."

"Ex-girlfriend," Thomas repeated, correcting her again. He glanced back at Eve. "What does it say?"

She flipped through the pages. "That's a bit trickier. Durer wrote in this thing for a long time, judging by the age of the book. A lot of his words are incoherent. Apparently, he believed that Salem Alistair possessed latent psychic powers. This included the ability to give life to nonliving things."

"Creation?" Thomas asked.

Eve shook her head. "More like the ability to animate things already in existence with his own consciousness."

"I guess that makes sense," Thomas said. "He called them his 'children' earlier."

"Right. Durer also worshipped an entity in the forest he called the Keeper of the Crows." She held up a few of the drawings from inside the old man's room. "I think this spirit is what's controlling Salem."

Thomas considered the words. "I think the killings are making the spirit stronger. If that's true, there's no telling what an army of scarecrows could provide."

"When we were kids, Salem used to tell me about something that wanted him in the forest," Jezebel said. "It scared him. Then tonight, Salem told me the spirit kept him alive after he was murdered. Don't forget, he called himself the Keeper of the Crows."

"Does it have anything to do with the pagan sacrifices of the early settlers here?" Thomas asked. "They were worshiping some type of demon, too."

"The book doesn't say a lot that identifies the entity Durer worshiped. From what it sounds like, the spirit can't possess anyone."

"It didn't possess him," Thomas said. "Salem Alistair was murdered by Logan Randall and his friends."

"Then the spirit must have corrupted his body," Jezebel said. "That thing we met claimed it wasn't the spirit of the forest, but it's not Salem Alistair either. It may have his memories and his brain, but the Salem I know would never have done any of this. He's been changed somehow."

"Then we have to stop him," Judge Underhill replied, breaking his silence. "By whatever means necessary. *That's* what you should be looking for in that book, miss."

"That's what I'm working on," Eve said, shooting him a look. "It's not as easy as it seems, especially in a moving car."

Thomas put his hand on her shoulder. "Relax. Just take your time."

The judge shook his head. "I suggest you hurry. If what you've said is true, this monster isn't going to stop until it has done whatever it takes to destroy you."

Suddenly, Jezebel slammed down on the brakes. As the car came to a screeching halt, she turned the steering wheel around and directed the car in the opposite direction.

"What are you doing?" Thomas asked.

"My mom!" Jezebel exclaimed. "If Salem still recognizes me, he'll remember who she is too."

"That doesn't mean he's going after her," Eve replied. "Maybe he doesn't even know where she is."

"Remember the crows? The Keeper has eyes all over the city," Thomas said. "He knows. Hand me the duffel bag."

"We should be focusing on getting out of here, not walking into the belly of the beast!" Judge Underhill protested. "If the Keeper was there, you would just be walking into a trap."

"If it was your mother, what would you do?" Jezebel asked.

Underhill didn't reply. Even Eve looked skeptical.

"We're going to save her, end of story," Thomas said. Jezebel glanced back with the ghost of a smile on her lips, her face full of relief.

There was silence in the vehicle for the next several minutes. Eve sat staring at the book in her lap, the beam of her flashlight positioned steadily over the old pages. The sheriff gripped the wheel tightly, and her eyes remained trained on the road ahead. Within minutes, the car was moving down a winding country road. Thomas gazed out at the dark landscape. Soon Jezebel turned off the road back toward a town street. With each house they passed, Thomas hoped any families hiding inside the homes were safe.

"You're right about the killings," Eve said. "Durer claims that the offering of blood strengthens the spirit of the cave. All of the murders only serve to make it more powerful. He also appears to claim that sacrificing life to the creature keeps you safe from harm."

"Really?" Thomas asked. "Let me see."

As often as I could, I would bring live food to the dark forest, read the passage. *There I would kill the animal, leaving its corpse for the crows. I have never dared to enter the cave.*

Thomas looked back at the pictures of the cave in the forest, which Eve had collected in the storekeeper's room. If Durer knew where the spirit's cave was, it was possible he left instructions on how to reach it.

"Those sacrifices didn't protect Durer in the end, though," Thomas said. "He was still murdered by the scarecrows."

"Unless," Judge Underhill said. "The spirit wanted *human* lives. Logan killed Gary Davis, and Salem seems to have left him unharmed."

Thomas doubted that very much indeed.

"It doesn't matter," Thomas said. "Even if we knew for sure that the sacrifices *would* keep us safe, none of us are about to murder innocent people."

The judge looked away.

"The question is," Eve said. "Which of them do we fight? Do we go after Salem Alistair or the spirit of the forest?"

"I'm not sure we're capable of fighting any of them," Thomas replied. "We don't even know where the Keeper's cave is. Seeking out Salem Alistair doesn't sound like such a good idea either."

***

Streaming winds pounded against the car, covering it with leaves that were in seemingly perpetual motion. Large trees looked onward in the back yards of the small houses on either side of the road, watchful guardians of the forest growing ever closer. Jezebel suddenly slammed on the brakes in front of a lonely white house. Light from the headlights spilled over the broken wooden fence.

"We're here," Jezebel said. She grabbed her gun. Thomas turned to Eve.

"Wait for us in the driver's seat," he said. "If this is a trap, we're going to need you to be ready."

"You can forget that," Eve said. "You're not leaving me. Not when these monsters are walking around."

"Don't worry," Judge Underhill said. "I'm happy to stay here where it's safe." He slid out of the passenger seat and walked to the front of the vehicle.

Jezebel broke out into a run toward her mother's house. Thomas and Eve took off after her, keeping their flashlights off.

"Be careful," Thomas said as Jezebel removed her keys from her pocket. "We need to be as quiet as possible." The wind picked up against the house. To Jezebel's surprise, the door swung open. It was already unlocked.

"Mom?" she whispered urgently, hoping that her mother didn't share the same fate as Percy Durer. In her heart, she still couldn't believe that Salem was capable of this. Surely he wouldn't kill her mother if there was even a shred of goodness left in him.

"She's not in the bedroom," Thomas whispered. With the rustling of the wind outside, they could hear nothing other than the sound of their own footsteps. It was too quiet. Thomas glanced back at the car.

"Underhill is gone," he whispered. "Jezebel, how did he know that Logan Randall killed Gary Davis?"

The sheriff froze. "I never told him that," she whispered. It briefly occurred to her that there was still a piece that didn't fit, but she didn't have the time to worry about it.

"Over here," Eve whispered. She pointed at the kitchen door. It too was hanging wide open. "Look outside."

Thomas pointed to a thin figure standing just outside the forest. Flipping on his light, Jezebel saw Emma Woods hovering under the large oak trees in the back yard. The frail woman's arms were stretched out, her nightgown swaying to and fro in the harsh winds.

"Mom!" Jezebel shouted. She tore out of the house in the direction of her mother. She was mere feet from her mother when Emma's body tumbled to the ground, revealing the Keeper of the Crows standing behind her.

Chapter TWENTY-THREE

The carved eyes of the pumpkin blazed in the darkness. Jezebel pulled out her gun, and the Keeper watched her gaze shift to the body at his feet. The Keeper remained in place, his uneven smile mocking her. Hundreds of crows flew overhead.

"I knew you would come. Best of all, you brought your friends straight to me. Along with that book." He looked up at Eve, taking in her startled expression.

"Yes, I know all about Durer's book. There is nothing I do not see. The very birds in the sky are my spies. The old fool was clever enough to record his knowledge, little good it did him. Give me the book, woman, and join your friends in death."

Jezebel howled in rage and lunged at the Keeper. He moved with inhuman speed and struck her in the shoulder, knocking her back against the ground. Tree roots burst out of the ground and wrapped themselves around her legs.

"You killed my mother, Salem! How could you?"

"You don't listen, do you? Although we share memories, I am not Salem Alistair. He lost control of his body the day you failed him. The day I was born."

The Keeper was so focused on Jezebel he failed to notice the two others moving closer.

"Cover me," Thomas whispered to Eve. He ran forward, firing at the scarecrow from his revolver. At the sound of the gunshots, the monster shrieked in anger. The Keeper's straw hands shot out at Thomas. He ducked under the first blow, but a root curled around his foot, causing him to stumble, and the next fist struck him in the abdomen. He was lifted into the air by the blow. The duffel bag fell a few inches away, just out of his reach. Thomas scrambled for the bag and used all his strength to pull the root farther out of the ground.

"Hand over the book," the Keeper hissed. "Or your friends will die the most horrifying deaths imaginable."

"You want it so badly?" Eve asked. She clutched the book tightly to her chest. "Then take it!" She hurled it into the air behind the Keeper. Instantly, a large tree root shot out from the ground and snatched the book. The Keeper took the book from the root and began flipping through the yellowed pages with interest.

"Kill them," the Keeper hissed. The crows flying above immediately started descending in a thick cloud. "I've saved something special for you," he said to Jezebel. The straw receded from his arm, exposing a white hand with sharp black fingernails. He stabbed Jezebel in the arm with one of the fingernails. Her blood dripped over the ground.

Straining with all his might, Thomas finally grabbed the duffel bag.

"Kill *this*," he whispered as he fired a flare gun at the scarecrow. The shot ignited, and the Keeper erupted in flames. The root around Thomas' foot came free, allowing him to grab Jezebel's shotgun. Thomas fired directly into the jack o' lantern. The Keeper was thrown back into one of the oak trees as bits of pumpkin sprayed into the air. While Thomas pulled Jezebel free, Eve grabbed Durer's book, which had fallen to the ground.

"We have to get out of here," Thomas shouted above the roar of the approaching birds. He followed Jezebel's eyes to the flaming scarecrow. The front of the pumpkin was obliterated, revealing the grotesque face of Salem Alistair underneath. It was not the frightened face Jezebel remembered in her nightmares. Salem was gaunt, his mouth surrounded by dark blood. His eyes were pitch black, in contrast with pale skin.

"My mother!" Jezebel shouted, unwilling to leave Emma's body. Thomas barely had time to pull her inside the kitchen before the wave of crows broke against the house. Windows shattered as the birds tore into the white house, scattering in every direction. Through the open door, Thomas could see the Keeper of the Crows begin to rise. The jack o' lantern regenerated around his face, once more forging the deformed grin.

"Where is the car?" Eve shouted. She hadn't overheard Thomas telling Jezebel that Underhill had abandoned them. After exiting the house, Thomas looked out from the driveway. He could see a blue truck parked at the nearest house several yards away. The crows turned around to encircle the house. Thomas wasn't sure they would have time to make it across safely.

We have to try, he thought, running outside. Eve and Jezebel followed, the athletic sheriff easily outpacing the others. The crows were getting closer with each second. When they reached the truck, Jezebel smashed through the window with her gun and unlocked the door.

"You know how to hotwire a car?" Thomas asked, as he watched her fire up the engine with ease. Just as the truck tires squealed against road, the cloud of crows hit them again. The force of the swarm almost knocked the truck over, but the sheriff managed to correct the vehicle's course in time.

"Is everyone OK?" she asked.

"Just scratched up," Thomas said. His knife wound from the novelty store still ached.

A low hiss from outside the truck ripped his attention away from his own injuries. The Keeper of the Crows was outside Emma Woods' house, running with supernatural speed. Jezebel stepped on the gas and brought the truck back onto the road.

"He's gaining on us!" Eve shouted. Even as the truck gathered speed, the Keeper quickly closed the distance between them. Eve fired several shots at the living scarecrow, but each shot went wild. The Keeper jumped over the truck. Instead of hitting the brakes, Jezebel accelerated. The truck ran over Salem, and the scarecrow's body rolled underneath the car. Thomas saw the creature rise up once more and start up after them again. The thing that kept Salem alive buried under the ground for all those years refused to let him die.

"Can't this thing go any faster?" Eve asked.

"I'm going as fast as I can!" Jezebel yelled. "It's not my fault he won't die."

This time, Thomas crawled to the back seat of the truck and opened fire with the shotgun. He hit the Keeper in the chest three times, knocking the scarecrow down to the road again. This time, the scarecrow stayed put.

"That ought to buy us some time," Eve said. "What now?"

Neither of the others replied. Thomas could see the sadness on Jezebel's face.

"I'm sorry about your mother," Thomas said. He laid a hand on her shoulder.

"He did it," she whispered. "He killed her. I know Salem is still in there somewhere, but that thing has taken him over completely. I can't let him suffer like this. Eve, what does the book say about stopping the Keeper? Does it mention it anywhere at all?" The truck turned right and headed back toward town.

Eve shook her head. "Nowhere," she said. "I don't think Durer believed the thing could be stopped."

"There has to be a reason why Salem wanted the journal so badly," Thomas interjected. Eve hesitated for a moment before turning back to the map she spotted earlier in Durer's bedroom.

"If the cave on this map is the one where the forest spirit dwells, it might have been what Salem wanted to destroy so that no one could find the cave."

"Why?" Thomas asked.

"Because it was afraid," Jezebel whispered. Her voice grew strong again. "If it was afraid, that means it has something to fear."

"We have no idea what the creature would be afraid of," Eve said. "If this thing is powerful enough to keep Salem Alistair from dying, it would be suicide to go up against it."

"Taking the lives of others in sacrifice makes it strong," Jezebel said. "What's the opposite of that?"

"I'm not sure," Thomas answered. "Don't forget, fire can take out the scarecrows. It seems to slow Salem down too, even if it can't kill him."

"That's a stretch," Eve said.

"Maybe," Jezebel replied. They drove in the direction of town. "We don't have a lot to go on right now."

Thomas froze. "Look at the town."

There were scarecrows everywhere. Many dragged various sharp tools behind them as weapons. He saw backhoes, shovels, and axes.

The smoke from the fire filled the air, forming a thick cloud in the dark sky. When the scarecrows began following the truck, Jezebel tried to maneuver away, but there were too many of them. The vehicle was almost cornered.

"Now Salem knows we're here," she said. "There's no way out."

Thomas feared she was right. There was no place to run.

Jezebel pulled into a parking structure and looked for a place to escape.

"Wait," Thomas said. "Stop the truck."

"Are you crazy?" Jezebel asked. "They'll be here in minutes!"

"I know," Thomas said. Their first meeting mere miles from the Alistair Farm seemed like years ago. "Even if we get out of here, Salem is still going to have every crow in the town searching for this truck."

"So we switch vehicles," Jezebel said, nodding.

Thomas shook his head. "It won't take him long to figure that out. Then we will never get to this cave. He'll have all of the scarecrows there waiting for us."

"What are you saying?" Eve asked.

"There's another way. I'll wait in here with truck. When they come out, I'll fight until the last bullet. You two can still try to escape. Salem couldn't destroy the other half of the bridge over the lake. I think his power stops at Cavern Lake. If you two can swim across it, maybe you can make it to Thistlewood. I'll try to get to the cave on my own. You two can take another car and slip away in the dark while they're all preoccupied with me."

"That will never work," Jezebel said. She tore the map pages out of the book. "You've been living here for what, four months? Can you follow that map without getting lost in the woods? I've lived in Gray Hollow for my entire *life*. I'm the only one of us who can make it there. If I destroy the thing in the cave, I can save everyone, including you."

"She's right," Eve said.

"No," Thomas replied. She couldn't be right. This was exactly what he *didn't* want. "Jezebel, you can't go out there on your own. You'll be killed. Like Eve said, it would be suicide."

Jezebel shook her head. She could hear the concern in his voice. "It's my responsibility."

"No, it isn't! Just because you're the sheriff doesn't mean you have to—"

"It was my responsibility a long time before I became sheriff. A long time ago, a friend was counting on me and I let him down. I've spent the rest of my life trying to make up for it. This is my chance."

"Jezebel, it wasn't your fault! Those boys *chose* to kill Salem Alistair. They did it. Not you."

The louder his voice grew, the softer hers became.

"There's no other way," she said. "Neither of you can get to the cave. I can."

"I don't want you to go," he finally whispered. She smiled warmly at him.

"Thomas, you've become one of the best men I've ever met. Whatever happens, I am glad we met."

Eve sat silently, watching the two of them. Jezebel put her hand on Thomas' face.

"I'll see you when this is all over," Thomas said. Neither one of them, he knew, were likely to make it. If one of them was going to survive, he hoped it would be her.

"Goodbye," she said, taking another flashlight, a lighter, and a revolver from the duffel bag. Then she was gone.

Thomas turned to Eve. "This is the last of the ammo," he said, reloading his weapon.

"Then we had better make it count."

"You can still get out of this," he said. "It's not too late to find a place to hide." They could see the scarecrows' shadows as the creatures found their way into the parking structure.

"No way," Eve said. The scarecrows were almost on top of them.

"Then hold on." Thomas flashed the truck's bright lights and revved up the engine. The truck plowed over the scarecrows in front of it as they raced back out into the street. Several of the scarecrows hung onto the truck. One grabbed the door handle, its lightweight body swaying in the wind. Another climbed onto the back of the truck using the tailgate, smashing the rear window with a pair of weed clippers. Eve shot the creature, which fell off the back of the truck. More scarecrows spilled out onto the street and surrounded the vehicle as Thomas headed for the edge of the town. He hoped the Keeper of the Crows was lying about there being no escape beyond the fallen bridge.

***

Jezebel wasted no time after leaving the truck. She prayed Thomas would remain safe. It would not take Salem Alistair long to reach the town. Most people would have tried to escape, but Thomas was risking his life to give her a chance. She wasn't going to throw that opportunity away.

As the scarecrows raced after the blue truck, the sheriff ran across the dark street. Jezebel carefully opened the door to the abandoned diner. Exiting through the other side, she found a small red convertible in the back parking lot. The vehicle would be perfect for her purposes. She took a careful look at the map then eased the car onto a back road. She had to find the cave before it was too late.

Jezebel kept her lights dim to escape the notice of the crows flying above. Her car sped through the whistling winds, quickly gaining momentum. She came to the old farm in minutes. Jezebel hastily parked and got out of the car, then bent down behind a cluster of trees and peered into the field in front of her. A massive cornfield covered the nearby pasture. On the other side of the cornfield was a dark forest, above which hundreds of crows soared.

Jezebel turned on her flashlight. She was almost into the cornfield when she heard the snapping of dry leaves behind her.

Then, nothing, as she felt the bullet tear into her back.

Chapter TWENTY-FOUR

The figures were everywhere. Blackness poured down from the heavens as the scarecrows approached. Each wore a malevolent sewn smile. The blue truck spun around. The screeching sound of the tires failed to drown out the jeers of the scarecrows.

The truck's engine roared as the vehicle headed toward the bridge. To Thomas' surprise, the colossal structure was virtually destroyed. An enormous hole loomed in the heart of the bridge; a black, empty space separating the sides leading to Gray Hollow and Thistlewood.

The scarecrows were drawing nearer. Thomas tried to throw the truck in reverse, but as he did so one of the creatures slid its hand over the handle and opened the door. The scarecrow wrapped its thin fingers around his arm in an attempt to pull him out.

"Thomas!" Eve shouted. From the passenger seat, she grabbed his other arm. Suddenly, the end of a farming hoe shattered Eve's window. Glass spilled into the truck. Time seemed to slow as the truck rotated around the edge of the bridge. Finally, the vehicle collided with one of the concrete columns at the base of the ruined structure.

Eve's grip gave way. Thomas fell out of the truck alongside the scarecrow. The pair rolled over the cement, and the creature ended up on top of Thomas. It stared down at him with lifeless eyes. The scarecrow wrapped its hands around his neck to choke him. Thomas almost lost consciousness but at the last second managed to kick loose from the creature's grip. Coughing, he scrambled to his feet.

"Get in!" Eve shouted. She had climbed into the driver's seat and was attempting to reverse the truck away from the wall. Thomas watched as a scarecrow latched onto the other door reached into the car and yanked her out of the window by her hair. Thomas shot the creature with the revolver, amazed he was able to hit the scarecrow with any accuracy. Unfortunately, the creature stayed upright. The monster did, however, release its grip on Eve. She rolled down the hill toward the lake and out of sight.

"Eve!" Thomas shouted. She didn't respond. As he turned to go after her, he saw the rest of the scarecrows drawing nearer. He returned to the truck and rummaged through the duffel bag in the back. There was only one flare gun left. Then his hands brushed against the lighter fluid containers Jezebel had placed in the bag.

Perfect, he thought. He quickly removed the containers from the bag. Straining from the force, Thomas hurled the containers toward the approaching creatures.

"Here goes nothing," he said. He squeezed the trigger on the last flare gun. The canisters exploded. Fire shot out into the night sky. Aflame, several of the monsters continued advancing. Thomas grappled with one of the creatures as it reached for him.

He heard a soft hiss carried by the wind and saw a tall form sailing through the air right at him. The creature hit Thomas with incredible strength. Thomas fell and hit his head hard on the pavement. His vision blurred. The Keeper of the Crows towered over him, flames licking his stained patchwork of rags.

Thomas pulled the trigger on the revolver. It clicked empty. He was out of time.

***

Jezebel collapsed into the cornfield, losing her grip on the flashlight. Her body fell to the ground with a thud. The cool soil seemed to still the pain for a moment. She crawled farther into the cornfield. Her body felt incredibly light, like she was being lifted into the air. Was she dead?

The gruff voice from somewhere behind her caused her to regain her focus.

"Come on out, Jezebel," Charles Underhill said lightly. She could see him standing just outside the cornfield as he glanced up at the multitudes of crows covering the black sky.

"Don't make this harder than it has to be." The judge stepped into the cornfield after her, glancing around in every direction. She took momentary solace in the fact that the place was a labyrinth; she realized he couldn't see where she had fallen.

"I'm sorry it had to be this way," Judge Underhill said. "But you heard what the woman in the car said. The Keeper requires sacrifice. He wants you. When you're dead, I'll be free."

She could hear his voice getting closer. Jezebel prayed it was too dark for him to see her, but she started inching away. Blood was pouring from the bullet wound.

"This isn't personal."

She heard him cock the gun.

"I always enjoyed working with you."

She watched as he stopped for a moment, apparently listening to the rustling of stalks as she backed away. Underhill fired again into the night.

"I didn't want to shoot Logan Randall either. We were actually planning to kill you together. When I heard you talking about Durer, I had to change my plans."

She couldn't see him anymore. Jezebel turned around and started heading back the way she came. If she could get out of the cornfield and back to her car, she might have a chance. The pain was almost overwhelming. When she rounded the corner, she saw that Underhill was waiting for her. He pointed his gun at her, wearing a cruel grin on his face.

"Tell me why," she whispered.

"I was in the car that Halloween night. I went to the Alistair Farm with the others. Why do you think I gave Rick a job? Or covered for Logan all those times? We killed Salem Alistair. And I'm not about to let that freak get me now, after all this time."

"You deserve this," Jezebel spat.

"You think I was going to allow something that happened twenty years ago get in the way of my success?" the judge asked. "Once I kill you, the Keeper will let me live."

A second gunshot echoed in the night sky.

***

Thomas' eyes opened, and he saw the jack o' lantern face glowing in the dark. He felt himself being dragged along the street.

"You aren't even from Gray Hollow," the Keeper hissed. "Can you see the way this town infects you?" Thomas clawed at the pavement in an attempt to free himself. Salem threw him against the blue truck.

"I've had my eye on you for a long time now. At first, I was willing to let you go. That part of me has been getting weaker and weaker with each killing. Salem would never have allowed me to kill Paul Morris."

Thomas spotted the sledgehammer inside the vehicle. He played dead, waiting for the scarecrow to draw closer. When Salem neared the truck, Thomas grabbed the sledgehammer and slammed it into the pumpkin head. Thomas stumbled backward from the impact. The Keeper reached up and dislodged the weapon from the remains of the pumpkin. His face was exposed once again; the twisted version of Salem Alistair swung the hammer back at the reporter. Thomas hurled himself to the ground and barely avoided being struck. He climbed to his feet and ran into the darkness beyond the bridge. The Keeper followed behind him.

"Now I am so much more than I—than Salem—ever dreamt of being. With each passing day I am more and more in control. The spirit of the forest will be pleased when I deliver your head."

Thomas could hear the monster laughing, a shrill, raspy laugh that made his skin crawl. Then a flock of crows passed by and flowed over the scarecrow standing in the street. The Keeper of the Crows allowed the birds to flock around him; Thomas supposed that was how they passed knowledge to him.

The Keeper roared with anger.

"Jezebel," he hissed. "You tricked me!" he screamed.

He knows what we're up to, Thomas realized. He knew he had to keep the scarecrow distracted.

"That means you're ugly and stupid," Thomas shouted. His voice echoed loudly. He backed into the night, watching the Keeper carefully. With the scarecrows gone, the Keeper was having difficulty finding him. "Everyone I talked to was right. You are a freak."

"Your blood will join theirs, and then I will rip Jezebel limb from limb. The boy would enjoy that."

The Keeper stared around as if waiting for a response. For a moment, there was silence. Then, an engine roared to life as Thomas revved the blue truck. Without giving the Keeper a chance to react, Thomas stepped on the gas and charged the scarecrow. Caught in the headlights, the Keeper of the Crows leapt into the air and landed on the hood of the truck. He pounded away at the roof of the cab, denting the metal exterior. His hands tore a hole through the top and almost took Thomas' head off.

"Time to start screaming," the Keeper hissed.

Thomas stared off into the night. Even in the nightmarish blackness, Cavern Lake was serene. He knew that if the Keeper killed him, he would go after Jezebel next. Thomas wasn't about to let that happen. Not after all the harm the creature had already done. He didn't have the power to put what was left of Salem down for good, but maybe there was a way to take the Keeper out of the equation temporarily, even if it meant doing the unthinkable.

The blue truck gained speed with each second. Thomas kept his foot glued to the pedal as he neared the bridge. He wheeled the car to the right and turned onto the bridge. The truck hit the bridge at full speed. The Keeper of the Crows realized what was happening one second too late. The truck sailed off the bridge, careening off into the night. Thomas fumbled at his seat belt. He managed to free himself just before he hit the water. Then everything went black as the icy depths began to pull the truck under the water.

The sensation of the freezing water pouring into the vehicle jolted him awake. Thomas looked around groggily, trying to maintain his focus. The Keeper slammed against the truck's windshield. The creature cracked the window, staring at Thomas with malevolent eyes. Thomas tried to pull back, still stuck in the seat. As the water poured in over his head, he took one last breath.

Then they were underwater. Suddenly, the truck collided with a giant rock ledge protruding from the lakebed. The Keeper was pinned between the truck and the rock, unable to get free. Thomas watched him from the driver's seat while he tried in vain to open the door.

Finally, he lowered the window and managed to swim up toward the surface. His lungs were almost bursting with pain. The surface seemed too far away. He would never make it.

The truck emitted an unearthly sound as it tumbled off the rock and sank lower. Thomas glanced down. Below, the Keeper was free again. Thomas swam upward desperately. His muscles were on fire. He wasn't moving fast enough to reach the surface, let alone escape from the monster quickly closing in on him.

Just as he neared the surface, a hand wrapped itself around his ankle.

***

Jezebel crawled through the field. Charles Underhill was exactly where she'd left him when she shot the man with her service weapon. It hadn't been difficult to remove her own gun while the judge was trying to find out where she was. She shot him before he could pull the trigger.

It was almost impossible to pull herself out of the cornfield. Jezebel had never felt so much pain. It was almost unbearable. Then she remembered the sight of her mother's body, and the sheriff mustered the will to stand. She had lost her flashlight but remembered the lighter was still in her pocket. Jezebel snatched a branch from the ground and fashioned a makeshift torch.

She limped through the field and stumbled into the forest. It was too late to avoid alerting the crows now. The gunshots had caused the dark forest to spring to life. If she didn't act quickly, Salem would be there soon.

Salem, she thought. The very name seemed to give her strength to continue. Jezebel made her way through the thorn patches, limping forward inch by inch. She could no longer see the map, but somehow she didn't need it. She could feel the evil ahead, festering as she walked deeper into the forest.

A crow flew out of the darkness, flying straight for her. Its beak tore into her flesh, and she cried out in pain. Jezebel fastened her grip around the torch. She failed Salem once. She would not fail him again.

Another crow hit her in the chest. She almost fell to the ground at the impact. An image flashed into her mind of the two of them playing as children, happily running through the fields of the Alistair Farm. Jezebel pressed on.

She could see the cave looming in the distance. The closer she drew, the more crows attacked her. They erupted out of the entrance of the cave, swarming all around her. Jezebel could no longer see anything amid the dark cloud. The crows tore into her, shredding her clothes and tearing at her flesh. Still she pressed forward.

Jezebel could hardly move against the weight of the endless sea of birds storming against her. Though the cloud threatened to put out the flame, the torch continued burning brightly. Her body cried out to her to stop, but she forced herself to continue moving. Barely clutching the torch, she inched forward little by little.

I made a promise, she thought. Her eyes were filled with tears. The birds kept coming. *I won't quit,* Jezebel swore to herself. Shakily, she put one foot in front of the other. Jezebel called upon her last reserve of strength and staggered into the cave.

Then all was quiet. Thorns grew up around the dusty insides of the cave, reaching out like claws. The birds were still there; she could feel them. There was something else there, too. Another presence. It was an entity far darker and more unsettling than even the twisted version of Salem Alistair.

"You should not have come here," roared the entity, its voice moving like the wind.

"Let my friend go," Jezebel demanded weakly. Her vision started to swim. She was dying.

"You cannot command me, girl. I have existed millennia before you were born and will endure long after you return to dust."

"What are you?" Jezebel waved the torch in the air. She fought to stay conscious.

"I have been known by many names. You may know me as the true *Keeper of the Crows. Your pitiful efforts will not stop me from casting this town into eternal darkness, Jezebel Woods. Salem Alistair will remain my servant for all time."*

"No," she whispered. "I'll stop you."

The shadow roared with laughter, splitting her ears with pain. *"What can* you *do? With each drop of blood spilled my power increases. You are nothing."*

"Maybe so," Jezebel said. "But you aren't taking anything. I choose to give my life freely to save Salem Alistair." She smiled, blood dripping from her mouth. "I'm betting that makes a difference." Jezebel held out the torch. She would burn away the entity and purge it with the flame.

She could feel the thing's fear.

"Fool," the spirit roared. *"Your sacrifice means nothing! Even if you drive me from this cave, the portion of my spirit trapped here is only a fragment! My consciousness will live on if it is destroyed. There will be no such return for you."*

"If that's what it takes," Jezebel whispered. Her eyesight blurred. "To save my friend."

She tried to walk forward, but she found she could no longer move. Her body wobbled, and she lost her balance. She felt herself falling for what seemed like an eternity. The darkness wrapped around her but could not touch her. Finally, she hit the ground. Her blood seeped into the dusty floor of the cave, and the torch rolled out of her hand. Jezebel's eyes closed as the flame spread to the dry thorns, covering the cave in fire.

The demon roared in pain. It could feel its hold over Salem Alistair fading. The darkness knew the impediment was only temporary. The Keeper of the Crows would live on elsewhere. Gray Hollow might be free, but this wasn't over. Its servants would see to that.

Then the shadow faded away, and was no more.

***

Thomas gasped for air as he broke to the surface of the icy lake. The freezing waters rose over him in waves. His muscles felt like lead. Then he felt a hand grab his ankle, pulling him back under the water.

The shell of Salem Alistair stared at him with hateful eyes. Using one last burst of energy, Thomas kicked free. He panted from exhaustion and swam toward the shore, where he collapsed from exhaustion.

A wave of water erupted across the shore as a large form emerged from below. The Keeper loomed over him. The wretched pumpkin mouth grew wide, exposing a mouth full of sharp, orange teeth.

Suddenly, the Keeper staggered back.

“No. Not when I was so close.” The scarecrow tried to lunge at Thomas, but an invisible force pulled him back. The wind ripped around him, and the Keeper threw his head back as a column of pure blackness erupted from his mouth and dissolved into the night.

The Keeper of the Crows fell still. Eventually, the wind carried his body back into the water. From the shore, Thomas watched as Salem Alistair’s body sank to the bottom of the lake.

EPILOGUE

One month later, Thomas stood at the edge of Cavern lake and peered down at the crystal waters below. Somewhere within the depths lay Salem Alistair's body. That was where it would remain, undisturbed and finally at peace. Jezebel had seen to that.

Thomas missed her more than he cared to admit. Jezebel's body was never found, but somehow he knew that she was gone. All his attempts to locate the cave concealed within Gray Hollow's vast network of forests were futile. Thomas wasn't even sure if there would be anything left to find. The darkness was gone, like a fog lifted from the town. In the end, Jezebel succeeded in freeing her friend from the Keeper's grasp. Together they saved the town.

Judge Charles Underhill's body was found outside a large cornfield. It wasn't hard for Thomas to figure out what had prompted the judge's odd behavior. Not when he did some research of his own and discovered that Underhill's father, Jeremiah, was close friends with Logan Randall's parents. Then Thomas remembered that it was Charles Underhill who had employed Rick Pepper. With Underhill working as a judge and Logan as a deputy, they thought they were all perfectly positioned to keep their involvement in Salem Alistair's disappearance quiet. They were wrong. As Thomas learned over the last few weeks, no secret could remain buried forever.

He didn't pity the judge or the deputy. They chose to run from their actions, whereas Jezebel took responsibility for hers. Wherever she was, Thomas hoped Jezebel was finally free of the guilt that haunted her for so long.

Rebuilding the town proved to be difficult work. The scarecrows killed many people, and Thomas mourned along with everyone else when Max Harper, Heavy Markham, Al Pittman, and others were laid to rest. Members of the Thistlewood police force appeared a few hours after the darkness lifted from the town. With Gray Hollow cut off from communicating for so long and the fierce weather on the other side of the bridge, Thistlewood's emergency personnel quickly concluded something was wrong. It took awhile for them to obtain motorboats and cross the lake.

It was impossible to explain what happened. Although some people told the media stories of terrifying scarecrows, the tales were largely dismissed. For his part, Thomas publically attributed the deaths to a group of microbursts and flat line winds that had torn the town apart. The people of Gray Hollow knew the truth and largely chose to keep it to themselves.

Several doves flew over the clear blue sky above. Thomas watched them until they disappeared from sight. He shifted in the snow, toasty in multiple layers of clothing. Below, the ferry passed over the water and carried passengers from Gray Hollow over to Thistlewood.

After he resurfaced from the lake that night, Thomas discovered that all of the scarecrows had been rendered lifeless. He led others in the community in burning the scarecrows to obliterate every last trace of the evil that had stalked the fields. They spent weeks searching through Gray Hollow, looking over farms and in cornfields. He started with the field where he and Jezebel were attacked for the first time.

They found hundreds of scarecrows remaining, excluding Salem himself. Thomas was surprised Salem Alistair was able to make so many in his youth. He didn't know if Salem had built them all while he was alive or if the entity in the cave had multiplied them somehow. Burning the scarecrows provided a catharsis of sorts for the town. With the memories of the lost still fresh in their minds, the people of Gray Hollow slowly returned to their regular routines. The small town resumed life as usual, with a few changes. Some policemen from Thistlewood volunteered to serve Gray Hollow temporarily until the town was back on its feet, and the makeshift ferry took over the role of relaying travelers between towns.

Thomas looked up at the bridge, the sensation of the icy depths below not forgotten. It would take some time to rebuild the large structure, a symbol of all that was lost.

"I thought I might find you here," he heard a familiar voice say. Thomas looked up to find Eve approaching him, her car parked at the curb. She sat down next to him on the snowy ground with a smile.

"I like to come here," Thomas said. "It helps me reflect. It looks like you finished early."

Eve had taken a temporary leave of absence from her job in the city to help him deal with the fallout. "Are you kidding? These stories are impossibly easy to write, Thomas. A debate to lower property taxes is the most heated topic in this place. Next to living monsters of straw, it isn't very exciting, is it?"

"Give me the boring stories any day," Thomas said.

"So," she asked. "Have you reached a decision?"

He nodded. "I have."

"You're staying, aren't you?"

"Yeah."

"You know there's nothing keeping you here. You've redeemed yourself, at least as far as I'm concerned."

"I can't believe I'm saying this," Thomas said. "But I think Gray Hollow is where I belong. I can do a lot of good here."

"So you're going to stay on as the permanent editor of *Hollow Happenings*?"

"Yes."

Eve sighed. "You know I'll be going back soon. What'll happen to us then?"

"I don't know," Thomas admitted. They had only just started to rebuild their relationship. "Let's just take it one day at a time."

They sat there holding hands in the snow, and Thomas felt himself smiling for the first time in a long while.

The nightmare was over.

ACKNOWLEDGMENTS

I would like to thank the members of my family who read this book first: Pam, Allie, and Jacob. Your feedback and encouragement helped make this book a reality. I would be remiss if I didn't thank my dad for his support through this process.

I would also like to thank Dr. Susan Wright and Amanda Lee for providing a second set of eyes. Your catches, comments, and suggestions were invaluable. This book is much better because of you.

A big thanks goes out to Sunbury Press for publishing this book. Thanks to Amber Rendon for a *beautiful* cover.

And finally, thanks to you, the reader! I hope you enjoyed what you read.

Until we meet again,

Kyle